The Long Journey Home

DON COLDSMITH

A TOM DOHERTY ASSOCIATES BOOK
NEW YORK

This is a work of fiction. All the characters and events portrayed in this book are either products of the author's imagination or are used fictitiously.

THE LONG JOURNEY HOME

A Forge Book
Published by Tom Doherty Associates, LLC
175 Fifth Avenue
New York, NY 10010

www.tor.com

Forge® is a registered trademark of Tom Doherty Associates, LLC.

ISBN: 0-812-57872-4
Library of Congress Catalog Card Number: 00-048459

First edition: February 2001
First mass market edition: May 2002

Printed in the United States of America

0 9 8 7 6 5 4 3 2 1

PRAISE FOR DON COLDSMITH

"Coldsmith's novel does an admirable job of focusing on the well-intended, but misguided Indian schools that forced children to subjugate themselves as they put on the often uncomfortable mantle of the white man's world."
—*The Sunday Patriot-News*,
Harrisburg, Pennsylvania

"For those of us who experience the Indian's path into the life ways of other Americans, Coldsmith beautifully captures and coordinates real worldwide events, change, nature, places, time, human nature and cultural clashes, in a brilliant creation of life which unmistakably has 'good medicine.' I left some things undone until I finished the book."   —Benny Smith, Keetoowah Cherokee

"Coldsmith's sketches of Wild West shows, early Hollywood and the flu epidemic of 1918 are excellent."
—*Publishers Weekly*

"This well-researched piece of historical fiction interweaves a compelling life story with many of the pivotal events of the early twentieth century."   —*Booklist*

"Here is a grand adventure pitting two . . . warrior castes against each other, with the fate of a continent hanging in the balance. The story should have been told before, but thank God it waited for Coldsmith to tell it."
—Loren D. Estleman, Spur Award–winning author of
The Master Executioner, on *Runestone*

"Coldsmith blends his extensive knowledge of history with daring speculation and a vivid imagination."
—Ron McCoy, Center for Great Plains Studies,
Emporia State University, on *Runestone*

"The author spins a compelling yarn."
—*Publishers Weekly* on *The Lost Band*

To Shatka Bearstep, Bert Yellowhawk, Jim Thorpe, High Eagle, Bill Pickett, Will Rogers, Iron Tail, Joe Looking Bear, Robert Conley, Benny Smith, and the many others whose stories have been reflected in this book.

[INTRODUCTION]

INTRODUCTION

This book was suggested to me a few years ago by a former editor and good friend. He envisioned it as a novel based on the life of an American Indian, Jim Thorpe, possibly the greatest athlete of the twentieth century. I balked at a biographical novel, but suggested a similar, but fictional, character with a comparable career. He could *know* Thorpe in an Indian school, follow Thorpe's Olympic triumph and downfall . . .

Only later did it occur to me that this era, the first few decades of the twentieth century, saw a tremendous amount of change, invention, and discovery. Radio, automobiles, airplanes, lighter-than-air dirigibles, manufacturing, moving pictures, exploration, science, on and on. No previous generation had seen such progress.

As I started the research for this book, every new bit of information seemed to fit somewhere else, like pieces of a jigsaw puzzle. (Let's see . . . If this character was there, at that time, he would have *also* seen . . .) I'm indebted to many people for their help, and for verification of my suspicion that *it must have been this way*.

I especially want to commend two sources: *Tim McCoy Remembers the West* by Tim McCoy and his son Ronald. Ron was able to verify many facts about which I inquired.

The other is a new book, released in 1999. *The Real Wild West*, by Michael Wallis, is already an award-winning reference volume, on the history of the 101 Ranch of Oklahoma and The Miller Brothers Wild West Show.

In all of my historical fiction, I have followed a single

principle: to be so accurate that no one could, by historical fact, prove that my story did not happen. This is still my goal. As outlandish as some of the events in the story of John Buffalo may appear, every one is based on fact and is verifiable. Without my credibility, I would have nothing.

Don Coldsmith

ONE

The boy squirmed in his seat. It was a beautiful day, ripe with the sights and scents of autumn. It was a day, he thought, when any boy of his age—nearly ten summers—should be outside, wandering the hills and the streams, maybe hunting squirrels in the timber along the river. Through the open window, he could hear the lazy, clattering buzz of a grasshopper in flight. That would be one of the big ones, with black and yellow wings.

The teacher was talking, in English, telling the class something about new books, as if they were a real treat, like something good to eat. Little Bull wasn't paying much attention. The weather outside made it hard to think about anything else. There were a lot of places he'd rather be than the schoolhouse. Almost *anyplace*, come to think about it.

He thought back about how he happened to be here. That missionary had come, and talked to the People around a story fire. Some of his stories were pretty good, about a man and woman and a snake who ate something called apples. Or maybe it was the man who ate the apples. He wasn't sure because he did not understand English well. Barely enough to follow the storyline. There had been a white woman with the missionary—probably his wife—who used hand signs to follow the story along. That helped some, but she wasn't very proficient at it. Still, everyone loves a story, and some of these were pretty good.

When an outsider camped with the People, there would be stories, which everybody could enjoy. Usually the stranger would tell his own Creation story, how *his* people entered the world. Little Bull found that fascinating. Usually, they had come from inside the earth, though sometimes there were big differences. One man said that *his* people were at the top of the blue sky-dome, and slid down the side to reach the earth. That one had been interesting. Another said that his people came up out of a lake.

Almost always, the stories included a Creator who helped the people in some way. It was generally assumed that this was really the same being, called by different names in each tribe or nation: Man-Above, Great Father, Grandfather. . . .

It was when the missionary began to mix his concept of God into the story about First Man and First Woman and the snake that things became even more confusing. The Creator became angry at the people over what they ate. Well, many other nations have foods which are forbidden, do they not? It was still a good story.

Then, one of the local storytellers thanked the missionary, as was the custom, and began to respond with their own Creation story.

"No, no!" the visitor exclaimed. "That is false. Blasphemy! Heresy!"

Little Bull did not understand such words, but he did realize that this was very rude behavior on the part of the visitor. It spoiled the entire tone of the evening. The People listened in shocked silence while the visitor ranted on.

"You people worship the wrong god!" he accused.

It became very quiet around the story fire, and then one of their leaders spoke. Standing Bear, one of the most respected of men, a holy man who always seemed to be able to see through to the heart of a problem. There was almost a twinkle in his eye, which may have been lost on most of the crowd. But he was polite, despite the rudeness of the visitor. He rose to his feet.

"We regret this, Uncle," he said calmly. "We did not know that there was more than one God."

There were a few quiet chuckles, but outright laughter would have been impolite. The story fire was over, spoiled by misunderstanding on the part of the visitor.

Despite the unfortunate beginning, the missionary stayed, and began to have some who followed his way of thinking. Mostly, it seemed to be those who thought they might receive more or better food rations from the Agency. The missionary seemed to have close connections there. So, he poured water on the heads of his converts, and pronounced them "saved." Most were unsure what this meant. However, nearly everybody realized that though the ways of the missionary were unknowing and impolite, his heart was good. He stayed for some time, and during that time he talked long and earnestly to those with small children.

"You owe it to them" he pleaded. "Let them learn the white man's way. They must grow up and live in his world. Place them in the school provided by the White Father."

That was how it had happened. Little Bull's mother was alone since the death of her husband, Yellow Bull, two winters ago. Pneumonia, it was said. She had two young children to look after. . . . She allowed the missionary to pour the water on her head and on those of her children, and had agreed to let Little Bull attend the government school. He would live there most of the year.

The first, stunning shock when he arrived at the school had to do with his hair. Little Bull was proud of his braids, lovingly combed and braided by his mother since he was small. They were plaited with strips of the finest otter fur with ceremonial care before he left for the white man's school.

"You would make your father proud." His mother smiled.

But as they were processed through a room where they changed to white man's clothes, each boy was shoved briefly into a chair. There, a white man with a pair of large shears quickly amputated each boy's treasured braids and tossed them aside. It was useless to resist, but a few cried. Little Bull was one of those.

At times, Little Bull wondered: Had his mother sent him away so that it would be easier to provide for her other children? He wished that his father was still alive. Yellow Bull had been a respected warrior, and there had always been people around their lodge to hear his stories. Especially the one about the fight with the soldiers at a place called Greasy Grass. That had been a few years before Little Bull was born. Yellow Bull had counted many coups that day, and there had been little trouble with soldiers since. But Yellow Bull was gone.

The teacher was walking down the aisle now, between the desks, and placing a new blue book on each. She was tall and bony, of indeterminate age, with a perpetually sour look on her long face, as if she had just tasted bile. Small, square eyeglasses perched near the upper portion of a long, straight nose. Her hair, a mousy brown, was pulled tightly into a bun at the back of her head.

It had been whispered that she had no man. Little Bull found that understandable. What man would want such a forbidding figure to grace his lodge, much less to warm his bed?

There were about twenty boys in the room, and each was to receive one of these books. No one spoke, except the teacher. *Someone should,* thought Little Bull. It would be only polite to express thanks, even though such thanks would not be completely sincere. The teacher dropped the last book on the desk in front of Little Bull.

"It is good," the boy murmured in the tongue of the People, by way of thanks.

The teacher whirled angrily. There was a short stick in her hand, one he was later to recognize as a "ruler." Before he knew what was happening, she had struck him across the knuckles with the stick.

"You will not use that heathen tongue here!" she snapped. "We speak only English, understand? You must learn to overcome the handicap of your inferior background. Do you understand me?"

Little Bull nodded, afraid and confused.

"Speak up!" the teacher demanded. " 'Yes, ma'am' is the acceptable answer."

"Yes, ma'am."

"That's better . . . Now, let that be a lesson to you all. You are here to rise above your savage beginnings, and to learn to live and work like civilized people. I will tolerate nothing less."

She went back to the front of the room and turned.

"Now, a part of such civilization is to have a good name." Her glance singled out Little Bull. "You, there. What is your name? In *English,* please!"

"I am Little Bull. My father was Yellow Bull."

There, that should impress people, that he came from the family of such a great man as Yellow Bull.

"No, no, that will never do," scolded the teacher. "That is a rather indelicate word. Hmm . . . A buffalo, I suppose?"

"Yes, ma'am."

"Buffalo. . . . And you will need a given name, as well

as the family name. Let's see . . . John . . . That is it. You are John Buffalo."

A few of the other boys giggled, but subsided quickly under the stern glance of the teacher. One by one, the names were Anglicized. Some were already acceptable in meaning, and were merely translated to English from their own language. Some, such as Bloody Hand, were modified, sanitized and, with the addition of a given name, this boy became Charles Hand.

By the end of the day, the teacher, Miss Whitehurst, seemed pleased with herself. There had been only one more incident which required the whacking of knuckles. John was never certain what precipitated that. The recipient was on the other side of the room. However, the ruler had the desired effect. No one else misbehaved for the rest of the day. The teacher had established her authority. One more rule was initiated before the end of the day: Hand signs were forbidden.

That was completely beyond the understanding of Little Bull, now John Buffalo. He could understand, in a way, the necessity to learn the ways of the white man. His mother had taught him well: *The white man is coming. . . . No, he is here! Those who do not learn to live by his customs will have no chance at all. . . .* But this thing of the hand signs seemed to defeat its purpose. Most of the communication on the frontier was dependent in some degree on hand signs. Why was their use prohibited?

Years later, John Buffalo finally realized the probable reason. Miss Whitehurst apparently did not *know* the signs, and found it wise to conceal that fact to maintain her rigid control.

By the end of the week, three boys had left the school. "Escaped," the others joked wryly.

For John Buffalo, this was not an option. *What you start, you finish,* his mother had impressed on him. There was a responsibility to bring pride and respect to the family of

Yellow Bull. To do this, it appeared, he must learn the white man's way. He must learn so well that he could outdo the white man at his own game. It was not only a challenge, but a duty.

TWO

At night in the dormitory, the students quietly used their own language. There could be trouble if they were caught, but the supervisor, who lived in a room at the end of the barrackslike hall was a little hard of hearing. After "lights out," when the supervisor's snores told that he was asleep, there was usually quiet conversation. John just listened, mostly.

"What will they do to the ones who escaped?" someone asked.

"Bring them back. Let Old White Horse whack 'em with her stick!"

There was muffled laughter.

"Shh . . . Don't wake the Bear."

The supervisor had earned this name because he was grumpy, a bit pudgy, short, and walked with a sort of swaying motion like a bear on its hind legs.

"He's out for the night."

"Hibernating?"

More laughter, more shushing, and a short period of silence.

"I don't think they'll try to catch them. Who would go after them?"

"I don't know. The Army, maybe."

More laughter . . . There was a break in the even snoring

from Bear's room. This brought instant quiet until the regular rhythm resumed. Finally, very cautiously . . .

"What do you think is the matter with old White Horse?"

"She needs a man."

The giggles could barely be suppressed.

"What man would want to bed *her?*"

"I don't know. Bear, maybe."

The laughter could hardly be controlled, now, but was finally stifled. Even John was amused at the thought of those two in such a situation. Some of the others apparently had the same mental image.

"He'd barely come up to her chest!"

"No matter. There's nothin' there anyway."

"Maybe she's a man!" another suggested.

"*Aiee!* You think so?"

"I don't know. I don't even *want* to know."

"Me, neither."

"Quiet down in there!" came a command from the Bear. "It's past lights out!"

After a long moment of silence, Charlie Hand spoke to John in a whisper.

"Do you think he heard?"

"Doesn't matter," observed John. "He doesn't know our tongue."

"Are you sure?"

"Well, no. But you're right. We have to be careful, Charlie. Let's try to learn their ways. If we learn enough, we can use it against them."

"How, Bull? I mean, *John.*"

"I don't know yet, Charlie. But the more we know . . ."

In the next week or so, Miss Whitehurst noted that certain of her pupils seemed to be working harder. It was difficult to determine their attitude because of the flat, expression-less looks on each face.

Have these savages no emotion? she wondered to herself. *No joy or sorrow, pleasure or pain?*

She did not even suspect that this was a deliberate, conditioned defense. If a person shows no hurt, it is harder to hurt him.

Regardless, she was pleased at the progress of some of her pupils in the area of reading, writing, and language skills. One of her best was the strange, quiet boy who had called himself Little Bull. A disgusting name, but one which had actually seemed a matter of pride for the boy.

Ah, well, she thought, *such is the savage nature.*

But she never had to punish John Buffalo again. She must admit, the boy was a quick learner.

John found the use of marks on his slate to express sounds intriguing. It was not long before the idea of letters and words to transmit messages to others was firmly established in his understanding. He pored over the blue book and began to find familiar words and phrases. Suddenly it came to him. *I can read!* He was quiet about it, not letting the others know too much. His heart was heavy for some of them, who struggled hard with the unfamiliar sounds. At times in his own recitation, he would pretend to stumble, so that the others would not think he considered himself superior. Besides, it seemed prudent not to reveal how much he was actually learning. Let there be something that he could keep secret. Someday it might be useful. He could not actually justify this feeling. It was only a dimly formed idea, perhaps stemming from his need for privacy.

In one area, he did not mind showing what he could do. When the class was turned over to the Bear each day for a period of exercise and games, John was in his element. As a small child in the Rabbit Society, the educational system of the People, he had excelled. He could outrun most of the children his own age, and some of the older ones. He was a better swimmer, could throw with greater accuracy and distance, and could best the others at wrestling. These skills were easily adapted to the games and contests of the white man. The hard, round ball, white with red stitches, was a handy weight to throw, and he could do so with accuracy. It was equally exciting to try to hit that same ball, thrown by someone else. A special club, long and smooth, was provided for the purpose. It was a game he enjoyed.

However, his favorite was a game called football. It reminded him of one time when the People had a good buffalo kill. One of the old men had shown the boys how to carefully remove the bladder of a large bull and fill it with air by blowing through a hollow reed. It was then tied, and the air-filled ball was great fun to kick and toss. Little Bull and the other boys had had a wonderful time with the toy, until a errant kick sent it into the fire, to end the fun. They were admonished to return to work, carrying meat to the area where the women were slicing it into thin strips to place on the drying racks.

The football was a more durable form of the inflated bladder. It was oblong, made of leather, and could withstand endless kicking. There were rules, Bear told them: an organized game between two teams who would try to carry or kick this ball to a goal. It was a more physical game than baseball. John Buffalo enjoyed them both. He was always among the first to be picked when it came time to choose sides for a competition, often ahead of older boys.

Even with all of this, however, the pleasures of learning and of competition in athletics could not compensate for the freedom he had lost. Many an hour he spent gazing out the window of the schoolroom at the distant hills. He dreamed of the days when he was small, of the sound of the patter of rain on the lodge cover. . . . Or the feel of a cool breeze as it drifted through the shaded interior of the lodge with the cover rolled part way up on a hot summer day. His parents' lodge, like most in recent years, had been of canvas, not skins. There was a unique smell of hot sun on canvas. . . . These were the things that he missed. . . .

There came a day the following autumn when everyone was admonished to look his best. An important visitor would be coming to the school. John was unsure as to the exact status of this visitor, but judging from the reaction of the Bear and old Miss Whitehurst, this was a man of considerable status. A chief, perhaps, a representative of the White Father in Washington. The teacher referred to him as "the Senator," whatever that might be. John gathered that this chief might have great influence over what was extended to the school in the way of food and supplies. The students were cautioned to be on their best behavior and to present themselves as clean, well fed, and happy. This struck young John as humorous, that one could be expected to have his heart soar with joy when requested. A bit ironic, actually.

His suspicions were confirmed as they lined up to greet the Senator. The Bear always marched them to other parts of the compound for meals, classroom instruction, the dormitory, or athletics. Today, all students were brought together at the parade ground, where athletics and games were held. Supervisors scurried to make sure their lines were straight as they stood at attention.

There was a troop of soldiers in their blue uniforms with yellow stripes on the trousers, impressive on their horses as they maneuvered into position for the inspection. John Buffalo smiled to himself in the knowledge that his father, Yellow Bull, had helped to defeat such units at the Greasy

Grass. *They ran like rabbits.* Yellow Bull had always chuckled as he told the story.

The Senator and his party arrived in an Army ambulance, chosen because it was enclosed. There was a chill wind in the air, suggesting that winter might not be far off. The Senator stepped down, and greeted the officers in charge of the military detachment. He was a tall man, wearing a dark suit, white shirt, and string tie. One of his helpers carried a buffalo coat over his arm, ready in case his leader had need of it.

The inspection did not take long. There was a brisk walk along the side of the parade ground where the pupils were arrayed. The Senator paused from time to time to take a second look or to speak to one of the youngsters. John hoped that the man would not single him out, but he did.

"What is your name, son?"

"John Buffalo, sir."

The man nodded. "Your father?"

Here was a dilemma. Miss Whitehurst had forbidden the use of the word "bull" as being indelicate, not to be used in polite society. But here, a greater authority figure was demanding it.

John Buffalo took a deep breath.

"Yellow Bull, sir. He was a great man. He was at the Greasy Grass."

"Greasy Grass?"

"The Little Bighorn, sir," blurted the aide.

"Is this true?" asked the Senator.

"Probably, sir. Warriors from this area—"

"Buffalo," snapped the Bear, "hold your tongue. The Senator does not want to hear such things!"

"On the contrary." The Senator smiled. "This young man speaks well for himself. Are you treated well here, John Buffalo?"

"Yes, sir," John said stiffly.

"Good. Keep up the good work!"

With that, he moved on.

John was confused. The visiting chief had spoken to him with approval, but he still might be in trouble with the Bear, White Horse, or any others with authority here. He doubted that he would ever understand the ways of the white man.

The inspection was finished, and at dinner it was announced that there would be a football game in the afternoon for the visiting dignitaries to watch. John Buffalo was proud to be chosen as one of the players for the demonstration. The wind had died somewhat, and the sun had emerged from behind the clouds. Maybe it would be a good day after all.

John's team had several good runs, but the height of the day came when he was able to place a dropkick squarely between the uprights. The opposing team had expected a run.

Later, he was summoned to talk to the Senator.

"Buffalo, is it? John Buffalo?"

"Yes, sir."

John noticed that one of the aides was scribbling in a notebook.

"And how old are you, John?" the Senator asked.

"About eleven winters, I think, sir."

"Mmm . . . Yes. Well, you are quite an athlete, boy. Good work. You have a talent. When you are a little older . . . Study hard. . . . You will hear from me." He turned to the aide with the notebook. "You have all of this, Tom?"

"Yes, sir."

John assumed that he was dismissed. He was a bit puzzled. He did not know for certain the meaning of "athlete" or "talent," but the context of the conversation had seemed good. At least, it appeared that he was in no trouble. In fact, the attitude of the Bear was almost respectful.

John Buffalo was made to think that he had acquired a friend who had great influence. He wasn't sure just what it could mean, but he had a good feeling about it. And hadn't the Senator emphasized, *You will hear from me*?

THREE

John worked hard and studied well. Once he had learned what was wanted, he could produce satisfactory results. "Satisfactory," of course, was a relative term. By appearing cooperative, he avoided penalties. Others, more stubborn than he, still had their knuckles rapped with the ever-present ruler in the bony hand of the teacher. Sometimes it was a tweaked ear instead. Old White Horse seemed to delight in sneaking up behind a pupil who was involved in some minor infraction and twisting his ear painfully.

But Little Bull, son of Yellow Bull, was a quick learner. A whack with the ruler, only one twist of the ear, was all that was required. At the same time, he had developed the technique of presenting the flat, emotionless facial expression which had been noticed by Miss Whitehurst. There was never a lack of emotion in him, but it had quickly become apparent that it was safest not to express it. The ways of the whites were so different. . . . A moment of joy or laughter or even despair must not be acted on, at least openly. It might be misinterpreted by the Bear or Miss Whitehurst. They seemed to take little pleasure in anything, most of the time. The rare words of praise or encouragement they uttered were as a result of behavior that was exactly as they thought a student should behave. Any deviation always brought frowns and ear tweaks. Since it was hard to tell what might be expected, the safest way was to show no emotion at all. A flat, stone-faced appearance was usually acceptable. At least, it avoided pain.

There was another problem, too, one he had not anticipated. If he appeared too cooperative, he was resented by the other boys. More than once during recitation, he would make an error intentionally, to stay in the good graces of his fellow students. This sometimes brought frowns and mild criticism from Old White Horse, but avoided resentment from his classmates. Very quickly, John Buffalo, né Little Bull, was learning survival skills in this new world into which he had been thrust.

The holiday season came, with the celebration of Christ's birth to a virgin. Of course, a part of their instruction was religious. That, perhaps, was the strangest of all the white man's strange customs. Everyone was expected to think exactly alike, it appeared, ridiculous as that seemed to John Buffalo. How could anyone tell another what he must *think?* There was no room at all for the fact that it might conflict with the advice of one's own spirit-guide. In fact, the teachers seemed to have no guides of their own. Their thinking was based only on the secondhand telling by the missionary of what had been told to him. How sad, he thought, for one not to have his own guide. He considered that perhaps the relationship of the whites with the spirits was not as well formed as among the People.

He made the mistake of asking Miss Whitehurst about it, and was astonished at the reaction. He had expected almost anything but this. . . . *Anger,* in return for a mild suggestion about how to please and attract the help of the spirits! All he had suggested was that the spirits might welcome the scent of a pinch of burning tobacco.

"Blasphemy!" snorted the woman. "You were sent here

to *overcome* such savage heathen notions. Now you must pray to be forgiven!"

But John Buffalo had learned an important lesson. The whites—at least, these—did not *want* to hear more about the realm of the spirit. This, too, brought a feeling of sadness to him: that anyone would feel that there was nothing more to *learn* about the Creator and the grandfathers of the spirit-world.

But having been rebuked severely added to his determination. He would not attempt to discuss such things as one's relationship to God. In such situations, he could always retreat into the emotionless stoicism that was becoming easier with each use. The other students too, found it useful in many situations. If in doubt, it was always safe to show no feeling at all. It was becoming a trademark in dealing with whites, and was now almost expected by the teachers. It was a safe barrier behind which one could retreat at any time.

The students were allowed a short visit at home during the holiday season. It was given grudgingly, and with the admonition that they must not backslide into the old uncivilized ways of the heathen while with their parents.

"That is a life which you must rise *above*," Miss Whitehurst warned, shaking a forefinger in warning.

She was met with the emotionless stoicism that she had come to expect. Sometimes she scolded, doubting that any of her charges might be able to rise above the handicap of their savage heritage.

John Buffalo, his friend Charlie, and another boy, now called "Thomas Evans" for no reason that the boys could see, walked home together. It required a full day. Tom's name, like John's own, should have been good enough. The family of Wolf Dung, Tom's father, had a proud tradition, like that of Yellow Bull. Somehow the whites did not seem to appreciate the pride in family that was expressed in the heritage of the Wolf Dungs.

The day was cold and snowy, and the trip took most of the day. John's feet were numb when he reached his mother's lodge. She insisted that Thomas and Charlie come in, too, to warm themselves before traveling on. It was found that all three boys had frostbitten toes, and Pretty Robe decreed that they thaw by her lodge fire before traveling on. Charlie was later to lose a toe and the tips of both ears from the exposure.

They were a day late in returning, for which they were severely reprimanded.

"You know you were due to return yesterday . . . *Monday,* not Tuesday!" scolded White Horse. "Have you not enough fingers to count a week?"

This was very confusing. Why should one day be better than another? They *had* returned, and at about the prescribed time. Is not one day much like another? Maybe it had something to do with the strange preoccupation of the whites over every seventh day. "Sun Day." It was to be devoted to God. On the rest, presumably, God was omitted or, at least, ignored. It was fitting to worship and give prayers of thanks for the Sun, the grass, and the buffalo. In fact, the annual Sun Dance was dedicated to that very concept. But should not *every* day begin with prayers of thanks and worship for those very things, not merely one in seven? Sometimes he thought he would never understand the whites and their approach to religion.

John began to grow rapidly during the next year. Hair sprouted on parts of his body where there had been none. His voice would break unexpectedly during recitation, which was embarrassing to him. The other boys giggled, but not very much. They were subject to the same affliction, or would be soon. Charlie was a little slower in his bodily changes, but Tom Evans (Wolf Dung) was already taller than John by a hand's span.

If they had been among their own people, this achieving of manhood would have been a time of recognition. In these surroundings, there was little recognition of that fact of life.

Except . . . With greater size and strength came increased athletic ability. It was clumsy at first, and his coordination was off just a trifle. One has to relearn the use of arms and legs that have suddenly become inches longer. However, it did not take long to realize that he could utilize the increased mechanical advantage. He could run, throw, kick, and tackle better, in the various sports which they were being taught. Now he enjoyed such activities even more. In a way, this was a mark in time. He was simply going through the manhood rituals of the whites instead of those of the People.

As John began to gain weight, filling out muscle on the lanky frame that he was developing, the Bear began to take an even greater interest in him. Mr. "Bear," they had learned, was actually the name of the boys' supervisor, though it was spelled differently than the animal. George Baehr . . . To the students, he would always be "The Bear," no matter what. John spent many extra hours of practice on the athletic field, and this impressed the coach. Anyone willing to put forth extra effort will very likely receive extra attention, especially if he shows talent.

The boy finally realized that the gruff exterior and the Bear nickname covered a sensitive, caring instructor.

"Try it this way, John. . . . That's it. . . . Left elbow a little higher as you swing the bat. . . ." Or, "Follow through with the foot *after* your toe strikes the ball."

Once, the Bear was able to procure a special pair of athletic shoes for the growing feet of John Buffalo. They were of harder leather than his moccasins, even more solid than the traditional moccasin of his people, which had a thick rawhide sole. These white man's shoes had uppers also made of heavy leather, and tight laces. At first, John was uncomfortable with the tight construction around the ankle, but the Bear explained.

"They will protect your ankles. Less injury, more winning football games."

John found that he could also kick considerably better and with more accuracy, and was quickly convinced.

By the middle of his third year in the government school of the white man, he was big, well-developed, and his coordination was improving all the time. His mother was proud when he was allowed to visit home for the holidays.

"You are so like your father," she said, a sad smile on her still-handsome face. "Yellow Bull would be proud, Little Bull."

John had a feeling of remorse, as if he were betraying the memory of his father. His mother's use of "Little Bull" was a twist of the knife, though she probably did not realize it. He was not only abandoning his father's heritage for the ways of the white man, but even his *name*.

John said nothing, and managed to enjoy the visit with family friends. His only sister—several years older than he—had married and had a baby of her own. This, too, weighed heavily on his conscience. Under the system of the old ways, it would have been the responsibility of Little Bull to teach that nephew. Now, he could not, because he would not be with the People, but away at the government school. He mentioned this to his mother, rather shamefaced and apologetic.

"No, you must not think so, Bull. It is important that you *learn,* because times are changing. You will have to learn the new ways, and *then* you can teach your nephew."

Sadly, he had to accept the fact that she was right. Yet there was another hurt which he did not mention. He found himself *enjoying* the ways of the white man, the athletic competition, the encouragement of the Bear, the special treatment he received as the school's star athlete. Sometimes even Miss Whitehurst smiled at him, and she was known to smile at hardly anyone. Practically no one, except Mr. Baehr, in fact. The boys' early speculation may have been fairly close. He had come to realize that "old White Horse" was not really old. Probably younger than his mother, who now seemed considerably younger than he had once supposed.

He managed to relax enough to enjoy the holiday visit, and talked more with his mother than he ever had. There was a new closeness, and she really seemed to understand his doubts and fears. She had done well to raise her children alone after the death of Yellow Bull. John left to return to school feeling somewhat better, supported by the understanding of his mother.

It was the last time he was to see her. A few weeks later, a message carried by his sister's husband informed him that their mother, Pretty Robe, had died during the influenza epidemic that had struck after the holiday visit.

The heart of Little Bull was very heavy.

FOUR

The loss of his mother caused a further separation from the People. At the time of the next holiday, John went back to the reservation to visit his sister and her family. It was a disappointment. There was enough difference in their ages that they had never been really close. In addition, the instruction of the young in the tribal structure separated the sexes somewhat after the first few seasons.

Now it was even more so. Little Dove was completely occupied with her family, was expecting another child, and knew little of the things that he was learning in the school. They had nothing to talk about. Dove's husband was no better to talk to. A friendly enough individual, Crippled Crow had no knowledge of anything outside the traditional ways of the People. Crow talked of hunting and of war, largely over now. He was good with horses, but without the buffalo to hunt, and no more fighting, horses were becoming more of a liability than a mark of affluence. And Crow, too, had no idea of the purpose of an education. At times he almost seemed to sneer at John for abandoning the old ways in favor of the white man's.

The closest that he felt to Crow during that entire visit, however, were the times on horseback or helping with the care and feeding of the animals. John had been riding since before he could remember. His mother had tied him, as an infant, on the back of a dependable old mare and turned the animal out to graze. The gentle rocking motion of the mare's walking as she grazed was a comfort.

Now he found that there was a sweet nostalgia about riding a good horse across the prairie. John had not realized how he had missed it. He recalled now some of the "medicine" that his father had taught him at an early age, to bring his spirit and that of the horse together. He used it, and it was good.

"You're good with horses," observed his brother-in-law.

"Not really," John said modestly. "I do a little medicine."

The subject was dropped, and that was as close as they came to understanding.

All in all, John felt the whole holiday visit as if he were spending it among strangers. Strangers, in fact, whom he found quite uninteresting. There was nothing to talk about.

It was almost a relief to have the visit come to an end. He actually looked forward to returning to school.

"How was your holiday, John?" asked the Bear. "Lots of good family visit?"

Bear was either ignoring, or did not know, the young man realized, of the death of his mother. Or maybe he had just forgotten.

"Good." John assumed the stoic expression reserved for whites. That was done effortlessly now, without even thinking about it.

His two closest friends, Charlie Hand and Thomas (Wolf Dung) Evans, had fared a little better at home, but not much. Charlie had been in a fight with a young man who had openly accused him of being a traitor to his People by attending the white school.

"That's not true, Charlie," protested John. "We'll have to play by white man's rules, and we'd better learn them."

"He knows that, John," Thomas answered. *"We* all do, but those out on the reservation haven't figured it out yet. I know what he's talkin' about. I got those looks, too: 'You sold out your people!' It ain't true, of course. We know that, but *they* don't."

"Don't say *'ain't,'* " chided Charlie. "Ol' White Horse will whack your knuckles!"

The three friends laughed together. Then it struck John. They had been talking in English, or the joke about White Horse and "ain't" would have made no sense. Somehow, this was a moment of sadness that was worse than anything yet. He did not quite understand what was happening, only that he was losing something that might have been important to him, and to his illustrious father, Yellow Bull.

He plunged back into his schoolwork and his athletics with a vengeance. In this sense, it was good to be back, and he tried to drown his gnawing feelings of guilt in hard work.

A few weeks later, after baseball practice, the Bear took him aside.

"John," he said seriously, "you're going to have a visitor."

"What?"

"A visitor . . . Senator Langtry. You must have made quite an impression on him."

"But I don't know any—"

Then it came to him. That time, soon after he had entered the white man's school . . . An important white chief . . . The man had noticed him on the athletic field and had spoken to him, encouraged him. It had given him a good feeling, and the man had promised to return. . . .

John had all but forgotten. The Senator had not returned, and he had assumed that this was much like most of the white man's promises. He had put it behind him, and had accepted that nothing would come of the chance remark.

"Oh! You remember now!" said the Bear, smiling in approval. A smile from the Bear was an unusual occurrence, possibly ranking up there with the visit from a Senator.

"What does he want from me?" asked John.

"I don't know, but it seems that he remembers you. *Likes* you."

"Is this good?" John was still suspicious.

The Bear actually laughed. "I would think so, John. A Senator is a powerful chief."

"Like the White Father in Washington? White Hor— Miss Whitehurst told us about him. President Cleveland?"

"No, John," the coach chuckled. "This is a sort of sub-chief. He works in Washington, too, though."

John now remembered that on the occasion of the

Senator's last visit, they had been told some things about him. What was it? They must be respectful to the visiting chief because the man had something to do with the supplies that they received from the White Father. Those supplies were sometimes meager, but the students were always told that they should be grateful. *Clean your plate.... Some boys are starving....*

He'd never quite understood how cleaning his plate was going to prevent somebody else from starving, but he had no trouble in cooperating. Sometimes it seemed that he could never completely satisfy the needs of his rapidly growing body. The vigorous athletic program also required more fuel than a sedentary life would have. Whatever the connection, if this visiting chief had some influence over supplies for the school, he'd try to please the man. He would do so anyway, of course. Politeness and respect for authority were a major part of his schooling, as well as in his early days at home.

"When is he coming?" asked John.

A year ago, he would not have asked such a question. The Senator would arrive when the time came. Now he was beginning to see time as the whites did. Morning for study, afternoon for athletics, Sunday for God. He still didn't understand such preoccupation with time, but accepted it.

"I don't know when," answered the Bear. "When the time comes, I guess, but soon. A few days."

John smiled to himself. He found it amusing that the Bear, a stickler for schedule, was forced into such a position. *The Bear, on "Indian time"?* Charlie would enjoy the irony in this.

This time, the arrival of the Senator's party was more exciting. The students had a better idea of what might be expected, and of the importance of the visit. After all, on his previous tour, the school was new and everything quite tentative.

The ceremony was much the same, the students drawn up in tight formal lines on the athletic field. The platoon of blue-clad cavalry wheeled smartly into position, guidons fluttering. Again, the guest of honor stepped from the Army ambulance, which had been his conveyance, and strolled along the lines of students. His piercing glance darted quickly from place to place, thorough and efficient. He seemed to recognize John Buffalo. He took an extra moment to sweep his eyes up and down the newly developed frame, nodded, and moved on. It was a disappointing anticlimax, which John felt deeply as the parade dispersed and the students headed back to their barracks.

"What's the matter, John?" asked Tom Evans.

"Nothing. Only I thought . . ."

"Wasn't this white chief here before?" asked Charlie Hand. "Yes . . . He talked to you, no?"

"I . . . I think so," muttered John.

They were back at the barracks building, waiting for the supper bell, when the Bear entered.

"John?" he called.

"Yes, sir?" John rose from the bench where he had been sitting.

"Come with me, John. The Senator wants to talk with you."

"Now?"

"Yes. Over at the Agency. The Superintendent's office."

"Am I in trouble?"

"No, no. Quite the opposite, I believe." The teacher smiled. "John, you told me that your parents are both deceased?"

"Yes, sir. Yellow Bull when I was small. My mother, Pretty Robe, two winters past."

"Yes, that is what I thought. They will ask you about these things."

"But . . . Why?"

"I am not at liberty to say, John. But this may be a great opportunity for you. The Senator is interested in helping you."

"Helping me do *what?*"

"Never mind. Come, now. They are waiting at the office."

The Bear was quiet as they walked the few hundred yards to the cluster of Agency buildings. John still felt some anxiety. Was there something that he was supposed to do and *hadn't?* He could think of nothing. And why was the Bear wearing such a self-satisfied smirk? That in itself was a highly unusual thing, and as such, raised many doubts and fears.

They reached the headquarters building, and stepped inside. After the brightness of the summer sun, the dim interior made it difficult to see for a few moments. Then he saw an open door to another room, where the Superintendent sat in a chair beside a desk. John recognized the man, though he had never seen him up close.

Behind the heavy desk, which he took to be that of the Superintendent, sat another man, the Senator. Both men rose.

"Come in, son," said Senator Langtry. "Sit down." He motioned to a chair. "Let us talk."

FIVE

John, isn't it? John Buffalo . . . Yes," mused the Senator, shuffling papers on the desk.

Impressed as he was by the domineering presence of this man of importance, the young man felt a touch of resentment. His pride would not let him miss this opportunity.

"Little Bull, sir, son of Yellow Bull."

The Senator stopped shuffling papers and looked up over the eyeglasses perched on his nose and ears. He seemed surprised. His mouth hung partly open for a moment.

"Sir, the boy—" began the Bear, but the Senator waved him to silence.

"So . . . Some *spunk*. That is good!" He looked back at the papers. "Ah, here . . . Yes, renamed 'John Buffalo' on admission to the school. Yes, 'Little Bull' would hardly be appropriate for a civilized man, you know. . . . Have to rise above all that. Hmm . . . Father deceased, I see, before the time of admission."

"Yes, sir," said the Bear. "His mother also, now. That's in another part of the record."

"Ah . . . My sympathy, John."

The man seemed genuinely concerned.

"Thank you, sir," said the boy. He was getting mixed feelings about this man. The Senator's spirit was a hard one to interpret.

Now the Senator pushed the papers aside and removed his spectacles, folded them, and placed them in a vest pocket. He leaned his forearms against the edge of the desk and placed his hands together meticulously, fingers spread, each fingertip touching its corresponding digit on the other hand. The hands were long and slender, looking out of place on a stoutly built man. The spread fingers reminded John for a moment of a spider, walking on a mirror.

"Son," said Senator Langtry, "I have a great opportunity for you."

I'm not your son, John wanted to say. *I am the son of Yellow Bull!*

Instead, he figured that for now, he'd better play along, until he could learn more.

"Yes, sir?" he asked politely.

"John, I have taken a great interest and no small amount of effort in a special project. A school, for boys such as yourself, who must have training to enter the civilized world. It is called the Carlisle Indian Industrial School, in Pennsylvania. Established a few years ago. Highly successful."

John had no idea where Pennsylvania might be, so he said nothing.

Langtry went on, "Young men are trained, as carpenters, masons, smiths, but also educated in the arts and the humanities, to an extent. One should be able to read the classics, of course, and to write and cipher."

The man appeared to be leading up to something, and John was curious.

"Now . . . Mr. Baehr tells me that you have been quite diligent in your athletic endeavors. Football, baseball . . . It seems that you have some natural ability in these areas?"

"Well, I . . ." John had no idea where this conversation was going.

"Never mind. It's obvious that you are willing to work hard to use your natural gift. In short, you're good at it, Mr. Baehr says. And, you'll remember, I saw you play during my last visit. Your dropkick won the game. But let me go on. I am interested in building the athletic program at Carlisle into one that can produce skilled, competitive teams. Especially football. It's been quite a few years, now—maybe twenty—since the Association was formed. The American Intercollegiate Football Association. Ever hear of it?"

"No, sir."

"Well, of course not. But teams from different colleges and universities meet to play. A great many schools are beginning to participate. Train travel is making it easier all the time. Now, here's my plan. I want to enroll you at Carlisle, where you can play football and learn a trade at the same time. How does that sound?"

"But I have no money, sir."

The Senator threw back his head and laughed heartily.

"I didn't ask you that, son! There will be no cost to *you*. We can even arrange for a bit of pocket money for your incidental expenses. No problem. Now . . . You have no parents, so no permission is needed. I will be your sponsor of record. Can you be ready to leave tomorrow morning?"

It was not really a question, but a command. The Bear was nodding encouragement and smiling.

"Yes, sir. . . . I guess so."

John had only a vague notion where this place called Pennsylvania might be. Somewhere in the East . . . The Bear had told him that the trip would require three or four days on the train. He had never seen a "train," other than a row of wagons carrying freight.

"I don't know, John," teased Charlie Hand. "I heard they eat Indian kids in Pessabania."

"Let him alone, Charlie," said Tom Evans. "You know that's not true."

"How would I know?" Charlie retorted. "I've never been there. Don't even know where it is."

"Back east somewhere," said John. "Anyway, that's what the Senator said."

"We'll miss you, John," Tom said seriously. "Will you come back and see us?"

"I don't know, Tom. If I can, I will."

John packed his few belongings into a small cardboard suitcase given him by the Bear. Miss Whitehurst gave him a little Bible, like those from which they studied.

"Don't forget to read it, John," she admonished. "Work hard. Make us proud of you."

She gave him a quick hug, to his embarrassment and to the glee of the onlooking students. John was startled and surprised to see a tear in the usually stern eye of the teacher.

"Look at that!" whispered Charlie Hand to Tom. "She's kissin' him!"

"No, she's not, she's just huggin' him." Tom giggled.

"Same thing. Well, almost."

Then, to everyone's astonishment, Old White Horse *did* kiss him—a quick peck on the cheek. The students cheered, and John blushed crimson as he climbed into the ambulance with the Senator and his aide. The corporal who drove the team flapped the reins and muttered, "Giddap," and the horses leaned into the harness and moved out. The military escort fell into double file behind.

It was hot and dusty in the enclosed vehicle. Even leaving the back door open did not help much. It seemed to suck in more dust.

"We'd have been better off in an open buggy," observed the Senator. "How did we happen to choose this, William?"

"We requested it, sir," said his aide. "Our last trip west was in winter, you remember."

"Ah, yes. It was needed, then. So *that* request is still

being honored." He chuckled wryly. "Never let common sense interfere with written orders, I suppose."

"Yes, sir. I'll see to it next time."

"Well, it will be better on the train. Ever ride on a train, John?"

"No, sir. Never *seen* one."

The Senator chuckled. "Ah, John, there are many things you'll see. The country is changing, growing. Modern achievements you can hardly imagine. Lights with no flame . . . A buggy that needs no horse to pull it . . . Trains that can run a hundred miles an hour . . . You will see great things in your lifetime, my boy!"

John had no idea how prophetic those words were.

The train was big and noisy and a bit terrifying, as it pulled into the little depot, bell clanging and brakes screeching. There seemed to be smoke and steam everywhere, people hurrying to and fro, porters handling baggage, men loading freight into and out of one of the rear cars.

"It'll be a little while, sir," said the ticket agent. "She takes on water here."

The Senator nodded and strolled down the platform, flanked by John and the aide, William. Their military escort had been dismissed on arrival at the station. The Senator explained to the young man how the big water tank beside the tracks was positioned to refill the boiler's supply.

The shiny black engine, with gleaming brass fittings and red trim, was a thing of wonder. Smoke rose from its stack, and steam vented from its boiler with a lazy hiss, waiting for reactivation of the steam chest. Directly behind the engine was the fuel tender, where the fireman sat, resting while he could, until he, too, could be reactivated. He was covered with black coal dust.

The engineer, relieved from his tasks for a few moments,

waved from the cab. A man in overalls walked along the platform with a long-spouted oil can, lubricating axles and other points of friction.

In a very short time, the crew had readied the train.

" 'Board!" shouted the conductor, and people hurried to climb up the metal steps and into the cars.

The car which the Senator and his party boarded was apparently one which had been added for the occasion. It was newer, and the seats, unlike those of the standard cars, were arranged with some facing the others and with tables between.

"A dining car?" The Senator was surprised.

"Yes, sir, but not operational," answered the aide. "The railroad people thought it might be more comfortable."

"Ah! Especially for me? Nice gesture. William, make a note. We must drop them a letter of thanks."

"Of course, Senator. Consider it done."

Now there was a rumbling sound as the engineer began to activate the power. Steam rushed from the steam chest into the pistons on the drive wheels, and the metal monster inched forward. Then a loud hiss of venting steam, and another few moments as the pressure was reapplied through the system of pipes and valves. Suddenly the wheels escaped from the friction that enabled them to propel the engine. The drivers spun rapidly, sending showers of sparks for a few moments and hurrying the venting of the steam with a mighty·rush. But the train was already moving. Slowly, like a falling tree, it gained momentum with the next push of hot vapor from the steam chest. Another vent, another gain in speed . . . Very quickly, the depot was left behind. The prairie began to slip past with ever-increasing rapidity, and the engineer blew the whistle triumphantly as his train fairly flew down the track.

John saw a couple of young men, probably fellow tribesmen, though he did not recognize them. They were riding like the wind, astride good horses, racing the train.

Stretched to their limit, ears flattened, moccasined heels drumming their flanks, the animals were still no match for the iron horse. They were quickly left behind.

The riders knew that they had no chance in such a race, he realized. It was merely an exercise, a carefree act of exuberance. It occurred to him that it was this sort of meaningless pleasure that he was leaving behind. For a moment, he felt a pang of regret. He yearned, envied the two young men, riding like the wind with the fresh prairie air in their faces. Would the experience, knowledge, and education that he had been promised in any way surpass the sheer pleasure of riding a fine horse with this reckless abandon? He watched the riders until they fell behind and out of sight.

SIX

The train rushed along the track, the monotonous double thump of the flanged wheels on steel rails becoming almost hypnotizing. There was no variation in the rhythm. Each span of track was exactly the same length as the one before, and the thousands before that.

Click-clack . . . Click-clack . . . Click-clack.

John had first been alarmed by the sound, but then had reasoned what its cause must be. It was preferable, anyway, to the rush and roar of the engine as they started and stopped at stations or at water tanks far from anywhere.

After a certain amount of time, the rhythm of the rails became a matter of interest. John found that he could tell when the *click-clack* was about to slow as they attacked a steeper grade. Conversely, it accelerated on the downhill slope. He began to liken it to the beat of the drums in the dance rituals of his people. More like the rattles, maybe. He began to imagine that there might be a song or chant appropriate to this odd double *click-clack* as each joint in the endless track was encountered, passed, and left behind. He began to hum, largely meaningless sounds, in cadence with the rhythm of the wheels.

Ah-ho-we-oh,
ta-me-ka-no!

He was drowsy, half-asleep, a dreamy semi-awake state that was at the same time restful and exciting. His eyes were half-closed, his body swaying. In spirit he was dancing to the heartbeat of the drums with all the quickening of the senses that his ancestors had felt. The flickering of light and shadow through the train windows as they passed trees and hills became the flicker of the firelight at the dance.

Ah-ho-we-oh . . .

"What are ye doin', boy?" asked William, the Senator's aide, with a chuckle. "Pretendin' ye're back on the prairie? Ye'd best get over that. Ye're to be tamed and civilized, ye know."

John was embarrassed, a little ashamed, maybe. The aide was certainly not one of John's favorite people. There had always been an air of snobbish superiority about him that was puzzling to the boy. He could see nothing admirable in the man. William was a servant to the Senator, hustling to do his bidding, at times almost fawning on the Senator's words. It was demeaning to have such a man belittling his drowsy musings.

"I . . . I was partly asleep," he mumbled apologetically. Instantly, he regretted it. He, son of Yellow Bull, had nothing for which to apologize. Certainly not to such a man as this, who now gave a chuckling snort.

The Senator, who had been dozing in his seat, roused suddenly.

"What is it?"

"Nothing, Senator," William said quickly. "We should be stopping for water soon."

"Ah, yes . . ."

The Senator shifted his body in the seat as his consciousness returned and he became reoriented. He glanced at John.

"Doing all right, John?"

"Yes, sir."

"Good. A tiresome trip. Well, we'll have better accommodations after we reach Chicago. We'll be there for a day. I have meetings and such. Then we'll travel on. But we'll have a Pullman then."

"Pullman?"

Some sort of contest, John supposed. He'd have to learn the rules.

"I've never played that," he confessed.

"No, no, John," explained the Senator. "The Pullman isn't a game, it's a car. A sleeping car on the train. We'll have beds and all. Much more comfortable quarters."

"Pullman!" snickered the aide, with a sidelong glance that was far from sympathetic.

John's cheeks burned with embarrassment. The Senator noted this and spoke with encouragement.

"You'll learn all these things, my boy, and more. Ah, it's a great, wonderful modern world out there."

"Pullman!" snorted William.

The Senator seemed irritated.

"Mr. Bagley," he said sternly, "I'll thank you to treat Mr. Buffalo with respect. He is our guest, and in our charge."

"Yes, sir," muttered William.

John could not suppress a sidelong glance of satisfaction.

Chicago was beyond all that John had been able to imagine. Huge buildings, some several layers high, people everywhere, hurrying somewhere else . . . The "lake" . . . More like what he had imagined the ocean would be, but fresh water, Senator Langtry said.

The Senator took him shopping to buy clothes more suitable for his introduction to Carlisle.

"But . . . I have no money, Senator."

"That's all right," chuckled the big man. "It'll be taken care of."

John wasn't sure he understood all of this, but he knew that it is impolite to refuse a gift. His mother had taught him that. He assumed that the Senator must be responsible.

"Thank you, sir," he said firmly. "But I've done nothing to earn this kindness."

The Senator laughed.

"Not yet, maybe. But you will, John. I expect you to become one of the greatest athletes in the country."

"Athletes?"

"Yes . . . You're good at football . . . baseball."

"Playin' *games?*"

"Of course, John. There's a great deal of interest in athletic competition between colleges now, and it's growing. I want to see some of the Indian schools on the cutting edge of this trend. As I've told you, the school at Carlisle is one of my pet projects. With well-chosen players, we can field a great team at football or baseball. They could compete favorably with Yale or Princeton. . . ."

The man rambled on, and John's mind began to wander. He had no knowledge of the names and places of which the Senator spoke, and it was easy to lose interest. He was gaining a general idea, though, one which intrigued him.

It nested neatly with the basic premise which he had gradually adopted: *To be successful with the white man, one must know his ways.* There had been times when he had fought this, but during the years in the Indian school, things had always been better when he had fallen back on that assumption.

He had always enjoyed competition, from the earliest days of his memory. Running, swimming, throwing, races of all kinds. It was part of the schooling of a young man of his people. The competition was for the purpose of producing strong, capable men for hunting and for war. As the son of Yellow Bull, and because of his family's pride, it was appropriate to do his very best. Above all this, however, was the fact that he *liked* it. The thrill of a well-placed throw or shot, farther or straighter or more accurately, sent his heart to pumping with satisfaction and joy. To be in front at the finish line of a race, ahead of everyone else, the wind in his face, was a special thrill.

There was now to be no more war, it appeared. The white man had won. Even Red Cloud, who had humbled the white man's whole Army, had now conceded that it was over. For a while, there had seemed no purpose in the development of the skills of manhood, and his heart had been heavy. Even the hunting was over, the buffalo gone, and there had seemed no purpose to life.

He could forget, when he was involved in the very physical sports, that it was temporary. In the end, meaningless. But, for the time that he was so engaged, his blood raced and his heart was good. That had gotten him through some of the hard times.

Now . . . He was just barely beginning to grasp a new revelation about the white man: They, too, admired physical prowess in anyone, and respected it greatly. If he were able to show ability, strength, and stamina—*manhood*—they, too, would respect him. He was already respected by the Senator. The man had said so. How fortunate, thought John, to have found a white man who understood.

The first night on the Pullman car was a startling experience. The Senator had seemed greatly impressed with such convenience, but until after the sun set and the reporter began to ready the car for the night, John had had no idea why. It had seemed more dignified not to ask any questions. Actually, it was a part of the stony, emotionless facade that he had developed for use in the presence of whites. His fellow students had done much the same: If in doubt as to what reaction is expected, *show none*.

Now he was amazed to see the Negro pull, push, and fold the seats in the Pullman car to create beds. Beds with white sheets and coverlets, and soft pillows to place under one's head. John wondered if the pulling of the beds into position was the reason for the term "Pullman," or whether the black man was the pull man. He did not want to reveal his ignorance by asking.

He was assigned an upper bunk while the Senator and his aide took the lowers.

"Good night, my boy," said the Senator genially. "In another day, we reach our destination."

The porter had showed him how to close the curtains that concealed his bunk, and John did so. In a way, sleeping in close proximity to others reminded him of his childhood and the lodge of his parents. He fell asleep, dreaming of his mother, drawing the door-skin closed for the night. The *click-clack* of the wheels became the sound of the clicking deer-hoof rattles that had hung beside the door. . . . Their purpose was for the use of any visitor, who could signal his presence by rattling the hoofs and calling out his name.

John's memory was playing strange tricks, pulling him back and forth, asleep as well as awake. He awoke once, started to roll over, and nearly fell from the bed. He lay there in the darkness, trying to remember what he was doing here, and why. He had been dreaming of a massive herd of buffalo, stampeding across open prairie. He was a child, in the lodge of his parents, and someone was trying to waken the family. . . .

Then the rumble of the herd became the trembling shudder of the train, and the clicking of the deer-hoof door rattle was the *click-clack* of the rails.

What am I doing here? he thought. *This is no place for the son of Yellow Bull!*

SEVEN

Eventually, the train trip came to an end. It was a pleasure to stand on solid ground again. John had lost track of time, the days and nights blurring together in a maze of swaying cars, clicking rails, the rush of the engine, and the wailing notes of the steam whistle. The blur of passing cities, grassland, forests, and farms fell behind in a similar confused array in his memory.

Back on solid ground, he felt that it, too, had been affected by the long trip. The ground would not stay steady, but seemed to be swaying, causing him to plant each step carefully as he walked across the platform toward the packed cinders of the street.

"The earth won't hold still, eh?" chuckled the Senator. "Don't worry, it won't last long. I'm told that sailors have the same problem after a long voyage, with the rocking of the ship."

There was a carriage waiting, and a polite driver who

helped stow their luggage in the rear. It was a short drive to the school.

There, the Senator took John to an office in one of the buildings, where he was introduced to a man behind a desk.

"Welcome, my boy," gushed the man.

It was plain to John that the motive in the profuse welcome was not really genuine. It appeared to be an effort on the part of the administrator to ingratiate himself with Senator Langtry. The Senator appeared not to notice, in his own effort to impress the school's administrator with the importance of his own prodigy. It was a very uncomfortable time, and John made full use of his stoic, expressionless face as the men visited briefly.

"How was the trip, Senator?"

"Not bad . . . Usual inconveniences, of course. Interesting to John, here. He'd never *seen* a train until now."

"Yes . . . Well, we'll certainly treat him well, Senator," said the other, with a laugh that was just a little too forced. "I've sent for the coach. He'll—Oh, here he is now!"

A burly man in trousers, a sweater, and a billed cap entered the room and glanced around curiously. A silver whistle hung around his neck on a black string that might have been a shoelace.

"Senator Langtry, Coach McGregor," introduced the administrator.

The two men shook hands enthusiastically. A bit too much so, John thought.

"And this," said the Senator proudly, "is John Buffalo, the student athlete I had written of."

"Yes," said the coach. "I recall . . . Football?"

"Yes, sir," said John modestly. "Or baseball. Anything . . ."

His voice trailed off, and he had an uncomfortable feeling that he'd said too much. Better to have stopped with "Yes, sir." He'd remember that.

However, the men seemed not to notice. They were busy talking about the weather, the political situation, and the program of the school.

"Yes, we're graduating skilled workers," said the administrator proudly. "They're easily employed. We have working arrangements with several factories in the area. Shoes, mostly. But, there's some demand for machinists, other light industry. And of course we can't forget the three Rs. . . . Readin', writin', and 'rithmetic!"

The three men laughed, though John didn't see anything very funny. Of the three subjects mentioned, only "Reading" began with an R. Maybe he'd missed the joke. Or, maybe that *was* the joke. White men, he thought, don't have much of a sense of humor. As always, his best course of action seemed to be to assume his defensive stoicism.

"Don't forget athletics!" reminded the coach. "We have a very progressive program."

"Yes, I know." The Senator smiled. "That's my purpose in bringing this young man. Your teams are competing well?"

"Yes, sir. We're traveling quite a bit for baseball, football, track and field. Other teams come here, too. Rail travel is making it easier all the time. We're considering a trip to Springfield College up in Massachusetts. Great athletic program there. . . . We'll play Harvard at football, soon."

"Very good!" Senator Langtry agreed. "I see a few female students on the campus. What is their course of study?"

"Home economics, mostly," the administrator answered. "Kitchen skills, serving . . . Our own dining hall is staffed largely by students. We're considering a nursing program. Possibly, even secretarial skills."

"Really?" asked the Senator. "They're that teachable?"

"Oh, yes. Actually, we think that many of our students approach the intelligence of whites."

"Yes, that's been my premise," said the Senator quickly, almost irritably. "But, the *females?*"

"Quite capable, sir," answered the administrator. "Accustomed to hard work, you know. Some, quite capable."

Here was a very puzzling thing. John found it hard to understand. Whites, he had learned, professed to hold women in high regard, and offered respect from a distance. He wondered whether any of these men realized that among John's people, women could speak in Council, vote, hold office, and own property. He had only learned in the past few years that white women had *none* of these privileges. Lakota women would surely not stand for such treatment.

Now, here were three white men, uncomfortably discussing whether women as a group were intelligent enough to learn. . . . Another of the jokes that whites would not understand. John smiled to himself.

"Yes, yes . . . Quite true, undoubtedly," the Senator was saying. "But . . . I must depart now. I've been away from my family for some time on this trip to the reservation school."

He turned to John and spoke, a little more slowly and a little louder.

That was another odd thing he'd noticed about whites as they talked to someone who did not speak English well. Somehow they seemed to think that speaking more loudly and more slowly would overcome the language barrier. John was somewhat offended by the Senator's use of this technique at this time. He was rather proud of his use of English. He had come a long way under the tutelage of Miss Whitehurst. He realized also that these men had been talking as if he were not even present. Almost as if he did not exist. It was a demeaning thing, a reminder that they considered him a lesser person.

But now he must try to concentrate on the Senator's words.

"John, I must leave you for now. These folks will help you get settled. Now, I'll be back soon to see about how you're getting on. You understand?"

"Yes, sir."

"Good. Work hard, now!"

"Yes, sir."

"We'll take good care of him, Senator," assured the coach.

"I know you will, Mac, and I thank you."

They shook hands all around, and the Senator rejoined his aide in the anteroom. The office had been too crowded.

For John, it was almost a moment of panic. In a way, the Senator had been his last link to home. His uneasiness was based on the fact that this great and powerful man seemed different, here among his own kind.

But he *had* promised to return soon.

The Carlisle Indian Industrial School was considerably different from the government school where Little Bull had become John Buffalo. The students here were older and, in most cases, had a good command of the English language. All had already attended primary schools, and Carlisle was directed more toward the preparing of a young adult to enter the world of the white man in the job market. However, it seemed that there was a great emphasis on physical fitness. Competitive athletics played an important part at this secondary level.

The track-and-field facilities were like none he had ever seen. A long oval running track of hard-packed cinders circled a smooth green area that formed the football field. There was a grandstand large enough to seat hundreds of people. A number of young men were running, jumping hurdles, tossing a discus, and putting the shot. Some of these were events that were completely unfamiliar to him.

He was especially interested in one area, where two or

three young men were throwing a long pole that looked like a spear or buffalo lance.

"What's that spear throwing?" he asked the student who had been assigned to show him around.

"The javelin? You've never seen that, I guess. Looks like a buffalo lance, don't it?"

Both laughed.

"There are other things you'll like here," said Little Horse. "The shot put . . . Like throwing a big rock. Races, of course."

Such competition was only for the young men, it seemed. Another of the mysteries of the white man's way, to John. Why should women not be as physically fit as men? Among his people, girls were taught the use of weapons for self-defense in case of enemy attack. Their work, too, was as hard as that of men. In addition, they must bear and nurture the children. How could white women be relegated to a lesser role by their own people?

The living facilities were a great improvement over those at the reservation school. There were dormitory rooms, to which usually four young men were assigned for sleeping quarters. There was a library and study hall, as well as a dining hall. In a different area of the campus were living quarters for the young women, strictly off-limits to male students, and vice versa, of course.

Little Horse was one of John's roommates. For some reason he had been allowed to keep his own name.

"What's your tribe?" Horse had asked at their first meeting.

"Lakota. What's yours?"

"Ah! My old enemy! I am Crow."

It could have been an uncomfortable moment, but it passed without further comment. By simple understanding, these two had more in common that either had with the white man.

"We have another roommate," Horse explained. "He's

working today. Charlie Smith . . . He's Cherokee."

" 'Smith'?" They gave him a white man's name?" asked John.

"No, he says it's a family name, from way back. I guess they've been in touch with whites a long time."

"There are four beds," John observed.

"Yes . . . We may get another roommate, I guess."

"You said this Smith is working?" asked John.

"Yes. We're all expected to help with maintenance, things like that. You'll see. It's easy work, mostly. But come on, now. It's nearly time for supper. They'll ring a bell pretty soon. You know how whites are about time."

There was a sound of footsteps in the hall, and a young man entered the room, looking curiously at John.

"Charlie," said Little Horse, "this is John Buffalo, our new roommate."

" *'Siyo!*" said Charlie Smith, extending a hand.

"Hello," said John, a little puzzled at the unfamiliar word of greeting. "You use your own tongue?"

Little Horse laughed. "We're not supposed to. Charlie's just showin' off. That means 'hello.' "

"I figured that," said John. "But, I got my knuckles rapped, once, for saying 'thank you' in Lakota."

The others chuckled.

"It's not so bad here," said Smith. "They don't push it. But . . . You're Lakota?"

"Yes. My father was Yellow Bull. You know Lakotas?"

"No . . . I just wondered. Aren't you and Horse supposed to be enemies?"

"Once . . . Not now," said Little Horse.

"I guess we're all in this together," said Charlie Smith.

EIGHT

In a few days a fourth roommate arrived, a quiet, intelligent young man who was introduced as Will Clark, a Chippewa. It was some time later that he referred to himself as "Ojibway," and was questioned about it.

"I thought they said 'Chippewa,'" observed Charlie Smith.

Will smiled his shy, likable smile, and explained.

"My people say 'Ojibway.' Whites call us 'Chippewa.'"

"Then they're the same?" asked Little Horse. "I had heard both, too."

Charlie chuckled. "Maybe it's too hard for a white tongue to say 'Ojibway,'" he observed.

Autumn was approaching, and it was wonderful to be outside. By shortly after daylight each morning, John was up, out, and running on the cinder track or across country. He sat through classes, impatiently waiting for the daily opportunity to take to the athletic field again. Coach McGregor worked with him closely, making helpful suggestions now and then. John particularly enjoyed some of the track-and-field events. He could throw the javelin farther than anyone on the campus. It was simply a matter of concentration. With the shaft in his hand and his arm ready, he became again Little Bull, son of Yellow Bull, and the polished javelin a spear or lance. He longed to try a real lance on buffalo. It was somewhat puzzling to him that the javelin contest was for distance only, not accuracy.

What good is distance if the lance finds no target?

"You're doing well, John," Coach McGregor told him one day, "but now, let's plan a little. Most of our track-and-field events are in the spring. It's good to stay in practice, but fall is usually for football. And since your sponsor, the Senator, is a football fan, we should work on that."

"What about baseball?"

"Spring and summer, mostly. For now, let's concentrate on football. Senator Langtry told me that your dropkick is pretty good. Actually, I think he said 'marvelous.' Come, show me."

They went to the field, and John practiced by the hour . . . Hold the ball, drop it at the exact moment as he took the step forward. . . . The idea, he had long ago realized, was to make the step a long one, with the right leg already swinging when the ball hit the ground.

"They used to play football with a soccer ball," the coach explained. "It's round, of course, and could be kicked from any angle. Now, with the pointed ball . . . Yes, that's it. . . . The ball should hit the ground just a heartbeat before your toe touches it. Good kick! Try it again! Now . . . Drop it with a little more tilt toward you. That's it!"

With John's natural instinct and the coach's skill at understanding the mechanism involved, he improved rapidly, both in accuracy and distance. By the time the season was ready to start, he could split the uprights neatly from any angle, and was improving considerably in distance. Part of that was undoubtedly the fact that he was gaining weight. Lean, hard muscle was filling out a frame that had once been lanky. John gloried in this strength and he could feel his blood race with the excitement of competition. The thump and shock of body contact felt good, and allowed him to work out a lot of the frustration he sometimes felt. He longed to ride a good horse on open prairie with the wind in his hair, to hunt as his father and grandfather had, and generations before them. To count coup on an enemy, even. He had a few confused emotions about that, but now it seemed unlikely that his lifetime would ever involve that.

There came a day when Senator Langtry again visited the campus. It was a total surprise to John, because no one had told him. It was a Saturday, the day of Carlisle's first football game of the season. This was not a major game, merely a friendly scrimmage with nearby Lakesburg College. Later in the season, the team would travel to Albright College at Reading, Beaver College at Glenside, and would also play Princeton, Harvard, and the U.S. Military Academy at West Point.

The squad was still warming up as Coach McGregor motioned John aside.

"Your friend the Senator's here." He motioned toward the stands with a nod of his head. "Better look sharp today."

"But he's not—" John began in protest, but the coach held up a hand to stop him.

"Never mind, John," McGregor said with a wide grin. "I know. Not your 'friend.' But he's taken a liking to you. He can be a big help. Don't look now, but when you get a chance, look for him. About a third of the way up, in the middle section. Box seats."

John took a quick glance at the crowd, and his eyes fell on the loveliest face he had ever seen. Even at this distance he was struck by the pure beauty of the young woman. Her face was flushed with excitement, and her smile was for the occasion, for the events of the day. But to him, it could only appear that it was for him, personally. For him only . . .

"Pretty, isn't she?" said the coach, seemingly from a far distance. "That, my boy, is the Senator's daughter."

"His . . . daughter?"

"Yes. They seldom miss a game."

"I . . . I guess I never wondered if he had a family."

"Oh, yes. That's his wife on the left, there. They have a son, too. At West Point, I understand."

"I see."

But John did not elaborate as to *what* he saw. Anyway, he could not have described his reaction. He only knew that up there in the stands, a young woman was watching his every move. Therefore, every move must be as nearly perfect as he could make it. He could not recall a time in his life when he had felt a stronger motive. On this important day, it was essential that he show his prowess. In the space of a few heartbeats, he had reverted to the young hunter-warrior. . . . He was ready to demonstrate his skill at combat to win the attention of the maiden who waited. In his mind's eye, he could already visualize this lovely creature as she participated in the traditional victory dances of his People. A woman, honoring her warrior as she reenacted his deeds of valor . . .

It had been a long time since he had experienced such thoughts of the People. Now, there seemed no other way in which he could have felt it. The pride and glory of the strength of his youth was matched by the sheer animal attraction to the beautiful creature in the box seat. He must be careful now. Must not be distracted . . . Not yet . . . First there was a battle to win.

The grassy field had been mowed and tended, and was now marked in squares with narrow stripes of whitewash. . . . The "gridiron." Now he must concentrate on the visiting team. For this afternoon, the enemy. Some of the students from Lakesburg were big, but no bigger than he. Besides, there was more than size at stake here. Agility, quickness, and intelligence, too, must all play a part. And for the moment, he must try to forget that the startling beauty in the center stands would be watching. Even so, he could almost feel those eyes on his shoulders as he went through the warm-up drills. At least, he thought he could. The eyes would be large and dark, as deep as the liquid eyes of a fawn. But no . . . the young woman was white, with hair the color of corn silk. Maybe her eyes would be blue. Maybe even green, like those of a Mandan girl he had met here at Carlisle. She claimed to be pureblood, but who knows? He tried to remember the color of the Senator's eyes. That might be a way to guess. . . . Light, as nearly as he could recall. A "white-eyes." Were they light brown or gray?

He missed the kick, and realized that he had lost his concentration. Damn! It was only practice, but he'd made that kick, from that angle and distance, dozens of times without a miss.

"Come on, John," said the coach, a little irritably. "You can't let the crowd bother you. Settle down."

John wanted to tell Mac that it wasn't the crowd, just one stunningly beautiful woman that was bothering him. But that would be no better in the eyes of the coach. Worse, maybe. And the thought of competing for a woman's attention should help, not detract, should it not? He was confused.

But now the whistle blew and both teams returned to the sidelines to huddle for last-minute instructions.

As an underclassman, John Buffalo would not start the game. Substitutions would take place only in the event of injury or exhaustion. John was torn by mixed emotions. He longed to get into the game, but would not want to do so because of injury to a teammate.

Lakesburg won the toss and would receive the kick. They drove down the field, mostly by brute strength, and were threatening to score when their halfback fumbled. The Carlisle players pounced on the ball and recovered. The stands went wild.

The players on the bench jumped to their feet to join the exultant cheering. As the noise subsided and they began to return to their seats, John turned a glance up behind him to the rows of spectators.

He wasn't certain that he could even locate the face that he sought, in the mass of humanity ranked there. He need not have worried. From the myriad of excited faces, one stood out. The eyes . . . Yes, they were blue. . . . Deep, clear blue, darker than sky, but lighter than night. . . . They were alight with excitement. Her lips were parted slightly as she leaned forward with anticipation, waiting for the next play. Such excitement and enthusiasm on the part of a woman, particularly a white woman, was probably considered unladylike. To John, it was charming and desirable. He had never been particularly attracted to white women. They often reminded him of Old White Horse, back in the reservation school.

When he thought of romance, he had always held, in his mind's eye, the image of one of his own: an Indian girl, probably Lakota. All of that was forgotten now. Here, up in the box seats behind him, sat a new ideal. The Senator's daughter seemed to embody all that he wanted. She represented his goal, to make good in the white man's world, by the white man's rules. And, even though the white man's woman often seemed pale and helpless, here was an exception. He could tell by the look in her eye that here was a woman who could stand shoulder to shoulder with her man, to fight the world, if necessary.

"Play's startin'," said Little Horse on the bench beside him.

In the space of a heartbeat, John was back in the world of reality. Dirt, sweat, hard work . . . The effort of the game in front of him. For a moment, he had let a fantasy overcome him. He realized now that in all probability his thoughts had been completely ridiculous. He did not even know the girl's name.

He turned his attention back to the game. Carlisle had taken over the ball, and now began the drive back up the field. Play by play, dig in, shove, pull, block, grinding square by square up the field . . . A change here and there . . . A lateral toss from the quarterback to the left halfback caught the defenders off guard and proved effective for a gain of some twenty yards. Later, there was a fumble on the snap: but when the pile of players was untangled, the ball was clasped tightly to the stomach of Carlisle's right guard.

The momentum of emotion carried the team the length of the field, yard by painful yard, and led to the first touchdown of the day. The kick for the extra point was blocked, but no matter. Carlisle had drawn first blood, and now held the momentum.

Not for long . . . Lakesburg made an adjustment in their lineup. A giant of a young man who had been playing at left tackle was shifted to right halfback for the offensive drive. The quarterback would take the snap from center and hand it to the big halfback as he charged forward. It proved impossible to stop the momentum of well over two hundred pounds of bone and muscle in less than three or four yards beyond the line of scrimmage. Carlisle shifted their bigger linemen to defend the crushing onslaught, but this weakened other sections of the line, and allowed other plays. Lakesburg scored, and their kick for the extra point was good: 7–6, in favor of Lakesburg.

The game now settled into a tough, grinding, punishing duel. Neither team could completely stop the other, and the afternoon ground on slowly.

On the bench, John fidgeted impatiently. He longed to join the battle, to feel the shock of body contact, to match his own bulk against that of the big halfback from Lakesburg. There were a few substitutions for minor injuries and for heat exhaustion, but the coach did not even look toward John Buffalo. He had made quite plain from the beginning that no one must *ask* to play. The upperclassmen had warned newcomers that to make such a request would insure that they would *never* be put in the game. It was the way of McGregor, and of any good coach, it was said.

So John said nothing, but sat and gritted his teeth, and watched the game grind its painful way toward the end.

Carlisle was ahead, 20–14, and shadows were growing long, when it happened. There were only two minutes to play, and Carlisle held the ball. Victory was in sight . . . but everyone was exhausted. The pass came from the center—a poor snap. The quarterback juggled the ball, and as he was hit by a smashing tackle, the ball popped high into the air. An alert Lakesburg guard caught it as it hung there and sprinted around the end and down the field. Perhaps "lumbered" would have been a better description, but the lineman was deceptively fast. There was no one near him as he crossed into the end zone. Lakesburg's kick was true, and suddenly the game had changed: 21–20, Lakesburg, with scarcely a minute left.

The day which had been so sunny was now darkening. The crowd was quiet. To add to the gloom, storm clouds were gathering to the northwest, and a chill breeze was beginning to whip the flag over at the administration building, and the pennants around the field.

Carlisle took the kickoff and halfheartedly ran it back some twenty-five yards. On the next play Lakesburg, already tasting victory, tackled lazily, and allowed another gain of fifteen yards. Carlisle's crowd brightened. Maybe . . . No, there was not enough time for more than one or two plays. It would take a miracle, but they'd make a valiant try.

Quickly, the pile of players unraveled, but one figure still lay on the ground, writhing in pain. Carlisle's left end . . . a broken leg? The officials stopped the game clock while a stretcher was brought onto the field and Joe Black-bird was carried off, to sympathetic cheers. Quickly, the coach called his squad together.

"Buffalo!" he beckoned. "You go in at fullback. Mordecai, you move to left end. Now, John, here's the play: The center passes the ball to you, past the quarterback. Can you kick us a goal?"

"I'll try. . . ."

"The wind's coming up," McGregor explained quickly. "If you catch it just right, John, you can use the wind to get a little more distance."

The whistle blew, calling the return to the game.

"Go *do* it, now!" called the coach after them.

Nearly sixty yards . . . A big assignment. *Too big,* thought John. But maybe not . . . He watched the pennants as he trotted out to the line and positioned himself. He'd be kicking toward the south goal, with the wind on his right shoulder blade. *Have to allow for the drift to the left. . . .* It was not unlike shooting an arrow, maybe, with allowance for a crosswind.

Lakesburg lined up confidently for one more play. Some of them were already smiling, showing the pleasure of victory. The quarterback called the signals. The center snapped the ball, past the waiting hands of the quarterback to the fullback.

To John, time seemed to slow almost to a stop. The ball floated lazily into his hands. He turned it, dropped it, and his right leg began its pendulum swing. He added all the force of powerful leg muscles. The ball struck the ground. A fraction of a heartbeat later, the toe of his shoe sent it on its way. It soared like a bird, too far to the right at first. Then it caught the wind, floating, rising, veering slightly *left. . . .* Maybe too far . . . No . . . Now, *long* enough?

The crowd gasped in amazement as the ball split the uprights, then roared in a mighty cheer of victory. John stood numbly as the spectators rushed onto the field in joyful celebration.

NINE

The spectators swarmed onto the field, yelling and cheering and congratulating the players. As the crowd began to thin, the team headed for the locker room to wash up and dress. John started across the cinder track toward the field house, with Little Horse at his side, still talking excitedly about the kick that had won the game.

"John! John Buffalo!" a voice called from the area of the stands.

The Senator was standing at the rail, motioning.

"Come here a moment," he beckoned.

Self-consciously, John shuffled across the track. He was sweaty, dirty but, after all, victorious. It would have been better to meet the stunning beauty who stood next to her father when he was clean and well groomed, but . . .

"Marvelous play, my boy!" the Senator boomed, extending a hand to pump John's in congratulation. "My, you've grown. . . . Filled out! That's good. School going well?"

"Yes, sir."

"John, I'd like to introduce my family. This is my wife, Mrs. Langtry, and my daughter, Jane. Our son is away at school. . . . West Point."

"So I had heard, Senator. Pleased to meet you, ma'am . . . Miss Langtry."

He nodded toward the women. It was "not seemly," he had been taught, to extend a hand to a woman in greeting.

At that moment, John could not have told anyone what the Senator's wife might have looked like. He was totally absorbed in drinking in the vision who stood at the Senator's other elbow. *Jane* . . . A perfect name for a creature perfect in form and beauty, he thought. Blue . . . The eyes were blue. He had been right about that. Her hair, which he had seen to be light in color from a distance, was beautiful in its coppery sheen. Long, uncut, but drawn up tastefully in a bun at the back. Her face was shaded by a wide-brimmed hat, but the healthy glow of sun-warmed skin showed familiarity with the outdoors.

Her smile, showing even white teeth, was one which easily gave the impression that it was for him alone. There are such smiles, of course, but in some way, this was special. The blue eyes searched deep into his soul, as if to verify the mystery that hung between them, yet drew them together. Her straightforwardness was a little embarrassing. To think that she could ever look with favor on an Indian boy with no family and no prestige was ludicrous.

There had been a time when he had been proud. The family of Yellow Bull had been respected, affluent, leaders in the nation. Now that was gone. It might not have impressed her, anyway, he told himself. But here she was smiling, the clear blue eyes showing not only respect and interest, but promise. He was sure that some unspoken understanding had passed between them.

The Senator was speaking now. . . .

". . . and I was wondering if you would join us for dinner. Your friend here, too, if you'd like."

The Senator nodded toward Little Horse.

"I . . . Yes, sir. I'm sure we could get permission."

The big man chuckled. "Of course. I'll take care of that

while you dress. We'll pick you up at the dormitory."

One last look into the blue eyes, so filled with promise, and he turned away. The image of the smile was burned permanently into his memory. He was ready now to fight the world. His heart soared like the eagle.

"Dinner" was at the hotel's dining room. The young men had never seen such elegance. White linen tablecloth, flowers on the table . . . Flowers which were clearly exotic species unknown to John's limited experience. He quickly realized that they had probably been raised indoors, artificially.

The silver table service was an array of beauty. John panicked for a moment, but then realized that he had only to watch the others, to see which fork to use first. He had never wanted so hard to please anyone as he now wished to please the sparkling beauty across the table. He quickly saw that Miss Langtry realized his predicament with the silverware, and was helping him. She would very slowly and methodically reach for the appropriate implement, holding it so that he could see. When he too reached for that utensil, the girl would nod and smile pleasantly. In no time at all, they were communicating, at a different level from the table conversation, which was light and insignificant. It was John's first experience with such intrigue, and it was a thrill beyond belief.

"I was proud of your accomplishment today, John," the Senator said between the main course and dessert. "Well done. Coach McGregor tells me that you're also interested in the track-and-field events."

"Yes, sir. But that seems to be seasonal. Springtime, Coach said."

"Yes. Quite true. But I have something in mind. Are you familiar with the Olympics?"

"The Greek contests? We read about them in literature."

"No, no," the Senator chuckled. "The *modern* Olympics. They're held every four years. A different place each year. The next one is to be in *Paris*, in 1900. The last one, incidentally, *was* held in Athens, a year ago. More coincidence."

"But what has that to do with . . . ?"

The Senator waved the query aside.

"Let me continue, John. As you know, I'm deeply interested in Carlisle, and specifically in athletics. It is my hope to help athletes with potential. And I would hope to have world-class competitors in the Olympics to represent our Carlisle program in track and field. I want the world to know about our Indian athletes."

"You mean . . . *Me?*"

"Of course, John. You and others. I'm always looking for talent."

John sat numbly, still not quite understanding, still distracted by the blue eyes and friendly smile of Miss Jane Langtry, across the table.

"The girl really likes you," said Little Horse later in the dorm.

"Nonsense!" snorted John. "She was just being friendly because of her father."

He knew better, of course. And Horse didn't even know about the chance encounter under the table. John's foot had chanced to touch that of Miss Langtry. He had jerked it back quickly, hoping that she hadn't noticed, or that she'd think it was an accident. But her smile suggested that it was no accident. It was a smile of intrigue and shared secrets. Oddly, it did not seem to him that she was experienced in such things. On the contrary . . . She was as new and fresh and childlike as he at the ways of romance. They shared something for a moment or two that was new to both; mysterious and wonderful and full of promise.

"She *does* like you, though," Horse was saying as John returned from his wonderful daydream. "Your attract-medicine is good. A lot better than mine."

"I don't believe so, Horse. I have hardly any, I'm made to think. You are far better looking."

Little Horse chuckled. "Not really. But it has little to do with looks, anyway, no? Your medicine and hers are good together. It could be felt."

John admitted to himself that it was true. There had been a wordless communication, a promise not yet fulfilled. . . . One that had hung there between them so plainly that it nearly shouted its presence. Little Horse had felt it. It seemed odd that the Senator and Mrs. Langtry had not been aware of it, too. But the Senator had been preoccupied with his talk of the Olympics, and Mrs. Langtry . . . Well, she might have noticed, but said nothing. John had been concentrating on the daughter, not the mother, and could not be sure. But, he had found that whites were less attuned to such things of the spirit, anyway. He had thought that to be strange. It was as if they were taught to deny things like medicine-feelings, rather than enjoying them as gifts.

Maybe it had something to do with the white man's strange approach to religion and God. Many whites, especially their holy men, seemed to think that if anything was fun, it must be wrong.

His thoughts were interrupted by Charlie Smith, who observed that neither John Buffalo or Little Horse had much attract-medicine anyway, and that he and Will Clark should have been selected for the dinner party. The four laughed together.

"Seriously," Smith said finally, "what did the Senator want? White men don't do favors with no reason."

"He wants John to work hard on his sports," suggested Horse. "He told us about the Olympics."

"What's that?" asked Charlie.

They explained the Senator's enthusiasm and his devotion to the Carlisle school.

". . . and the next Olympiad, in 1904, is to be held in St. Louis," Little Horse finished. "I think the Senator wants John to try to qualify."

"At football?" asked Will.

"No . . . track and field," explained Horse. "They don't play football in the Olympics. I am made to think John will hear more about it."

At the suggestion of the coach, John and Little Horse wrote notes of thanks to the Senator.

There were other football games. In fact, one nearly every weekend through the autumn. John was getting in more playing time. He had proved himself by means of the dropkick, but the injured player was out for the season because of a broken leg. John found himself carrying the ball more. He was quick on his feet, and the coach praised him for his running ability. He could be best described as "slippery," dodging tackles and threading his way among opponents, rather than relying on brute force. But he still enjoyed putting a smashing tackle on an opposing quarterback.

Senator Langtry attended a few more games, always visiting with John at some point, encouraging him on to bigger and better things. He did not bring his family again. He was apologetic that his legislative duties had prevented not only time with his family, but his attendance at many of Carlisle's athletic events.

John, making progress in matters of politeness and the social graces, asked that his best regards be extended to Mrs. Langtry and to their daughter, Jane.

"Why, thank you, John. That's very thoughtful of you. The ladies were quite impressed with you and Mr. Horse at our dinner outing. I will certainly carry your message."

John dared not think that his *real* message to Miss Jane Langtry might find its way, but he knew of no way to make that contact. It would be unseemly to write to her directly, unless invited to do so. Maybe, if the Senator actually did carry John's regards, she would understand. If not, nothing lost. . . .

The Senator made one remark which certainly gained the attention of John Buffalo.

"Next spring, if my schedule and yours permit, perhaps you'd enjoy a visit to our farm. You've been around horses, I trust?"

The remark about horses was accompanied by an odd sidelong glance, as if it were a joke. John was puzzled. He had been with horses all his life, until he was sent away to school. He longed to be with them again.

Years later, he realized the subtle meaning behind the remark. The honorable practice of stealing horses to prove one's manhood, practiced among the natives of the great plains, was not understood among whites, and was frowned upon.

TEN

Late in the fall football season, Carlisle's squad traveled by train to Massachusetts to play a team at Springfield College, a professional school for youth leaders and clergy. This college, the coach warned, was at the forefront of physical education in America. Many of the instructors and coaches in the widespread programs of the Young Men's Christian Association were receiving their training at Springfield.

"We can expect to be competing against some top athletes," warned McGregor. "These folks are hardworking and innovative."

This prediction proved true. Although friendly and accommodating, the men of Springfield College proved to be tough on the gridiron. There were new formations and maneuvers, as well as brute strength. As the shadows grew long, the game seesawed back and forth, the lead and the momentum changing several times. The clock ran out with the game tied, 35–35.

Carlisle would spend the night before traveling home, and there was entertainment planned. After a friendly banquet with a lot of good-natured fun, it was announced that there would be a special demonstration at the gymnasium. A new game . . . An activity for the winter months when the weather prevented outdoor sports, and young athletes needed something to keep in shape. They moved to the gym, and a young instructor, James Naismith, from Canada, explained how it had originated, mostly by accident.

As a graduate assistant at the college, Naismith had been working part time at another job at the downtown YMCA, with younger boys. At the end of the class sessions, it was sometimes difficult to induce the students to return the soccer balls to the storage boxes without a lot of delay and horseplay. The instructor had decided to make it a contest, dividing the class into two teams: Who could put the equipment away faster?

From there, things began to change rapidly, and somewhat unexpectedly. Several of the youngsters found that they could speed the process by throwing the soccer balls into the bins from a distance. At this point, many instructors might have stopped the fun, but to Naismith it was merely another challenge. Why not make that a part of the game? With a storage box at each end of the gym, he had announced the game of "box ball."

A few rules evolved, and sometime later, he conceived another idea. Around the balcony of the YMCA gym was a running track, banked at the turns, for the track-and-field runners to use in inclement weather. Why not fasten the boxes to the rail of the balcony? Someone stationed above at either end could retrieve the ball after each score, to hasten the game along. He had requested the custodian to find two uniformly shaped boxes, but none were immediately available. The custodian suggested that perhaps a pair of bushel baskets might suffice. Always flexible, Naismith quickly agreed. They could, he observed, change the name of the game to "basket ball."

The game could be played, Naismith continued, with almost any number of players. They had experimented with as many as twelve to fourteen on each side. However, it had proved more practical and a more open and exciting game, if there were no more than five or six on each team.

Rules were evolving. No body contact. No walking or running with the ball, but it could be bounced repeatedly. . . . The students were calling this a "dribble."

After the brief explanation, the demonstration began, with six on each team. The game was amusing—sometimes hilarious—as the ball moved back and forth, up and down the floor.

John admired Naismith's ingenuity and managed to visit with the young coach for a few moments after the game. An idea was forming in his mind. Until now, he had really not begun to visualize any long-term goals for his life. He was enjoying his athletic activities, but had really not thought seriously beyond his years in school. After that, what?

Now, he was being exposed to a group of professionals, teachers of athletics. They were interesting, interested in their student athletes, honest, hardworking. They had been good to him. . . .

Maybe I could learn to be a coach, he thought.

On the train back to Pennsylvania, he pondered considerably about it. He was lost in thought, staring sightlessly out the window at the passing countryside, when the coach slipped into the seat beside him.

"You're looking mighty serious, John," said McGregor. "Something wrong?"

"No, sir. Just thinking."

Neither spoke for a little while. There was little conversation in the entire squad, with tired athletes dozing in the comfort of the sun-warmed railroad car.

"You played a good game," said Mac.

"But we lost," John answered.

"No, it was a tie."

"That proves nothing, though."

"On the contrary, John. It proves that two teams are equally skilled."

"It's better to win," protested the young man.

"Of course," smiled the coach. "It's a lot more fun. A better feeling than almost anything. But it's not all about winning."

"It's *not?*" John asked in surprise.

"Not entirely. There are more important things. Winning is not as important as how you played the game. Whether you did your best, whether you played fairly, or tried to cheat. Respect for your opponent, as well as whether you earn *his* respect."

John sat, pondering. A matter of *honor . . .*

"Remember," the coach went on, "the team we played, where their field was a bit sandy?"

John remembered it well. The opposing players, on their own turf, had sometimes found occasion to kick or scuff sand into the faces of the linemen as the ball was snapped. They also seemed to be prone to infractions of the rules when the referee was not watching.

"But we beat them," John protested.

"Yes . . . but you didn't *respect* them. They hadn't earned your respect. Now, can you remember teams we've played when we were beaten, but still respected the other?"

"Yes."

He thought of a couple.

"John, *you'd* never throw sand in the opposing player's eyes, would you?"

"Of course not."

"Why?"

"Well . . . There would be no honor in it."

"Exactly. That's what I meant. Winning is not as important as how you play the game . . . with honor and respect."

Somehow, John thought of his father. Yellow Bull had once tried to talk to him about this. He had faced enemies in battle, rather than on the playing field. He spoke of "worthy opponents," and of some for whom he had no respect. John had not understood the words of Yellow Bull then, when he spoke of men "with no honor in them." He wished that his father had lived longer, to help him understand some of these things.

And there was this other thing, too. "Coach," he blurted, "do you think I could learn to be a coach?"

McGregor smiled, pleased.

"John, this time *I'm* honored. In answer to your question, yes, of course. Not only that, I think that you could be a great coach. An example for students. You have pride and honor, as well as skill."

"But I'm not . . . I don't—" He started to mumble in protest, but the coach interrupted him.

"That's exactly the point, John. You're good at what

you do, and you know it. But you don't flaunt it. You know what I mean?"

John's mind drifted back to some of his earliest memories, among his own people, when his father had been still alive. One of his father's friends had been a powerful leader, a medicine man. Someone had referred to him as a holy man, and the leader had denied it.

"No, I am nothing special. I do a little medicine . . . that's all."

Little Bull had questioned his father later.

"Is he not really a holy man?"

"Of course he is!" Yellow Bull had chuckled. "He has the gift of a very powerful medicine. But to admit it would be boasting. That would weaken his medicine, so he must deny it."

Pride without boasting.

"It is sometimes called modesty." Coach McGregor drew John back to reality. "Some have it, some don't."

From that time on, John noticed that the coach asked him to help some of the younger athletes.

"John, come over here a little while. Can you give Edward, there, some hints about the javelin?"

This gave him a great deal of pleasure and pride. Even so, he tried to be modest about it.

"Tilt the point just a little bit higher, Ed. I find I can get a little more distance out of it that way. You might try starting your stride just a bit earlier. . . . See how that works for you. . . ."

Soon the younger students seemed to feel that it was an honor to have John Buffalo comment on their workouts.

He found that such activity also improved his own performance. He saw the reason. If he was forced to study in depth the factors which improved performance in others, they could also be applied to his own.

Some of the other physical instructors and coaches began to ask his help, too, and John's self-esteem soared. He tried hard not to show it. "It was nothing. . . . I try to notice things. . . ." He must not misuse what he was beginning to see as a gift.

But the idea in his head was becoming more well-defined. This would help him to become a successful coach. He talked to McGregor about it, and was pleased with the coach's reaction.

"I don't see why not, John. You have a few more years of schooling, but . . . Well, let's keep it in mind."

Toward spring, John received the letter with Senator Langtry's official seal on the envelope. It was an invitation to spend a weekend at The Oaks, the home of the Senator and his family, in the eastern part of the state and near the Maryland border. The Senator promised an opportunity to see and ride some "fine horses," and to discuss John's progress and his future.

"I am also contacting the office of Carlisle's administration," the letter continued. "The Dean of Students there will help you with arrangements and with acquisition of train tickets, *et cetera*. . . ."

It was a great surprise. John had expected that possibly he would be asked to accompany the Langtrys back home after a ball game or some other visit. But this . . .

He was still pondering it when a message arrived, hand-carried by a wide-eyed student assistant secretary.

"You're to report to the office," said the young man. "Are you in trouble, John?"

"I don't think so."

He tore open the envelope and read the simple request: *Please report to the office of the Dean.*

"Wait," he said. "I'll walk back with you."

ELEVEN

John stepped from the train, carrying his small suitcase. He was somewhat uncomfortable in his new clothes: "gentleman's clothes."

His roommates had teased him considerably as he prepared to leave, but the Dean had been quite specific. The Senator had requested that John Buffalo be outfitted properly to attend a weekend at The Oaks, and had also funded the shopping trip.

"You do clean up pretty good, for an ignorant savage," teased Little Horse.

"Stop it, Horse. It wasn't my idea."

"You probably won't even speak to us when you get back," chided Will Clark.

"I just hope he don't give Carlisle a bad name and embarrass us all by fartin' at dinner or somethin'," Charlie Smith said soberly.

"He won't do that," said Will. "He'll be holdin' his cheeks too tight, thinkin' about that girl."

"Stop it, fellas!" protested John. "I've been asked to go, and—"

"Yeah, somebody's got to do it," moaned Horse in mock sadness. He shook his head. "John's willing to sacrifice himself. We *do* appreciate it, John."

Now he stood on the platform, wondering what to do next.

"Mr. Buffalo?" a deep voice asked.

He turned to see a uniformed Negro coachman in a red swallow-tailed coat with gold buttons. The man was wearing a black silk top hat and shiny black knee-high boots.

"I'm John Buffalo," the young man said cautiously.

"Yes, suh." The coachman smiled. "I'm to carry you to The Oaks. Here, I'll tote your bag, suh."

John was taken completely off guard by this tone of deference. He relinquished the valise, and the two walked toward an area where there were several coaches and buggies with waiting horses.

"How are you called?" he asked the black man clumsily.

"I'm Henry. Work for the Senator."

"Yes, I figured," said John. "I'm John."

"Yes, suh," said the darky. "I figured."

Both grinned.

Henry placed the valise in the rear and opened the door for his passenger. John looked inside at the opulent fittings and velvet upholstery. There was no one else present.

"I . . . Can I ride up there with you?" asked John.

"Reckon so."

The rolling hills drifted past the carriage, bright green in their spring splendor. Neat, well-kept farms nestled among the small patches of timber. There were large barns, painted a dull red, close to white houses whose appearance seemed to radiate a warm comfort. . . . A good spirit, unafraid of hard work. Many of the barns were ornamented with one or more circular designs, in bright colors and geometric symbols. It reminded him of some of the designs painted on the lodge covers among his own people. *The People* . . . Now, that seemed a lifetime ago.

The coachman noticed his interest.

"Ever see them before?" he asked. "Them signs on the barns?"

"No, sir."

"Them are hex signs. Askin' for health an' prosperity an' all . . ."

"You mean like a prayer?"

"Huh! Well, maybe so. Dutch use 'em. . . . Bring good luck, they figure."

They moved on, leaving the young man to wonder anew at the strange ways of the white man. As many and as different as among the red man, it seemed. And the countryside continued to flow backward past the carriage.

A half hour's ride on a well-traveled road brought them to a lane where the team turned in almost without reining. An arched gate of wrought iron proclaimed "The Oaks" over the drive, which was lined with well-spaced old oak trees. White fence rails separated green pastures on both sides from the white gravel drive. On their left, a trio of yearling colts pranced and trotted alongside the coach as it traveled toward the house. Barns, sheds, and corrals sprawled behind the house, which was one of the most magnificent that John had ever seen. It rose three stories into the air in majestic dignity, white and pristine. All of the other buildings wore the same pure white. The wide front porch, which reached completely across the front of the mansion, boasted a series of massive columns, like those pictured in some of the books in the Carlisle library. More of the great oaks flanked the house and shaded some of the smaller structures.

"This here's the big house," Henry explained as the horses trotted smartly around the long, curved drive toward the porch.

There was a twinkle of amusement in the eyes of the coachman as he watched the reaction of his passenger.

"I figured," said John.

Three people now emerged from the doorway to greet the coach as Henry brought the team to a stop at the steps. John recognized the Senator and Mrs. Langtry, but his attention was riveted on the third figure. *Jane* . . . What a beautiful name. One befitting the angel who bore it. Odd . . . He had thought and dreamed many times of her radiant beauty, but now . . . Ah, his memory must be faulty . . . She was even more beautiful than he had expected. John tried not to stare.

He stepped down from the coach to a stone platform which ran along the center portion of the broad steps to the porch. He realized the convenience of such a structure. Persons seated inside the coach could step out at the same level with no difficulty.

"Senator . . . Mrs. Langtry . . . Miss Jane," he greeted clumsily. Or, at least, he felt so.

"John! Good to see you, my boy!" boomed the Senator, extending a hand. "Come! How was your trip?"

"Just fine, sir," John said self-consciously.

A servant came from inside the house.

"I'll take your valise, sir," the man said. His complexion was somewhat lighter than that of the coachman, but his face displayed some negroid characteristics. Yet his voice lacked the deep-throated resonance of Henry's rich accents.

"Thank you, Reuben," said Mrs. Langtry. "Just put it in the east guest room."

Reuben nodded deferentially and stepped back into the house. John was embarrassed. At least, he could have carried his own suitcase. This was an entirely new world for him. He had a difficult time understanding why he, John Buffalo, né Little Bull, was considered superior in some way to Henry, the coachman, or to Reuben, whose status was still a bit unclear. Both were men of middle age. It was not that John failed to enjoy the special attention and honor that now befell him. He was flattered. . . . It *felt* good. But it was uncomfortable. He had done nothing to earn the attention and honor that was coming his way. Among his own people, at this stage in his life he would be seeking the advice and counsel of such men. Their life experience could be quite helpful to a young man trying to find his way. Well, he never would cease to be amazed at the ways of whites. He'd try to relax and enjoy the extra attention.

"Come, let us sit," said Mrs. Langtry with a sweeping gesture toward a white wrought-iron table on the broad veranda. "We'll have some lemonade!"

She picked up a tiny crystal bell from its place on a doily in the center of the table and gave it a gentle shake. A young woman in a black-and-white frilled dress, and with a white lace cap on her hair, popped out the door.

"Yes, ma'am?"

"Some lemonade, Carlita, if you would."

"Yes, ma'am."

The girl darted back inside, and the Langtrys and John seated themselves at the table. The Senator fumbled with the heavy gold chain that looped across his vest and pulled a large gold watch from its pocket.

"Mmm," he mused. "Still early . . . Let's have lemonade, and then I'll show John around the stables. Still time for that before dinner."

"But Papa," protested Jane. "He'll want to change for dinner."

"Of course, my dear!" boomed the Senator. "Still time for that, too. But I want our guest to see . . . Oh, yes! I understand . . . Well, of course you may come along!"

"I'll defer," said Mrs. Langtry. "I need to check on things in the kitchen. Oh . . . Here's our lemonade, now."

The tour of the stables was a thing of wonder. Barns and stables, so clean and orderly . . . John had *lived* in far worse places. Stalls and paddocks were clean and dry, the animals well groomed. The small pastures, too, were immaculate, trimmed and fenced with white-painted posts and planks.

The horses were magnificent. The Senator talked at great length about breeding and bloodlines. These were horses bred for racing on the track, he explained. Much of it, John did not understand. There were sires several generations ago, it seemed, which had greatly affected the white man's racehorses. Senator Langtry talked of the Byerly Turk and the Godolphin Arabian, and something called a Barb. There were stallions brought from some other part of the world to England, where they sired colts from English mares. The families had been intermixed now, but the Senator was proud of the Arabian strain in his own horses.

One stallion in particular, a magnificent gray called Thunder, was the Senator's pride and joy. He recited the animal's pedigree for three generations back with a great sense of accomplishment.

Thunder, whose name was actually Blue Thunder, was out of Gray Lady, by Blue Cyclone, by Trade Wind . . .

"There's a bit of Barb a little further back," the Senator continued. "On the dame's side, of course."

Much of this was lost on young John Buffalo. Still, he did understand lineage was important. His father, Yellow Bull, had been especially proud of his buffalo runner, Owl Dung, so named because of white spots on the glossy black rump. Owl's sire had been obtained in trade from some Blackfeet, who claimed to have stolen the animal from someone farther west . . . Shoshones or Nez Perce. The story was garbled . . . completely lost, now. It no longer mattered.

Little Bull, son of Yellow Bull, stood gazing at the stallion, and it was good. He had not realized how much he had missed the contact with horses these past few years. He loved the familiar smells, the warm, not-unpleasant ammoniac scent of sunlight on a well-ordered paddock.

Thunder nickered softly as the party turned to move on. John glanced back. Somehow, the animal's presence reached out to him as a kindred spirit. It had been a long time since John had communicated with a horse, and it came as something of a shock. He had almost forgotten. . . . It was the white man's way to ignore, or even to deny such things. He had fallen into many of the white man's ways of thinking because it was easier than trying to explain or to understand. He had determined to be successful in the white world, but was it to result in the loss of something else?

May it go well with you, my brother! He directed the thought toward the stallion, feeling clumsy with the unaccustomed effort. He was greatly pleased, then, when a similar sensation came back at him.

And with you . . .

"Well," said the Senator, "let's go back and get ready for dinner. You like horses, eh, son?"

"Yes, sir," said John. "I was raised among them."

The Senator laughed. "Yes," he agreed, "I'd assume so."

John was unsure whether it was a compliment or a criticism. Maybe he'd never know.

TWELVE

Dinner was an experience in itself.

"I could have eaten everything they gave me with one knife," he told his roommates later.

There was an array of eating utensils even beyond that of his previous experience with the Langtrys. Again, he managed to follow the actions of Jane, across the table from him. She was quite aware of his problem and helped him, as before. John would pause and watch her actions, an enjoyable pastime in itself. She would slowly and deliberately select the appropriate fork, and quite pointedly hold it in the proper position for use. Much of it seemed ridiculous to him, but he was trying hard to learn. He had not forgotten his basic goal: to learn the white man's ways so well that he could be successful at them.

Some of the foods he could identify, some not. There was wine, too, to be sipped with the meal. It was warm and tingling on his tongue, and gave him confidence. He was tempted to gulp it from the stemmed glass, but noticed that the others only sipped. He could come to enjoy this, he admitted to himself.

There was one moment of consternation when a servant leaned over to offer some clear liquid in a shallow bowl. It was after the main portion of the meal. . . . Soup? Was he expected to take the bowl? Until now, each course of food had been placed on the table before him. He should have been watching the server more carefully. In something of a panic, he glanced around the table. There were no other similar bowls in sight. What was he expected to do?

His face flushed and he felt that everyone was looking at him. For a moment, he considered leaping to his feet to run from the room. Maybe the others would think he had become ill. That would be better than . . . *Wait. Stay steady,* he told himself. He glanced across the table, and his eyes met those of beautiful blue. Frantically, he reached out in his need. *Help me!* he asked silently.

The expression on Jane's face was not exactly one of amusement, but it was reassuring. A very slight twinkle in the blue eyes, a conspiratorial smile that flickered around the corners of her lips. . . .

Very slowly, she lifted both her hands to the edge of the table, fingers pointing down. . . . Moved them together . . . A dipping motion, a slight wiggling or stirring movement, then raising them to return to her lap . . .

John looked again at the bowl before him. A single flower blossom floated on the surface. *Water* . . . Not to drink, but to wash. A finger bowl! He had never used one, or even seen one, but now he remembered that Old White Horse, back in the reservation school, had mentioned such a thing when she was first teaching them the use of silverware in "polite company." She had even used almost the same wiggling motions of the fingers now used by Miss Jane Langtry.

Now more confident, John gently dipped the fingers of both hands into the bowl, glancing across the table to verify as he did so. He received an almost-imperceptible nod of approval, which was more gratifying than anyone could have known.

The water was warm and soothing, and all seemed right with the world as he dried his fingers on the linen towel draped across the servant's arm.

"Thank you," John told the man quietly as he moved on. The servant nodded.

John looked across the table with a smile that sent the same message. *Thank you!* The returning smile said plainly that the message had been received. The girl nodded, ever so slightly. John's heart was lifted, filled with the knowledge that they were communicating on such a level. He had not really expected to find whites who understood this sort of mind-talk, a thing of the spirit. And, that it would be this exotic creature with whom he established such an understanding was beyond belief. He smiled across the table at her, and she smiled back in return. His heart was very good.

"Alan is coming home tomorrow," said the Senator. "A short visit between the school terms. You've not met Alan yet, have you, John?"

"No, sir. He's at West Point, you had told me?"

"Right! Upperclassman now. He'll graduate next year. Make a great leader," the Senator added proudly.

"Yes, sir," said John, and then felt rather foolish. For all he knew, Alan Langtry might be a complete idiot.

Probably not, though. To be accepted at West Point, even with the Senator's influence, the young man must have some leadership qualities. Yet undoubtedly, Alan's path had been easier because of his father's influence. John had been long enough in the political system of the whites to see such things. Actually, he was a beneficiary, himself.

"I do hope," said Mrs. Langtry, "that our country won't become involved in the trouble in Cuba."

John was puzzled for a moment. There had been talk about trouble on the Spanish-held island of Cuba, but that seemed far away. He failed to see how Mrs. Langtry's statement fit into the table conversation.

"Now, now, Mother," the Senator said patronizingly. "That would only give a young officer a chance to prove himself. To advance quickly."

It took a moment for John to realize. There *was* a connection, a very solid one. A young officer graduating from

West Point would be assigned his first command. If there was no military activity, no need for concern on the part of his parents. On the other hand, no opportunity to prove himself, either. He might remain a lieutenant for a long time.

With a sort of wonder and amusement, John saw a familiar pattern here. As a small child, he had listened to the old men as they smoked and talked in the lodge of Yellow Bull. They had talked of horse-stealing raids on the Crows and the Blackfeet, sometimes the whites. Even Cheyennes, though that was long ago, and the Cheyennes had even been allies at the battle of the Greasy Grass. It was all gone now. Even Red Cloud had signed a treaty with the Army.

But how reminiscent of conversations in Yellow Bull's lodge, this discussion around a white linen table. . . . The men thinking of combat and honor, the women proud, yet concerned over possible harm to the young warriors. Maybe it had always been so, among all people. For some reason he thought of the Bible story of David and Goliath.

And, what was a young red man to do now? Stealing horses to prove manhood was a thing of the past, frowned on by the whites, even to the extent of being punished by hanging. But he, John Buffalo, had found a way to exert his manhood, on the gridiron or in the track-and-field events. He had the determination and the skills.

Oddly, the Senator's next question seemed to pertain to the same line of thought.

"John, have you thought about what you might like to do after you graduate? What sort of work?"

"That's a long way off, sir. At least two years."

He was hesitant to speak of such high ambitions.

"I know," said the Senator. "But one must plan ahead."

"Yes, sir," John said quickly. "I had thought of teaching. . . . Coaching, maybe."

"Oh, yes! Coach McGregor had mentioned that. Physical education. Excellent. Didn't he also say that you were helping him?"

"Only a little, Senator. A few suggestions here and there. I'm not qualified to teach."

"Ah, but you have the skills. You can show others how you do it. Show your confidence, lad! And when the time comes, you may count on me for a recommendation."

"Thank you, sir. I appreciate it. But that really is a long way ahead."

"Not as long as you think, John. But let's not dwell on it. For now, let us menfolk adjourn to the library. Please excuse us, ladies?"

"Cigar, John?" offered the Senator as they entered the room.

"Thank you, sir."

A smoke . . . A social smoke, among the men of the lodge. A rolled stick of tobacco leaves, instead of a pipe, but the same ceremony, it seemed.

The Senator clipped the ends from both cigars, lighted both, and settled into a leather chair, gesturing to another for his guest. Curls of bluish smoke spiraled toward the dark ceiling.

John had not smoked a cigar before. It was fragrant, stronger in taste than a pipe. As far as he could tell, there was only tobacco in the cylinder. He would have preferred a bit of sumac or willow, maybe cedar or grape leaves. No matter. It was a social smoke, with the host's tobacco, and it was good.

He looked around the room, dark in the corners where the light of the gas lamp did not reach.

"We're thinking of electricity," said the Senator, noticing his glance. "It seems to be the coming thing."

John was bewildered. Why would anyone want a better light? He had never seen gaslight until he came to Carlisle.

Before that, the open fire, and at the reservation school, candles and coal-oil lamps. The world was moving faster and faster. . . .

"Care for a brandy, John?" asked the Senator.

It was not really a question. The Senator was already pouring from a decanter into two snifters on a sideboard by the big desk.

John looked around the room. The walls were filled with books, shelves reaching clear to the high ceiling. He wondered whether there was anyone who had read them all. He wanted to ask, but decided against it.

Senator Langtry now handed him one of the glasses. It was different in shape, nearly globular, with a short stem. John noticed that his host held the glass, cradled in his palm, with the stem between his fingers. The big man seemed to enjoy sloshing the dark liquid around in the bottom of the glass and then smelling it, finally taking a sip. John copied the ritual. Yes, a lot different from wine. . . . He sipped carefully and was instantly glad that he had not gulped more than a tiny bit. The liquid was warm in his mouth and throat . . . and pungent. "It goes *up* instead of down," he would tell his roommates later.

He settled back comfortably in the big leather chair to listen to the Senator's talk about football and track. It was easy, warm, and comfortable here. He had only to respond occasionally to the Senator's pointed questions.

"Don't you think so, John?"

"Oh, yes, sir!"

He could certainly learn to live like this.

They finished their cigars and the brandy, and the butler appeared in the doorway, as if on cue.

"Anything else tonight, sir?"

"I think not, James. Good night."

"Good night, sir. Master John, I'll show you to your room when you're ready."

"Oh . . . Yes . . ." John rose quickly, only a little unsteady. "Good night, Senator."

He knew the way to the room, of course. He had changed and cleaned up there earlier. But this must be a ritual for guests. Perhaps it did make sense. A confused guest might easily blunder into the wrong room among the several along the big upstairs hall.

He followed the butler to his room, and James turned up the gaslight and turned down the bed.

"Good night, sir."

He slipped out quietly and closed the door.

There was a deep feather mattress and pillows, covered with white sheets. On the dark, carved headboard of the big four-poster, gargoyles presided over the scene. Odd things to carve on a bed, John thought, but he was too tired to worry about it.

He had only one regret. He would have treasured even a short contact with the Langtrys' daughter before retiring, but it was not to be. He fell asleep, anticipating what tomorrow might bring.

THIRTEEN

Alan Langtry arrived the next morning for a brief holiday. The family was excited, of course, and in the excitement of the reunion, their guest naturally felt out of place. But it was not a new feeling for John Buffalo. He had felt that for much of his life.

After the first excitement of Alan's arrival, however, this feeling began to subside again. Initially, the cadet had a slightly superior attitude, but it was only temporary. Very quickly, Alan Langtry became as friendly and hospitable as his parents and his sister. Within an hour or so, John was quite comfortable with them. They seemed to genuinely enjoy his company.

The two young men talked of school, which was hardly comparable, and of athletics, which were very much the same. Football was becoming important at West Point, and they discussed whether Alan and John might compete next year.

The three young people went riding in the afternoon, and here they could really begin to relate. There is a theory among horsemen that there is something about the outside of a horse that is good for the inside of a man. This was a prime example. They laughed and joked and rode over the countryside, free of troubles and responsibility for a little while.

The gear for riding "English" style puzzled John. The uncomfortable saddle, the two sets of reins . . . (Years later in a similar situation, he heard an old cowboy comment, "If you can't handle a horse with one set of reins, you sure as hell ain't gonna do it with two!") But he managed, paying attention to the actions of the others. Most of his experience with horses had been in his childhood, usually bareback or with a simple saddle pad. The bridle had often been only a soft-tanned thong, tied around the animal's lower jaw as a "war bridle."

But he could recognize and appreciate the quality of the animals. The tall bay gelding which he rode was a magnificent mount. John wondered how it would feel to chase a buffalo, a bow or a lance in his hand. He had never experienced that thrill, except in childish pretense. He thought of his father, and wondered what Yellow Bull would have thought of this bay as a buffalo runner. He guessed that this horse, Major, might have been too tall for the warrior. As nearly as John could remember, Bull had favored a more compact, muscular mount.

But the days of chasing buffalo were gone now. They had become quite scarce even before John had been removed to the government school. He could remember only a time or two when as a boy he had seen free-ranging buffalo. They were not very impressive. Thin and ragged, their woolly winter coats shedding in patches. There were no more than six or eight animals. A group of young men had raced out and managed to kill two as they fled before the riders. The camp had eaten well for a few days, and even managed to store a little meat.

Usually, though, such "hunts" were held at the Agency. A few scrawny steers would be driven to the reservation and penned near the Agency's office. The word would go out quickly that the government beef issue had arrived, and the people would gather. One steer at a time would be released, to be chased down and killed by young men on horseback. The cowboys who had delivered the ration would watch with glee, yelling and cheering at the pitiful remnant of a proud people. . . .

"Go git him, Chief!"

Then the women would butcher the kills, salvaging every scrap possible of the never-quite-sufficient ration. The elders would shake their heads sadly. John remembered the despair in his father's face as he had watched. There had been no initiative left, nothing on which to base his dreams. Quite possibly, he now realized, this was part of the reason for the death of Yellow Bull at a rather young age. His spirit had been dying for a long time. His son was just now beginning to see how difficult it must have been for one of the warriors who had defeated the yellow-haired chief, Custer, at the Greasy Grass. It had been a victory, yes, but the beginning of the end for the People . . . All the more reason for his son, now John Buffalo, to reject the old ways and to excel in the world of the white man.

"Race you to the stables!"

Alan Langtry's challenge jolted him out of the daydream. John put his heels to the bay, and the two horses leaped forward to the contest. Langtry's big gray was a jump ahead, having caught the other by surprise. But Major had been on the track and recognized a race. Ears flattened, the bay stretched his neck and ran. He was smooth . . . All his gaits had been smooth as the riders trotted and cantered, but now . . . *Aiee!* Like a well-oiled engine but without the noise and the steam, the magnificent animal challenged the competition. Stride by stride, a hoofbeat at a time, they gained on the gray. His nose came even with Langtry's stirrup, then the shoulder of the horse, now neck and neck. . . . They passed the gate to the training track and thundered into the yard in front of the stable in a dead heat.

"Say, you're pretty good!" Alan laughed. "Are you this good at football?"

"Of course he is!" Jane stated flatly, pulling her mare to a stop beside the others. "Wait till you see him!"

"That might be a while," said her brother. "But it could be, John, that our next contest will be on the gridiron!"

They walked the horses to cool them out, unsaddled and turned the further care of the animals over to the stable grooms.

It had been a good day, and John felt a warm kinship with the cadet whose background was so different from his own. Their natural competition as budding athletes was a friendly one, their conversations open and interesting. John sensed that Jane felt it, too, and was pleased. He realized that the girl wanted the two young men to relate well. She was obviously close to her brother, and it was with great satisfaction that he saw her approval of their budding friendship. It could have no other meaning—*she* was attracted to their guest. He had already sensed that, of course, and could hardly believe his good fortune. He longed to spend more time with her, in private, to share his ambitions and dreams, to gain her approval for the things he hoped to achieve.

"What do you intend to do, after college, John?" Alan asked at dinner that evening.

"Well, I'd thought of coaching," John said hesitantly. "I—"

"He's helping McGregor some, now," interrupted the Senator.

"Football?" asked the cadet.

"Track, mostly. A little football . . ."

"He's as good at track as he is at football," boasted the Senator.

John was uncomfortable. He would have liked to explain that the coach had simply asked him to give bits of advice to some of the younger athletes. But the Senator . . .

"I see this young man as a potential Olympic athlete," said Senator Langtry broadly, addressing Alan. "Track and field . . . We'll bring him along!"

The idea flitted through John's head that nobody had asked *him*, but it was lost in the realization that here were people who *cared*, and he was grateful. Besides, his relationship with Jane Langtry showed all signs of becoming more than friendship. Her smile, the promise in her eyes as she looked at him, plainly said so. He longed to spend some time alone with her, if only to talk.

That opportunity finally came. It was purely an accident, or at least he thought so. In retrospect, maybe not. He had gone to the stable to be near the horses. He was now aware that he had missed them more than he realized. His horse medicine had always been good, but had suffered from disuse. He must find a way to be around them more if he could, he decided. Unused, a gift of the spirit loses its power. He was using his athletic ability, and it was growing in strength. Yes, he must find a way.

He was standing at the stall of Major, the big bay he had ridden earlier, absently stroking the velvet nose while they communed wordlessly. The horse stood, eyes half-closed, as absorbed in the reverie as the young man.

"Oh, *there* you are!"

John turned, startled.

"I—Yes, we . . . I was . . ."

He felt stupid and clumsy, having been startled back to reality, caught off guard by Jane's silent approach.

She quickly put him at ease.

"It's okay . . . I understand," she said gently.

He was made to think that she really *did* understand. There was an expression in her face that said so. And she had said "okay—," an odd place to hear it. A slang usage, not quite acceptable in polite company. It was used some by whites, but he had not expected to hear it from the girl. His friend Charlie Smith used it sometimes. A Cherokee word, John thought, *okeh,* meaning, in essence, "It is good."

And it *was* good. They talked. . . . Later, he could not remember specifically what they talked about, but their spirits melded together in an exciting, yet comfortable calming blend. It was as if they had known each other always, had been friends, maybe lovers. They were *comfortable* together. *This is how it should be,* he thought.

Suddenly, a look of alarm came over her face. Then she laughed. . . . A rippling laugh like the cool, clear water over polished pebbles in a mountain stream.

"I forgot!" she admitted. "My mother sent me to find you to get ready for dinner."

Impulsively, she leaned forward and kissed him. It was not a deep, lingering kiss, but a quick, warm recognition of the feeling between them. It was, however, full on the lips, exciting, tender, filled with the promise of what might be ahead. John was mesmerized. Not only had he never been kissed in that way before, but it was so unexpected. . . . Warm, inviting, suggestive. He took her in his arms for a moment, but she pushed him away gently.

"Not now," she whispered. "We have to go. Come on!"

She gave his hand a gentle squeeze, and in her eyes was a look that spoke volumes. *Later . . .*

She turned and led the way toward the house.

Dinner again was jovial, but very formal. John tried hard not to stare into the blue eyes across the table. Naturally, it was necessary occasionally, in the course of the polite table conversation. However, in these brief moments, she managed to convey their closeness and private understanding, the joining of their spirits as they met and communicated in some other plane of being. He felt that his heart would burst with joy. At least, would soar to another realm, with *her*. . . .

The Senator was speaking now, bringing him back to reality. . . .

"Wh-What?" John stammered, embarrassed. "My thoughts were elsewhere."

"Not surprising!" chuckled the Senator. "A lot going on in your life, eh?"

"Yes, sir," John said politely. To himself he added, *You have no idea, Senator!*

"What I asked," Langtry went on, "was whether you have met a young man named Penny . . . William Penny?"

"I think not. Should I know him?"

"Possibly. New at Carlisle. Another athlete."

"Oh, yes, I think so. Will, we call him. Sac and Fox?"

"I suppose so." The Senator dismissed the question as if one's nation of origin was of no matter. "An athlete. From Oklahoma, or somewhere."

"Yes, sir. That's the one, I think. I don't know him well.

Coach asked me to help him with the javelin a time or two."

"Good! Yes, I think he's another who has a great future in athletics, as you have. I'm counting on you, my boy!"

FOURTEEN

Returning to Carlisle, John fell back into the routine. Study, practice, run, compete, attend classes, study. . . .

He located young Will Penny, only a year or two behind him, and mentioned that Senator Langtry had inquired about him.

"Yes, I talked to him once," Penny said. "After a meet, maybe. What does he want?"

"Nothing, I guess. Just likes to help athletes. He's interested in the Olympics. Been very kind to me."

He did not add his private thought: *And he has a daughter I would die for.*

"All white men want something," Penny suggested.

"Maybe just the satisfaction of seeing his pick-out-of-the-crowd becoming successful," said John. "I think his heart is good."

He did not reveal how close he had become to the Senator's family.

The months passed. Summer came and went. There were few classes, but some students remained on campus for special projects, and some, like John Buffalo, because he really had no place to go. He worked for the college for low pay, but it provided room and board. When he was not otherwise occupied, he spent time in the gym or on the track, running, exercising, lifting weights, keeping in shape for the coming football season. Some of the other athletes remained in the area, working at odd jobs or farm labor. One of these was Penny.

"John!" he greeted one morning. "You need a job?"

"I'm working here. . . . You have one?"

"Yes."

"Farmhand?"

"No, even better. I'm playin' softball, over by Harrisburg. And I get paid!"

"For playin' ball? They pay you for *that*?"

"Sure. Want to come over with me and try out?"

He was sorely tempted, but . . .

"I better not, Will. I told Mac I'd stay on campus. I'm workin' out here to keep in shape."

There was one marvelously bright event that summer. A neat white envelope arrived unexpectedly, addressed to John Buffalo, and a student who worked in the mailroom informed him about it.

"A letter?" asked John. He never received any mail. There was no one. . . .

"Yep . . . some kind of foreign stamps."

There must be some mistake, thought John. Who would write him? The foreign postage, especially, made him certain that the letter was addressed in error, intended for someone else.

He stopped by the mailroom, actually asking someone its location to find it. Yes, the square white envelope was addressed to him. His name was inscribed with beautiful penmanship in a flowing hand, using blue ink. It was sealed with a neat blob of blue sealing wax, imprinted with a fancy-styled monogram. It took him a moment to decipher that letter: a capital "L" in English script. L . . . *Langtry*.

At about the same time, he realized that the envelope was faintly fragrant with an oddly familiar perfume. . . . Yes! The fragrance used by Miss Jane Langtry, suggestive of roses and lilies of the valley, with a hint of musk. . . .

He found a quiet corner and opened the envelope.

Dear John,

    We are touring Italy this summer, my parents and I. Alan is in school. I think of you often, and our time together at The Oaks. I would love for you to be here to share the beauty of Rome and its many wonders.

    I look forward to seeing you at Carlisle this fall.

Respectfully,
Jane Langtry

He was stunned. He had never received a letter before. The thrill of it was almost overwhelming. Alone in the study room, he read and reread the note, inhaling the faint perfume that invoked memories of the exciting time he had last experienced that subtle fragrance and, the *content* of the message. A solid declaration of friendship, a strong suggestion of more, and a wish to see him again, soon. He felt that it carried a much deeper message than the words alone could tell. . . . A matter of spirit.

Now he thought of her even more often. He wished for time to pass, to bring on the football schedule for more than one reason, now.

It was a beautiful day in early fall when the crowds gathered for Carlisle's first football game of the season. The school had done well the previous year, and there was much interest. The crowd gathered early, arriving by train, by wagons, buggies, coaches, and on foot.

John had been awaiting the arrival of the Langtrys since dawn. He had heard nothing, but assumed that the family would be on hand, because of the Senator's absorbing interest. And, he hoped, because of a somewhat different interest on the part of Miss Jane Langtry.

When he did encounter the trio, it was completely unexpected. He was coming out of the locker room with the team to take part in informal practice before the final coaching session. As they crossed the running track, they encountered the flow of gathering spectators approaching the stands.

"John!" called a young female voice. "John Buffalo!"

He turned to face the trio. The Senator, Mrs. Langtry, and Jane . . . Had he forgotten how beautiful she really was? In some way, she had matured a bit, her face and figure even more striking than ever. She rushed toward him and gave him a quick embrace.

Startled, he returned her hug clumsily with one arm. His other hand was occupied with his helmet, dangling on its strap. But over Jane's shoulder, he could clearly see the expressions on the faces of her parents. Mrs. Langtry's was one of startled surprise and puzzlement. Maybe that was a logical reaction. However, the expression on the Senator's face was chilling. Not only surprise, but consternation, and an anger approaching rage. His ruddy jowls flushed as purple as the wattle on a turkey-cock.

What could be wrong?

"I . . . I have to go," John mumbled. "I'll see you after the game?"

Senator Langtry gave a noncommittal harrumph that could have meant anything.

Mrs. Langtry said nothing. She was as pale as the Senator was florid, her eyes a frightened rabbit's.

Jane seemed not to notice anything unusual. "Of course!" she chirped happily. "We'll see you then!"

Something was wrong, and John was not certain what. It must have something to do with Jane's overt display of affection on the track. Yes, that was probably it. . . . The Langtrys were an affectionate family, except for the Senator himself. He always seemed a bit too pompous and formal to exhibit affection. Such a display as that on his daughter's part would probably be considered inappropriate. He rather dreaded the meeting after the game. He feared that he would be chastised, though he had had little to do with the public display of affection. Jane might be due some severe criticism, and his heart was heavy for her.

The game was a disaster. John's thoughts were far away. He was clumsy, inattentive, missed signals, and at one time nearly ran in the wrong direction after a spin to escape the grasp of the opposing tackle. In another generation of football, the coach would have benched him for a substitute. But at that time, substitutions were only for injury.

He played on doggedly, looking to the stands to try to locate the Langtrys from time to time. He finally located them, halfway up the stands at the fifty-yard line. They seemed very quiet, but then so was the rest of the Carlisle crowd. There was nothing to cheer about.

"What's the matter with you, Buffalo?" the frustrated coach demanded at half time.

The score was 21–0 in favor of the visitors, a team that Carlisle was favored to defeat easily.

"I don't know, Coach."

"Are you sick?"

"No, sir."

"Well, let's get in there! You're not playin' your usual game! And you others . . . Just because Buffalo's havin' trouble, no reason you should quit. *Help* him! You got to try even harder. This isn't a one-man show, you know. . . . We're a *team!*"

After the half-time break, they played better football, but not by much. They were completely outclassed and out-maneuvered by a lesser team, and any recovery was too late and too little. It was the upset of the season.

John's own performance was even worse in the second half. He *must not* keep looking to the stands at the fifty-yard line. Even when he did manage a glance, it was not comforting. Possibly, this could be sorted out when he met the Langtrys after the game. He'd apologize, assure her parents that he had no ulterior intentions where their daughter was concerned, and maybe things would be all right again. Anyway, he hoped so.

They left the playing field in disgrace, heads hanging in defeat. But at least it was over. The embarrassment would last a while, but was less urgent at the moment than this misunderstanding with the Langtrys. With these thoughts in mind, John made his way to the track in front of the stands, trying to phrase an apology in his mind.

The sullen, disappointed crowd was dispersing quickly and quietly, unaccustomed to the indignity of such a defeat. John looked and waited as the last of the spectators trickled out of the stands and through the alleyway to the street. He had not seen the Langtrys leave. Maybe they were outside. . . . He hurried to the street, but they were nowhere to be seen.

Then it occurred to him that during the last quarter he had consciously avoided looking at the stands. They must have departed early, with some of the other disgruntled fans. He would have thought this unlike the Senator.

Maybe he had missed them at the track. . . . He hurried back into the stadium, but it was almost empty.

He encountered a dejected Coach McGregor, who tried to put a better light on a bad day.

"There'll be better times, lad. I don't know what your problem is, but come in tomorrow. Let's talk about it."

"Yes, sir. . . . But I was looking for the Senator. I was to meet them after the game."

"Oh . . . I don't know, John. I think they left early. Maybe some government business."

"Did he get a message or something?" John blurted clumsily.

"I don't know. I was watchin' the game, unlike some I could name."

McGregor used sarcasm as a teaching tool.

"Yes, sir. . . . I'll be in to see you in the morning."

Charlie Smith had seen the Langtrys leave, and had wondered, but knew nothing more. Little Horse, who had seen the spontaneous embrace on the track, attempted to tease him about that, but met with such sullen fury that the subject was dropped quickly.

The conference with McGregor was brief and to the point. *Get back to work and forget distractions*. John was unable to share his thoughts and fears, but promised to do better. He plunged back into training with all the pent-up energy of frustration, but found little help. His heart was too heavy.

John considered writing a letter of apology to the Senator, or to Jane, or to both. He rejected that approach for a number of reasons. Primarily, he felt that he had nothing for which to apologize. There was no one to whom he could talk about it, to share his doubts and fears. He withdrew into his protective shell, becoming more and more alone.

A few days later, John was called into the office of the Dean, an unusual circumstance. Coach McGregor was seated in a chair by the desk, looking very uncomfortable.

"Mr. Buffalo," began the scholarly, stiff-starched administrator, "you have been selected to transfer to another college to further your athletic career."

"But why . . . Where? I don't understand."

He looked to McGregor in consternation.

"It's none of my doin' lad," the coach said, his anger barely controlled. "I need ye here."

Mac's brogue always became heavier in times of emotional stress. The athletes had joked about that. But this was no joke.

"This is an official request, through the Bureau," the Dean went on. "I suppose it's an effort to distribute talent—in this case, sports talent—to some of the lesser schools."

"But in mid-season—," McGregor sputtered.

"I don't understand, either," admitted the Dean. "But, we must honor the request. We'll miss your talent on the gridiron, Buffalo."

It was a halfhearted statement. The tolerant dislike of the academic community for athletics was a familiar joke.

The Dean continued, "You'll transfer to Haskell Indian Institute."

"Where in hell is *that?*" McGregor erupted.

"It's at the edge . . . Let me see"—the Dean peered over his spectacles at the papers on his desk—"Kansas . . . Lawrence, Kansas . . . Hmm . . . A two-year *junior college?*"

There was surprise in his voice.

"What's goin' on here?" demanded McGregor.

"I'm sure I don't know, sir," the Dean said formally. "Now, let us get on with arrangements for the transfer."

FIFTEEN

Some explanation came forth the same day with the arrival of a note to John Buffalo. He recognized the envelope, the seal, the handwriting of the address, and the faint scent of the perfume.

My dear one,
  My heart is heavy. My father was furious over my unladylike behavior and over our friendship, which he considers inappropriate. I deeply apologize for having embarrassed you, and for any trouble that he may cause for you. I know not what that might be.
  He is talking of sending me abroad to school, which I suspect is to keep us apart. But know that my affection (dare I say "love?") for you will be forever.
  I will write you when I can.

Yours always,
Jane

John sat staring at the page. A few days ago he had been at the top of the world. His life ahead of him, a promising career . . . Now it was like ashes in his mouth. The worst was not even to his career, but the loss or destruction of the budding romance. The pinnacle of that thrilling episode had been the experience of a lifetime. To have a beautiful woman throw her arms around him with such feeling in a public place was embarrassing. But it was also such an honor . . . *Aiee!* But then it was spoiled by the reaction of her parents.

He still did not understand about that. He had thought that the Langtrys liked and respected him. Their quick withdrawal had confused him completely. What had caused the change? It could be nothing but the scene of affection at the stadium. And that was not even of his own doing.

"You're *leaving?*" Charlie Smith was astonished. *"Why?"*

"I don't know, Charlie. Just a request through the Bureau."

"But . . . Where?"

"I don't know. Some school out in Kansas. Haskell, it's called."

"*Haskell?* I know that one, John. It's only about a hundred miles from the Cherokee Nation. But . . . That's only a two-year school. A *junior* college! I don't understand. Maybe Senator Langtry could—"

Charlie stopped short and the two stared at each other.

"Yes," John said sadly. "I'm afraid so."

"Because of that little hug on the track the day of the game?"

"I don't know, Charlie, but it looks like it. They left early, you know. I had a letter from Jane."

"I heard you got a letter," Charlie said with a smile.

"Well, it wasn't good. She's going to school in England or somewhere. I wrote to her but haven't heard back."

"He's sending her away?"

"I guess so."

Charlie took a long breath.

"Whew! Well, damn it, John, you've got to face it. The Senator doesn't want his precious daughter keepin' company with a savage redskin."

John's temper flared. "It's not like that, Charlie!" he insisted.

The Cherokee said nothing for a few moments, and then

finally spoke, but more softly. "You know it is, John. I'm sorry. I thought the Senator was different."

"But I didn't think he'd do *this*, Charlie."

"Me, neither." Charlie sighed deeply. "I guess white men are all alike, after all. They all *look* alike, you know."

It was a wry attempt at humor, a reverse twist to the white man's impression of the hundreds of Indian cultures. But it was a poor joke, and fell on deaf ears.

"At least, I can write to her," John said.

That, too, proved to be wrong. The next day, John's letter was returned, unopened. Across the face of the envelope was scrawled in a firm hand: "Return to Sender."

His heart was very heavy.

Only a few days later, John found himself on a train, heading west again. It was different country. His sense of direction was acute, but his knowledge of geography and the political boundaries which had been drawn by the whites was sketchy. Borders, which could not even be seen, seemed a ridiculous concept to John and his friends. Charlie had told the others of a situation in which the white man's government had awarded adjacent tracts of land to his Cherokee Nation and to the Osages. Through error, the land assignments overlapped, which led to border warfare between the two. And both were right.

"Huh!" said Little Horse. "Borders are a white man's disease, anyway."

"Maybe so," agreed Charlie. "But our word for 'Osage' now translates to 'Nation of Liars.' "

The others had chuckled, but it was a sour joke.

The miles slipped behind with the *click-click* of the wheels on joints in the rails, a bitter reminder of the hope he had felt two years ago on the journey east. He was being exiled. There was no other interpretation. Through no fault of his own . . . His only crime had been the affection of the Senator's daughter. Even in that, his own part had been passive. The active role was Jane Langtry's. It was of little help that she, too, had been banished from home and country. That was a wry twist to the dark jokes played by fate.

Haskell Indian Institute was located on a flat tract of land south of the town of Lawrence, Kansas. Between the two was the campus of the University of Kansas, perched on a hill. Between this hill, impressively titled Mount Oread, and the Kaw River, sprawled the town of Lawrence. It had been burned by William Quantrill's Confederate raiders, and some two hundred of the residents had been killed during the War Between the States, but Lawrence had now recovered and was rebuilding.

The area had also suffered from the loss of the riverboat industry, as the navigable rivers were bridged by the railroads. Riverboats which once plied the Kaw, unable to pass under a railroad bridge, had been sold or transferred to companies operating on the upper Missouri. But the town was still well located. The area around the junction of the Kansas (or Kaw) River with the Missouri was the gateway to the rapidly expanding West. Another day's journey westward from Lawrence would bring a traveler to Topeka, the state capital.

In the midst of all this expansion, there was a thrust for education. Within easy traveling distance were several colleges and universities, and the whole area was interested in athletic achievement. The strength of young manhood was prized greatly on the still-lusty frontier.

Within the radius of a day's train travel were at least eight or nine colleges and universities with strong athletics programs. The University of Kansas, almost within view of Haskell, had a small but growing athletic program.

"Our toughest rival is Baker University," said Walter Goingbird, his first new acquaintance. "That's a Methodist school about twelve miles south of here. We play them in football and baseball. It's close enough for us to walk over to the game. They walk here, too, when we play here."

"Who else does Haskell play?" John asked.

"Well, the strongest are the church schools," Walter explained. "There's a lot of 'em pretty close. . . . Park College, over on the Missouri side. They're Presbyterian, and so is the one at C of E—that's College of Emporia, a bit farther away. We play Washburn at Topeka. Now, that's a city college. There's a Baptist University at Ottawa, south of here, beyond Baker. . . . Town of Ottawa . . . Then Lane University at Lecompton, between here and Topeka. They're United Brethren. Let's see. . . . Oh, there are state Universities of Missouri and Nebraska. KU, of course. Kansas has an aggie college, too, a ways west of Topeka."

"And all of these have football?" John asked. "Not just track and field and baseball?"

"I think maybe so, John. Football's catchin' on pretty fast. First game in Kansas was here. Kansas and Baker, about eight years ago, they said."

"Who won?"

"Oh, Baker, of course. They're the bigger school."

Maybe it won't be so bad, John told himself. Still, he was only half-convinced. And still, he smarted from the rejection and undeserved penalty for the simple infraction of having been born with red skin.

By comparison to Carlisle, back in the more civilized part of the country, Haskell was somewhat primitive. But the instruction was good, the athletic program active. That is, within the limits of money for equipment. That had always seemed to be a problem everywhere, even at Springfield College.

One major difference at Haskell was something he had not foreseen. Many of the student athletes were older— some in their thirties, perhaps even forty years old. He remarked on this to Goingbird, who chuckled and nodded.

"Yes," he agreed. "That's right. There are a lot of men in the plains nations. . . . Kiowa, Apache, Southern Cheyenne. . . . Even some Osages, who were sort of caught in between. Some refused to cooperate and stay on reservations, but then later figured they'd have to play along. So, some of them are in school here. They have some pretty wild stories, but it's hard to get 'em talkin'."

"I'd suppose so," agreed John.

In age, some of these men were contemporaries of his father. It startled him to realize that some of these older students might conceivably have ridden with Yellow Bull and the others against the cavalry at the Battle of the Greasy Grass, called the Little Bighorn by the whites. Surely not . . . He dismissed the idea as too unlikely to consider seriously. But . . . Maybe?

There was nothing he could do to attempt contact with Jane. His letter had been returned, and there was no point in trying again. He mustered what faith he could, hoping against hope that she would try to contact him.

SIXTEEN

John worked hard to gain a place on the football team at Haskell. It was virtually impossible, because the season had started before his arrival, and the team had been chosen. Barring injuries, his place this season would be on

Haskell's bench. The coach was understanding, but was having a fairly good season, and was not likely to make changes in a winning lineup.

"Be patient, Buffalo," he said. "Keep on the way you're doing, and you'll be in there next season."

This concerned John because he realized that he would probably have only one more year of collegiate play. Still, he did enjoy the few times that he was able to enter the game. He worked hard, made some good plays, but was usually placed on the line, with the gritty brute force required at those positions. There was little opportunity to demonstrate his skill at ball handling, broken-field running, or the dropkick which had brought him attention at Carlisle.

Students were not forbidden to go to town, but it was not encouraged. Many simply saw no reason for it, and preferred to stay "with their own kind," as the whites put it so quaintly.

John would just as readily have stayed at the school, but his friend Walter Goingbird was more familiar and more confident among whites. His Cherokee people had been in contact for centuries, and were considered one of the "civilized tribes."

"Funny thing, though . . . They don't exactly *treat* us civilized," said Walter, a twinkle of twisted humor in his eye.

They were on one of those visits to town in early spring. Walter was explaining how to interpret whether they'd be welcome or not.

"See that sign in the window of the café?" asked Walt. "*Colored people served in sacks only.* Now, you have to guess: Do they figure 'colored' means just Negro, or does

it mean redskins, too? You might even hear 'red nigger,' "
he added.

They walked on into town. On Massachusetts, a main
business street, the buildings were larger and more opulent,
displaying a measure of wealth and success. There were
cafés and restaurants and stores, and a fine hotel.

The two students did not intend to eat. Their meals were
taken at the school cafeteria, but Walter continued to explain.

"Now, that sign"—He pointed to one in the window of
an upscale restaurant—"*We reserve the right to refuse service to anyone.* . . . That means about the same as the other
one. You might be served there, but might not."

John had no desire to find out.

A man approached, walking on the flagstone walk from
the other direction, apparently headed for the restaurant.
There was something familiar about him: the way he
walked, the athletic motion in his stride. John was puzzled.
How could he know this man, far from any place he had
ever been?

The white man paused, seemed confused. He had appeared to be about to enter the restaurant, but now turned
toward the approaching duo.

"Do I know you?" he asked John, still looking puzzled.

When he spoke, his voice recalled the connection for
John . . . A game . . . Yes . . . Springfield. The demonstra-
tion game of "basketball" . . . This was the man who had—
Naismith!

"Mr. Naismith?" asked John. "What are you doing
here?"

"I live here. But how do I know you? You attend the
University?"

"No, sir. I'm at Haskell."

"Oh, yes . . . You were at Carlisle? Football! Of course.
We talked for a moment after the game. Butler, is it?"

"No, sir. Buffalo. John Buffalo. But . . . *You're* at the University?"

"Yes, I came as athletic director. But how did you happen to come to Haskell?"

"A long story, sir . . ."

"Forgive my prying. You have another season here?"

"I guess so."

"Well, best of luck to you, son. Not when you play us, of course, eh?"

All three laughed.

The rising "eh" on the end of the sentence may have been the last vestige of the coach's Canadian accent. It went unnoticed by John.

"And your friend, here?" Naismith asked politely.

"Oh, yes . . . Pardon me. This is Walter Goingbird. He's at Haskell, too."

"Yes." Naismith extended his hand. "Pleased to meet you."

Walter shook hands and nodded a greeting.

"Good to meet you, sir."

"You play ball, too?"

"A little."

"Good . . . Well, have a good season." He turned to John with an afterthought. "You were thinking of coaching, weren't you, Buffalo?"

"Yes, sir."

The coach nodded. "Well, stay in touch, eh?"

"What did he mean, 'stay in touch,' John?" Walter asked as they walked on.

"I don't know, Walt. I met him when we played Springfield College, and he seemed interested in what I was planning to do. He complimented my play. . . . I'd had a pretty good game. He seemed interested that I'd thought of coaching."

"Maybe he wants to offer you a job!" teased Walter.

"Quit it, Walt! He's just being nice."

As they walked on, another thought occurred to him.

"Say, Walt . . . I just remembered. When we were at Springfield . . . You know that new game, 'basketball'? He's the one who started it. They showed us a demonstration game."

"You figure they'll play it here?" asked Walt.

"Maybe. He used it for younger students, though, at the Y in Springfield."

"A kids' game?"

"Pretty much."

They headed back toward Haskell.

But in the back of John's mind, a thought was forming. He *would* stay in touch. Maybe he could gain some good advice.

The letter came several months after his arrival at Haskell. It was an envelope similar to that sent to him by Jane Langtry just before he left Carlisle. He could even imagine that it smelled the same, the faint floral scent of her perfume. But the stamp on the envelope was unfamiliar, and in some foreign denomination. He did not recognize the postmark.

It was addressed to him, John Buffalo, at Haskell, which was odd. Even more puzzling was the handwriting—a feminine hand, but not that of Jane Langtry. He was certain of that. He had read and reread that brief note until it was nearly worn out from refolding.

Curious, he opened the envelope. The letter was longer. His heart beat faster as he saw the handwriting. Yes, *this* was hers. . . .

My dearest,
    It has been so hard. I am in Paris, studying here.

My father has been so unreasonable in his efforts to keep us apart. I have written you repeatedly, addressing my letters to Carlisle. They are always "returned to sender." I know not whether they are returned from Carlisle, or whether I am watched here. Maybe, both. I suspect that you may have experienced similar treatment.

Now I may be more successful. I have a friend here at last, to whom I have confided our problem. I learned, through my brother, that you were transferred (dare I say "banished"?) to Haskell Indian Institute, on the far prairies. I regret, my love, that my family has been the cause of this. There was no wrong on *your* part. I was far too forward. But, I feel so close to you. And alas, we are being punished for things that have never happened. We have never even *kissed*.

But I digress. . . . My friend, Emily Brighton-Jones, a British schoolmate, has agreed to help. She is sending this letter. You can reply, writing to me, but addressing the envelope to Emily. She will be discreet.

Oh, my dear . . . I do hope that you, too, share the uplift of the soul that I experience when I think of you. I feel that surely you must, or I would not feel it so strongly. I have heard that your people are powerfully in tune with things of the spirit. My mother says that this is blasphemy, but I know what I feel. I am also convinced that there will come a time when we can be together. Of this I am certain, no matter how long it takes.

But I am rambling. . . . I pray that this effort is successful, so that we can communicate.

Yours always,
Jane

He sat numbly, staring at the letter in his hands. His heart quickened. She had *not* forgotten. She even seemed to *understand* the things of the spirit of which she spoke. She was *not* like other whites, appearing either smugly superior or pitying, or both.

He questioned his ability to express his feelings as she had done, but he must try. He was confident now that she would understand any deficiencies in his ability to communicate on paper.

Even so, he rewrote the letter three times before he was satisfied.

My dear one,
    My heart soared like the eagle to see your letter, and to know that our spirits are one. I am made to think that you do understand.
    My letters, too, have been returned. This, I *cannot* understand.
    I hope and pray that with the help of your friend, Emily, we can talk through letters. I will eagerly await your answer to assure ourselves that this will let us be in contact until we can be together.
                    Your obedient servant always,
                          John

He addressed the envelope to Miss Emily Brighton-Jones, sealed it, and then began to wonder. . . . How much postage? He had decided against a return address. That might alert anyone who was watching Jane Langtry's mail. However, it would also prevent its return, and he would never know whether the letter had reached her.

Finally, he walked to the main post office in Lawrence, and inquired as to proper postage to Paris. The postal clerk gave him an odd look, checked in a book, and told him the amount: nearly a dollar in all.

"Don't you want a return address on it?" the clerk asked with a sly grin.

"I . . . No, it's not needed," John said quickly.

He hurried back to the school and tried to calculate: How long would it take his letter to cross the continent, then the Atlantic by steamship, on to Paris by train, and the reply back to Kansas in the reverse order. Weeks ... Months, maybe.

But now he could wait.

He had something to hold on to.

SEVENTEEN

John realized that it would be weeks or even months before he could expect an answer to his letter. He threw himself into his studies and his constant exercise and training routines. He did so with more enthusiasm now, knowing that contact had been established. Still, the waiting was slow and frustrating.

The summer break was approaching. Some students returned to their homes, but most stayed at Lawrence, or in the area. There were many summer jobs on farms in the surrounding hills, and John had no trouble finding work, for room and board and a little pay. He tried hard to do what was expected. It helped that he had placed himself on a demanding, scheduled routine. He had not fully realized the importance until he chanced to overhear a conversation between his employer and a neighbor. John was cleaning and oiling harnesses in the barn. It was hard not to overhear the talk just outside.

"I heard you hired one o' them Indians from over at Haskell," the neighbor was saying.

"Yah," said Hans Schneebarger. "Dis vun ist goot vorker."

"I heard tell they ain't very reliable as to showin' up on time."

"Mebbe so, mebbe not. Dis vun ist goot."

Inside the barn, John was very quiet. Even though the conversation was favorable to him, he was embarrassed. It *was* demeaning to be classed as part of a group that was being considered irresponsible. He could see how this had evolved. Among his people, time of day was defined loosely. When will the council be held? *When the time comes*. The sun comes up; it goes down. The white man is preoccupied with the numbers on the face of his clocks and watches.

John had tried hard to learn the white man's ways. His years in the government schools had helped. It startled him a bit to realize that he had been successful enough to be singled out as one who "ist goot" about promptness. He was uncertain whether to accept the compliment or to resent the lumping together of all Indians as unreliable. Then it occurred to him that he was guilty of the same thing. He had a tendency to lump together all *whites*. White men do this. . . . Do that . . . *White men pay too much attention to their clocks*. . . .

This line of thought was interrupted by the conversation outside.

"I tell you vun t'ing," Mr. Schneebarger was saying, "dis boy, John, ist der best I ever seen mit horses. He can *talk* mit dem!"

"Aw, c'mon!"

"Yah! Ist true."

The two men walked on to look at something over at the hog pen, leaving John in wonder. His employer rarely gave him a word of praise, but apparently was quite impressed with John's horsemanship. It was something that he had never thought much about. Horses had been a part of his life in younger days, and he had missed them. Here, he was enjoying the renewed contact. The smells of a sweaty animal; the not-unpleasant, slightly ammoniac scent of warm sun on the hard-pounded earth of the corral brought back memories. The sense of smell recalls perhaps more deeper memories than any other, and he was reliving the more pleasant times of his childhood. He had not realized recently how much he had missed the horses of the People.

Somehow, the summer passed. He wrote another note to Jane via Emily Brighton-Jones, still not knowing whether his first one had been received.

In early August a letter arrived, recognizable by the French stamps and postmarks. His friend Walter Goingbird walked out to give it to him. It was addressed in the handwriting of Jane's coconspirator, Emily. There was something about the envelope that made John suspect that the envelope had been tampered with, but he could not be sure. Possibly, there was merely the wear and tear from being tossed around in a mailbag and lying in the musty hold of an ocean liner.

That evening he sought privacy at the top of the hill behind the Schneebarger farmstead and opened the letter, his heart racing. The faint scent of her perfume lingered even now.

My dear one,

I know not whether any of my letters may have reached you. I have not heard from you. I have to consider that you may not want me with the same passion that I feel for you, and this tears my heart to pieces. I prefer to think, and this is my dream, that we *are* one, and that we are being prevented from contact.

I know that my mail is being censored, both incoming and outgoing. This may not even reach you.

Since I have not heard, I must assume that either you have received none of my notes, that you did not try to answer, or that you tried unsuccessfully. I choose to cling to the latter interpretation. Your mail, too, may be censored, you know.

I do not know how long I will be able to continue in this wretched condition, not knowing. Maybe, someday, our trails will cross once more. Until then, know that I want you, need you. . . . But for now, I fear that my father has won. I will continue to write, but without the confidence that I once felt, until I can hear from you.

Yours always,
Jane

At the top of the hill, John voiced a long, wailing sob, like a song of mourning, which in fact, it was. It echoed across the woodland, the grassy meadows, and the cornfields of Hans Schneebarger. Horses raised their heads to listen.

"Vas ist das?" Helga asked her husband.

"Ist nothing. Dot Indian . . . John. Zum sort of chant . . . Like it vas dere church, maybe."

"Yah," she agreed. "Dot's likely. But he better come. His supper he vill miss!"

Back at school in September, John threw himself into his training with gusto, but it was no good.

"What's the matter, Buffalo?" yelled the coach after a fumble during scrimmage. "You're just not concentrating!"

After practice, the coach took him aside. "John, is something wrong?"

The coach was calmer now, having gotten past the rush of frustration over a poor performance. What could be wrong with one of his star athletes?

"No, sir," John said grimly.

There was no way he could explain his feeling of help-lessness, the terrible loss that gnawed at his heart, with no possibility of remedy.

Likewise, there was no way for the coach to reach him. From past experience, it was apparent when one of the Indian students adopted this attitude. This was an emotionless stone-faced front, a stoic defensive posture that was completely impenetrable. It was futile to try to breach that facade.

"Okay," said the coach helplessly, "if there's anything I can do to help, you know where to find me."

A strange young man, he thought, *but no more so than a lot of others. More sensitive, perhaps.*

He wondered what had occurred during the summer break that had so changed the world of John Buffalo. Maybe he could drive up to the Schneebargers' and ask about any unusual happenings. But it would have to wait. The football season was in full swing just now. They had to prepare to meet Missouri's Tigers, and it looked as if Buffalo wouldn't be ready. Maybe he could use George Bacon, or Edward Whips-Along. . . .

John was doubly frustrated now. He watched from the bench, knowing that he could do better than the players on the field. He *had* done better. But then, on the heels of that thought, a realization: that had been when he was filled with the emotion and energy of a thrilling love. That love still existed, but was now unattainable.

On one of his few free afternoons, he took a hike into the hills south of Haskell. He realized that he should probably have been in the library, but his spirit called for renewal.

The warm autumn sun found him on a hilltop, watching the big red squirrels so common to the area. They were busily gathering acorns from several varieties of oaks. Leaves were changing color. . . . The slope across from him to the east was a tapestry of gold and scarlet and the yellow of cottonwoods and the green of an occasional cedar. It was good.

A thought came to him, a quotation. . . . He did not remember the source, and it had made no sense to him at the time: *Those who can, DO. Those who cannot, TEACH.*

Why should this have popped into his head, as he sat here nursing his misery? This—his last competitive season in school—was not to be a good one. It was probably too late now to salvage anything from it. But his greater goal— to become a coach . . . Regardless of this season, he would have to do something else next year, anyway.

Maybe he could find employment. Mr. Schneebarger had seemed satisfied with his work, especially around the horses. The man had hinted that he could maybe come back next summer, but John had paid little attention. He was too depressed at the time to even think about it.

Besides, the pay was poor. Room and board, but meager cash. Not that money had ever been important to John. Still, one must eat. But it was an option.

Maybe a better one, however . . . *Those who cannot, TEACH.* . . . When he had heard that saying, it had meant those physically unable. But could it not as well mean those no longer in school? He'd enjoyed the coaching that he had done. He had seriously considered it as a career. Only recently had the distraction of his thwarted romance driven it from his mind.

He realized now that he had been depending considerably on Senator Langtry to guide his athletic career. Maybe, Olympic competition. Now that was gone, too, along with his lost love. He shook off his bitterness. Surely there were others to whom he could turn.

Naismith! Of course . . . The man had expressed interest in him, had offered him kindness and help, not once but *twice*. Once in Massachusetts and again since the coach's arrival at the University.

Yes . . . He'd walk over to the University and ask to talk to Dr. Naismith. Maybe there would be some sort of assistant-coaching job for which he could apply.

He rose with new purpose, and hurried back to the Haskell campus.

EIGHTEEN

John waited in the outer office, under the watchful eye of a guardian secretary or assistant of some sort. The secretary, a young man with unruly hair and a face badly scarred by the pitting of smallpox, was busily sorting papers and arranging them in folders, presumably in alphabetical order. From time to time he glanced up toward the visitor, a bit suspiciously, perhaps. That look was not unusual. *You are different. . . . I'm watching you to see that you don't try anything. . . .*

John wondered if he and his fellow students at Haskell might exhibit a similar attitude toward whites. This struck him as ironic, and might have seemed more so, if he had not been overwhelmed by the enormity of his present problem. He withdrew further into his protective shell.

Conversational voices behind the door marked *J. Naismith, Dir. Athletics* rose a trifle in volume, yet with good humor apparent. The visitor must be preparing to leave. Now the door opened. A young man shook hands with the coach and turned away, with a glance and a nod at John Buffalo.

"A fella to see you, sir," said the pockmarked secretary.

Naismith looked up, puzzled.

"Yes?"

"A few words with you, sir," John mumbled.

"Yes . . . Come in. . . . Mr. . . . ?"

Confusion was plain on the coach's face as he struggled to place his visitor.

"Buffalo. John Buffalo."

"Ah, of course! Haskell . . . Before that, Carlisle, right? Football and track, wasn't it? Come in."

"Yes, sir."

Naismith gestured toward a chair, and circled around his desk to his own seat. He folded his hands, elbows on the desk, and leaned forward.

"How's your season going, Buffalo?"

He seemed curious as to why a player from another school would be here to talk to him in mid-season. Perhaps even a bit suspicious.

"Not the best, sir."

"But I thought Haskell was having a pretty good go at it, eh?"

"Oh . . . Yes, sir. Not bad. I thought you meant myself."

"Well . . ." The coach seemed confused. "Well, I did, to some extent. Both, maybe."

"I see. . . . But . . . I'm not starting," John blurted. "I haven't played much."

Now the coach appeared astonished. "You're *not?* An injury?"

"No, sir. Coach felt I wasn't ready."

"*You?* Not ready? Buffalo, I've seen you play."

Naismith leaned back in his chair with a chuckle, and then forward again.

"You're not in trouble?"

"No, sir," mumbled John, "not that way."

He was embarrassed, wishing he hadn't come. The coach, experienced in talking with young men, took another approach.

"Let's see. . . . This is your senior year. Your last season, eh?"

"Yes, sir. I'm not certain how it stands. I was at Carlisle for two years. . . ."

"Yes. And *then* you transferred to Haskell? I don't understand—it seems backward, somehow."

"I had no choice, sir," John said stiffly. He was very uncomfortable with the way the conversation was going.

Naismith nodded thoughtfully.

"Yes, I understand."

John had the impression that maybe the coach actually *did* understand, and he felt a little better. Maybe he could state his problem.

"My reason for coming wasn't about this season, sir. I know it's my last collegiate competition, good or bad. I was thinking of next year. I . . . Well, how does a man go about looking for a coaching job?"

Naismith leaned back in his chair with a more relaxed chuckle.

"Oh, so that's it, eh? You're looking for a job for *next* year. A good plan, Buffalo. But . . . Let's see. . . . Your credentials are confusing. You won't have a degree. Really odd. Why would they—? Well, never mind. What I'm getting at is that you won't be qualified academically, even as an assistant. You might work as a trainer or manager while you take enough credit hours to hold a degree. You could work on your track events toward the Olympics at the same time. McGregor told me you're pretty good. Discus, wasn't it?"

"Well . . . Javelin's probably my best event. That and cross-country."

"Yes . . . I suppose you realize that distance runners don't really peak in their careers until they're nearing thirty?"

"I'd heard that, sir."

"Well . . . Let's see, now. . . . Your first move will be to inquire. You need to know how many credits you'll have at the end of this academic year. How many more you'll need for a degree. Where did you intend to enroll?"

"I hadn't even thought about it, sir. I didn't know where to start."

"Well, it would need to be where you can find a job of some sort. Preferably, in athletics, eh? Several colleges in the area . . ."

"Would there be anything here?" John asked. "As a job, I mean."

"Maybe . . . Let's find out about the credits and requirements. Ask your registrar at Haskell for a transcript, and we'll take it from there. Meanwhile, keep working hard."

Naismith rose, which seemed to indicate that the interview was at an end. The coach opened the door into the outer office, where another young man was waiting, and now rose excitedly from his chair.

"Coach!" he said breathlessly. "They offered me a job. Basketball coach!"

Naismith threw up his hands in resignation.

"I keep telling them. You don't *coach* basketball. It's just a *game!* Well, come on in." He turned to John. "Buffalo, let me know when you have that transcript, eh?"

It was not the easiest task to get a copy of his records.

"They won't be complete until next summer," grumbled the clerk in the administrator's offices. "What do you want with your records anyway, Buffalo?"

"I've been asked to submit them," John said stiffly.

"Well, we can't just give them to *you*. We'd have to send them to an accredited institution."

"Then send them to Coach Naismith at the University."

"There'll be a charge. A dollar."

"Okay, I'll pay it."

"Be a couple of weeks."

"Then go ahead, *please*."

The dour clerk shrugged noncommittally and went back to his pens and paper.

In due time, with much insistence, the needed documentation was ready. He was even allowed to hand-carry the sealed envelope to the University.

"It has to stay sealed," warned the clerk.

"Of course," said John brusquely, laying a hard-earned silver dollar on the counter.

He made his way back to Naismith's office as soon as his schedule permitted.

"Oh, no, not here," said the pockmarked secretary. "Take it over to Administration."

"May I speak with the coach?" John asked.

"Huh!" grunted the other. "He's out of town."

The door to the inner office was closed, but John had no reason to question the secretary's statement.

"When . . . Never mind . . . Would you tell him that John Buffalo was here? That I have the papers he requested."

"Yes, I'll leave him a note."

The young man smiled. Maybe he wasn't really as gruff as he tried to appear. Just doing his job.

John asked directions and found the appropriate office, where he handed his envelope to another clerk.

"I'd like to speak to someone about completing a degree."

The other nodded.

"Have a chair," he gestured, as he turned toward an inner office, carrying the envelope.

It seemed to John that he waited a long time. He could hear a conversation in the inner office and eventually a tall, thin gentleman with fuzzy sideburns and a full, bushy mustache emerged with some papers in his hand. He peered at John over small but thick spectacles, as if he were observing a scientific specimen of some sort.

"Let me see. . . . You wish to *enroll*?"

John took a deep breath, trying to conceal his anxiety and his emotions.

"I wished to inquire how many more credits I would need to finish a degree," he said politely.

The man looked from John to the papers and back again, his distaste obvious.

"But"—he stammered—"these credits are from, uh, *Indian* schools."

Somehow, the distaste with which the man said "*Indian*" made it sound like typhoid or cholera.

"You must realize that this is a *University*. We could accept very few of *these* credits."

He gestured with the papers, his attitude implying that he feared he might soil his hands just by examining the forms.

"But . . . There are three years of study there," John protested.

"Of course," said the educator, speaking slowly and a little loudly, as if that would help the misunderstanding. "A year at Haskell and, uh, two more at, uh, *Carlisle,* is it? *Indian* schools. These are not acceptable credits, for the most part."

"I will have *another* year's credits in the spring," John offered.

"Yes, uh, *Haskell* credits. You may have enough entry-level hours for a semester or two. But . . . Some of these you have will not be eligible. If you had taken this class, for instance, here at the University, you would have needed other prerequisites first."

He pointed to the top page on the sheaf of papers.

"But I took that course! I scored well."

"Yes, but without the prerequisites, this other freshman course can't be accepted."

"I would have to take it *over again*?"

"Well, yes . . . But only after taking the prerequisite, Beginning Mathematics."

"*Beginning*?"

"Of course. One must start at the bottom, in any field. Except, of course, digging a well."

The man giggled, amused at his own cleverness.

John Buffalo assumed his stone-faced stoicism, his protection.

"Do you want these?" asked the man, offering the papers.

"I wanted information," said John. "Maybe I got it. I have wasted three years?"

"Not at all." The man smiled. "You can read and write."

The message was plain: *And most savages can't.*

John would have liked to have more information about just how many of these credit hours *could* be transferred, but he realized that it was not forthcoming.

Maybe, when Naismith returned, he could be helpful. He stopped to leave the envelope and the papers at the coach's office, with the pockmarked clerk.

NINETEEN

They won't accept your credits?"

Naismith was indignant.

"Only a few, they said. Not more than a semester or two."

"Well," the coach pondered. "I can see their position. Not that I agree with it, John. . . . Much of your study has been at a training level called 'normal school.' Not comparable to the University. But to further confuse things, you've competed in football and track for three seasons. In your fourth, now. And this, at college level. And from Carlisle, back *down* to two-year training level. I don't understand that rationale at all."

John said nothing. He had a pretty good idea of that rationale, but it would do no good to attempt to explain. He had been punished for his poor choice of parents, and an unacceptable romance.

Jane . . . He still thought of her often. He had mourned her loss and had tried to move on. There had been a brief time when *no* woman even looked attractive to him, but that had passed. Now his attraction was guarded. More objective, a bit defensive, in the stoic, emotionless "Indian" way. He did not expect . . . Did not even *want* to feel about any woman as he had felt about Jane Langtry. That was the love of a lifetime. The urges he felt now were purely animal.

"John?"

"What? Oh, yes, sir."

His mind had wandered and he had been lost in thought.

"Are you all right, John?"

"I . . . uh . . . I think so, sir. You were saying—"

"I asked whether you knew how many credits the University will accept, eh?"

"Oh . . . No, sir. They didn't say. Not more than a year's work, I gathered."

Naismith shook his head.

"Well, first you should finish the year at Haskell. Receive your two-year degree. That lends some dignity. Then you could probably find a job as a trainer. Possibly we can help with that. Pay would be poor. . . . Little chance for advancement. But you could continue your education and your physical training, compete in open track events, look ahead to Olympic level."

"You mentioned further education, sir. What would be needed to coach?"

"At least a college degree, I'm afraid, John. But you wouldn't have to do it all at once, eh?"

"What about the cost?"

"That, of course, is a potential problem. Have you any resources?"

"Resources?"

"Yes. Any income . . ."

"Oh. Money."

"Well, yes, to put it bluntly."

"No, sir. At Haskell—"

"Ah, yes. The Indian schools. Carlisle, too, of course . . . This is outside my experience, John. But you know there are fees, tuition, expenses at colleges and universities?"

"Yes, sir. I've just had no occasion to deal with it."

"I understand. Well, in most cases, the cost is by the credit hour. You'd pay only for the courses you take. Probably a registration fee."

"How much money are we speaking of?"

"I can't say, offhand. But within reason. You can do this, John. Finish your year at Haskell, and I'll inquire around. A trainer's job, or even a locker-room attendant would be a start, eh?"

The coach rose, indicating that the interview was at an end.

"Thank you, sir."

"Stay in touch!"

They shook hands and parted.

Now, with at least some sense of direction, John could try harder to concentrate on football. First, however, it was necessary to get into some games, and that was difficult. The Haskell team was well seasoned and well coached. Players were in good condition, and there were few injuries. John found himself in an odd dilemma, almost hoping for the injury that would thrust him into the game, yet feeling guilt for that very hope.

In practice, he worked with a vengeance. In scrimmage against the starters, he tackled and blocked as if the game actually depended on it. After a particularly hard tackle, he was helping the ball carrier to his feet when the coach rushed onto the field.

"Take it easy, Buffalo. This is just practice, you know." He turned to the dazed player. "Are you okay, Soldier?"

"Yes, sir. I think so. Damn, John, we're on the same side, remember?"

"I—I'm sorry, Soldier," muttered John. "I didn't mean . . ."

"I know. It's okay."

If he could only take out his frustrations in a game or two!

But he warmed the bench and, in observing, learned. Football was still in process of development, and the rules were at times unclear. Haskell played teams with bizarre variations to their uniforms. Straps and handles dangled from the suit of one team's ball carrier. His teammates could grab and pull, push, carry—even *throw* the quarterback through or over the line of scrimmage.

Another team wore jerseys with the outline of a football, complete with lace up the middle, stitched on the chest. This created difficulty in identifying who actually had the ball.

Some of their games were with semiprofessional teams, with strange equipment and techniques. One of these, the St. Louis Athletics, had pointed helmets with a lace up the back like that on a football. When the ball was snapped, several players would yank off their helmets, tuck them under an arm, and run wildly. Which one should be tackled? And, if you guessed wrong, there could be a penalty for holding.

When the season was over, John reverted to distance running to stay in physical condition for the coming track-and-field season. Each morning he rose early to run at least ten miles before classes. In inclement weather he still ran, counting laps around the gymnasium.

Christmas came and went, observed but little celebrated by the students, most of whom remained at school for the holiday break. There was a Christmas dinner with some special treats. Oranges, not a usual delicacy in the school cafeteria, and for each, a sack of hard candy.

With the help of James Naismith, John managed to obtain more information about his academic status. At the University of Kansas, he would be allowed credit for what would amount to a year's study. There were three more courses for which he could receive credit by taking "prerequisites," which would have been required if he had taken the courses at K.U.

"You could take some of those now," suggested Naismith. "This term."

"Uh . . . Sir, I couldn't."

"Not enough time?"

"Well, that, and . . . I have no money, sir."

"Yes, I suspected as much. Which leads me to another matter. I may have a job for you."

John brightened.

"Here?"

Naismith smiled. "No, it's customary to fill our jobs with our own students, you know."

Of course, thought John. *How stupid of me.*

"This would be at Lane University," the coach went on. "Over at Lecompton, west of here. Walking distance. Ten miles, maybe. A church school. United Brethren . . . A good school. They need a trainer and locker-room manager. Here, I'll give you the name to contact."

Naismith pulled a sheet of paper toward him and scribbled on it, then folded it and handed it to John.

"Here's your introduction. Hand this to the coach over there, eh?"

It was three weeks before the weather permitted such travel. When there was finally a break, he crossed the bridge at Lawrence and followed the road west, on the north side of the Kaw River. The road was thawing in the watery rays of the pale winter sun. It was muddy in places and slippery in others, and it was difficult for him to maintain a runner's pace.

It was not difficult to locate the brown sandstone University building when he arrived at the town of Lecompton. Easily the most imposing structure in town, its construction had been started as the state's Capitol Building. Shifting politics moved the capital to Topeka, a few miles west, and the unfinished building was sold to the Church of the Brethren for their University. The Brethren were originally allied to the Methodists, but based around German-language congregations, and more pacifist, similar to the Quakers.

John was not particularly interested in all of this, but listened patiently as an enthusiastic student escorted him to meet the man to whom he would give Naismith's note.

Coach Braun rose to shake hands, and unfolded the note, scanning it briefly.

"Ah, yes! Coach Naismith spoke to me of this, Buffalo. As I understand, you are not to enroll as a student?"

"Possibly, sir. I will graduate from Haskell this spring,

but will need further credits to enter coaching."

"Ah, yes, I remember now. You seek a trainer's job while you continue. A few classes here, then?"

"If possible, sir."

"I don't see why not. A bit unusual perhaps, but . . . Didn't Naismith tell me you had attended somewhere else? Some eastern school . . . Springfield?"

"No, sir. He was at Springfield. I was at Carlisle, and we played them at football."

"I see. Well, this isn't much of a job, this trainer's position. Usually I use one of our own students as a part-time helper. But that man is graduating. We are talking of next term, I assume?"

"Yes, sir."

"This could mean room and board, perhaps a couple of dollars a week. . . ."

"Coach Naismith suggested that I might work toward a degree from here. There would be enrollment costs?"

"Yes . . . I gather that your resources are limited?"

Not limited; nonexistent, thought John.

"Uh . . . Yes, sir."

"Well, it might be possible to consider a waiver. At least a partial one. Nothing definite, you understand. We'll see. After all, this is months away, you know."

"Yes, sir. Thank you."

As he left Lecompton, his spirits rose. The journey back to Lawrence was much shorter and easier because his heart was soaring.

It had been a long time since he had anything good about which he could think. Maybe he had come to a point in the trail where things could again become good for him. He smiled to himself, and lengthened his stride toward the Haskell campus.

TWENTY

Maybe his world was beginning to fall into place again. He still thought of Jane sometimes, but less often, maybe. There was not the rending, tearing sense of bereavement that he once had felt. There was regret for the loss, but it was a loss of something that had really never been, except as a hope and expectation. In his more thoughtful moments, he told himself that such a love could never have been, anyway. Her world was far removed from anything that he could ever be. He had been taught this, in many ways, since his first day in the government school on the reservation.

Now, however, he had envisioned a new goal and a realistic chance at achieving it. He could work for the summer again, maybe save a little money. He'd move to Lecompton as the harvest was over and the fall term began at Lane University. It was a plan. He was certain that in a position as trainer he could begin to do some coaching.

John worked hard at his own training, pleased that his abilities at track and field were improving. In distance runs, his wind was better than ever, and his coordination smoother. He almost never fell at the hurdles now. The javelin soared to greater distances as he developed muscle strength. He placed in the track meets against other schools around the region.

Shortly before the end of the spring term, it occurred to him that it might be good to contact Coach Schmidt at Lane again, to verify their previous conversation. He was accustomed to a daily ten-mile morning run, and usually another in the evening. He could easily head across the river and west, ending the morning session at Lane. The return trip could be at any time later in the day.

It was a glorious morning in May, cool and sunny, and the sun was pleasant. John could glory in the use of his developing strength and condition. He reached Lecompton and slowed to a walk to cool down as he neared the campus at Lane University.

"Ah, yes," said the coach, half-turning to set down a burlap sack of equipment. He extended a hand. "Good to see you, Buffalo. But I'm afraid I have bad news."

"Bad news?"

"Yes. The trainer's job . . . It's filled."

"I don't understand. I thought—"

"I'm sorry, John. I told you, we give preference to our own students."

"Yes, sir, but you said—"

"I don't know what you thought I might have implied, John. But the position is filled. Maybe next year."

There was no point in further talk. That much was plain. It was also plain that the "preference" was quite selective. The pimply faced young man beyond the lockers, stuffing soccer balls into another gunnysack, was a Nordic type with blue green eyes and flaxen hair. It was as plain as if someone had said: *You're just an Indian.*

John's shield of stony stoicism descended over his face as he turned away.

"Maybe later, son," the coach called after him.

John wanted badly to shout at the man, *I am not your son! I am the son of Yellow Bull!* But it would do no good. He walked away.

———

The road back to Lawrence was much longer than it had been on the morning run, and not nearly so smooth. What had been a beautiful day, with sights, scents, and sounds of spring, had deteriorated considerably.

As he passed Mount Oread, he considered turning aside to talk to Coach Naismith, but elected to defer it. Possibly, when he regained his composure, he would consider it. Yes, he probably owed it to the coach to tell him of this latest twist of misfortune.

It was nearly two weeks before John had recovered to the point where he felt comfortable in approaching the man.

"Really? I'm sorry, John. Did he give you any reason?"

"One of his students . . ."

"Ah, yes. Well, that can't be helped. What will you do now?"

"I don't know. I can work for the summer for one of the farmers, but then, I don't know."

"Sorry I'd have nothing here. There are other colleges around, though. I'll keep an eye open. Stay in touch, eh?"

John talked to his own coach, but they had never been really close.

"Too bad, Buffalo. I'd hoped that would work out for you at Lane. If I hear of anything . . ."

"Yah!" said Mr. Schneebarger. "Ist goot. Ve got a horse to break, too. Ven ken you start, John?"

"Two weeks. I could come this weekend, two days."

"Mebbe so, Saturday. Sunday, nein. Ist day to rest."

John had always found that odd. Most whites, especially the more churchly types, set aside a day for "rest" every seven days. Routine chores must be done, of course.

Milking, feeding, and gathering eggs. In most families, there was no plowing or planting or hoeing. The main activity was church, which sometimes lasted most of the day. Prayers and singing and endless sermons.

He participated, to an extent. It was easier. Old White Horse had taught him that. But he still wondered. Why does the white man talk to his God only once a week?

There was a ceremony as the graduation took place at Haskell. The students wore robes and funny mortarboard hats, and marched to music. Speakers praised the graduates, and urged them to go out and make their instructors proud; to show that they had overcome the handicaps of their collective origins. They marched out again, soberly, to the same music.

John had made few close friends during his time at Haskell. He had been too distracted by personal problems and disappointments. There were short good-byes and good wishes from a few classmates, and an unexpected word of encouragement from the coach.

"Buffalo, I don't pretend to know all your problems, but . . . Well, I know you've got possibilities. Whatever it is, don't give up. You can do it!"

"Thank you, Coach," muttered the embarrassed John.

If the coach only knew. But maybe he did, in some way. Coach had seen a lot of young Indians go out into the world to challenge a game in which the cards were stacked against them.

"Give it your best. I expect to hear good things about you."

"Yes, sir. I'll try."

———

His good-bye with Walter Goingbird was not much longer. Walt was perhaps his only real friend here.

"Where will you go, John?"

"Back out to Schneebarger's for now, I guess. You?"

"Home to Oklahoma. Lots of changes goin' on there, I hear."

"Good or bad?"

"Both, probably."

The two chuckled together.

"Always that way, John," added Walter.

John nodded, but reserved his thought that if something good was to occur in his life, it was past due. He was more than ready for the good part.

John moved into the small crib in the barn where he had spent the past summer. All in all, not a bad place. It was used as a tack room, and the walls were hung with bridles and pieces of leather harness and hand tools used in the constant necessary repairs of equipment. The familiar smells of leather and neat's-foot oil brought back memories of last season. . . . Of the unexpected letter that had dashed his romantic dreams in an instant and sent him into depths of despair from which he was not yet ready to recover. He tried to push that behind him.

He did not know how long he would be here. His departure last fall had been because of the beginning of the school year. Now there would be no urgency. If Schneebarger needed him longer, so be it. Here his heritage stood him in good stead. *What will happen will happen. And only when the time comes.* Meanwhile, he was here. He could work with the horses, using his gifts of athletic ability and his ability to see into the thoughts of the animal. That, too, he regarded as a gift.

Last year he had barely become acquainted with the family's three children. Looking back, he decided that Mrs. Schneebarger had probably planned it that way. There had undoubtedly been some distrust or at least doubt about the hiring of an Indian. Schneebarger had probably decided on that move without consulting his wife. Gradually, the buxom Helga had become more friendly. There had actually been tears in her eyes when John moved back to school in September.

Now she was much more open and friendly, her smile and demeanor welcoming him back. He was careful to treat her with respect, as he had been taught. The position of women among his own people was somewhat different than among whites. Indian women could speak in council, could vote, own property. In some tribes, *all* property. By contrast, white women seemed to have little control of their lives, beyond their kitchens and firesides. That had been very confusing to him, especially since the first white woman he had ever seen had been Miss Whitehurst. Old White Horse was a special case, and did not fit the pattern.

The Schneebargers' home, however, was the closest contact he had experienced to an ordinary white family's patterns of behavior. He quickly realized that the previous year had been a test and that he had passed. He was now accepted almost as family, and it was good.

The older two children finished the school year at about the time John moved into the tack room. They were home for the summer. Hans—"Little Hans" to distinguish him from his father—was about ten or eleven, John estimated. He was smart and strong and very much wanted to do "man things," to make his father proud.

Gretchen, a year or two younger, was equally eager to become a young *hausfrau*. The "baby," Wilhelm, was actually about three or four. He had been born after the family came to America, John was told.

"Ve talk only English at home, now," explained their mother. "Before . . . At first ve talk Cherman. Den, Liddle Hans goes to school. De odder kids, dey laugh at him 'cause he can't talk good, und he don't understand. Now, ist better, *nein?*"

They, too, John realized, were going through a process much like his own. These people, of another origin, were trying to learn the ways of this new country. It had not occurred to him that some whites had the same problems.

Besides all this there were the Negroes, former slaves and children of slaves. He knew that they had special problems. Some had joined the Indian tribes and had intermarried, especially among the Seminoles and Creeks. He had known a couple of students at Carlisle who were very dark-skinned. He was just realizing what extra problems *they* would have in the white man's world.

"Liddle Hans was having trouble mit reading," his mother went on. "The teacher sent home his books for the summer. Maybe you help him some?"

John realized that this was a great honor, a sign that he had been accepted by the family. He was flattered.

"I'd be glad to help, Mrs. Schneebarger."

"*Ach!* Call me Helga. Everybody does."

"Okay, Helga. May I look at the schoolbooks?"

"Sure. Over dere . . ." She gestured.

There were four books. *McGuffey's Reader* and a spelling book. He'd used those himself. An arithmetic volume and another, titled *History of Kansas,* by Noble L. Prentiss. Curious, he opened the history book. A printed sentence on one of the first pages indicated that this was the official history text for all schools in the state.

Curious, John scanned the table of contents and noticed a chapter titled "Indians of Kansas." He found that page. The chapter was only three or four pages long, mostly omitting more than mention of the dozens of tribes and nations who had migrated or been forced in, out, and through the area.

The chapter closed with a summary paragraph:

The story of their wars and huntings and migrations has little interest to civilized people. When they passed away from Kansas and the world, they left nothing except mounds of earth, rings on the sod, fragments of pottery, rude implements. They fought each other, disputed possession with wild beasts, were stricken down with fell diseases, but their history never became of interest or importance to the world, because they did nothing for the world.

John sat staring at the page for a few moments before he closed the book.

Some things never change, he reflected.

TWENTY-ONE

The breaking of the colt was to start immediately. Schneebarger had apparently planned it that way, waiting until his hired man was available.

"You vork mit him a liddle at first," suggested the farmer. "He knows you from dat last summer."

John was somewhat at a loss as to how to begin the education of a workhorse. A horse is a horse, but one may be far different from another, not only in size, color, temperament, and body build, but in its ultimate use.

At this time and place, a man might breed a mare to

produce the kind of foal he needed. Bred to a light-boned, trim stallion, she might produce a carriage horse with considerable style and grace. To a medium-sized saddle horse, an animal useful for riding, roping, or herding cattle, a "cow-horse." The same mare, bred to a heavy draft horse of the European cold-weather type would produce a "workhorse" . . . Big footed, hairy, muscular, this animal would never excel at speed, but could pull massive loads in harness. A good mare could even be bred to a jack donkey to produce mules, a sterile hybrid with some of the best qualities of both parents.

"Oh, yah," said Hans as he turned away. "Before you start dat, mebbes you could t'row de cow ober the fence some hay?"

"Yes, sir, I'll do that."

He was often amused at the German's stubborn attempts to speak English. This was a problem which he could understand, having had it thrust on himself at an early age. He smiled as he visualized Old White Horse attempting to force her tutelage on someone like Hans Schneebarger. Hans was apparently having a lot more difficulty with the transition than his wife, Helga. And Little Hans would probably have little or no accent at all.

John himself felt that his English was pretty good, compared to some of his classmates. He had spoken it exclusively for several years. He still had Lakota, of course, and had picked up a little Kiowa, and rudimentary Cherokee words and expressions. Some of these, such as *okeh*, indicating agreement, had been adopted by whites almost without their realizing it.

Now John stood looking at the yearling colt, already the size of a good buffalo runner. A gelding, already neutered when he was small, should be no problem to handle. Hans was gentle with his horses, and his behavior would probably be transmitted to the youngster as confidence in humans. The colt would learn by example.

Hans had no patience with anyone who would mistreat an animal. John had once seen him soundly thrash a man who, on the road to Lawrence, had been beating a horse. The stranger's wagon was stuck in mud and, instead of trying to free it by lightening the load or applying leverage to the wheels, the man was applying a heavy whip. Schneebarger stopped his own team and jumped from the wagon to pull the other man from his seat. With hands the size of slabs of bacon, the German cuffed him soundly, jerked the whip from the man's grasp and tossed it into the mud, followed by the culprit himself. Then, as the man floundered, yelling and cursing, Hans motioned to the startled John to take the reins of the stranger's team. While John handled the horses, Hans stepped into the mud and applied his powerful muscles to the trapped wheel. With a sucking noise the wagon rocked free, and the German slogged back onto the road, ignoring his victim in the mud. He motioned John back to his own wagon.

"You drive," he said.

Hans himself sat on the tailgate as they moved on, scraping mud from his boots and clothing with a stick. Nothing was said for a mile or so, and finally, anger cooled somewhat, he spoke again.

"A man kin holler ven he needs help," he philosophized. "A dumb baste cannot."

This statement had seemed to need no comment, and John made none.

Now he smiled to himself, remembering. Already, he could feel that his medicine with this colt was good. It would only be a matter of familiarizing the animal with the routine of harness and pulling.

John began by tying the animal, already broke to halter, in one of the stalls. He dumped a bucket of oats into the feed box and began to rub his hands over the neck and shoulders while the colt ate. He whispered in its ears, words of comfort in Lakota, breathed in the animal's nostrils. . . . The colt continued to chew contentedly on the oats. Confidence, pleasant association . . .

On the next day's session, John took some pieces of harness with rings and buckles and fastened them together as a teaching tool. He had never done this before, but reasoned that a workhorse must learn to have straps and buckles and metal rings dragged over and around and beneath its body. Again, he let the colt see and smell the contraption before he began to drag it over the animal's back and down the hip and stifle. The colt stiffened, ears erect, but then resumed eating. In only a few sessions, it was possible to toss a harness across hip and shoulder and buckle it.

Placing the bit in the colt's mouth was another matter. The metallic taste and unfamiliar shape of the snaffle seemed an obstacle. John was sure that once in place, in the proper space behind the teeth, it would not be uncomfortable. His people often used metal bits, and he had seen them used at The Oaks. . . . (A painful jab of sweet memory—now lost—flitted over him.) He considered using a thong as a war bridle, but decided against it.

Instead, he obtained from Helga a small jar with a little sorghum molasses. A smell, a thin smear of the sweet thick syrup over the snaffle . . . By the third session, the colt would trot eagerly toward the bit to take it in his mouth.

In two weeks, John could drive the harnessed colt around the barnyard, pulling a log on a chain. He was ready to place the colt in team harness with a more experienced animal to finish his training.

"Yah! Ist goot!" marveled Hans.

A few days later, Hans called to John as he was harnessing the team to the cultivator. A neighbor had stopped by.

"John! Heinemann, here, likes de vay you handle dat

colt. He wonders could you mebbe help him mit vun colt of his?"

"Well . . . I'll try. If it's okay with you, of course."

"Sure."

"What's the problem?"

"Not sure, John," said Heinemann. "He's spooky. Fights anything you try. Oh, yes, he's a saddle horse. You have any experience with them?"

John smiled to himself. Nearly all of his experience was with horses that were ridden. The training of the young workhorse had been new.

"Some," he said aloud. "I'll see what I can do."

"Good. Come on over when you get a chance."

"Ven de work's all done, I send him ober," said Schnee-barger.

All three chuckled. This was a common oft-repeated remark, never taken seriously. An inside joke, which was understood by all. The work was never all done on a frontier farm or ranch. It isn't, even now. Something always beckons, and part of the management was—and is—the selection of the most urgent among those chores that need attention.

"Maybe Sunday?" asked John, with a glance at Hans. The Germans tried to observe the sabbath within their ability to defer some of the more major jobs. Some things *must* be done daily, of course.

"Yah! Ist goot, ef you want, John."

The colt in question was a stocky, well-built two-year-old, recently gelded and completely undisciplined. *He'd make a pretty good horse,* John thought. This was the useful sort of animal sometimes referred to as a "chub," a stout animal that could be used as a cow horse or to work in double harness to pull a light wagon. Sometimes, both. *He'd probably have made a good buffalo runner,* John thought.

Just now, the animal stood in a small corral, ears erect and attention riveted on the newcomer. Everything about him radiated fear and suspicion.

"You raise him, Mr. Heinemann?" John asked.

"No, no . . . I just bought him from a trader. Looks like he could be dangerous."

That would explain a lot. No telling what the horse's background or experience had been. It was not impossible that this was a wild colt, recently captured in a horse hunt on the prairie farther west, still partly unsettled. With the buffalo gone, wild horses had proliferated. There were still a few wild horse hunters capturing the animals for resale to settlers, because good horses were always in demand.

No matter his origin, this colt would be a handful. He had possibly been mistreated, probably been handled roughly, and the distrust he now had for the human race shone plainly in the wide-set eyes.

"Well," said John cautiously, "we'll see."

He tried to think of some of the tricks he had seen his father use. There was much medicine involved, a communication and mingling of the spirits of man and horse. Yellow Bull had had a special medicine bag, containing a few items that he used sometimes. A "chestnut" from the foreleg of an old stallion, the odd misplaced toenail at the knee which is a remnant of ages past. . . . A grayish lump of dried "milt," the bit of tissue found sometimes on the tongue of a newborn foal, its purpose unknown. Tradition has it that the milt teaches the foal to suckle, even before birth. Regardless, such objects carry the medicine which had allowed Yellow Bull to become the horseman that he was. . . . They carry the primitive spirit of the horse, present since Creation.

Yellow Bull's horse-medicine bag had accompanied him to the Other Side on the burial scaffold. John could certainly have used some spirit-help now, and hoped to remember some of the skills he had seen his father and other men use in a horse's training . . . Skills not entirely dependent on the medicine of milt and chestnuts from an old stallion.

"Just leave me with him for a while to get acquainted," he told Heinemann.

"Go ahead!" Heinemann shrugged and turned away. "There's a rope on the post, there. Stuff in the tack room if you get that far."

Heinemann didn't seem as if he had a lot of confidence.

"Thanks!" John called after him.

Then he wondered if his thanks had sounded sarcastic. He turned his attention to the colt, who still stood watching him.

"Okay, fella," he said softly. "I'm comin' into your camp, but I mean you no harm."

He crawled between the poles of the corral and stood upright, moving very slowly. The horse's ears flattened against his head and his nostrils flared.

John stood very still. He must not show fear. Especially just now.

TWENTY-TWO

The average cowboy would have roped the horse, snubbed him to a post, and by brute force and awkwardness forced the creature to submit. The very term "breaking" of a horse implies dominance over the animal being trained.

Maybe a more accurate word for the manner of readying a horse for use among John's people would have been "taming." This is not to say that there was no force involved in their methods. It is necessary to exert control over other creatures at times for their own or for mutual good. The American Indian would not have become the finest horseman in the world without this. In a group of animals *within* any species, some exert dominance over others. This is necessary for the common good.

But in the case of the unusual relationship between the American Indian and his horse, the key factor is the closeness of the partnership. Among the plains tribes, a child might literally ride before he could walk, as Little Bull had.

A warrior or hunter might picket a favorite horse or two next to his lodge for safety against theft, or for extra care and special feeding in winter. Among the Pawnees, a few horses were often kept *inside* the big earth-bermed lodges of the extended family.

All of these customs led to a closeness of spirit between man and horse. With this background, when the time comes for the taming and training, it requires mostly communication. The necessary ingredient is to make it easier to do what is wanted than to do the opposite.

In this case, however, it would be an uphill battle. For this horse, nearly every contact with man had been in an unpleasant situation. His probable capture as a wild horse fairly recently, the struggle against ropes, the castration, the confinement . . . Now the animal stood, suspicious, expectant, probably wondering what unpleasantness was about to happen next. He might even decide to try a preemptive strike at this new two-legged creature.

John began to hum softly, soothingly, as he had seen his father do. *It's not the words,* Yellow Bull had explained, *it's the song.* . . . A soft, rhythmic cadence, halfspoken, half-sung, a reassuring song that joins the spirits of man and horse.

*I mean you no harm, my brother. . . . We can search
together. . . . I will show you . . . Our spirits mix well,
with no harm to each other.*

The horse paused, curious. He could not hear the song at
this distance, and was frustrated. Something was happening, and he did not understand. The situation must call for
some sort of action. The animal broke into an easy lope,
circling the corral. It might have appeared, as the horse
rounded the curve of the fence, that he was rushing or
charging at the man almost in his path. It was a challenge,
but one to which John must not respond. He must show
no fear, but equally, no aggression.

*This is your camp. . . . I have entered it. . . . I mean
no harm, but here I stand. . . .*

The horse barely turned aside as he brushed past. It was
the critical moment to show no fear. The animal's shoulder
bumped against John's, and he held his ground, not avoiding nor inviting. It was an expected contact, a test. He had
often been blocked harder by an opposing defensive back.
In that case, though, he could respond. Here he must remain neutral, nonresponsive. The horse rushed on, circling
the arena. John waited.

*See . . . There is no harm to either of us. You are still
here; so am I. Come again. . . .*

This time there was no contact, but a slight slowing of the
canter as the horse passed. John was certain that he saw a
questioning look in the big dark eye as it passed. He
moved a step farther into the arena during this circuit. The
horse must change its course slightly to avoid collision. It
did so, without seeming to notice.

*See? You have done what I ask, and no harm comes
to either of us. Is it not good?*

After a few such passes, the horse stopped and stood on
the other side of the enclosure, waiting. John moved very
slowly, taking a step toward the animal, pause a little, stop
and wait. He was within a few feet when the horse could
stand it no longer, and bolted away to begin the circling
again. This time, only a few circuits and then the stop, in
another place. Patiently, John approached again.

*We are going to do this, my brother, no matter how
long it takes.*

This time, only a couple of circuits and a stop. And this
time, John was within a pace or two before the animal
broke and ran. After a few such tries, he was able to touch
the sweaty neck. Of course, the startled horse flared away,
but soon stopped.

At the next touch, the hand was allowed to remain there
a few moments. When the horse moved on, John removed
his hat and wiped his own sweat from his brow.

Then another touch to the neck, a gentle stroke. He took
a step back and extended the hand toward the horse's nose.
The animal smelled, actually extended its head for a better
sniff at the mixture of sweat from man and horse.

*Ah, you see? Our spirits blend well, no? And still, no
harm comes. We can work together, you and I. . . .*

By the time shadows lengthened, John could pass his
hands over most of the upper portion of the colt's body.
He had breathed into the nostrils, whispered his song into
the ears, and could lead the colt with a short rope around
its neck.

Heinemann returned to the corral.

"How's it goin', John?"

"Pretty good."

The man glanced at the horse and back to John, a puzzled look on his face.

"You ain't bucked him out yet?"

"Didn't figure to. We've been gettin' acquainted."

"Well, now, John . . ."

There was plain doubt in Heinemann's voice.

"He's come a long way," John said cautiously.

John walked slowly over to the colt, stroked his neck, and petted his nose. The horse rubbed its face against his shirt and stood, eyes half-closed, obviously content.

"Well, I'll be damned!" Heinemann exclaimed.

At the sound of the man's voice, the horse came alert, cautious, defensive. John patted him comfortingly, and he relaxed again, still cautious.

Before he left that evening, John had placed a halter on the horse and had removed it, and was able to wipe a saddle blanket across the animal's back.

"I'll come back tomorrow evening," he promised.

Within a week, John was riding the colt under saddle, swinging a lariat, putting the animal into a walk, trot, and canter.

"I wouldn't have believed it!" marveled Heinemann.

"Yah, like I said, dis John ist good mit der horses!" Hans Schneebarger chuckled.

His reputation spread. Another farmer with a problem horse, and yet another. Schneebarger viewed all of this with mixed emotions. He could bask in the reflected glory of having "discovered" this talent, but it also had a tendency to interfere with the work on his own place. Finally, he laid down the ground rules.

"Yust on Sundays," he cautioned. "Mebbe sometimes after supper if I don' need you here."

"Yes, sir. But . . . Could I bring a horse here to work with in the evenings? Dave Jones has one—"

"Sure!" interrupted Hans. "Dat's fine. I yust need you ven I need you."

By the summer's end John had tamed or trained several animals. His reputation was growing. This led to talk with horsemen, horse traders, and cowboys who happened by, and in this way he learned of the contest.

"Over by Topeka," the trader told him. "You'd ought to go over. They'll have a buckout, ropin', mebbe some steer wrasslin' . . ."

"What's that?"

"Jest what it says, I guess. Somebody said there's a nigger from some big ranch in Oklahoma that does it with his teeth."

"Aw, c'mon!"

"No, really. He calls it bulldoggin', on account of the way he bites the critter on the nose."

"You seen him do this?"

"No, but I talked to fellas that did. Let's see . . . What was that nigger's name? Bill somethin' . . . Packett? No that ain't it. Pickett! Yeah. Bill Pickett. The 101 Ranch . . . Miller Brothers. They've started some kind of a Wild West Show."

"A show?"

"Yeah. You know about Buffalo Bill's Wild West Circus?"

As a matter of fact, John did. Some of his father's friends, in fact, had worked for Buffalo Bill Cody, riding with painted faces on horses painted as if for war, whooping and circling the arena for the pleasure of the crowds. His father had frowned on such nonsense, but some prominent leaders of the plains tribes had joined Cody's circus as entertainers.

"Heard of it, yes," said John.

"Well, you'd ought to go over there this Sunday," insisted the trader. "Maybe they'll give you a job playin' Injun."

The man slapped his knee in amusement at his own joke, and then paused, a little embarrassed.

"You *are* Injun, ain't you? I heard your ways with a hoss was some of that Injun 'medicine.' "

"Maybe so."

"No offense, son. But I just thought . . . Well, hell, go over and watch if you want to. It's nothin' to me either way."

John felt that the talkative horse trader had backed himself into a corner and was uncomfortable, then talked himself in deeper as he tried to talk his way out.

"Maybe I will go over," John said mildly.

The other man relaxed a little.

"Good," he said. "I reckon you'd like it."

TWENTY-THREE

John's trip to Topeka was memorable, to say the least. He rode a borrowed horse.

The Miller Brothers 101 Ranch Circus was a magical extravaganza, a performance to quicken the heart and delight the senses. Sweating men and horses; exhibitions of roping, trick riding, and handling livestock; bucking horses and bulls; and the event that had precipitated John's interest, the bulldogging of steers by Bill Pickett.

The mixed-blood Pickett was becoming famous on the show circuit. He had demonstrated his specialty in Canada and Mexico, as well as at dozens of events throughout the American West. As a ten-year-old in Texas, Willie Pickett had watched a bulldog, trained to work cattle, catch and hold a young steer by the nose for several minutes. The dog fastened its teeth into the animal's upper lip, which seemed to completely immobilize the steer.

I could do that, thought the boy.

When opportunity offered, Willie tried it. No one around . . . A calf, more his size . . . He found that it worked as well for him as it had for the dog. As he grew a little older, he demonstrated to a bunch of local cowboys that he could immobilize calves in this way while they were "worked" and branded.

At the Taylor, Texas, Fair in 1888, Will Pickett had been asked to demonstrate his peculiar skill. He was seventeen at the time. In this demonstration, a steer was roped and tied, and Pickett would mount its back. Then it was released, Pickett holding to the horns. Somersaulting over the head, he would grab the steer's upper lip in his teeth and, with a twist, he would throw the animal to the ground and hold it.

He worked for a while on a ranch near Rockdale, Texas, and Lee Moore, the owner, began to book appearances for him at county fairs in the area, finally branching out into Colorado and other states about 1900, charging admission fees as a specialty act. After the 1902 season, Pickett signed on with Dave McClure, the cowboy promoter, who was famous among rodeo and show people as "Mr. Cowboy." This brought him better bookings and more notoriety. In 1904, at Cheyenne Frontier Days, his exhibition resulted in this testimonial from the *Wyoming Tribune:*

The event par excellence of the celebration is the great feat of Will Pickett, a Negro who hails from Taylor, Texas. He gives his exhibition this afternoon and twenty thousand people will watch with wonder and admiration a mere man, unarmed and without a device or appliance of any kind, attack a fiery, wild-eyed and powerful steer, dash under the broad breast of the great brute, turn and sink his strong ivory teeth into the upper lip of the animal and, throwing his shoulder against the neck of the steer, strain and twist until the animal, with its head drawn one way and under the controlling influence of those merciless teeth its body forced another, until the brute, under strain of the slowly bending neck, quivered, trembled, and sank to the ground, conquered by a trick. A trick, perhaps, but one of the most startling and sensational exhibitions ever seen at a place when daring and thrilling feats are common.

Initially, McClure had been cautious. He described Pickett as a "half-breed," which implied Indian and Caucasian. In most of the United States, an individual with as little as one-sixteenth Negro blood was legally a "colored" person. Athletic contests between whites and coloreds were not only frowned on, but illegal in many places. Very quickly, his fame was so widespread that it didn't matter, though the stigma of his Negro ancestry still hung over him.

At the time the demonstration took place, John had learned much of this background. Pickett, now called "Bill" instead of Will or Willie, was booked as "the Dusky Demon, the most daring cowboy alive." By this time, he was working from horseback, stepping from his horse's back to that of the steer while a "hazer" on the left kept the half-ton animal running straight. (In modern steer wrestling events, much smaller animals are used, and the approach is from the *left*. Pickett approached from the right " 'cause mah hoss is taught I'm gettin' on an' off his left side.")

John was quick to note that Bill Pickett's skin wasn't

much darker than his own. Part of this could be accounted for by the burning and tanning of constant work in the sun. Still, there was something. . . . The man's features seemed more Indian than negroid.

"Hey, there," a voice called.

John looked around. It was the horse trader who had urged him to go to the show originally.

"Ain't this somethin'? I told you about that Pickett. Want to meet him?"

"You know him?"

"Shore! Come on!"

John followed the trader, a little embarrassed. He doubted that this somewhat shady character really had such connections. His suspicions were confirmed when they approached the place where Pickett had tied his horse. The Dusky Demon was loosening the cinch on the sweating animal, and looked around as they approached. The mildly annoyed expression on his face verified John's suspicion that the braggart horse trader was no more than a casual acquaintance.

"Bill, this here's a boy that wants to meet you. Name of John Buffalo. He tames horses."

Then the trader's gaze shifted. "Hey, there's a feller I need to see!"

He left quickly, but in the opposite direction. John and Pickett stood, both a bit confused and embarrassed, looking after the retreating figure.

"You know him?" Pickett asked.

"Not hardly," answered John. "He's a horse trader."

"Reckoned that," smiled the Dusky Demon. "He been hangin' aroun'."

He studied the young man for a few moments.

There was, somehow, an understanding between them, as if they had always known each other.

"You Cherokee?" asked Pickett.

"No, Lakota. You?"

Pickett nodded. "Cherokee, white, some colored . . . Less'n half, we figger."

"I . . . Mr. Pickett, I was amazed at your performance."

The dark man smiled, showing even white teeth under his mustached upper lip.

"No trick to it. An' call me Bill."

"Thanks. I'm John Buffalo."

"Howdy, John. About this bulldoggin' . . . You could do it. Jest grab him and bite him on the nose. . . . Hope it ain't a snot-nosed steer."

Both chuckled.

"You don't use a rope at all?" John asked.

"Naw. A rope's okay for hangin' folks, I guess, but when ah'm chasin' a steer it jest gits in the way."

"I see . . ." He didn't, exactly. "You travel a lot?"

"Quite a bit, with the Millers' 101. They be good folk. Ah was doin' on mah own before. Been to Canada an' Mexico."

"Mexico?"

"Yeh . . . They got them fightin' bulls down there."

"You rassled *them?*"

"Naw. Jest the steers. But they be purty ringy. Rassled a bull elk in El Paso, though. Don' try *that*. He got too many horns!"

"Okay, I won't," said John, quite truthfully. He had no such intention.

"Say," said Pickett, "you hear about dat earthquake an' fire at San Francisco las' spring? Ah was *there!*"

"You were?"

"Yas, I *was!* Say, that was somethin'! Look like the whole world be goin' up in flames. All them folks outa their homes, no place to go. . . ." He shook his head. "I don' want no more o' that."

"I reckon not," agreed John. "But, I was lookin' at your

horse, here. How'd he get the scar on his chest?"

"Ol' Spradley? He's a 101 colt. Had a bad injury when he's a baby. Big chunk o' fence rail stuck in his chest. Splinter-like. Nobody noticed, an' he got so puny they was goin' to kill 'im, put 'im outen his misery. I axe could I have him, an' Mr. Joe he say yes, he no good anyhow. Ah cut that chunk o' board out, an' he heal' up purty good. Runs spraddle-legged, though. Thass why I call 'im Spradley." He patted the gelding affectionately. "He a good boy." He paused and spoke cautiously. "That ol' hoss trader, he say you got a way with 'em?"

Now John was cautious.

"Sort of, I reckon. I just try to get inside their heads, talk to 'em. . . . Easier'n tryin' to do it by force."

"Sometime you needs force." said Pickett.

"Sure. You couldn't *talk* a steer down. But, startin' a horse out calm-like is goin' to make it lot easier ef you have to bust him later."

"Thass true."

A man approached and spoke to Pickett.

"Bill, they'd like to have you in the arena again. Are you up to it?"

"Reckon so. Lemme give ol' Spradley a bit mo' rest. It's purty hot."

"Sure. When you're ready." He turned to look at John. "Do I know you?"

"Prob'ly not. I just came over for the show."

"You know Bill here?"

"I do now. We just met."

"Mistah Miller, he's the hoss trainer that no-'count trader was talkin' of," said Pickett.

"Not really," protested John.

"Wait a moment. You tame wild horses, right?"

"Well, not exactly . . ."

"Yes, I expect you're the one. Look, let's talk about this. I need a few more Indians for the wagon-train scene.

You'd fit in that. But I was wonderin' if you could do that horse-tamin' act in the arena. Run in a wild horse. . . . You want a job? By the way, I'm Zack Miller. I run the show, my brother Joe is the rancher, and George is the book-keeper."

"I . . . I see," muttered John. This was pretty sudden. A *job?*

"Mr. Miller, I'm from over near Lawrence, on a bor-rowed horse. I . . ."

"No matter, son. We'll figger a way to get the horse back, if you're interested."

"Well, I suppose I am. In hearin' about it, anyhow."

"Good! Let's go talk about it. John, is it?"

"Yes, sir, John. John Buffalo."

TWENTY-FOUR

Y ou're *what?*" demanded Naismith. "Leaving?"

"Considering it," answered John. "I wanted your ad-vice."

"A *circus?*"

"Not exactly, Coach. The Miller Brothers 101 Ranch . . . Wild West Show. They have some good people. I can't seem to find a job as a coaching assistant."

"Well . . ." Naismith seemed just a little uneasy about that remark. "You might try it for a season. Working with horses, you say?"

"Yes, sir. I'm told that I'm good with them. I do have some pretty good luck, I guess."

He had decided not to go into too much detail about his "luck" with animals. He had learned caution when talking to whites. Any white man, even one whom he trusted to give good advice. Naismith might have John's best interests at heart, but there were things that the coach might never be able to accept or understand. Especially about things of the spirit. Somehow, whites seemed to be afraid of things that they didn't understand. Sometimes it seemed to be mixed up with their religion, as a sort of denial of the obvious presence of the power of the spirit. To think in terms of good or bad luck, however, was acceptable.

"And they pay well?"

John paused. Zack Miller hadn't been very specific about that. It would depend on his skills, the showman had implied, but there were dozens, maybe hundreds of men and women in their employ. The Indians who played a part in the reenactment scenes seemed content. Bill Pickett, a "man of color," was obviously pleased at his connection with the Millers and the 101. There seemed to be a general tone of respect for each other on the part of the 101 crew, and this seemed to come from the Millers themselves.

"Apparently so, sir. No specific figure was mentioned, but their employees seem satisfied and—well—*proud* to be working there."

Naismith nodded. "That's a good sign. Well, John, I hate to see you abandon the goal of coaching. But you don't have to leave it permanently. Stay in shape—you'll probably do *that* easily. And stay in touch. You have talent. Maybe later, eh?"

John had the feeling that the coach's heart was right. It was plain that he, too, realized the overwhelming obstacles that faced a young Indian in the white man's world. Naismith had made the effort, and would do so again, but some things are not to be. At least, not easily.

They shook hands warmly and John turned to go.

"Say, John," the coach called after him. "You might talk to a fellow who's doing some coaching. Allen . . . Forrest Allen. They call him 'Phog.' He's coaching at Haskell as well as at Baker, and has done some work for me. You'll probably stop by Haskell anyway, eh?"

"Maybe so."

He did stop by to tell the Haskell administration what he was doing, and to tell the coach good-bye. He also asked about Coach Allen.

"Not here right now, John. He's based down at Baker. A good man. Coachin' basketball for us this winter."

John smiled. "Naismith still says that's just a game. But maybe I can talk to Allen later."

"Maybe so . . . Best of luck with the cowboyin', John!"

"Thanks . . ."

He did not think it worthwhile to contact Coach Allen now. It would take most of a day, and he had a lot to do. He must explain to Schneebarger what he intended, gather his few belongings, and return to Topeka before the 101 departed. Transportation back to the Ponca country of Oklahoma Territory would be by special train, carrying the entire Wild West Show.

During the train trip, he was approached by Zack Miller, who motioned him over and slid into the seat beside him.

"Glad to have you join us," Miller began. "Buffalo, isn't it?"

"Yes, sir. John Buffalo."

"Mmm . . . Got that in a government school, I reckon. You're Sioux?"

"Yes, sir.

This man seemed to understand, so John decided to elaborate.

"Once I was Little Bull, son of Yellow Bull," he added, showing a bit of pride.

Miller smiled. "That's good," he said simply. But John knew that he understood.

"Well, you see our Show. The 'Wild West.' My brother Joe figured that we'd ought to do somethin' to preserve the cowboy life, the Indian ways, show how to handle stock, work cattle, an' all. Joe says, 'Boys ten years old and younger have never seen a genuine Wild West show, and we are going to make it possible for them to see one!' We have a variety of acts, a bit broader than Cody's Buffalo Bill show. You've seen that?"

"No, sir."

"Well, no matter. What we have is a real workin' ranch . . . 110,000 acres. We aim to show folks what a ranch is an' does, *plus* the specialty acts. Ridin', ropin', tricks, Pickett doin' his bulldog thing. Gawd, I dunno how he does that! You a friend o' his?"

"No, sir, we just met."

"Well, he savvies folks purty good, an' he seems to like you. Anyhow, we're always lookin' for new acts, an' if they come right offa the 101, so much the better. We do have a buffalo herd, but mebbe we'll get a couple of camels and an elephant or two. But never mind . . . Tell me about your act."

"Well . . . I really don't have an act, sir."

Miller took a puff on his cigar, blew a cloud of blue smoke, and tapped the ash into the tray on the arm of the seat beside him.

"But somebody said you tame wild horses. That true?"

"Maybe, but it ain't exactly an act, Mr. Miller. I tame 'em 'cause they need tamin'."

"No matter. Them steers of Pickett's don' really need to be bit on their nose, either. It's a demonstration . . . shows what *can* be done. Now on the wild-horse thing . . . We can talk about it later. Sounds like I need to watch it.

When we get down to the ranch, we'll run in a couple of range-runnin' yearlin's, and you can show me.

"I can do that," John agreed.

"Okay . . . Meanwhile, you can do some odd-job ranch chores. The boys will show you the bunkhouse an' get you settled."

He started to rise and then paused.

"You don't mind playin' Indian when we take the show out on the road?"

"No, sir."

It was a truthful answer. *Not for people who come this close to understanding,* he thought.

The 101 Ranch itself was an experience like no other. It was hard to comprehend its sheer size and the hundreds of people who were employed in the operation. There was a headquarters complex resembling a small town, with houses, a store, barns and stables and granaries, a running track for horses, and arenas for practicing the various acts for the Millers' shows. The demand for bookings had resulted in the formation of a second troupe, so that the Miller Brothers Wild West Show and Circus could be on tour in separate parts of the country at once. The 101 had its own railroad sidings as well as locomotives and rolling stock. "Headquarters" was still in the White House, the original home of the Miller family, built by George W. Miller, father of the Miller Brothers. Mother Molly Miller still lived there.

There were vast herds of horses and longhorn cattle, a small buffalo herd, and carefully segregated herds of pure-bred Angus and Hereford cattle.

John learned, gradually, that the Millers had conceived the idea for a Wild West Show of this magnitude by attending the World's Fair in St. Louis, a few years earlier. They had also made some valuable connections there. In

1905, with national media attention, the Millers hosted a gala celebration which drew 65,000 people to the ranch. The national convention of newspaper editors was in attendance, and some thirty trains brought spectators. President Theodore Roosevelt, already a fan of the concept of the Wild West Show, asked the Governor of Oklahoma Territory to call out the Territorial Militia to help with security and crowd control.

"Remember Geronimo, the ol' Apache chief?" asked the cowboy who was showing John around the ranch. "He was here."

"I thought he was in jail."

"Well, he is, I guess. But the Millers—Mr. Joe, I guess—got permission to bring him for that roundup. They got the chief to shoot a buffalo, and barbecued it for them newspaper folks."

"But he must be about eighty," John protested.

"Guess so. But he rode in one o' them horseless carriages. A Locomobile, it were called, I'm thinkin'. Ol' chief was outa practice . . . missed a couple o' shots."

"Bow and arrows?"

"No . . . A new Winchester. That'd be his last buffalo kill, they said. 'Course, it was his *first,* too, you know. Apaches didn't have buffalo where they lived." The cowboy chuckled. "But I reckon it shore impressed the crowd. What's your job goin' to be, John?"

"Workin' with horses, I guess. Not sure yet . . . This happened purty sudden."

"Yep." Slim nodded. "Zack gets an idea, he moves on it, don't he? But . . . Say, you must be the wild-horse tamer! That it?"

"I guess that's what Mr. Miller had in mind," admitted John. "But I really don't . . ."

"Yeah . . . Indian medicine-tricks. I gotta see this. You're Sioux, ain't you?"

"Yes. Lakota."

"We got quite a few Sioux already. Pine Ridge, Rose-bud."

These were reservations, and John knew his people by their band names: Oglala, Hunkpapa, Brulé . . .

"Mebbe you'll know some of 'em."

"Not likely . . ."

John was having some very strange feelings. Would he have much in common with Lakotas from the reservations, now that he had been detached from his people for several years, and subjected to the white man's ways? Time would tell.

Meanwhile, he moved into the bunkhouse with the cowboys. He dressed and acted as the whites did, and felt more at home here than in the cluster of lodges down by the river. He felt an odd pang of guilt, as well as a bit of scorn for those not able to assimilate into a modern world.

It did not occur to him that perhaps *they* were taking advantage of a rapidly changing social situation, as were the Millers and their 101 Ranch.

Of one thing he was certain: On the 101, everyone seemed to be respected for his skills and abilities, not for his race or ethnic background. The Millers employed whites, Mexicans, Negroes, and Indians, treating all with respect not found in most places he had been. Some non-whites even had considerable status. With some surprise, he learned that the Pickett family had their own home on the 101.

Maybe this was his own ticket to the future.

TWENTY-FIVE

Over the next few weeks, John met a lot of people with remarkable talents. It was an atmosphere of unreality, as if most of the hundreds of people in the gigantic ranch operation were playacting, at least part of the time. For some, all of the time. This is not to say that theirs were easy jobs. They developed, practiced, and perfected skills not seen elsewhere, for the purposes of The Show. Trick riders, fancy ropers, marksmen (and women) who could perform amazing stunts with a rifle or pistol. Some spent days and weeks of special training sessions for the purpose of readying an animal performer for a specialty act that would last only a matter of minutes in the arena. A horse that would "play dead" or roll over on command . . . A dog that would dance on his hind legs, wearing a top hat . . . The skills involved were largely those of the trainer.

In other cases, the skills were the result of long years of hard work on the backs of galloping horses. A headstand, a bounce from one side of the horse to the other, touching the ground at both sides, at a full gallop. Perhaps the "suicide drag" stunt . . . Many of these were young women, who seemed especially agile at this sort of trick riding. There were names which would become well known later as their fame spread. Lucille Mulhall, billed as The Original Cowgirl, could rope as well as any man and better than most, a world champion rodeo performer. Jennie Howard Woodend was another, actually an aristocrat from a wealthy and prominent Eastern family, who preferred the life of the West. She performed as a trick rider and worked maintaining fence for the 101 as "Jane Howard." Lillian Smith, who was dressed as an Indian and was billed as "Princess Wenona," outdid even the famous Annie Oakley with her shooting skills. Other veteran women performers were Julie Allen, Edith Tatlinger, and Zack Miller's wife, Mabel.

There were always a cadre of young women striving to perfect their skills to the extent that they could become one of the featured acts on The Show. Meanwhile, they worked for pay at ranch jobs alongside the men, who were many times engaged in similar pursuits. But the Millers were quite strict about the impression that their female performers might give to the public. They were never to appear wearing lipstick or rouge, and must dress discreetly, to avoid any impression of the cheap or tawdry.

Some of the men were working similarly toward becoming feature acts. Most would never become headliners, but there was always a need for large numbers of horsemen. They filled out the cast of hundreds for the reenactments of wagon trains, Indian attacks, cavalry charges, and frontier skirmishes. When the Wild West Show was not on the road, the same riders were carrying out routine ranch jobs, working cattle, branding, and fixing fence. The day-to-day work required to operate the far-flung 101 Ranch with its thousands of cattle and horses demanded a lot of cowboys.

There was always excitement in the air. The Millers were creative, and seemed to want to try any new innovation that came along. They were always experimenting with new seed crops and the newest farm machinery. This drew the attention of people with like minds, who would drop in unexpectedly just to show the Millers a new machine, or an automobile, driven by steam or kerosene or gasoline.

The 101 employees seemed to expect to be called on to do each other's jobs when there was need. Sometimes it seemed that the entire operation was a gigantic play. On

John's first tour with The Show, Zack Miller took him aside.

"John, would you mind puttin' on a soldier suit this time? I've got plenty of Indians, with the Oglalas and White Eagle's Poncas, but I need a few more cavalry for the rescue scene."

"Sure," John said quickly.

"Good!" Zack clapped him on the shoulder. "Go see Tom Mix. He's got the uniforms."

Mix handed him the folded blue trousers and jacket.

"The hat you're wearin' is okay, John. Check the duds back in after the last performance."

"Right."

"Say, weren't you an Indian last time?"

"Still am, I reckon. Zack needed some more soldiers."

This sort of thing was expected as the norm. It was not until later that he had time to wonder what Yellow Bull would have thought of his son's pursuit.

As he turned away, John noticed a stranger with a bill cap worn backward, carrying an odd-looking black box on a tripod.

"Who's that fella?" he asked. "What's that he's carryin'?"

Mix chuckled. "Aw, that's Will Selig. He's takin' movin' pictures."

"Movin' pictures? How can that be?"

"You don't know about movies yet? They're the comin' thing. Pictures on a screen, like a lantern-slide show. Special camera an' all. He turns a crank on the side, there. . . . Same way when they show it. The crank makes the pictures move. You'd ought to go in town, sometime they're showin' one at the opera house."

There was little to indicate that in a few years this same Tom Mix would be recognized as "King of the Cowboys," and that Tom and his horse, Tony, would be the highest-paid act in the rapidly expanding "movie" business.

"Say, John," Mix called after him, "weren't you goin' to do some kinda horse-tamin' act?"

In the frantic pace of the 101's activities, that had almost been forgotten.

"I guess so. Nothin's been said about it."

"Aw, Zack's busy. Look, I'll mention it when we get back from the show."

"Okay . . . Thanks, Tom."

Looking south across the Salt Fork of the Arkansas River, there could be seen a hill, the highest point around the 101 headquarters. It seemed to call out to John, but it had been weeks before he had the time to ride over and explore. When he did manage to go there, it was worth the wait.

It was away from the hustle and bustle, a quiet that he had not felt for a long time. He had not realized how much he had missed the chance to be alone with his thoughts. He could see in the distance below him the beehive activity of the ranch. But here it was quiet, and he could be alone.

It was not often that his chores and responsibilities around the ranch allowed him to slip away. He was careful not to let it seem that he was a slacker in any way. His duties first, then maybe he'd be able to find an opportunity that drew him to that hilltop.

On this occasion, it was early autumn. The diverse grasses of the prairie were beginning to turn color, from bright greens to an endless assortment of pinks and yellows and reddish hues. These muted tones of the grasses were accentuated by patches of crimson sumac and the bright gold of cottonwoods along the watercourses.

He rode past the Oglala Indians' camp near the river, crossed to the south side, and headed for the hill. Part way up the slope there was a clump of shrubby sumac, turning scarlet with the changing season. He dismounted to tie the horse, allowing it enough slack to graze on the prairie grass, now curing to standing hay. The animal began to crop the reddish seed heads of turkeyfoot grass, and John made his way on up the hill.

The climb was longer than he expected. A rise that appears insignificant from a distance on the prairie may be much more imposing close at hand. Objects are dwarfed by the vast panorama and reach of the land. The eye sees gently rolling grassland, a full half-circle of horizon at one time. One glance encompasses hundreds of square miles, some of which may be quite rugged.

He reached the top, and stood for a moment, panting to regain his breath. He had thought that he was in fairly good condition, but this activity had used different muscles and motions. He recovered quickly, however, and found a place to sit while he enjoyed the sunset. The rock was warm from the autumn sun and felt good against the slight chill of the south breeze. He wondered idly what sort of winter there might be in this place. It was farther south than he had ever wintered.

To the north across the Salt Fork, the ranch headquarters sprawled before him, a bustle of activity. He was reminded of an anthill, with its seemingly aimless comings and goings, but all a part of a complicated effort to accomplish some purpose, no matter how obscure.

There was a movement below him, nearer at hand, and he focused his gaze. A human figure, ascending the hill as he had done . . . He felt a flash of resentment at the intrusion, but quickly realized that he had no exclusive right to be here. Still, it was unfortunate. He had been enjoying the solitude. There had not been a time since he arrived at the 101 when he had managed to be alone.

The figure approached, heading straight toward him now. A woman . . . He had seen her in the practice arena. . . . Trick rider, maybe. She was attractive, in the split riding skirt and embroidered blouse used by many of the girls. In their actual trick riding, her garb would be more like that of the cowboys. The loose, flowing fabric of skirts and blouses would be dangerous as the rider swept across, over, and under the horse and saddle. Even a momentary snag on the saddle horn or on the cantle could interrupt the rhythm and cause a serious accident.

The girl reached the top and straightened, took a deep breath, and came directly toward him, still breathing hard. John wondered if she had sought him out on purpose.

"Sorry," she said between gasps for air. "Didn't know there was anybody up here, till I saw your horse. Don't want to bother you."

"It's okay," John found himself saying, not quite truthfully.

"Sometimes," the woman went on, "I jest have to get away. Too many damn' people."

That had been his own motive, he realized, with a bit of surprise. Here was someone who felt as he did.

"That is true," he said cautiously. He pointed to a spot on a rock near him. "Sit?" he invited.

"Thanks."

She sat, and both were silent for some time, studying the brilliant colors of the rapidly changing sunset. Orange and gold and purple and red shifted and danced majestically as thin layers of cloud moved and evoked even more colors than can be imagined.

John began to study the young woman's reactions to the majestic scene, and was pleased. They were much like his own. He turned more attention to her. . . .

She was possibly ten years older than he, rather mannish in her bearing, and tanned by the summer sun. Her hair, tied up in a bun and topped by a flat wide-brimmed hat, was a pleasant medium brown. Her eyes . . . It took him a little while to determine the color. It was even more difficult because of the changing colors of the sunset. The eyes, too, seemed to shift and change color. He decided that they must be a gray green. Then he wondered why it would matter.

He thought back. . . . He had not felt a real attraction to any woman since his world was shattered over the loss of Jane. For him, the blue eyes and golden hair were the pinnacle of feminine attractiveness. Anything less was not worthy of consideration. He might admire a buxom figure or a well-turned ankle, but it was not the same.

His feelings were similar as he studied this woman. She seemed pleasant, friendly, down-to-earth. . . . Not unattractive . . . A sincere smile . . . One who understood the need to get away from the frenetic rush of people . . . One who understood . . .

"Have you come here often?" she said softly as the shadows deepened on the east slope of the hill.

"My first time," he said. "I've wanted to. I knew it would be good. Have you been here before?"

"Yes. It makes the world right."

He nodded.

"I—I don't know your name . . . ," he blurted.

She laughed, a soft rippling music like clear water over white pebbles.

"Hebbie," she said.

"Hebbie?"

" 'Fraid so." She was quiet a moment, and went on in a musing tone. "I was christened Hepzibah. That's a Bible name, I reckon. But I ain't wearin' *that*. I changed it to Hebbie."

She paused and looked at him studiously, possibly with a bit of suspicion.

"Don't know why I told you that. Nobody here knows it."

She paused again, a twinkle in her eye.

"If'n anybody turns up knowin' it, it's your fault, an' I'm after your hide!"

They laughed together.

"No cause for worry," he said.

"I don't know your name," she said. "You're the horse tamer, ain't you?"

"People keep tellin' me that, but we haven't got around to it yet. But, forgive me . . . I'm John Buffalo."

Hebbie nodded.

"I'd heard the John part," she noted.

"I think I've seen you practicin'," he said. "Trick rider?"

"Ridin', ropin', rifle shot. I'm tryin' 'em all. But say, it's uphill when you got all the talent in the world just above you. I prob'ly will never ride an' rope as good as Lucille, and hey, I thought I was a good shot until I saw Wenona. But they need cowgirls for the parade, and I have to say, it's excitin', ain't it?"

She paused, seemingly lost in thought.

"But kinda lonely," she added softly.

There was no way to tell her that he felt exactly the same way. The same feelings had brought them both to the top of the hill. Then he realized that there was no need to tell her. She already knew.

She rose suddenly and extended a hand to him.

"Come on," she said. "Let's walk."

He rose, with Hebbie still holding his hand, and they turned to walk along the flat hilltop. It was perfectly level, a narrow oval half the size of a football field.

"Look!" she pointed with all the excitement of a child. "The evening star!"

They stopped, still holding hands, and watched the other stars appear suddenly, one at a time, in the darkening sky.

And it was good.

TWENTY-SIX

Their friendship was something of a surprise to John. He had never before had a woman for a friend. His attachment to Jane Langtry was a romance, but this was different. He was attracted to Hebbie physically, but not to the extent that—

He sighed. It was not appropriate to try to understand it. It was simply there, a closeness and understanding that had happened without either of them realizing it. He knew without discussion that Hebbie felt much the same. She, too, had been surprised at their immediate sharing of feelings.

Actually, it was an unlikely relationship. She was half again his age, and their backgrounds had little in common. She did confess to a little Cherokee blood on her mother's side. There had been a time on the frontier when it was a step up the social ladder to marry into the Cherokee Nation. The thrifty, hardworking Cherokees were far more affluent than the dirt-scrabble whites who were homesteading on the border near them. They never discussed it, but in his heart, John suspected that that infusion of Indian blood helped to establish the union of spirit which had characterized their first meeting.

Their paths crossed occasionally, in the day-to-day activities of their work. Sometimes, on the rare occasions when nothing much was going on, they rode together, sharing new places, new sights and sounds. They sometimes went to the hill, which was often referred to as Cowboy Hill, because of its landmark status. Cowboys in the vast open country could see the hill from any direction, as far as thirty miles away. For a rider who might be slightly disoriented on a cloudy or overcast day, it was a reassuring beacon.

It was a reassurance to the pair of friends who loved to go there, too. In a way, it represented their odd and mismatched friendship. Nothing demanded or expected: just a mutual trust and respect, a solid rock in a world that sometimes seemed to be made of quicksand.

They talked . . . About nothing in particular. They still knew little about each other, but enough. They had known that from the first. Neither felt any need to conceal, nor any urge to reveal. And, much of the time they were together, they were communicating in silent trust, without talking.

"Hebbie, you ever been married?" John asked one Sunday afternoon as they rode.

She looked at him curiously.

"Nope. Never found the fella I'd want to inflict that on."

They rode in silence for a while, and she spoke again.

"You?"

"What?"

"You . . . You been married?"

"No!" he blurted, a bit more emphatically than he intended. "Why?"

"Nothin' . . . You asked me, is all."

She was quiet a little while, and then spoke again.

"Well, it's not quite true. There was a cowboy. Fella a lot like you, I reckon. We grew up together. Folks all figgered we'd end up married."

There was a long silence, and curiosity finally prompted John to speak.

"So . . ."

Hebbie took a deep breath.

"That damn' war with Spain. He had to go show what a man he was. Damn' show-off got hisself killed, is what."

"Hebbie . . . I'm sorry . . ."

"It's okay. I don't think about it as much as I used to."

There was nothing to say, and they rode in silence for a while. Finally she spoke.

"But thanks for askin'," she said softly, closing the subject.

Someday, maybe he could tell her about his own tragedy. But not now.

"John, Mistah Zack lookin' for you," Bill Pickett told him one morning.

"I do something wrong?" asked John in surprise.

"Don't think so. The boys jes' run in a bunch of range colts. Reckon he wants you to help with 'em."

John sought out Zack Miller, who was leaning on a corral fence studying a dozen young horses. They were a mix of yearlings, two- and three-year-olds, and it appeared that they had never been handled. For all practical purposes, they were wild horses. They stood, ears up and nostrils flaring, suspicious, defensive, ready to jump at the slightest sound or movement.

"Ready to try one of them, John?" Miller asked.

"Might as well, I guess. Which one?"

"How about that roan filly?"

Zack pointed to a well-built two-year-old.

John studied the animal. . . . Foxy little ears, pointed in at the tops . . . Large, wide-set eyes . . . Intelligent face . . . Good slope to the shoulder, and a long hip tapering to a low-set tail. A horse his father would have admired.

"She's okay," he said.

"Where you want her?"

"The little pen over there. Don't rope her."

"Do that yourself?" asked Zack.

"Mebbe. Let's sort of see what happens."

They separated the young mare from the others by means of gates and the sorting chute, and into a small circular breaking pen. She exhibited a moment of near-panic at being separated from the others, calling out to her companions. For a moment it appeared that she might try to jump the eight-foot enclosure, but she decided against it.

Good, thought John. *She's got a little judgment.*

Still alarmed, the young mare circled the pen at a lope, occasionally whinnying to her companions. John waited, watching.

"Go ahead, John!" called one of the cowboys, laughing.

"Let him alone!" admonished Zack Miller. "It's *his* act!"

The filly finally settled, slowed, and stopped, watching her tormentors cautiously.

Now John moved slowly, slid between the horizontal poles into the pen, and rose to his full height. He was carrying a soft cotton rope. He took a step toward her.

Disturbed by this intrusion, the animal began to run again, circling the arena. John had stepped inside her periphery, and she now followed the fence. Gradually he moved back toward the fence, into her path. She brushed against him, a glancing blow that knocked him off balance for a moment, but he stood fast.

Show no fear, he reminded himself, *but present no danger, either.*

On the next circuit, the filly moved around him without threatening.

Good . . . We have an agreement, then?

The running became less excited and more brief with each episode. He would take a step or two, the filly would run, but not so fast or so far now. He kept crooning softly to her in Lakota. When he finally touched her neck she panicked again for a moment, but stopped and stood after a couple of circuits. The touch had enabled him to obtain a smear of her sweat. He paused and wiped his brow, mixing their scents. . . . Medicine. He extended his hand and she sniffed curiously.

See? Our medicine is good together. . . . We do each other no harm. . . .

Another touch, a pat on the neck and shoulder, an asking of permission, on the level of the spirit. He rubbed gently, and the animal seemed to enjoy it. The ears were an obstacle, but not for long. Soon he was rubbing her ears, tossing the soft rope over and around her neck and across her back.

He looped the rope around her neck just behind the ears and used it to lead her toward where Miller stood, one foot on the lower rail.

"That's about it," he told the showman. "Want me to go on? Prob'ly better to do it later at another session, but—"

"No," said Miller. "I see . . . Damn! Twenty-three minutes! You could prob'ly halter her now?"

"Sure. You want—?"

"No, no," Miller interrupted. "I see your work. Amazing!"

Some of the cowboys at the rail began to applaud, and the filly spooked and pulled away. John let her go. This was no time for a confrontation.

He slipped out between the rails, and Miller met him with a handshake.

"Great job, John. I want you to go ahead with her training. When will you be riding her?"

"A few days."

"You don't buck 'em out?"

"No. Easier not to, I figger."

"I see. Well, she's yours."

John wasn't certain whether it was a gift, or whether the little strawberry roan was to be his assigned 101 mount in the show. He could find out later.

The boss started away as the onlookers dispersed, but then turned and came back.

"You realize we can't use you in the show, John?"

"But I thought—" *I thought that was the whole idea of my being here!* he wanted to shout.

"Then . . . You mean I'm *fired?*"

"*What?* Christ, no! Where did you get that idea?"

"You just said—"

"No . . . We just can't use horse tamin' as an act. Takes too long. Folks pay money to see *action.* Horse tamin' is quiet and slow. But no, I still want you *ridin'* in the show, and workin' with horses on the ranch. You're *good*, boy. Mebbe as good as they come, with horses. But it ain't a *show* act. . . ."

He turned away, muttering to himself, "Damn! Twenty-three minutes."

Someone approached, and John turned to see Hebbie. Her eyes were sparkling with excitement.

"I didn't know you were here, Hebbie," he mumbled.

"Wouldn't have missed it," she said warmly. "John . . . Well, you were just wonderful!"

She gave him a quick little hug and kissed his cheek.

John blushed crimson.

"Careful!" he protested. "That's prob'ly against the rules or somethin'."

"I don't think so," she laughed. "And . . . Tell you what—I don't *care.*"

They looked at the little roan.

"I heard Zack say she was yours," Hebbie said. "Reckon he meant to ride for the 101, or to keep?"

"Don't know," admitted John. "He gave Spradley to Bill

Pickett, but that's a different case. Don't matter much, I reckon. Looks like I'm gonna be here awhile."

"That's good," she said quickly.

It sounded as if she thought he might be leaving. She must have heard his conversation with Miller.

"Well," he said, "everybody's got to be someplace, I guess."

TWENTY-SEVEN

It was autumn now. The leaves on the blackjack oaks were dry and brown, but still hanging on. In past times, these scrub oak thickets had made a good natural windbreak for teepee dwellers. Now, they provided shelter for wintering cattle and horses on open range.

Most afternoons were still warm and sunny, and John used the good weather to continue the training of the little mare, now called Strawberry.

The show season was over, except for a regional celebration or two, where the entire troupe would not be required. Usually John was asked to go. He was versatile, able to portray an Indian, a cowboy, a settler with an ox team, or a blue-clad cavalry trooper. There was a general feeling that he was a favorite of Zack Miller's, and consequently of Tom Mix's, too. He had spent some time with a visiting young cowboy with a friendly grin and a droll sense of humor. His name was Will Rogers. He was a friend of the Millers, and he did amazing things with a rope. Several of the ropers had taken some lessons from Rogers, including Lucille and Hebbie, as well as Mix, John, and a couple of the other cowboys. John was interested to note that Rogers and Pick-ett were good friends. They had met, someone said, when both had been performing at Madison Square Garden or somewhere. Rogers, once billed as the "Cherokee Kid," had traveled and performed in Africa and South America, but was now primarily appearing in New York. He had immense appeal to Easterners, as they looked to the ro-mance and adventure of the West.

Some of his stunts were unbelievable.

"John, get on your horse there, go off thirty yards or so, and ride past here at a fast canter," suggested Rogers.

Spinning a rope in each hand, he tossed both as John thundered past on Strawberry, catching the horse in one loop and the rider in the other.

There was a low sigh of admiration from the gathered crowd, many of whom had remarkable skills themselves. There was little envy in evidence. Rogers was so friendly, likable, and modest that he always left people feeling bet-ter about themselves and about the world.

"John, come to town with us!" said Tom one Saturday evening.

Some of the boys often rode over to Ponca City, or to Bliss, for a few drinks or to play a few hands of stud poker.

"No, I'll stay here," said John.

He didn't care much for drinking, and was always a bit self-conscious about being in public with whites, even cowboys who were his friends.

"Aw, c'mon, John. It'll do you good."

He didn't want to appear uncooperative. Maybe it would do him good.

"Okay," he agreed. "I'll get my horse."

———

They rode into the little town of Bliss and tied the horses outside the bar. It was not quite dark, but the mellow light of kerosene lamps gave a warm glow to the room, a welcome. Behind the bar over the mirror was a painting of poor quality, an overweight, scantily clad female with a smile that was more like a leer, as she looked down on the bar.

The bartender saw John's glance, and chuckled.

"She gits to lookin' better after a few drinks," he advised.

The other cowboys roared with laughter.

John sipped his fiery whiskey slowly, not really enjoying the evening, and wondering why he had bothered to come to town. Maybe after another drink or two . . . He tossed down the glass and the bartender refilled it promptly.

He was beginning to feel better, except for the mild buzz in his ears. A poker game was starting over in the corner. Maybe he'd sit in. . . . He was more comfortable now, ready to relax and have some fun.

Tom Mix strolled toward that table, but suddenly glanced out the window and stopped dead in his tracks.

"Oh, Jesus!"

"What is it?" asked the bartender.

John was caught up in the general rush to the window. There on the sidewalk in the fading light knelt a heavyset woman in a sunbonnet and a full dark dress. She carried a large handbag, which now lay on the walk beside her.

"What's she doin'?" asked someone.

"She's prayin'," said Mix in a hushed tone.

"What is it?" called the bartender again.

"It's bad, that's what it is." Mix answered. "That there is Carry Nation!"

"Oh, damn!" muttered the bartender. "Not here!"

He began to move quickly, taking an armful of selected

bottles from behind and under the bar, and scurrying to the back room with them.

John was confused.

"What's goin' on?"

"That there," said Mix, "is that temperance lady, from across the border in Kansas. We need to get outta here."

"But what's she—" John was watching through the window fascinated.

The woman outside had risen now, looming to nearly six feet tall. John stared in amazement as she reached into the handbag to draw forth a large hand ax. Holding it above her head, she charged through the front door. The drinkers scattered like quail, some retreating through a side door, some slipping out the front after the attacker had passed.

But her target seemed to be not the drinkers, but the bar itself. She rumbled around the right end of the counter while the bartender retreated around the left.

The hatchet swung in a mighty horizontal arc, smashing a dozen of the bottles on the shelf under the mirror. Glass and assorted liquor showered down over the ample front of her dress, and across the polished surface of the bar itself. The mirror was next.

"Oh, no!" whimpered the bartender. "The mirror—"

Silvery shards tinkled to the floor.

"May this be the fate of the Demon Rum!" thundered the woman.

Her hatchet swung again and more demons joined those on the planks. She paused, looking up at the painting as if in doubt. One swing of the ax left a cleft in the blatantly exposed skin of the painting's brazen woman that was not exactly anatomical.

The heavy arm descended, and a keg on a stand behind the bar splintered, amber fluid gushing out through the rupture.

John was still standing open mouthed as the hatchet swung again and again.

"This to the foes of the Lord!"

"Come on, John!" one of the 101 cowboys called from the doorway.

A table crashed over, spilling drinks, cards, and poker chips across the floor. Recovering his senses, John slipped outside. Men were untying horses from the hitch rail and hurriedly climbing aboard to sprint down the street and out of town. He mounted Strawberry quickly.

There was another crash and the sound of breaking glass from inside.

"What the hell is goin' on?" he asked in bewilderment. "Why isn't she arrested?"

"She usually is," said Mix. "That's what she wants. . . . Publicity. She's against drinkin', even medicinally, I guess. Sheriff's prob'ly hidin' out. I wouldn't want to try to stop her, would you?"

"But . . . Where'd she come from?"

"Up at Medicine Lodge originally, I think. Mebbe she still lives there. They're dry. 'Prohibition.' But she travels all over the country, puttin' on this act."

"You seen her before?"

"No, but I heard. She's put a lot of places out o' business. The law's usually skeered of her. Reckon we can see why."

John nodded agreement. He felt sympathy for the bartender, who was probably also the owner. He was surely ruined now.

"I heard her first husband was a drunk," said one of the cowboys.

"Reckon she'd *drive* a man to drink!" retorted another. "She shore got *my* attention."

"Want to ride on over to Ponca City?" somebody suggested.

"Naw, it'd be too late."

"She might foller us."

The ride back to the 101 was quiet. There was nothing to talk about, now that the excitement was over. The happy anticipation of an evening on the town was forgotten in the grim contrast of the ride home.

"Damn!" muttered someone. "How'd that ol' bitch do so much damage so fast?"

"Really?" asked Hebbie excitedly the next evening when he recounted the adventure. "You *saw* her?"

They were sitting on the sun-warmed stone shelf atop the hill, one of their favorite retreats.

"I sure did. Say, she was somethin'. You wonder about what she'd do to somebody with that hatchet."

"But she don't use it on people, does she?"

"So they say. Just the Demon Rum, I guess."

"John, you usually don't go drinkin' with the boys," she said tentatively.

"Naw . . . They sort of talked me into it." He chuckled. "Really, we didn't even get started drinkin', hardly. And when Carry got through, there wasn't much to drink. I tell you, Hebbie, she scared some pretty tough cowpunchers."

"I'm sure of that," she chuckled.

They were quiet a little while, watching the fading panorama in the western sky. With the fading sun, the night's chill came rapidly at this season. She snuggled against him, shivering a little, and he encircled her with an arm. The shared warmth of their bodies was good, and she nuzzled closer.

The sun's last rays made highlights on her hair, and he studied her profile. Strong nose and cheekbones, a determined chin . . . Really, she was a quite attractive woman. As she leaned toward him, her face turned, bringing her full lips nearer his. What was a man to do? He kissed her. It was a warm and sensual kiss, like none he had ever had.

Of course, he had little with which to compare and, at the moment, Jane Langtry was the farthest thing from his mind.

As she turned, into his arms, her breast brushed against his hand, and he instinctively cupped it in his palm. The kiss ended, but the hand remained.

"Did you really want to do that?" she asked softly.

"What? This?"

He gave a gentle squeeze.

"Yeah. I sort of thought we were just friends."

"Well . . . We are . . . I mean . . ."

He was embarrassed now.

"It just seemed natural."

He started to remove his hand.

"No, no," she said. "It's okay."

They sat a little longer, and he kissed her again. There was more passion now. Both were breathing more heavily.

"Oh, John," she murmured.

Then suddenly, she pulled away.

"Wait a minute. . . . How old are you, John? Not twenty yet, I'll bet."

"Well, maybe not . . . I'm not exactly sure. They didn't keep good records. What the hell are you gettin' at?"

"Hmm . . . Guess I ain't quite old enough to be your mother. Damn' sight nearer than I'd like, though. Never mind. I'm just thinkin' out loud."

"But—"

She placed a finger on his lips.

"Shh . . . Don't talk. Yes, we're friends, an' that's good. But, looks like we're startin' somethin' else here. An' . . . Well, I reckon you haven't had much experience. Gov'ment schools an' all."

"Well, I . . ." He was embarrassed to admit how really meager his experience actually was. "I can learn, can't I?" he joked.

"Sure," she chuckled. "An' you don't mind if I coach you?"

"Can't think of anybody I'd rather," he said. "And we're still friends."

"Oh, well," Hebbie said. "What the hell . . . Shut up and kiss me."

He did, long and softly and very satisfactorily.

Finally they came up for air.

"Wow!" she said, "you don't need much coachin'. That's pretty good. No, *real* good. Now, put your hand here. That's right . . . Now, other one here . . . Oh, yeah, that's good . . . Now, kiss me again. . . ."

It was a long time before either spoke, and then it was Hebbie again.

Tears were wet on her face.

"Oh, John . . . I'm so glad we found each other."

TWENTY-EIGHT

Maybe it was a mistake last night," she told him the next day. "Is this goin' to spoil us as friends?"

John was caught completely off guard by such a question. He had realized that he was inexperienced, clumsy, probably inadequate in her eyes. Yet, he had gotten the impression that she, too, had been caught up in an ecstatic adventure, where both body and spirit had merged into a magical moment.

"I . . . I don't hardly reckon so," he said clumsily. "I know I didn't know much about it, but—"

"Hush!" she said, laughing and blushing under her tan.

"That ain't what I meant. *I* was prob'ly takin' advantage of *you*."

"No, no . . . You'd never do that, Hebbie."

Now the old twinkle was back in her eyes again.

"Well, I dunno," she said in mock seriousness. "I might, you know." She slipped a hand under his elbow and into the crook of his arm as they walked past the paddock.

"Never can tell," she added.

John felt better, though he was still puzzled by the enormity of the situation. He had never felt like this before. This was not the way it was supposed to feel to fall in love. But, if this was not falling in love, what *was* it? Hebbie was plainly teasing him, implying a hint of things to come. Maybe that was part of it, the teasing and laughing together . . . *Aiee*, growing up was such a chore. Especially with no one to really advise him.

Back among the People, he would have had an advisor. An uncle, according to tradition. But his mother had had no brothers still living, even before he was taken away from the reservation. One of his uncles had been killed in a skirmish with soldiers before Little Bull was born. The other had died of some white man's illness before he was old enough to remember. Typhoid or pneumonia or something, he supposed.

His thoughts moved back to the present, and to Hebbie, his friend and now his lover. What was supposed to happen now? Would they be expected to marry? He wasn't sure. There was no male friend with whom he felt close enough to ask. Some of the cowboys occasionally visited women in town, and on one occasion he had accompanied a couple of them to the bawdy house. He didn't know what the other cowboys had told the girls, but they had offered to pay for his visit. The whores had teased him about his inexperience. He was at the same time excited, stimulated, and repulsed at the sweaty, heavily perfumed women. *This is not as it is supposed to be*, he thought. He had been unable to perform.

Now, here was a totally unexpected situation. A completely satisfying friendship had suddenly blossomed into something else. Into a wildly thrilling, yet warm and satisfying exploration of an entirely new level of relationship. It was something he did not know how to handle.

The next day, he finally thought of a solution. It was one so simple that he wondered why he hadn't thought of it sooner. He could ask Hebbie. She was the focus of his puzzlement anyway, as well as his best friend. He'd ask her about it, when occasion offered.

"Hebbie, I need to ask you about somethin'."

It was evening, two days after their experience on the hill. He had encountered her out behind the horse barns, and they were walking together in the twilight. It was growing chilly.

"Sure. What's that?"

"Well, about the other night . . ."

"Yeah?"

Her tone softened with her probing question.

"I'm not sure what I mean, here," he went on. "But . . . Well, what's supposed to happen now?" he blurted.

She giggled, and then seemed to realize how serious his question was. Her nervous giggle stopped.

"What did you want to have happen?"

"I . . . I just don't know, Hebbie. Nobody has ever told me the rules about this."

"What do you mean, 'rules'?"

"Well, my people have customs. A young man has a teacher . . . An uncle, maybe, who tells him about love and courtship and marriage and all. I don't have anybody, and I don't know your white customs on this."

She started to laugh, and then stopped short again.

"You're serious!" she said, surprised.

"Well, of course."

"I see . . . An' the cowboys ain't much help, are they?" Now she was sympathetic and understanding.

"They're friends, but there's nobody I'm really close to. Nobody who'd know to help me with this. You're my only real friend."

He thought for a moment that there was a tear in the corner of the gray-green eyes. Hebbie smiled, a little sadly.

"John," she said seriously, "I'm proud you'd ask me. Now, there prob'ly ain't rules, like the ones with your people. An' we've maybe broke some, to some white folks' way of thinkin'. But . . . Well, we know each other purty good. I guess we don't have to do anything about this right now. That okay?"

"If it is with you."

She nodded, then shifted the subject. "John, how old are you, really? I asked you before, an' you ain't sure, you said, but you got some idea, right?"

"Sure. Eighteen, maybe, give or take a year."

"My Lord! I'm robbin' the cradle!" Hebbie said, half to herself.

"How old are *you?*" he asked.

"John," she said evenly, "you ain't supposed to ask a woman her age."

He was confused.

"You mean . . . That's a white man's rule or something?"

Hebbie smiled, perhaps a little cynically.

"Well, yes. Reckon you could say so."

"I'm sorry. I didn't know. Among my people, the old women are proud of their many winters."

"And among mine, too. But you're talkin' *old* women, John. A *young* woman ain't goin' to cherish her years. Not for a long time."

"I see. And you're a young woman."

"I'd hope to tell you! Some days . . . But never mind. Look . . . I ain't goin' to see my twenties again, but I ain't quite old enough to be your mother. That close enough?"

"I guess so."

"Okay. An' there's some that are gonna look with disfavor on our bein' together."

John bristled indignantly. "That's no business of theirs!"

"Exactly! But there's always some that feel they have to judge everybody else's doin's."

"That's *their* problem!" he said.

"True. But things go smoother if they don't have too much to think about."

"What are you sayin', Hebbie?"

"Just that . . . Well, you and I know how we feel about one another, but we don't have to tell the world. So, we just be friends in the open like we been all along."

"And things go on the way they are!" he agreed.

"Sure. With the exception that you an' I know better. We behave ourselves in public. Okay?"

Since they were well behind the horse barn, and twilight was deepening, she gave him a quick hug and a kiss on the cheek.

John longed for more and would have held her more closely, but she pushed him away gently.

"Later," she promised in a whisper.

"John!" called Tom Mix, "How'd you like to go to Mexico?"

John had been gentling a colt in one of the small pens, and paused to look up at the approaching cowboy.

"Why?"

"We're goin'! Joe's takin' the show to Mexico City. It's a heap warmer there. We'll be back by Christmas, though. Want to go along? Usual pay."

"Who's going?"

"Purty near the full troupe. Ropers, riders, some o' the Indians. Couple of the dancers . . . I reckon they like strippers even in Mexico."

They both chuckled. Ever showmen, the Millers had signed several carnival acts that season. Exotic dancers, a "tattooed man," jugglers, and a magician.

"I dunno. Mostly the Wild West bunch. Pickett's goin' . . . A bunch of the cowgirls. We'll take the Hunnerdan'-one train."

John wondered whether one of the cowgirls would be Hebbie. He couldn't ask Tom. Well . . .

"How long?" he asked.

"Dunno. Couple o' weeks, maybe."

"Sure. Why not? Am I a cowboy or an Indian?"

Mix laughed.

"I dunno. Maybe both."

"When do we leave?"

"Next week, I guess. You'll want to take Strawberry?"

"If I can."

"Sure . . . I'll keep you posted."

The train ride was yet another experience. They were stopped at the border by customs inspectors who rifled through everything on the train, looking for any attempt at illegal entry.

Joe Miller walked from car to car, explaining that there was a rebel Mexican group threatening an insurrection. The authorities were suspicious over the importation of hundreds of horses and riders, many of whom were armed.

"They've always got somethin' like this goin' on," Joe Miller fretted. "It'll be okay, let 'em search."

So the Mexican customs authorities searched, even prying up floorboards in the cars to look for contraband. Some of the women performers were indignant over the way they were patted and poked and squeezed, and Joe Miller was sputtering with rage.

"Did they do that to you?" John asked Hebbie angrily.

"Nope . . . They were too occupied with the dancers," she told him. "There's much to be said for not bein' *too* purty."

"But you're—"

"Hush!" she cut him off. "Folks will think you're carryin' a torch for me or somethin'."

The inspectors went so far as to explore supplies in the commissary car, much to the consternation of the cooks. Mexican soldiers thrust bayonets into containers of lard and other foodstuffs, to ensure that no weapons or forbidden items were hidden there. Considering the temperaments of American cowboys and of Mexican soldiers, it is perhaps remarkable that an international incident did not occur on the Miller Brothers show train. That it did not may be attributed to the discipline and experience of the 101 show troupe. Also, maybe, to the expertise of Joe Miller. Joe always operated on the theory that anything can be accomplished. It is necessary only to discover the right means. It is possible that some Mexican palms were greased with silver on the railroad siding that day.

In any event, the train moved on to Mexico City and a spectacular welcome. The newspapers were fascinated by the huge cast of characters who arrived on the train. The people were tired of the rumors of rebellion and war, and were ready to play. Performances began and, in a short time, attendance at the Wild West Shows were exceeding that of the bullfights.

This was not an acceptable thing for the professional matadors. They especially resented Bill Pickett and his bulldogging act, and began a campaign of slander. Journalists became involved, and there quickly evolved two sides: one supporting Pickett, the other deriding him as a fake.

The bullfight crowd insisted that the Dusky Demon would have no chance against a real Mexican fighting bull. An indignant Joe Miller came to the defense of his people, especially Pickett. Argument led to challenge, and it quickly became apparent that the two sides were on a collision course.

At Miller's urging, Pickett agreed to a bizarre contest. He would attempt to bulldog a fighting bull, chosen by a committee of the bullfight operators. The newspapers went wild, encouraged by interviews and by advertising purchased by Joe Miller. This would be an event to outshine both the bullfights and the Wild West Show. The betting became heavy as the date of the contest approached.

By the appointed day, there was more excitement and coverage by the newspapers for this event than for either the Wild West Show or the bullfight itself.

TWENTY-NINE

Joe Miller met with the bullring aficionados to finalize the rules.

Despite the derisive ridicule of the matadors, who worked on foot, with a cape, Pickett would approach the bull on horseback. He would be allowed hazers on horseback, but must handle the bull with bare hands and, of course, his teeth.

He would control the animal for a specific period of time, the length of which was a point of contention. Miller became irritated and finally issued a challenge that was hard to refuse, and included a wager: If Pickett could stay in the ring with the bull for fifteen minutes, five of which he would spend *on the bull's head,* as the promoters demanded, the Millers would take the entire gate receipts of the day. This, in addition to a side bet suggested by Joe Miller: 5,000 pesos. The bullring operators quickly agreed.

Meanwhile, Pickett was having some doubts. Before leaving home, he had had a nightmare in which he was being chased by a huge black bull. His wife, Maggie, had believed that the creature represented the devil himself. The Dusky Demon did not like the way things seemed to be shaping up. The Millers tried to reassure him. It was only a dream, after all. . . . Wasn't it?

The Plaza El Toreo was packed with spectators, some supporting Pickett's challenge. Most, however, were loyalists to the traditional spectacle of the bull ring, and already offended by the unorthodox challenge of the gringos' Dusky Demon.

Prominent government officials were present, including President Porfirilo Diaz of Mexico. The 101 troupe attended in full force to cheer on their champion.

It did nothing to raise their spirits when a group of costumed matadors entered the bullring before the contest, solemnly carrying a black coffin lettered *El Pincharino,* "The Gored One." This bothered Pickett, recalling his dream and Maggie's concern. Zack Miller treated his doubts with more encouragement and a sizable dose of rye whiskey.

The bull selected for the contest was called *Frijoles Chiquitos,* "Little Beans," because of some odd bluish freckles on his black hide. This encouraged Pickett. The bull in his dream had been a solid color: jet black.

It was agreed that Pickett would be allowed hazers on horseback to direct the bull's run while Pickett made his jump. These would be Joe and Zack Miller and Vester Pegg, veteran 101 cowboy. They quickly found that *el toro bravo,* the fighting bull with centuries of deliberately bred bad disposition, cannot be hazed like a Texas steer. The animal immediately attacked the horses. The picadors in a standard bullfight are mounted on horses protected by padded armor, and the horses are often blindfolded. The American cowboys, and especially their horses, were out of their league. Pegg's horse was gored and disabled immediately. The goal changed quickly from one of directing the run of the bull to that of avoiding his enraged charges. The three horsemen maneuvered for position, trying to get Pickett into a position for his leap to the horns of *el toro*.

In the melee and confusion, the four animals twisting and turning, the bull suddenly abandoned one selected victim to attack another. The victim was Pickett's horse, Spradley. In the process of turning, the horse's hindquarters were exposed, and the bull's vicious horns sank home. Spradley fell, going down to a sitting position as his injured hip muscles failed. Pickett jumped to the sandy arena, and to the mercy of the maddened bull. The crowd roared approval.

Pickett scrambled and the bull turned, now eager to reach a man on foot.

Hebbie, seated in the stands next to John, grabbed his arm.

"He'll be killed!" she yelled.

But Pickett dove straight at the bull, between the horns, and fastened himself around the neck with both arms.

This was much like having the traditional bear by the tail. He couldn't turn loose without being killed. He could only try to hold on. He was unable to move into position for the bulldog bite to the nose. The bull was whipping head and horns wildly from side to side, trying to dislodge this annoying creature, but Pickett hung on, with no other alternative.

The crowd was turning ugly and began to throw objects into the arena. Seat cushions, rocks, bottles, sticks and canes, "even open knives," by one account. Something struck Pickett in the face, drawing blood. Another facial wound, partly healed after a previous performance, reopened, and the bleeding increased. The crowd cheered.

Then some heavy object, said later to be a beer bottle, struck Pickett in the side, fracturing ribs and opening yet another bleeding wound. A journalist from the *New York Herald* wrote:

> He groaned in sudden pain, gasped for breath, cast a last, imploring, agonized look at us, his long-time friends, and loosed the iron clasp which had defied the fury of as fierce and strong a bull as ever pawed the earth of El Toreo.

Frijoles Chiquitos, although weakening, now suddenly began to revive and turned toward his tormentor, who lay helpless on the ground. Vester Pegg stripped off his red shirt and leaped into the arena, shaking it at the bull to divert him. This allowed Pickett to stumble to the shelter of the barricade and safety. Pegg, too, escaped the rush of the tired bull.

But now the crowd became really ugly, turning on the other gringos who were scrambling to escape a rain of debris.

"Over here!" John yelled to Hebbie.

The other cowboys and cowgirls were retreating to an area in the El Toreo facility which provided relative safety behind an iron gate. At least they could huddle together in defense.

Pickett was concerned primarily with the injury to his horse. An old man, apparently a healer, offered to help. He placed two ripe bananas in Spradley's open wounds, and soon the horse was able to struggle to his feet. He fully recovered later, with only scars.

Meanwhile, President Diaz was forced to call out two hundred mounted soldiers to restore order. It was several hours before it was safe for the 101 troupe to leave the shelter they had found from the angry mob.

But in the end, Pickett had more than qualified to win both the bet and the gate receipts, some 48,000 pesos. He had been in the bullring for more than a half hour, and had spent seven and one-half minutes on the head and horns of the bull.

It was two days before Christmas.

Three days later, following the last performance of the Wild West Show, without Bill Pickett's act, they boarded the train for home, stopping at San Antonio and at Fort Worth.

They were scheduled to stop for an appearance in Gainesville, Texas, also, but the Millers canceled the show and moved on. The weather had turned bitterly cold, and the battered troupe was glad to see the home ranch again. It had been a tough tour.

Only a few days later, in the middle of the night, John woke in the bunkhouse. Something was wrong. . . . He couldn't pin it down, but there was a feeling of tension in the air, an urgency. . . . A sense of danger, and a warning.

He rose quietly, shivering in the January cold, and pulled on his socks. The plank floor was too chilly to go barefoot. He shuffled toward a window, and became aware of a yellow orange light. . . . Surely it wasn't time for sunrise yet! Besides, the glow seemed to come from the wrong direction. Confused, John wondered for a moment whether this was a dream or vision of some sort.

Now the source of the orange glow seemed to be flickering, like the light of a campfire. . . . *Fire!* As this dreaded thought screamed its way into his consciousness, there came a simultaneous echo from outside.

"FIRE! The White House is on fire!"

In the space of a few heartbeats the street outside was filling with people, yelling, running, trying to bring some order to the unthinkable chaos. Some carried buckets, to try to organize a bucket brigade, but there was no ready source of water. Even the tanks for livestock in the nearby corrals were frozen or kept nearly empty to prevent the risk of bursting from a deep freeze.

"Who's still inside?" someone yelled as the cowboys tumbled from their beds and pulled on clothing as they ran.

"Dunno."

A window crashed on the second floor of the venerable old White House, and a burst of flame roared out into the night. John could see the figures of people stumbling out the front door, silhouetted against the hellish orange glare inside. Someone was helping a partly bent figure across the porch and down the steps. That would be Mother Miller, her granddaughter Alice at her side.

John ran with the crowd, now gathering in front of the house. It was only too apparent that the cause was hopeless.

The Millers had been entertaining a party of friends from the East, and a succession of people kept pouring out of the smoke-filled house. Some were barefoot in the frozen darkness.

"Where's Little Sol?" yelled George Miller, turning from helping Mother Miller off the porch. "He woke us!"

George's faithful pet dog had wakened those in the house just in time.

"He must be still inside!"

"George! Don't go back in!"

"I've got to."

George pulled away and dashed back inside. He came back quickly, carrying an armful of clothing and dragging a small trunk. . . . His mother's jewelry.

"Can't find the dog," George panted, coughing from the smoke. "He saved us!"

Quickly, it was over. The massive three-story White House crashed to a pile of embers in the space of a few minutes. The fire had started in the furnace room in the basement. The loss was almost inconceivable. Personal possessions, family mementos, and a small fortune in antique furniture, prized by Mother Miller, had been lost. Perhaps the worst loss of all: the records and documents of the 101 Ranch. George, the bookkeeper of the operation, had made his family's home in the White House, and all records were kept there. The house and contents were only partially insured.

But, almost miraculously, there was no loss of life, except for the hero of the disaster, Little Sol, George Miller's dog.

THIRTY

It was a bleak January at the 101. Everyone was already beaten to exhaustion from the Mexican tour. It had been financially successful, but to the members of the show troupe, exhausting and dangerous. Bill Pickett would take months to recover and heal from his near-death adventure in the bullring.

The fire seemed to have been the last straw, but there was more to come. That very day, word came from the nearby town of Bliss, that one of the 101 employees had died in a rooming house there. He was Henry Breslow, foreman of the "canvas unit," in charge of all the tents and equipment as the Wild West Show traveled. Henry was a young bachelor, not yet thirty, and a critical link in the show operation. His death was rather sudden, from a tonsillitis infection. Like the rest of the exhausted show troupe, Henry had had little stamina left with which to fight one more battle.

Despite these depressing events, and the continuing bitter cold of the winter, life went on. The ranch office was re-opened temporarily in Joe Miller's home in Ponca City, and preparation for the coming season moved ahead.

The ashes of the White House were hardly cooled when plans began for reconstruction. Joe Miller would supervise the new building, and swore that it would be fireproof. So safe, in fact, that "a bonfire could be set in every room without damaging the house." An architect was hired, and within a month plans had begun, encompassing the latest in modern construction, including plumbing, hot and cold running water, electricity, ventilation, and steam heat. All of these systems were self-contained, even the electrical generators.

The building itself was larger than the original White House. It was three stories tall, built of reinforced concrete and steel with an asbestos roof. The third floor "attic," a dormitory-style facility, held enough beds to sleep one hundred visitors during special occasions.

With all the modern features, the new White House was built in a Colonial style and, in appearance, would resemble a southern plantation home.

That spring, there was other excitement, too, as modern developments startled the country and the world. Henry Ford, a manufacturer of automobiles, was mass-producing a family vehicle that he called the Model T.

Inspired by the success of the Wright brothers' experiments with "aeroplanes," other aeronautical engineers were quickly discovering flight principles that led to more successes.

All of this in turn created a demand for petroleum products to fuel the futuristic machines. During the absence of Joe and Zack Miller on the Mexican tour, George had been approached by E. W. Marland, an oil prospector, with a proposal for exploration drilling on the vast 101 ranch.

The Millers were always eager for new innovation, even with their love of the old ways of the Wild West. They felt a need to preserve the record of that West, even as it seemed to be slipping away. The death of Frederic Remington at forty-eight, one of the West's great painters, called this to the attention of the public that year. With the diversity of the vast 101 empire, they were in a position to promote this preservation. Their far-flung enterprises in livestock, farming, ranching, and entertainment were a major influence on a rapidly evolving modern America.

The Millers were fascinated by the idea and engineering of motion pictures. In turn, some of the pioneers in that budding industry were attracted by the Old West. Theirs seemed to be a natural medium to preserve what was left. This led to an alliance between the early movie pioneers and the Millers, with the same goals approached from different sides.

"John, you want to be in one of them movin' pictures?" asked Tom Mix.

"What do I have to do?" John was suspicious.

"Nothin' much. Nothin' you ain't been doin' already in the show. This here's Mr. Selig." He introduced the producer with a wave of his hand.

John recognized the name, which was well known at the

101. Selig had been at the ranch during a flood on the Salt Fork, and had offered fifty dollars to any cowboy who would attempt to swim his horse across the flooded river for the camera. There were no takers until Tom Mix accepted the challenge.

Mix had blindfolded his horse, worked him a little to get him used to the blindfold, and then urged the animal into a hard run, off the bluff and into the flooded stream. Then they swam to the other side. Selig had kept cranking his camera, capturing the entire event on film.

"Here's the scene," said Selig. "We'll bring the wagon train around the shoulder of the hill, and then have the Indians attack, from the west, there. The wagons will try to circle, and we'll burn a couple of them. . . . Pour some oil in the wagon beds to make a black smoke. . . . Then the cavalry comes in, pennants fluttering, shooting, from over there, and the Indians flee. . . ."

"Pretty much like the show, then?" John asked.

"Yeah," said Mix, "except for burnin' the wagons. "We'll have a few riders fall off of horses like they was shot."

"Who's gonna do that?" John asked suspiciously.

"We've got a couple of cowboys to do it," said Selig. "They get extra pay, of course. You want to try it?"

"Don't think so," said John. "I take enough lumps without doin' it on purpose."

"Fair enough," chuckled Selig, "but if you change your mind, it's a rising profession."

"Am I a cowboy or an Indian today?" John asked Tom.

"Prob'ly cavalry," Mix answered. "We're long on cowboys, and White Eagle's bringin' some Poncas over to ride with the Oglalas."

"When does this happen?"

"About noon, a little after," said Selig. "Our light will be best then."

"Good. I'll be there."

"Oh, John," Mix called after him as he turned away, "borrow a bay to ride instead of Strawberry. You're Army issue today."

The cavalry was quite strict about the colors and markings of their mounts. A strawberry roan in a platoon of sorrel or bay horses would be inappropriate. Of course, a mare would be too. Cavalry animals were all neutered males. But this would not be so noticeable in an action scene as an animal that was off color.

There was always a bit of excitement when the act started. There was more today, just knowing that they could watch themselves later in a darkened theater. It was an eerie feeling, different from the usual thrill of the act in the arena of the Wild West Show. This would take on more importance because it would be preserved.

Sitting on his borrowed bay, John watched the wagons wind their way across the rolling prairie and around the hill. Then a shot, a yell, more shots, screams from the wagons, teamsters lashing their horses into a canter, attempting to circle for defense.

Now the Poncas swept down, whooping and firing. The cottony white puffs of smoke could be seen a few heartbeats before the sounds reached the ears of the cavalry on the hill.

One of the wagons overturned, breaking away from the madly galloping team. The passengers and the driver jumped clear, and it took John only a moment to realize that this was one of William Selig's "stunts." The moviemaker was hunched over his camera, cap on backward to allow his eye closer to the viewfinder, steadily cranking the machine of his own design.

One of the wagons caught fire, then another, and black smoke rolled from under the burning canvas. The Poncas were shooting flaming arrows from the hill, but it was apparent that the fires in the wagons were set by Selig's crews. It certainly produced an exciting film, though John doubted that the Poncas had often launched flaming arrows at anyone.

Now the cavalry bugler blew the charge. It would not be heard on the screen, of course, but served to raise the emotions and quicken the pulse, adding to the realism. The blue-clad troop swarmed down the hill, firing their carbines, and the Poncas wheeled away in retreat.

It was an amusing diversion, but as the scene ended and everyone laughingly returned to more normal activity, John felt a pang of regret, and some smattering of guilt. Would the moviemakers ever film an act where the Indians *won?* What about Custer?

Meanwhile, the cast and crew of the Wild West Show was gathering, after the winter break. The cowboys and cowgirls had largely remained on the ranch, but many of the specialty performers had spent the winter in warmer climes, working the off season. Now, with the 1909 season pending, they began to gather. The Millers and their partner and advance man, Edward Arlington, were constantly recruiting new acts. The cowboy band was already an attraction, as well as Vern Tantlinger, boss of the cowboy unit and expert with the boomerang. His assistant would catch the boomerang in flight.

There were also sideshow acts; Magicians, jugglers, ax throwers, a minstrel troupe, trained mules, lion tamers, and dancing bears.

Bill Pickett was still recovering from his wounds, but there was no shortage of other headliners. "Prince Lucca," of Russia, led a troop of Cossack horsemen.

Zack Miller himself performed in the ring, displaying marksmanship on the back of his trained Arabian stallion.

Vern Tantlinger had also recruited a number of Sioux

Indians from the Pine Ridge Reservation, to ride with the Poncas and other Indian performers. Princess Wenona, "world's best female shot alive," would continue to be a crowd pleaser.

Taking advantage of the opportunity to film working cowboys, cattle, and buffalo as backdrops for his scenes, William Selig produced three movies that spring on the 101.

Oil exploration was in progress, too, occasionally spoiling the movie crews' plans for a scene. On top of all this, the farm operations continued to expand, with new crops and new varieties.

Celebrity guests were common at the ranch after the restoration of the White House, and there was always an increasing air of excitement. It was easy to become intoxicated with the excitement of being a part of what appeared to be a rising star: the 101.

John and Hebbie were pleased to be a part of such excitement, and to be with each other. Once more, John mentioned marriage.

Hebbie hesitated a long time, and finally sighed deeply.

"Oh, John, I don't know. I was burned, once. I'm afraid . . . Oh, let's not spoil what we've got."

She kissed him softly.

"I'll think about it, though. . . . Thank you. . . ."

THIRTY-ONE

The 1909 show season was a mad blur of excitement. Crowds everywhere were large and enthusiastic. It was easy to fall into the contagion of excitement that was always present when the Millers were around. Several unrelated events contributed to the enthusiasm and fascination of the public with the Wild West and the Hundred and One.

A French motion-picture company in Mexico City, to film the bullfights, had recorded Bill Pickett's ordeal with the Mexican fighting bull. Moviegoers worldwide, and especially in America, were treated to repeat performances of Pickett and Spradley and the near-tragedy in the arena. It would be late in the season before Pickett was able to perform again, but the film called attention to the show and filled the bleachers in the big tent.

Yet another unrelated event sparked interest in motion pictures, Wild West, and the 101. Former President Theodore Roosevelt was an enthusiast of the West and of big-game hunting. When he announced his intention to go on an African safari to hunt big game in 1909, motion picture pioneer William Selig, filming on the 101, petitioned to be allowed to go along and record the expedition's activities. He was refused.

Undaunted, Selig hurried back to his Chicago studios and prepared another approach. He hired an actor resembling the famous Teddy, and constructed a movie set with tropical plants and an old lion. African tribesmen were portrayed by Chicago Negroes. Innovative camera angles, skilled editing, and the unfamiliarity of audiences with both Africa and with motion pictures created an illusion that was remarkable in its effect. The film, *Hunting Big Game in Africa,* was held for release at the proper time.

When word came from the Dark Continent that Roosevelt had bagged a lion, Selig was ready. Theatergoers thrilled at the mistaken impression that the film they were watching was film of the Roosevelt hunt. This inspired Selig to create more outdoor and jungle films with a menagerie of zoo animals and file footage from foreign lands edited into his flexible story lines. Many of these were produced, at least partially, on the vast and varied landscape of the Hundred and One.

The entire fascination of the public with the spectacle of outdoor adventure drew record crowds to the 101 Wild West Show performances, and it was a great season for the Millers and for their cast of performers.

In late autumn, Vester Pegg approached him with a proposal.

"John, how'd you like to see South America?"

"What do you mean?"

"Some of us are goin' to sign on with another show . . . The IXL Ranch Show."

"Leave the Hundred an' One?"

"No, no, John. Just for the winter season. It's their summer down there, you know. We'll be back by April, before the tour starts here."

John was cautious.

"I dunno . . . Who's goin'?"

"Well, the Tantlingers, the Parry girls, Jim Garrett, Frank Maisle, Chet Byers, George Hooker . . ."

"Them are all headliners, Ves. Why would you want me?"

"You're a good hand with horses, and we'll be takin' several. Need some help."

"Can I think about it?"

"Sure. No hurry. We won't leave till next week."

John sought Hebbie's opinion.

"Maybe you could go, too," he suggested.

"No, no, John." She smiled. "They'll want headline acts and a few hands to look after the stock. You fit that category, but I don't fit neither one. Not good enough to headline, and not really a stock handler. But you go on. It'll be a great way to spend a winter."

"But . . . I'd miss you, Hebbie."

"Yeah, sure. You'll have them little senoritas cattin' after you so fast. . . . You'll have a great time. Go on ahead, John."

"Are you tryin' to get rid of me, Hebbie?"

"Hell, no. Just, you get a chance, you oughta take it."

"But I—No! I won't do it, without you. Wouldn't be any fun."

"None at all? Maybe a little?" she teased.

He grinned. "Well, maybe a *little*. But it ain't worth it. No, I'll tell Ves not to count me in."

Hebbie said nothing, but only smiled. He could tell from that smile though, that he had made the right choice.

The crew of headliners returned from South America in early April, looking tanned and healthy and ready to start the show season. They met the rest of the troupe in St. Louis to prepare for the season opener on April 16.

"Boy, that was a tour down there," Vester Pegg told him. "You'd've liked it, John."

"Well, maybe next time."

There was little time to catch their breath before the show rolled on to enthusiastic crowds everywhere. St. Louis . . . Dayton, Springfield, Columbus, and Cambridge in Ohio . . . Pittsburgh, Philadelphia, Washington, Baltimore. . . . New England . . .

With awareness of other "Wild West" shows on the road, the 1909 tour had been rechristened the 101 Ranch Real Wild West Show. After all of the above appearances in less than six weeks, it was a seasoned but tired troupe whose show train arrived in Brooklyn for a week's booking. In the early morning, they detrained and set up on the old circus lot at Fifth Avenue and Third Street, later abandoned to progress. It was Sunday, so no performance was booked until the following day.

"Hey, John," someone called. "Mr. Joe wants a meeting at noon. Pass the word!"

What now? It had been a busy and hardworking season so far, but there was always the possibility of an unpleasant surprise. Where the Millers were involved, anything could happen, and frequently did.

John's muscles tightened involuntarily. Was this to be an announcement that the tour was over and everyone was on his own? What would he do in New York City? More to the point, was this an announcement that the show was in financial trouble and that no one would be paid? There was considerable apprehension as the troupe gathered under the Big Top.

John took Hebbie's hand as Joe Miller strolled out into the center ring. There was a hushed silence as he faced the crowd of more than a hundred troupers: headliners, sideshow operators, Cossacks, Indians, roustabouts.

"Y'all have been doin' a great job," Miller began.

It was like waiting for the other shoe to drop. But . . . *What?*

"But we got us a half-a-day off," he continued.

Absolute silence.

"So let's have fun! Let's all go to Coney Island! It's on the Hunnerd and One!"

Now a cheer arose, and a few war whoops from the Sioux, who weren't quite certain what it was about, but saw the joy in the faces of their fellow performers. The crowd scattered to change and dress for the occasion.

Meanwhile, Joe Miller had tipped off the newspapers that the troupe would be traveling to Coney Island for an afternoon of recreation. They were followed by a bevy of reporters as they gathered in the circus lot and headed for the Third Street railway station. The ticket agent reacted initially with a certain degree of alarm. After all, a crowd of more than one hundred people in strange and colorful costumes, many of them Indians in tribal dress, was an imposing sight. Very likely the railroad employee had transient thoughts of what had happened to Custer only a few decades ago. He might have been even more anxious had he realized how closely some of these people were related to those on the Little Bighorn.

Joe Miller, leading the high-spirited crowd, stepped up to the window to placate the agent with cash. Tickets to Coney Island for everybody.

Coney Island, at the southern end of Brooklyn, had been a resort and recreation area for many years. Actually, it was not an island, but a peninsula, now mostly connected to the greater landmass. It boasted six miles of carnival attractions, fun houses, dance halls, rides, and freak shows.

The Hundred and One troupe detrained at about four o'clock, and went straight to Thompson and Dundee's Luna Park, the largest of the carnival ride complexes. They were met at the entrance to the park by a band blaring carnival music and were welcomed by Fred Thompson himself. Curious New Yorkers gathered to watch the fun, and to follow the crowd of show people from one attraction to another.

It was a strange situation. More than a hundred physically fit, active people, who made their living by being whirled, jolted, bumped, jarred, and battered. . . . Now, for recreation during their half-day vacation from work, they submitted themselves to a myriad of purchased indignities. In this, they were whirled, jolted, bumped, jarred, and battered and, for the next several hours, had a wonderful time. The 101 troupe rode every ride, saw every attraction, and relaxed thoroughly, with no responsibilities.

They played like children that evening. Champion rider George Hooker, enjoyed the gentle ride on the wooden horses at the merry-go-round.

A newspaper reporter who spoke Spanish quickly attached himself to the Mexican vaqueros and acted as their interpreter for the evening.

The Indians were fascinated by the rides. Women with babies fastened securely in cradle boards rode the steep Helter-Skelter slide. One of their favorite rides was Luna Park's Chute-the-Chutes, a slide with cars which plunged into a pool of water. Red Eagle and some of the younger Indians rode it again and again. The more dignified Chief Plenty Horses had a different opinion: One ride on the Chutes was enough for a man of his rank.

The Ferris wheel was one of the popular attractions. John and Hebbie spent some time in one of the gondolas near the top of the wheel. While the operator seated each next batch of passengers, there would be a pause of a minute or two. It was a romantic interlude, looking out over the ocean, or in the other direction, over the lights of New

York as darkness fell. At the top of the great wheel, it was as if they were the only couple in heaven, but looking down on the mere humans below. He kissed her, long and warmly, and it became one of their most exciting experiences as each long pause heightened the romantic interlude. Their breathing became heavier. . . . His hands began to wander, and their bodies pressed closer in the gondola's chair.

Finally Hebbie pulled away, still breathing hard.

"My God, John! Not here. He's gonna start this thing whirlin' again in a minute. We don't want to be part of the show!"

"You don't think it would make a show?" he teased, sitting back to catch his breath.

"Too good, maybe. You'll land us in jail. Now, behave!"

Her words were harsh, but her tone was soft and loving.

"Later," she finished.

As they dismounted from the Ferris wheel, Vern Tantlinger approached, a worried look on his face.

"John, have you seen Pickett?"

"No . . . We . . . Uh . . . We been on the Ferris wheel. Why? He's missin'?"

Vern did not seem to notice their flushed faces and mild embarrassment.

"Don't know," he answered. "Nobody's seen him since we got off the train. I'm a bit worried. I'm askin' around. You know how Bill can be about drinkin', and he's not used to big cities."

"And nobody's seen him?"

"Not since the train."

"Could he have stayed on the train?"

"Hell, anything *could* happen, John. I sent Walker to look for him."

"Hank Walker?" Hebbie burst out. "Vern, that's like putting the monkey in charge of the bananas!"

Hank "Rocky Mountain" Walker was the driver of the Deadwood Stage in the show, skilled at his job, and completely reliable—but he enjoyed a good time.

"Aw, Hebbie, Hank ain't that bad," Vern assured her. "He'll find him. But, let's not tell Joe Miller. He's got enough to think about."

But some time later, it was discovered that no one could find either Pickett or Walker.

Miller led his troupe to dinner at the Surf Avenue Restaurant well after dark, and ordered their famous Coney Island shore dinner for all hands. Someone had told him about the missing cowboys, and he alerted the police to keep an eye out for them. He also requested that they keep back the crowds of curious New Yorkers so that his crew might enjoy their meal.

They had barely started on the massive plates of seafood and bowls of chowder when in strolled the two missing cowboys.

"Should've expected it," said a relieved Tantlinger. "Neither one of them two ever missed a meal."

Walker explained that he had found Pickett standing on a corner on Surf Avenue, counting all the automobiles, and so fascinated that he had lost track of time.

As they left the restaurant and headed back toward the train, someone called from the crowd on the street.

"John? John Buffalo? Is that you?"

Curious, John paused and turned aside. The voice sounded familiar, but the light was poor under the incandescent bulbs of the electric streetlamps.

A young man detached himself from the crowd.

"John? What are you doing here?"

"Charlie Smith?"

"None other," grinned his former roommate. "You're with the show, here?"

"Sure. Couple of years, now."

"You're not coaching?"

"Nope. Couldn't find a job."

"Good!" said Charlie.

"What?"

"Then you don't know Coach McGregor's been lookin' for you?"

"No . . . What for?"

"He's got a job for you!"

"A job? Doin' what?"

"Coachin'. He asked me to let him know if I heard from you."

THIRTY-TWO

What are you doin' with this outfit?" Charlie demanded. "But no . . . Back up . . . You left Carlisle in a hell of a hurry. Nobody knew why, and we couldn't seem to get any answers."

The old heartbreak washed over John in a wave like those that rhythmically rolled over the Coney Island beach and receded again like the wave. It had been a while since he had thought about it.

"That's a long story, Charlie. Doesn't matter much now. But what are *you* doin' here?"

"Doin' Coney Island, like you. I'm teaching, and on a vacation weekend."

"Here? New York?"

"No, at Carlisle. Came down to look at some new equipment we're considering. Going back on the train tomorrow. But, John, tell me about you. We found out you'd been at Haskell, but they didn't know where you went after you left there. And this"—Charlie swept an arm at the tired but happy cowboys and Indians moving up the street— "Somebody said this is the Hundred and One Wild West Show?"

"That's right. I work for the 101."

"C'mon . . . You're funnin' me."

"No, I'm not, Charlie. I train horses at the ranch."

"Oh, yes. I've heard you say that; you like horses. So, you don't ride in the show?"

"Well, yes . . . I do. We all do several jobs, help one another in a pinch. The Millers are tough but fair, Charlie. They're payin' for this Coney Island trip."

"Really? That's a heap o' money, John."

"Yep . . . They don't mind spendin' it if it keeps the gang workin' and happy."

"But . . ." Charlie paused and his eyes swept over his friend from head to toe. "You're a *cowboy* in the show?"

John laughed. "These are my workin' clothes at the ranch. In the show, I'm a cowboy sometimes, or an Indian, sometimes a cavalry trooper."

Charlie's face registered his shock.

"My God, John! What would Yellow Bull say?"

"Well . . . Dunno. I'd guess he thinks I'm tryin' to beat the white man at his own game. But Charlie, these folks are different. They have some respect. Look . . . See these Indians? Poncas. Those over there are Sioux. They're all in the show. We've got Mexicans and Russians. A few breeds and Negroes. There's Bill Pickett over there— colored and Cherokee, they say."

"I've heard of him. . . . Wrestles steers with his teeth, somebody said? Some trick?"

"No trick, Charlie. He does it. Damn' near got killed when we were in Mexico."

"Heard about . . . Wait! *You* were there?"

"Sure. Several weeks. Say, we'll be here a week. Come on over. I'll get you a pass."

"Come on, John, we'll miss the train," called a woman's voice.

"I'm comin', Hebbie. Charlie, come back to camp with us. We've got more talkin' to do. And yes, I'd like you to meet Hebbie, my . . . uh . . . friend. Hebbie, this is Charlie Smith. We went to school together, back at Carlisle."

"Pleased to meetcha, Charlie. Sure, come bunk with us. Always room for one more on the road."

"But, I—"

"Come on, folks," yelled Vern Tantlinger. "We're loadin'! Bring your friend, John."

"Well, okay," Charlie said. "I *do* need to tell you about McGregor."

They talked until far into the night.

"You don't know why they decided to transfer you out West?" asked the puzzled Charlie Smith.

"Not really," John said, not quite truthfully. He thought the reason was pretty certain, given the circumstances.

"Couldn't your friend the Senator help you out on that, John?" Charlie asked, half teasing.

Then his face changed.

"My God, John. It was—"

"Never mind, Charlie. Let's talk something else."

"My heart is heavy, my friend. Let us speak no more of it."

"Good. But . . . You spoke of Mac. A *job*, you said?"

"Yes! He's been trying to find you. Asked me if I knew, because of our friendship. He knew you'd transferred to Haskell, but they'd lost track of you."

"And you're working for him? McGregor?"

"No, no. I'm teaching English. But we have a really

good athletic department now. And a rising star. Name's Jim Thorpe. Sac and Fox, from Oklahoma, I think. A whiz at football and baseball, but Pop Warner likes him best at track and field. Distance runner . . . All your old events, John.

"Wait a bit. Was Pop Warner there when you were? Director of Athletics? Great head coach . . ."

"Well, he *had* been. I was at Carlisle only two years, you know. But didn't he leave about the time I got there?"

"Oh, yes, I forgot. He was at Cornell. . . . His alma mater, I guess, for about three years. But he's back, now, building. There's this Thorpe kid. Small, but wiry. Aw, there's too much to tell. Let me back up. . . .

"I said, Pop Warner is building our athletic program. It's big, but getting even better. Our Indian kids are enthusiastic. All they ever wanted was a fair chance to compete with the white man. We can relate to that, no?"

Charlie went on without waiting for an answer.

"Funny thing one of the Sioux students told Pop Warner: 'You had the press agents. . . . When the white man won, it was always a *battle*. When we won, it was always a *massacre*.' But back to the subject. . . .

"You maybe heard about President Roosevelt organizing an American Olympic Committee a few years back?"

"Something of the sort. He's been down to the Hundred and One."

"Doesn't surprise me. He's been everywhere. But he wants America to support sending amateur athletes to the Olympics. It helped that the Olympiad was held in St. Louis a while back. Now, the next one is to be in Stockholm in 1912. If Carlisle can field some entries for the tryouts, we think we can make a good showing. And, we'll have this Thorpe."

"You will have?" John was confused.

"Well . . . Yes. He was sent on a summer job in the outing system. Pop and Mac have some people out looking for him . . . think he might have gone back to Oklahoma. You haven't run across him?"

That was an inside joke. It was commonly thought by most Easterners that anything west of the Alleghenies must be in close contact with the rest of the West.

" 'Fraid not. I'll keep an eye out," said John.

"We'll find him," assured Charlie. "His parents are dead, but he's got relatives down around Stroud and Garden Grove."

"But what did they want *me* to do?" asked John.

"Well, you used to help Mac. The coaches remembered that you used to help them with the young runners. They used you as a trainer. They've got some funds for an assistant, and Pop wants Jim Thorpe in the decathlon in 1912. If we can find him, that is."

"Two years," mused John. "I don't know, Charlie. I'd need to know more."

"Of course!" said Smith. "But it's right in your field."

"What field? Playin' cowboy and Indians?"

"No, you know, John. And it's a chance to travel . . . Europe . . . England. The summer Olympic games are in Stockholm."

"Where's that?"

"Sweden, of course."

"Never was much on geography."

"Yes, I recall," jibed Charlie. "But there's more incentive now."

"That's true. Well, tell Mac to write me."

"Where?"

"The 101 . . . No, that won't work; we'll be on the road. After this week, we got to—"

"Wait!" Charlie interrupted. "You'll be here a week?"

"Guess so."

"Okay. I'll travel back to school tomorrow, and tell McGregor where you are. He'll probably want to write you before you leave New York. Where do you go next?"

"I dunno. Someplace in New England, I think. He's really serious about this, Charlie?"

"Of course, John! This is important, I tell you!"

On Tuesday, just before the matinee performance, a young man on a bicycle approached him.

"You're John Buffalo?"

"Yes . . ."

He looked over the young man's clothing, which appeared to be somewhere between a military uniform and that of a railway conductor.

"I have a telegram for you. Sign here."

John did so. The messenger handed him a yellow envelope, remounted the bicycle, and pedaled away.

"I never had a telegram before," said John, staring at the envelope in his hand.

"Well, open it," suggested Hebbie.

"Oh . . . Yes. I'll open it."

He ran a fingertip beneath the flap at one corner, and ripped the top fold open. Inside was a folded yellow paper.

DONT LEAVE NEW YORK STOP
WILL BE THERE THURSDAY STOP

                                                    MAC

McGregor did arrive on Thursday, on a noon train, and made his way to the tent city on the circus lot in Brooklyn. There he inquired as to the whereabouts of John Buffalo, and was directed to the horse pens.

However, the performance was just beginning, and John was in the arena, taking part in the grand entry.

McGregor waited impatiently.

"Go on over and watch the show," suggested one of the roustabouts. "He ain't goin' nowhere. We'll tell him you're lookin' for him."

Mac sauntered over to the massive Big Top and found a seat near the performers' entrance. The distinctive odors of sweaty horses, popcorn, and dust mingled with the unique smell of sunshine on canvas, in a not-unpleasant potpourri. There is nothing on earth like the smell of a circus under canvas.

Likewise, there is none of the human senses that stimulates the nostalgic memories of the past like the sense of smell. MacGregor was a child again, watching his first circus. This was a somewhat different show, but the memories came flooding back as he watched. Mixed with the circus atmosphere was another odor; the smoke from the Millers' lavish use of black gunpowder. It was a circus and the Fourth of July all rolled into one.

"Mac?" someone said, disturbing his reverie.

"What? Oh, yes, John!"

McGregor was jarred back to the present.

"Charlie Smith said you were lookin' for me." John extended his hand. "I got your wire."

"Oh, yes . . . Yes," said McGregor, gathering his thoughts and remembering his responsibilities. "Is there someplace we can talk?"

"Sure. Come on."

John led the way to a part of the circus lot away from the noise and traffic of the performance, and they sat on a couple of the wooden shipping boxes used to carry small items of tack and equipment.

"Charlie tell you what I want?" asked the coach.

"A little."

"Well, it's simple. This Jim Thorpe is a wonderful athlete, John. Best since you were there. You have no idea how I hated to lose you. You had the potential. . . . But that's behind us now. No use cryin' over spilled milk. Now, we've got Thorpe. We've beaten about every school there is in football. Army, Navy, Notre Dame, Harvard, all of 'em. Feels good, John. But he's Olympic material in track and field. You were always good to give some pointers to the younger athletes. And I figured you'd be coachin' somewhere. How'd you get into this—Never mind, we don't have time."

John smiled wryly.

"Came pretty close to a job or two out in Kansas, but they wanted somebody with lighter skin."

McGregor was silent for a moment.

"I know, John," he said a bit sadly. "Our students have that problem sometimes. But in this case, it's a plus. You can not only understand Thorpe's problems of that kind, but can coach him, and pace him on the distance events. I want to see him in cross-country, decathlon, and pentathlon. You can help him with all those."

"I don't know, Mac. I've got a pretty good job here, workin' with good people. I'd sorta hate to give it up."

McGregor looked as if he'd just been kicked in the stomach.

"But, John . . ."

"Two years," John mused. "What then?"

"Then you'd have some status as a coach! What better reference than having paced an Olympic champion, John?"

"He hasn't won it yet."

"No, but he could, with your help."

"When do you have to know?"

McGregor chuckled.

"Yesterday . . . As quick as you can, John."

John nodded.

"I'll want to talk to the Millers. I don't have a real contract, and they're pretty good to deal with on a handshake, but . . . Well, you understand, Coach. I can't let 'em down if they're countin' on me."

"Of course not. When can you talk to them?"

"Maybe this evening. When do you go back to Carlisle?"

"Don't know. I didn't know how long it would take to find you."

"Okay. Can you get back to me tomorrow? The show's here through Saturday, but I'll know by noon tomorrow."

"That's good, laddie!"

Mac rose and extended his hand. John shook the hand, pleased. He remembered now that the coach used the term "laddie" very seldom, and only when he was greatly pleased.

Now, back to the arena for the closing ceremony. Then, before the evening performance, he'd have to find a way to talk to the Millers.

And to Hebbie.

THIRTY-THREE

Joe Miller was easy.

"Wonderful opportunity, John! Of course, we'll miss you. But you know where the old Hundred and One is. We'd welcome you back anytime. It's a two-year job?"

"Yes, sir. Maybe it would lead to a better coaching job, but hard to tell."

Miller laughed.

"Never knew you were an athlete, boy! Of course, all our 101 gang are, in a way. But, well, good luck!"

They shook hands.

"I'm not sure I'm goin', sir. A couple of things I have to find out about. But I wanted to ask you first."

"Of course . . . Proper way to do it! I hope it works for you, John."

The tough part was Hebbie.

"Why, John! I never knew this about you!"

"Knew what?" he asked, and then felt stupid about how he'd said it.

"That you had that sort of ambition."

"You knew I'd played football. Track, too."

"Sure. At the Indian schools. But I never knew you wanted to coach. Never knew you could. You have a lot of talents, John."

She snuggled close, in the darkness under one of the big show wagons.

"A lot of talents!"

"Stop it, Hebbie, we need to talk."

"Okay, I'll behave. Talk away."

She now sat primly upright.

"Hebbie, be serious. I need to decide about this."

"What's to decide? Just do it!"

"But I don't want to leave you."

"Hey, we did all right before we met. We can again."

"Hebbie . . . I thought we meant more than that to each other."

Now she became more serious.

"John, I'm not wantin' to belittle what we have. It's wonderful. But we'll both get along."

"I don't want to just 'get along', Hebbie. I need you. Let's get married, and you can go, too."

There was a long pause in the darkness, and she took his hand.

"John," she said finally, "you've asked me before, and it was a real temptation. We're good together. You know me better than anybody ever has. I had some doubts. I'm older'n you, and you're better educated, but we do suit each other pretty good. I'm beginnin' to think it *could* work. But I'm goin' to say no again for now."

"But *why?*"

"Timing's bad. You don't want to get married and run right off—"

"But you'd go with me!" he interrupted.

"No, no, John. A training camp is no place for a woman. It's bad luck, anyway, I'd expect, like a woman on a ship."

He wondered what Hebbie knew about training camps and women on ships, but wasn't sure he wanted to ask.

"Anyway," she continued, "I ain't exactly sayin' no, John. I'm sayin' not now. I'll wait for you. We can write."

"You'll stay with the Hundred and One?"

"Sure. It's more or less family now, ain't it? I'll be okay, John."

She snuggled close again, and this time he didn't protest.

It was difficult and confusing to stay in touch with McGregor for the rest of the circuit. John felt a responsibility to the 101 to finish the agreed-upon show season. It took a couple of letters back and forth to finalize the arrangements. That in itself was not easy, because the show was on the move. John kept McGregor informed as to their schedule, as the summer rolled on.

It was agreed that after the Minnesota State Fair appearances, John would travel by train to Pennsylvania and Carlisle, to join the coaching staff and the athletes with whom they worked.

He had no contract as such. Most of the 101 Ranch employees operated on a cowboy handshake, and thought nothing of it. Many could not have read their contract, anyway. Basically, contracts were reserved for a few of the headliners. Despite this, however, the strength of the implied agreement was in many cases stronger than words on paper. Unless circumstances were extremely unusual, once the season started, everyone expected to finish it on the show circuit with the rest of the "gang."

Finally, John simply wrote McGregor to that effect. *I'll be there this fall. . . .*

This removed some of the pressure to be doing something. The time he found to be with Hebbie, and to deepen their understanding, was valuable. Their relationship became closer with the knowledge that soon they must be apart for a while.

He found that he dreaded the parting as the time neared for his trip east. He proposed again.

"No," Hebbie said firmly. "I said not now. You got work to do. I'd be a distraction."

Then she gave him a seductive wink.

"But . . . Just ask me again when you get back!"

She put him on the train, kissing him good-bye with a few tears.

"It'll be okay, John. I'll take care of Strawberry. Can I ride her in the show?"

"Sure. You'll have to cue her left lead sometimes."

"Yes, yes . . . Get on the train, now. And, I'll take your saddle back to the ranch. I'll be waitin'!"

He watched her as long as he could, standing on the platform, waving good-bye. His heart was very heavy, and he nearly decided to jump off the train and go back. But it was accelerating now, and a glance at the cross ties flickering backward beneath the iron wheels quickly changed his mind. He tried to concentrate on what lay ahead, but for a long time he could think only of something Hebbie had said: *Ask me again when you get back.*

It was nearing October when John found himself backtracking his journey west a few years ago. He arrived at the station and hitched a ride to the campus.

The familiar brick buildings looked smaller than he remembered. It was difficult to put things into perspective, after a few years of worldly experience. The bittersweet memories came flowing back. . . . This had been an important place in his life, and in the lives of many people. Facts which he had known before but which had seemed unimportant now loomed large. More than a century ago, these buildings had been the headquarters of General Washington's Army during the Revolution. That had seemed long ago and far away to him when he had been told of it. . . . Much more important now. . . .

He watched the students in their blue uniforms at close-order drill, heard the bugle calls which regulated the day's schedule. It was a dreamy return to days long gone, and which could never be recovered. . . .

"John! John Buffalo!" a voice called from the practice area for track and field, drawing him back to the present.

"Good to see you, laddie," said McGregor, pumping his hand enthusiastically. "Let's get you settled, and then talk some strategy. Here . . . let me take one of your bags."

Reluctantly, John relinquished the smaller of his bags.

Across the way on the old field that John had known as the "gridiron," a football squad worked out.

"Is your boy—Thorpe, is it?—Is he working at football or track?" John asked.

McGregor looked somewhat embarrassed.

"Well, John," he said haltingly, "I . . . We . . . That is . . . John, he's not here."

"Not here? Where is he?"

"It's hard to explain. Come, let's walk on over to your quarters while we talk. You're familiar with the 'outing system': Students hire out for the summer term to work?"

"Of course. I did that at Haskell. Not quite the same . . ."

"Yes, yes. . . . Well, Thorpe didn't come back."

"Something happened to him?"

"No, we'd have heard. But, he never got to that job. We figure he got on the wrong train. John, you'd have to know this Thorpe. He's a bit unpredictable. Actually, a bit like yourself."

"But, Mac . . . He just didn't come back, this fall?"

"Well . . . Not last year, either."

"My God, Mac! He's missing for *two* years?"

"John, it's not quite like that. We know he's been working in North Carolina. Just between us, I think Pop Warner has a pretty good idea where he is."

"But you expected him back when the fall term started."

"Yes, we did. He'll turn up, sometime, when he thinks it's time." McGregor paused with a mischievous grin. "Surely you know about that."

The white man's preoccupation with time was a frequent joke.

When will it happen?

A white man states a day and hour. Ask an Indian, and he shrugs. . . .

When it's time.

It was often said of the red man: "He's on *Indian* time."

John was sifting this information through his mind.

"Then . . . If your athlete's not here, I guess there's no job for me?"

"Oh, yes, John. Warner still wants you, for when we do find Thorpe. Meanwhile, we have some others with great potential. Pop sees this Olympiad as a team effort, not just one star headliner. You'll be working with others. You can not only coach, but act as a pacesetter for some of the distance runners. Oh, here's one you need to meet!"

He motioned to a runner just coming off the track. The young man was short, slender, and wiry, and came trotting over.

"John, this is Louis Tewanima. He's a distance man. . . . Hopi . . . You'll be working with him. Louis, John here played football at Carlisle a few years back. He'll be a trainer and assistant coach—whatever Pop Warner decides to call him. We'll use him to pace some of the distance runners."

Tewanima merely nodded, but John held out a hand and the little Hopi shook it.

"Guess we'll be seeing a lot of each other," suggested John.

"Yes," said Tewanima.

"Well, let's get you settled," Mac said to John. "You can get acquainted later."

The meeting with Coach Warner was brief and to the point.

"Mac tells me you're good with young athletes," Warner said abruptly. "I won't try to tell you how to do it. If I had to do that, I wouldn't need you. We've got this Thorpe . . ."

"He's here, then?"

A strange twinkle appeared in the eyes of the wily coach for a moment and quickly faded. John had a feeling that there was a strong possibility that Thorpe's disappearance for a while may have been at Warner's suggestion—or, at least, consent—while the young athlete grew and matured.

"He'll be here," Pop Warner stated positively.

THIRTY-FOUR

Louis Tewanima proved to be both a challenge and a joy to work with. His command of English was far from fluent, and Louis seemed to consider it unimportant that he attempt to change. There was a story that when he attempted to go out for track, he was told by Pop Warner that he was too small.

"Me run fast good," the little Hopi had stated. "All Hopis run fast good."

Warner had given him a try, and quickly realized that there was nothing boastful about "run fast good," but merely fact. The coach had been unaware at the time that a traditional Hopi game involves running long distances while kicking a ball ahead of the runner.

Tewanima had never weighed more than 110 pounds as his training weight, but exemplified the truism that dynamite comes in small packages. His specialty had become the ten- and fifteen-mile distances.

"Last year, we had a meet over at Harrisburg," McGregor recalled. "Louis missed the train, so he just *ran* the eighteen miles to Harrisburg and got there in time to win his race. He was entered in the two-mile. He'd probably have run back to Carlisle, but we managed to corner him and put him on the train for the ride home."

John laughed and shook his head.

"Mac, how can I teach anything to a runner with that kind of talent?"

"Maybe you can't," McGregor admitted, "but he needs some help sometimes to understand what it's about. Warner wants to qualify him for the Olympics. You know that involves a lot of pacing and timing. You're pretty good at that. Now, while we're lookin' to find Thorpe, you work with Tewanima. He's still thinkin' in terms of cross-country, and a lot of the distance events will be on the circular track. Louis has a hard time understandin' the sense of that. I guess he figures, why run in a circle when you can *go* someplace with it?"

"Well, there's somethin' to be said for that," John observed.

"That's true. But you know what I mean. We took a team to New York to run in Madison Square Garden last spring. Tewanima was entered in the ten-mile competition. He looked at that little track—ten laps to the mile—and just shook his head. He went over to Warner and told him, 'Me afraid get mixed up go round and round. You tell me front man, and I get him.' "

"What happened?" John asked.

"That's just what happened," laughed Mac. "When the race began to line out, Pop Warner would catch Tewanima's eye as he came past, and point out some runner who was leading him. Louis would pass him. Lapped the whole field one at a time, and turned up the heat at the finish. . . . He set a new indoor world's record that day."

John was laughing.

"Just ride herd on him, as you'd say in your cowboy talk," Mac went on. "Pace him on his workouts. I've seen you work with runners. You'll find ways to help him."

John had his doubts. It was a long time since he'd done any running. Among the 101 cowboys, he'd step up into the saddle to go anywhere, even a few hundred yards. This would require the use of muscles he hadn't called on for several years.

The first week was torture. On the morning after his first attempt to pace Tewanima, he awoke with a dull ache up the insides of both thighs. When he attempted to move, his muscles jerked into unbelievably painful cramps. Stifling the gasp of agony that threatened to reveal his condition to others in the dormitory building, he rose and hobbled a few steps to get everything working.

By the week's end, his conditioning had progressed far enough that he felt more confident. Warner seemed satisfied with his work as a trainer and assistant, and he settled into the routine of the school year.

———

He wrote Hebbie occasionally, and she attempted to do the same. He had not realized until now just how limited her schooling had been. He felt a certain amount of guilt for having placed her in a situation that called attention to her lack of education.

Dere John,
   it was gud to here of you. I am fine here. I am ridin straw berry, teachin her to rop offn her. Shes a gud horse. I hope yur work is goin gud. I miss you.
                                          Senserely,
                                          Hebbie

Somehow, the clumsily lettered and poorly spelled note, written on a sheet of ruled tablet paper, struck him emotionally as nothing else could have. Only now did he fully realize how much he missed her. In the time since he had been at the Hundred and One, Hebbie had become one of the most important things in his life. He should not have left her. . . .

There was a short time when he actually considered leaving Carlisle to return to Hebbie and the 101. He abandoned the idea for a variety of reasons. He was needed and appreciated here. Hebbie would give him the scolding of his life if he let these people down. Besides, his pay was pretty meager in the nondescript job that was part of Pop Warner's program to field an Olympic team. Each day and week contributed more to the shaping of that goal.

He wrote to Hebbie more frequently. He knew that she could read much better than she could write. In the dim recesses of his mind, he began to imagine ways that he could help her further her education when they were together. Always, there was that goal, distant but achievable. Some day they *would* be together.

Meanwhile, his letters could serve a useful purpose. She'd read them, which would help her reading skills. It would also help him to feel closer to her. He was missing her terribly.

My dearest Hebbie,

I got your letter yesterday, and it was wonderful to hear from you. I miss you a lot, even as busy as I am with Tewanima and the other runners. He's the Hopi I told you about.

We still haven't seen anything of Jim Thorpe, but Pop Warner says he'll turn up. I wondered why they call him "Pop," and somebody told me: When he was playing football at Cornell, Warner was a little older than the others on the team. He was about twenty-five, I guess, and they joked about his being the 'old man' of the squad. So, he's still called "Pop." Sometimes, "Pappy."

Things are going pretty well here, but it's lonely. I'm thinking maybe I'll come back to the 101 for Christmas, but I don't have a very good idea what they'll expect here. I still wish you were with me. We'll talk more about *that* when I see you, too!

We did have a close call a while back. We'd taken a track team to a meet in New York City, and stayed overnight at a hotel. In one of the rooms, three of our students who had never seen gaslights before didn't understand how it worked. They blew it out when they went to bed and damn near suffocated in the night. Luckily, they'd opened the window, or they'd probably have been dead when we found them. Of course they could have blown up the whole hotel, too, if one of them had struck a match!

I'd better quit now and get to work. Take care of yourself, and stay away from those cowboys! Ha!

I love you,
John

The Christmas trip never materialized, and the winter dragged on into spring, with the return of the outdoor track events. There was still no sign of Thorpe.

Hebbie's letters seemed to reflect her willingness to at least try to improve on her scholastic abilities.

. . . The school teacher at the 101 is helping me . . . I don't want you to be ashamed of my ignorance. I never had much schooling . . .

She told of rewriting her letter for the approval of the teacher . . .

. . . and she says I'm doing better. I do miss you, John.

Love,
Hebbie

It was summer before the event occurred that began to give some sense of purpose to John's return to Carlisle. The track team had had a good spring season. John considered rejoining the Miller Brothers for the show season, but there was pressure for him to remain at Carlisle.

Under the leadership of Pop Warner, the Carlisle Indians were becoming established as the power to beat in collegiate athletics. They were formidable opponents in football, track, and, more recently, basketball. On the gridiron, they had shown well against all of the country's top teams, including the military academies. Carlisle was being described as on a par with the YMCA's Springfield College, the premier athletic school of the nation.

Even so, John was frustrated. He had been recruited to assist in training and conditioning a star Indian athlete. So far, he had never even met the young man, and no one seemed to know where he was. "He'll turn up" was becoming a well-worn excuse. There was a bittersweet amusement in the fact that in this case, the white coaches seemed unconcerned, as if they were the ones on "Indian time," while John Buffalo fidgeted and worried.

But there came a day . . .

John was hailed on the campus by Arthur Martin, secretary to the Athletic Department.

"John! Great news! They've found Jim Thorpe. He's on the way here."

"Great! Where is he?"

Now Martin was laughing. "In Oklahoma! Exendine ran into him on the street in Anadarko."

"What was he doing there? For that matter, what was Exendine doing there?"

"I don't know. Maybe looking for Thorpe. We knew he has family in that area. And Albert says Thorpe's in great shape. He was a little small when he was here before."

John's thinking took a strange direction for a moment. How was it that Albert Exendine, track coach and holder of many school records, happened to be in Anadarko, Oklahoma, at the right moment? It was not beyond belief that Pop Warner would intentionally hold someone out of competition until he had gained some size and maturity. And Thorpe had been described as small. But that was two years ago, it now appeared.

"Do we know anything about Jim Thorpe's eligibility?" he asked Martin.

"Well . . . he played football here for two seasons. . . . Mostly intramural the first year, I guess. But he should have two years of eligibility left. Unless, of course, he's been in college someplace else."

"Is that likely?" asked John.

Martin laughed. "Not a chance. If he competed in athletics, we'd know it, because he'd be winning."

Just the sort of scheme that would appeal to Pop Warner,

John guessed. Track-and-field athletes mature later than some. Why not farm out a potential winner until he gets some maturity and then send somebody to bring him back. . . .

THIRTY-FIVE

That is Jim Thorpe?" asked John. "I was led to think he was small."

"Well, he *was*," Mac admitted. "When he came to Carlisle, he was just a kid. The records in the office say he was five foot, five and one-half inches. He grew some, I guess, before he left. But that's a while back, too. Lord, he's filled out now! No wonder Exendine was impressed. Jim's probably six feet, and nearing 200 pounds, wouldn't you say?"

"Sure is . . . Like a steer just off summer pasture."

Again, the suspicion crossed his mind that the two years when Thorpe had been "missing" may have been a part of Pop Warner's long-range plan.

Thorpe's version was simple. He'd been at the Carlisle railroad station with a group of students waiting for transportation to their summer "outing" placements. He'd been scheduled to work at farming, for which he had no great fondness, and was approached by a couple of friends who were similarly disinclined. They said they had jobs in North Carolina, not connected with Carlisle's outing system. On a whim, Thorpe had decided to go along for the ride with Joseph Libby and Jesse Young Deer. At the summer's end, he'd gone back to spend the winter with family and friends in Oklahoma instead of returning to school. He'd helped around the farm of an aunt, but became restless as summer came on, and returned to North Carolina for the season. The part-time job there evaporated in midsummer of the second year, and he'd returned to Oklahoma, where he'd encountered Exendine.

The timing was fortunate, especially for Warner's 1911 football season. His 1910 season, eight wins and six losses, had been one of Warner's worst, lacking the skills of Jim Thorpe.

"But I thought Pop wanted him for track," John protested to Mac.

"He does," chuckled Mac. "But he *needs* him for football. It's okay. Jim likes football better than track, anyway. He can do both."

Jim proved to be a big, easygoing teddy bear of a man, with a friendly grin and a tolerant attitude. Except, of course, in competition. John studied Thorpe's running style on the football field, where he could observe unnoticed. He had been described as difficult to tackle, slippery, and unpredictable in his running. John expected to see a light-footed, shifty broken-field expert.

On the contrary, Thorpe seemed to simply run *over* opposing tacklers. His running style was with knees high, utilizing the length of his thighs. More than one opposing player who simply tried a clean, open-field tackle from the side was rewarded with a ride off the field on a stretcher. After such a collision, even an expert tackler became cautious.

Carlisle's 1911 football schedule was one of the toughest in its history. Despite the previous lackluster season, Carlisle was spotted as the team to beat. Thorpe did not yet have a prominent name, but the crowds and the sportswriters knew Stansil "Possum" Powell, Carlisle's great fullback. Also due to attract attention were Pop Warner's innovative techniques and trick plays, the "Warner system of modern football." Already, rules had been changed to prohibit some of Warner's shenanigans, such as the "hidden ball," shoved up the back of Charlie Dillon's jersey and removed by a teammate after he crossed the goal line.

More recently, Warner had developed extensive use of the "forward pass," created by high-school teams in the Midwest some years earlier.

But this season promised to be like no other. On their schedule were teams boasting no less than twenty-two allAmericans: Georgetown, Pittsburgh, Lafayette, Pennsylvania, Harvard, Syracuse, and Brown. And many of their other opponents were equally strong.

Their first game was against Lebanon Valley College on September 23. The Indians defeated Lebanon 53–0. Four days later, Muhlenburg College fell to Carlisle, 32–0.

The season continued. Highly rated Georgetown fell 28–5. A Washington newspaper began the sports stories of October 15:

Not since Custer made his last stand against Sitting Bull at the Little Big Horn has a battle between redskins and palefaces been so ferociously fought as that which was waged on Georgetown field yesterday afternoon when the chiefs from Carlisle savagely forced Georgetown's weak, though gallant cohorts to bite the dust 28–5.

One week later, Carlisle defeated a fine Pittsburgh team, 17–0.

Commenting in the *Pittsburgh Leader*, sportswriter Henry I. Miller noted:

To say that Thorpe is the whole team would be fifty percent wrong, but he certainly is the most consistent performer trotted out on the Forbes gridiron in many a moon . . . Thorpe carried the ball two of every three times for the visitors . . .

The *Pittsburgh Dispatch* concurred:

This person Thorpe was a host in himself. Tall and sinewy, as quick as a flash and as powerful as a turbine engine, he appeared to be impervious to injury.

The next contest was in Lafayette's home field at Easton. No opponent had crossed that goal line since 1908. The final score was Carlisle, 19–0. A disappointed Easton sportswriter commented:

The entire team seemed to be built around Thorpe, the redskins' big halfback. Thorpe was a bad man for the Lafayette tacklers to stop . . .

Penn . . . Jim Thorpe suited up, but was sidelined because of a badly sprained ankle in the Lafayette game. His teammates, now exuberant with the taste of victory, still defeated Penn, 16–0.

November 11, 1911, was the date scheduled for Carlisle to play Harvard, the defending national champions. A recognized powerhouse, Harvard's "Crimson" had allowed opponents to score only fourteen points in the previous six games. Coach P. D. Haughton had assembled a squad with depth at every position, comprising three complete units. By contrast, Carlisle's traveling squad consisted of only sixteen players.

Having missed the Pennsylvania game because of the injury inflicted at Lafayette, Thorpe was limping and heavily bandaged. Harvard had the home-field advantage, and more than 30,000 fans jammed the stadium, one of the greatest crowds in football history.

Haughton elected to play the game in an odd way: He started his *second* team, reputed to be as good as his first. Substitutions were from his *third* squad until the fourth quarter, when he would bring out his fresh first team against the tired and battered Indians.

Scoring was low, with both teams struggling against the defense of the other. Thorpe was unable to cross the Harvard goal line, but did kick four field goals with his bandaged leg: one in each quarter.

At the half, Harvard led, 9–6. Carlisle managed to put together a good third period, scoring a touchdown plus one of Thorpe's field goals from the thirty-seven-yard line. The quarter ended with the score 15–9 in favor of Carlisle.

At the start of the fourth quarter, the Harvard first unit ran onto the field. Only two players remained who had been in the game before: the quarterback and the right guard.

In this quarter Jim Thorpe kicked the longest field goal of the game, from forty-eight yards. The spectators reported that the ball soared higher than the uprights of the goalposts as it passed. Even Coach Warner stated that it would have been good from twenty yards farther out.

Harvard fought back, scoring another touchdown, but the game was over, won by the margin of Thorpe's 48-yard field goal.

Thorpe had done all of the kicking for the Indians, and had carried the ball on three out of five plays.

Shocked by the defeat of his elite squad, Coach Haughton could only state for the press, "I realized that here was the theoretical superplayer in flesh and blood."

Thorpe had an interesting comment on the game. He later told a reporter:

One of the men who bothered me most was the umpire. If you remember, he was clad in a red sweater and golf trousers that looked enough like moleskins to disturb anybody at a critical moment in play. I am sure that I dodged him at least a dozen times in my open-field runs. . . . I asked him to change the sweater several times, but he apparently forgot what I had said to him.

The Pennsylvania newspapers heralded the win with great glee:

CARLISLE GOES CRAZY, VICTORY OF TEAM WILDLY CELEBRATED BY STUDENTS

Headed by the famous Carlisle Indian band, the entire battalion of Indian boy students snake-danced through the principal streets of the city in weird contrast to the ostensible purpose of their procession, which was that of an escort to the recumbent figure of Crimson Harvard laid out on a stretcher borne by redskin bearers.

Their next game was against Syracuse, and Pop Warner confided to his assistants that he thought the team was becoming careless. He predicted a slump.

To make matters worse, it had rained all week, and the field at Syracuse had been described as a "sea of mud." This could become a major problem. The Indian athletes played for fun, and mud was no fun. This had become a factor a few years earlier, when one of Carlisle's opponents, aware of this idiosyncrasy of the Carlisle squad, watered their field with fire hoses for three days before the game. The Indian attitude was reflected by Little Boy, Carlisle's big center, when he stated flatly, "Football no good fun in mud or snow."

Syracuse won the game, 12–11, on the muddy field. This was the only loss for the season. Carlisle had scored 298 points to their opponents' 49, and the name of Jim Thorpe was now recognized everywhere.

John had spent a season of worry over Thorpe's health. The injury in the Lafayette game was of great concern. That ankle would need to be in top condition to even qualify for tryouts for the Olympiad. The mechanical stress of one play at a time was a far different matter from the prolonged pounding necessary in the hurdles and the distance events.

All of this did not seem to bother Thorpe. Many years later, biographer Robert Wheeler was to write:

> Christmas, 1911, found Jim, dressed as Santa Claus, passing out toys to the Indian children. When "Santa" was unmasked, he was serenaded, cheered as the "great All-American" and presented with an American Flag.

Thorpe's one regret for the season was that he blamed the one loss of the year, against Syracuse, on himself. He had missed the extra point that would have tied the game.

THIRTY-SIX

In later years, it was written that the 1912 spring track season at Carlisle provided merely a warmup for Jim Thorpe, leading to the Olympics in Stockholm. That, of course, was a deliberate understatement. There was a lot of training to do before that even became a possibility.

Thorpe limped off the field after their last 1911 football game with a heavily bandaged leg, but was training hard by January. It would be necessary to attend the Olympic try-outs at one of three regional sites: Stanford in California, Marshall Field in Chicago, or Harvard Stadium in Cambridge, Massachusetts. The athletes from Carlisle would compete at the nearest, the facility at Harvard.

First, however, they must prepare outdoors on the cinder track when the weather permitted. When it didn't, they ran laps in the gym and practiced the jumping events and hurdles.

There were four major track meets on the East Coast that spring, and Carlisle athletes competed in all. Thorpe did well in all, demonstrating his versatility and improving through the season.

At the Boston Athletic Association's meet, he claimed a gold medal in the 100-yard dash, a silver in hurdles, and bronzes in high jump and shot put.

Next at Pittsburgh, three gold medals: 12-pound shot, 60-yard hurdles, and 60-yard dash. John was impressed. Seldom does the same athlete win both the dash events and the heavy shot put.

At Middle Atlantic, three more gold medals: both 12- and 16-pound shot, as well as 75-yard dash, and a silver in the standing jumps.

In the Carnegie Meet, a short time later: gold medals in shot, high jump, and 220-yard hurdles. Silver in the broad jump and in 220 yard dash, and a bronze in the 100-yard dash.

Jim Thorpe's versatility would stand him in good stead in the variety of events in the decathlon.

Two athletes from Carlisle qualified for the Olympiad

at the Harvard tryouts. They were Jim Thorpe and Louis Tewanima.

On the morning of June 14, 1912, the United States Olympic team boarded the ship that would take them to Europe, from New York harbor. She was a Red Star Line steamer, the S.S. *Finland*, chartered by the American Olympic Committee, and carrying 164 athletes and their coaches and trainers.

Some of the athletes had a certain amount of anxiety over the ocean crossing. A few, of course, were already veteran world travelers; but to some, the ten-day crossing without a glimpse of land was a bit frightening. John could not forget that only a few weeks before, a huge ship—the largest and safest in the world, according to all reports—had sunk on her maiden voyage. There had been great loss of life, and for days, the newspapers had carried stories of tragedy, heroism, and miracles. Someone fortunate enough to have missed the ship as she sailed. . . . Someone else, who had not planned to be on the ship at all, but had boarded at the last moment. . . .

It was no comfort to know that only two months earlier, the *Titanic* had struck her fatal iceberg in the same general area as the route to be followed by the *Finland*.

Since athletes must train to stay in top form, they trained on shipboard. There were endless laps around the cork-covered deck for the runners, makeshift jumps, hurdles, and tennis courts—even a canvas tank in which the swimmers could exercise. Riflemen practiced on targets towed behind the ship.

For some events, it was virtually impossible to practice:

shot put, javelin, hammer throw, and discus. (Despite this, the United States team won three gold medals in shot put and hammer throw.)

A legend arose later that Thorpe had refused to train on shipboard because he "didn't need to." Several other athletes, however, recalled challenge sprints with Thorpe. There are, in fact, photographs of Jim running laps on the deck of the *Finland*, wearing his military cadet's uniform.

There would be no loafing on the *Finland*. Mike Murphy, trainer for the United States track team, would not have permitted it. Besides, the Carlisle athletes had Pop Warner to keep them alert and moving.

When they docked at Antwerp, Belgium, there was a three-day layover to regain their equilibrium before starting on to Stockholm, another four days on shipboard. This time, by order of the coaches and Mike Murphy, the head trainer, there would be no strenuous training until the games themselves began.

On July 6, 1912, teams from twenty-eight nations entered the new stadium at Stockholm, erected for this occasion and financed by a national lottery. A crowd of 30,000 packed and overflowed the stands. The athletes marched through the mighty arch and around the track, thrilling to the sound of a 4,000-voice chorus singing "A Mighty Fortress Is Our God."

They passed the royal box, where King Gustav, Crown Prince Gustav Adolphus, and Grand Duke Dimitri of Russia were seated. The athletes saluted as they passed, with hats over their hearts.

There were speeches of welcome and presentations, and finally His Majesty the King formally opened the games. The crowd burst into a roar and quieted again.

Then the events were called by the clerk of the course: "All out for the hundred!"
The Fifth Olympiad had begun.

All of this was nearly overwhelming for John. He had seen many crowds and many shows, but never anything to compare with this. His blood raced, and he longed to be competing. There had been a time when . . . No, he probably could never developed the skills to compete in such a tournament. It was enough of a wonder to be here at all. . . . Still, there was a pang of regret over what might have been.

It recalled to him his lost love, Miss Jane Langtry, and what else might have been. He hadn't thought of her for a long time. He wondered what the world had brought her.

This, in turn, brought his thoughts back to Hebbie. He had missed her terribly, but not until this moment did he realize how much. He wanted to share *this* with her. . . . But his feelings assured him of one thing: He would ask her to marry him the very next time he laid eyes on her.

The first events for Carlisle's Jim Thorpe would be the following day; the pentathlon was a new event, a mix of five unrelated efforts. The Scandinavians were expected to dominate, with their lead competitor a big Swede, Hugo Wieslander, already famous in worldwide competition.

The five events were running broad jump, javelin, 200-meter dash, discus, and 1500-meter race.

In the broad jump, Norway's Ferdinand Bie, with a jump of 22 feet, 5.7 inches, established the tone of the competition. No one had approached this distance until Thorpe, the unknown American, stepped to the line.

John held his breath. He knew that Thorpe, like the other Indian athletes, cared nothing about setting a record of any kind. The goal was to beat the other competitors. It was a major advantage to compete late in the event, when the spectators had virtually declared Bie the winner.

Thorpe's tremendous speed and the strength in his legs would stand him in good stead here. His momentum would gain distance. He soared—there is no other word—the winning distance of 23 feet, 2.7 inches, nearly a foot beyond his nearest rival.

The next event, the javelin, was virtually conceded to Sweden's Wieslander. This was the Third Olympiad to offer the javelin throw, and since 1906 it had been dominated by the Swedes. It was a bitter disappointment to the American team. Thorpe's throw of more than 153 feet was beaten by nearly 10 feet; Wieslander's javelin sailed to 162 feet, 7.30 inches.

This defeat and determination on the part of the Americans created a spectacular finish to the next event, the 200-meter dash. It was described later as "the most thrilling race of the entire games." Jim Thorpe's winning time was 22.9 seconds. Two other Americans, Donahue and Menaul, finished in a dead heat at 23 seconds flat. Two Canadians finished fourth and fifth, with 23.2 and 23.5 seconds.

The discus, one of Thorpe's best events, brought another first, with a throw of 116 feet, 8.4 inches. His teammate, Avery Brundage, placed second for the Americans, and other efforts "were not even close," John wrote to Hebbie.

The last event of the pentathlon was the 1500-meter race. It was deliberately chosen to demonstrate versatility. It may not be the same athlete who lifts the weights and throws the hammer who can stand the pounding run at distances such as this. John realized that this mix was much like comparing the skills of a racehorse to the pulling power of a heavy draft horse. A horse which could do both jobs would be rare indeed. But here, it would be expected from human athletes: throwing, sprinting, and, in addition, the prolonged stamina of a distance run. He gave silent thanks for the manner in which the runners had trained at Carlisle. Let somebody else set the pace. Maybe, running behind the leaders, then passing as the leader tires . . .

The 1500-meter run would consist of four laps around the cinder track. Thorpe's position was next to the outside lane, a poor position when it came to a challenge. As the gun sounded, he seemed to slip on the blocks, and was well back in the pack as Brundage and Bie charged into the lead. The pace was fast on the first lap, which pleased John. It pleased him, too, that Jim did not seem to be concerned, but settled in behind the leaders, following the strategy they had practiced. He made his move during the second lap. . . . *Not too early, Jim.* . . . Brundage had fallen back and Bie, the Canadian, was alone in the lead. During the third lap, Thorpe drew even. At the start of the fourth circuit it appeared that Jim Thorpe had just begun to see this as a contest. He now began to really pour on the effort, drawing well ahead of the pack.

They crossed the finish line with Thorpe several strides ahead of the nearest competitors. Two American teammates finished second and third, and a totally exhausted Bie was forced to settle for sixth place. The crowd went wild!

Now for the accounting. . . . In the pentathlon, one point was awarded for a win, two for second place, three for third, a low score being the goal. Jim Thorpe, with a score of 7, had the advantage of 15 points over the nearest competitor, Ferdinand Bie, the Canadian, at 21. Other scores were 29, 29, 30, 31, and 32.

The Scandinavians had been expected to sweep the event, but it had been dominated by Americans and Canadians. James E. Sullivan, America's commissioner to the Olympics, commented that this ". . . answers the allegation that most of our runners are of foreign parentage, for Thorpe is a *real* American, if there ever was one."

His record was to stand, for generations yet unborn.

But now it was time to prepare for the grueling three-day decathlon, to begin the following Saturday.

This time there would be ten events:

> First day: 100-yard dash
> Running broad jump
> Shot put
>
> Second day: Running high jump
> 400-meter run
> 110-meter hurdles
>
> Third day: Discus
> Pole vault
> Javelin
> 1500-meter race

Saturday dawned dark, gloomy, and overcast. Attendance had fallen off because of the threat of rain. It was necessary that the athletes compete rain or shine, because of the tightly scheduled Olympiad. Other events must be followed on schedule.

John was greatly concerned about the effect of the weather on Jim Thorpe, with the Indian athlete's natural aversion to contests in the rain: "No fun . . ."

Possibly even greater was the effect of the situation on Pop Warner, who muttered and paced and worried.

With justified concern, as it turned out. Shortly before the start of the games, the heavens opened and it began to pour.

THIRTY-SEVEN

The decathlon . . . Day one . . .

As was to be expected with the onset of rain, Thorpe got off to a bad start. In the first event, the 100-yard dash, he was nosed out by one of his own teammates, E. L. R. Mercer, a specialist at the sprint. This was not unexpected.

In the next event, the running broad jump, the rain really began to cause problems. The takeoff board was slippery, and many of the contestants were scored with faults. Thorpe was faulted twice, and on the third try jumped a qualifying distance of 22 feet, 2.3 inches. It was not good enough. Lomberg, of Sweden, bested Jim's jump by 4.4 inches.

Thorpe was discouraged. He was not accustomed to losing. If he could not do better in the shot put, he might as well forget the decathlon. He was wet and miserable, and it was hard to see any fun in competing in the continuing drizzle.

"Come on, Jim," suggested John. "Let's get you into some dry warmups before the shot put."

By the time the clerk called, "All out for the shot put," Thorpe's attitude had improved. Still, he knew that he must do well in this event. He put the 16-pound shot 42 feet, 5 and $\frac{9}{20}$ inches, scoring first place and beating Wieslander's toss by 2½ feet.

He was exuberant in the locker room. Pop Warner, soaking wet but happy, laughed at Thorpe's explanation.

"Maybe it was the dry uniform that helped me win."

Maybe it was.

Day two . . .

High jump, another first with a jump of 6 feet, 1.6 inches. The clear and balmy weather undoubtedly helped.

The 400-meter run saw Mercer, the sprint specialist, winning over Thorpe with a time of 43.3 seconds, compared to Thorpe's 45.3.

In the next event, however, the 110-meter hurdles was a specialty of Thorpe's, if he could be said to have one. His time in the Olympiad, 15.6 seconds, established a record that would stand for thirty-six years, when it was to fall by a mere tenth of a second.

The crowd was beginning to recognize and to cheer Thorpe.

Decathlon events are scored against a standard, with a maximum 1,000 points per event, a possible total of 10,000 points. An athlete breaking or equaling the standing record receives 1,000, with points deducted for lesser scores. At the finish of the second day, even with performances that disappointed Thorpe, he had totaled 5,302.87 points. Mercer, the sprinter, with spectacular wins, had accumulated 4,752.20. Lomberg of Sweden ranked third, with 4,664.39.

Day three . . .

The first three of the four competitions would be field events: discus, pole vault, and javelin. These were specialties of the great Wieslander, and events which Thorpe did not consider his best. Despite this, he managed to score one second place and two thirds, coming in closely enough to the leaders to accumulate more total points.

The last event of the games, just before the award ceremonies, would be the 1500-meter race. His performance in the same event in the pentathlon had been so spectacular that the crowd had picked him as their favorite. It had been a grueling week, and it was anticipated that he would likely be slowing from exhaustion. Instead, Thorpe bettered his own time in the previous 1500-meter run, by more than four seconds: 4 minutes, 40.1 seconds.

Thorpe's final point score in the decathlon was 8,412.955 out of 10,000, 688 points ahead of the runner-up, Sweden's Wieslander, with 7,724.495. Five other athletes were bunched in the 7,000 range, including Americans Donahue and Mercer.

These were the last events of the Olympiad, and the presentation of honors that afternoon was carried out by King Gustav. The *New York Times* reported:

> When James Thorpe, the Carlisle Indian and finest all-around athlete in the world, appeared to claim the prizes for winning the pentathlon, there was a great burst of cheers, led by the King. The immense crowd cheered itself hoarse.

King Gustav regained his dignity and presented the laurel wreath and gold medal. He also presented a life-size bronze bust of himself to Jim Thorpe.

Later, the ceremony was repeated for the decathlon: the wreath and medal, as well as a silver chalice studded with jewels, in the shape of a Viking ship, a gift from the Czar of Russia.

The King himself appeared nearly overcome with emotion. Breaking tradition, he extended a handshake.

"Sir, you are the greatest athlete in the world!" he pronounced.

Jim Thorpe's response, equally emotional but humble and barely audible, was typical:

"Thanks, King."

He was to state later that it was the proudest moment of his life.

Americans had dominated the 1912 Olympiad. As an extra honor for the Indians of Carlisle, Louis Tewanima won the silver medal in the 10,000-meter marathon.

The Americans decided to take advantage of the publicity that had been generated by Thorpe's spectacular showing.

"John," said Pop Warner, "I've booked a couple of exhibition meets for Jim. You want to stay over with us, or go back on the *Finland?*"

"Hadn't thought about it, sir. What's Tewanima going to do?"

"Louis will stay with us. He'll compete in the exhibitions, too. He's really enjoying all this, I think."

"Aren't we all, Pop?"

They chuckled together.

"Yes," John went on. "It's hard to let go of the excitement. I'll stay with you. How long?"

"Couple of weeks ... I'm working on the schedule. Everybody in Europe wants to see Jim run, I guess."

Thorpe was unable to accept all the invitations: to compete, to meet dignitaries, even to dinner. There were simply too many. The party from Carlisle was entertained like royalty. They saw some beautiful country, tasted fine wine and unfamiliar foods with exotic flavors, met dignitaries and, in general, had an all-around good time.

It was pleasant to bask in the reflected honor that was bestowed on Jim Thorpe. It was not unlike traveling with the 101 Wild West Show, and seeing the awe in the eyes of children as they gazed at the colorful performers, the animals, and the assorted equipment. Only this time it was more personal, and it was even better. He wished that Hebbie could be here to share these experiences with him. That was the fly in the ointment, the slight twinge of guilt that he felt as he saw and experienced Europe at its best.

Even to an experienced traveler like John, who had traveled the show circuit, transportation in Europe was an amazing phenomenon. He was quite familiar with trains, their major mode of travel with the 101. The ranch owned its own rolling stock and many miles of track.

In the past few years, too, there had been a proliferation of automobiles, powered by a variety of energy sources: steam, coal oil, or gasoline in the new internal-combustion engines; even electricity. That was an amazing thing to John: a battery of glass jars filled with acid, which occupied the covered rear deck of the automobile, much like the baggage boot of a stagecoach. These were connected by wires or cables to each other and to the engine, an electric motor which produced the rotation of the rear wheels. One major advantage of this electric carriage was its complete silence, compared to the noisy clatter, smell, and smoke of the steam and gasoline autos. They often frightened women and children, and caused stampedes by runaway horses. John had seen towns where automobiles were forbidden by city ordinance. In the major cities, of course, they were becoming more and more commonplace. Their stop in New York before boarding the ship for Stockholm had shown that. There was a noticeable increase in the number of automobiles in just the two years since Bill Pickett had counted their numbers on the 101 "gang's" excursion to Coney Island.

Aeroplanes, too . . . John had seen several in the past two years. The Wright brothers had opened a virtual Pandora's box with their flights only a few years ago. There had even been a flier, a friend of the Millers, who had landed at the 101 Ranch last year.

John doubted that the flimsy-looking things, made of sticks and piano wire and covered with canvas, would ever be practical. Interesting, though.

Here in Europe, there was a greater density of population. Not only more people, but more trains, automobiles, and aeroplanes. Everybody seemed to be going somewhere.

However, John was completely unprepared for the sight that occurred one afternoon while they were attending one of the exhibition contests. He realized that people around him were looking up at the sky, and beginning to chatter in their own tongue. Just as he was about to look up, Tewanima grabbed his arm and pointed, talking rapidly in Hopi.

There in the sky overhead was a huge silver cigar-shaped craft. It was hard to judge its size, but John estimated that it must be as long as a football field. There seemed to be engine noise from it, though it was hard to tell over the noise of the crowd at the track meet. A compartment with windows much like a Pullman car hung below it, and he thought he could see people looking out the windows.

"What the hell is *that?*" John exclaimed in wonder.

"An airship of some kind?" suggested Pop Warner.

"You've seen them before?" John asked.

"No . . . read about 'em. Let's ask Sven, here."

They turned to the young man who had been assigned as their interpreter.

"Airship? Yes . . . *'Zeppelin.'* There is regular service in Germany. Some flights to here, sometimes to Paris."

"What means *'Zeppelin'?*" John asked.

"A man's name. He made it. How do you say . . . ?" pondered the interpreter.

"Invented it?"

"Yes. That is it. Invented."

The great silver ship sailed smoothly overhead and on

into the distance, and John had a strange feeling that the world he knew would soon be obsolete.

Only now did he understand fully the urgency that the Millers felt to preserve their heritage, that of the American West. In this rush to modernization, everything familiar was slipping away, and quite rapidly.

THIRTY-EIGHT

The noon Cumberland Valley train drew to a stop at Carlisle, Pennsylvania, on Friday, August 16, 1912, brakes squealing and her venting steam chest hissing. A cheering crowd of 15,000 greeted the travelers as they stepped down to the platform. There were students and townspeople and dignitaries, and banners proclaiming "Hail to Chief Thorpe," "A Carlisle Indian," and other slogans. The band was playing.

There were speeches of congratulation, led by Superintendent Friedman of the Carlisle Indian School.

"This is an occasion for congratulation. It is a national occasion. The things we celebrate here and the heroes we welcome to Carlisle concern the whole country. . . . We have here real Americans, known as Indians, but whose forefathers were on the reception committee which welcomed to this soil the famed first settlers who arrived on the *Mayflower*.

"We welcome you, James Thorpe, to this town and back to your school. You have covered yourself with glory. . . ."

The speeches went on for some time, and the excitement lingered even longer. It was a good day.

"But, John, I don't see why you couldn't stay. Admittedly, it's not a high-pay coaching job, which you'd certainly be qualified for. But, it could lead to something better. Give it time, son. We're about to start football season. Thorpe has another year of eligibility. So does Tewanima. You work well with both."

"I'm honored, sir," John told Pop Warner, "but . . . Well, I made a commitment."

"Where will you go?"

"Oklahoma . . . the Hundred and One."

"More cowboyin'? . . . Wait! There must be a girl. . . . Ah! Of course! That would be it," laughed the coach. "Well, you can always tell a man in love, I've heard, but you can't tell him much."

John was blushing scarlet, even though he knew that Warner was sympathetic to his plight. But he had made up his mind.

"Thanks, Coach," he said, "but I really do need to get back there. Hope you have a good football season."

Carlisle did have a good football season, though not a perfect one. In fourteen games, their record for the 1912 season was 12–1–1. They scored a total of 504 points to 114 by their opponents.

Kyle Chrichton, who witnessed the Lehigh game, where Lehigh was heavily favored, later wrote his impressions:

The Indians were the first team I ever saw that disdained dressing-room rites between halves. . . . They simply wandered off to a side of the field when the half ended and had a hilarious time among themselves until the whistle blew. Anybody who thinks the Indians are a solemn race is nuts. Do you know how they called signals in that game? They'd line up and then Old Jim would yell "How about through left tackle this time?" and off they'd go, right through that spot. Next time Jim would yell "Right end, huh?" and away they'd go again. After the first few times, Lehigh realized they weren't kidding and rushed all their defenses to the spot, but it never did any good. They'd pick up three or four or five yards at a clip, and then Jim would break off for a real good gain. And if they got stopped with that monkey business, they'd run sequence plays, three or four quick plays, without a signal. There'd be a wide sweep to the left, line up quick, bang; to the left again. Before Lehigh woke up, the Indians had another 30 yards and were chuckling among themselves.

West Point was probably the toughest foe the Indians met that season. Gus Welch, the quarterback, recalled:

Pop Warner had no trouble getting the boys up for the game. He reminded the boys that it was the fathers and grandfathers of these Army players who fought the Indians. That was enough.

One of the Army athletes, who played right halfback, commented years later:

Except for [Thorpe], Carlisle would have been an easy team to beat. On the football field, there was no one like him in the world. Against us, he dominated all of the actions.

The halfback's name was Dwight Eisenhower.

When John stepped off the train at Bliss, Oklahoma, Hebbie was there to meet him. With a mixture of laughter and tears, she flew into his arms. . . .

"Oh, Hebbie!" he moaned in ecstasy.

He woke with a start. He'd fallen asleep in the seat of the railway coach, and was dreaming. Embarrassed, he took a quick look up and down the aisle of the rocking car, wondering if he'd really spoken aloud.

Some of the other passengers were drowsing, too. It was hot and dusty. It might have been worse except for the hot breeze generated through the open windows by the train's motion. A plump middle-aged woman across the aisle was smiling coquettishly at him. He *must* have said something aloud. Either that, or she was trying to establish a connection. Maybe both. He couldn't remember what he might have said in his dream, and had no idea whether anyone had heard him. It was a very uncomfortable situation.

The train slowed. Probably time to take on water. Maybe also a thirty-minute stop for dinner at one of the fine Harvey House restaurants along the rail system. He hoped so. It would help to be able to get out and walk around a bit. But he saw the frequent mandatory stops with a certain amount of impatience. He longed to be back on the 101 with Hebbie.

There was also the fact that he had not heard from her for some time. He had been traveling, of course, and Hebbie would know that his mail could not be forwarded. However, he had expected that there would be mail held for him at Carlisle. He was uneasy when there was nothing. Several weeks had passed while he was in Europe. Surely, she would have at least had a letter waiting for him. Deep in the back of his mind was an uneasy doubt. He had been away a long time. . . .

———

When he did actually step from the train onto the platform at Bliss, he hoped against hope that she would be there to greet him. He *had* written her to tell her approximately when he'd arrive. Actually, it would be a slim chance that she would guess which train would carry him back to Oklahoma. Still, it was a disappointment—

"John? John Buffalo?" called a voice. But it was a male voice.

He turned.

"Gus!"

A team and wagon stood at the loading dock, and the driver was stacking boxes from the platform into the wagon bed. On the side of the wagon was the ever-present logo: 101.

"Didn't know you were comin' back today," Gus said cheerfully. "Want a ride out to the ranch?"

"Sure. Thanks, Gus. Can I help you load?"

"About done, now. Reckon your timing's as good as ever. You got more baggage?"

"No, this is it," John said.

The cowboy set the last box in the wagon bed, and the two men took their places on the seat. Gus clucked to the team and the horses leaned into their collars for the hour's drive to the ranch.

"Well," said Gus, "we heard all about the Olympics and Jim Thorpe. That must have been some show."

"It sure was, Gus. Sometimes I can hardly believe it, even now. How are things on the Hundred an' One?"

"Busy! The show's still on the road, of course. But, damnation, John . . . Let's see . . . You've been gone a year, right?"

"Nearer two."

"Oh! Well, there *is* a lot, then. You mind that some of the show folks were headin' for warmer winters . . . South America, even? Well, Joe Miller got the idea of winterin' in California. Cheaper and a sight easier than here. Joe even bought a house there, moved his family."

"*Left* the 101?"

"Not really. They live *both* places, go back and forth with the seasons. But, John, you'd never have expected . . . There are other outfits—show outfits—winterin' there. Al G. Barnes's Circus, an' the "Two Bills" Wild West . . . Buffalo Bill and Pawnee Bill, y'know."

"They merged?"

"Yep! Never figgered that, would you? They're all in sort of the same area. Town called Venice. But say! You remember them movin'-picture folks . . . Bill Selig an' them? Well, a bunch of them are out there. I guess the weather's mild enough they can shoot pictures damn' near all winter. A bunch of our gang are out there, doin' that. Tom Mix . . . Say, you know what a talker an' show-off he allus was? Well, he shore found his place, with the picture folks. Some of our others, too. Hoot Gibson, Hoxie . . ."

"They all quit the 101?"

"Well, not necessarily. More like the 101 joined *them*. The Millers, especially Joe, travelin' back an' forth, are really into the movin'-picture thing. Partnerin' in some of the picture work. Now, you see them new log cabins over southwest, there?"

Gus pointed to some structures in the distance.

"Yep . . . What are *those?*"

"Just that. Cabins. The movin'-picture business was goin' on here in the summer an' in California in the winter. But some of them city folks get a little upset at scorpions an' rattlers comin' in their tents. So the Millers built them cabins. Use 'em for scenery, too, for shootin' the movin' pictures. 'Movies,' they call 'em now, y'know."

"You been to California, Gus?"

"Sure. A couple of times. We took a whole herd of buffalo, some longhorns, and about thirty of the Indian families and their lodges out there last year, on contract to one of them movie outfits. Horses too, of course."

The talkative cowboy was in his element. John longed to ask him about Hebbie, but Gus was too busy in his enthusiasm about the new directions the 101 empire was taking.

" . . . and say! You know about the Tournament of Roses?"

"What's that?"

"Well, one of them California towns—Pasadena, I think it's called—has this big parade, celebratin' that they can grow flowers in the wintertime. They end it up with a big chariot race. Have it on New Year's Day. . . . Well, you know how Joe feels about parades. We took damn' near the whole outfit last time, while you were gone. 'Course, half the show was already there. But remember Lillie Francis? Great-lookin' cowgirl! Well, Mel Saunders, the Roman-rider, and ol' Oscar Rixson, the bronc tamer, was both courtin' her. They all agreed that she'd marry the winner of a horse race they'd have at the Roses thing. Turned out to be a bigger drawin' card than the chariot race!"

"Who won?"

"Mel did. He's the better horseman, I reckon. But say, what a party we had! They was married next day, and we partied till we put 'em on the train back to the 101 for the honeymoon."

Gus paused, lost in thought.

"Let's see, now. . . . George Miller bought a new kind of car—Cadillac, they call it. Always the latest, y'know. Say, you heard about the fire on the show train? Up in Wisconsin . . . One of the canvas cars caught fire. They stopped near a crick, an' ol' Beasley—used to be Princess Wenona's husband, you 'member, he got a bucket brigade goin'. . . . Saved the train, I reckon. But a few days after, they had a wreck. Derailed five cars, killed some of the horses. Had to put some more down, they was hurt so bad.

An' at night, in a storm, with lightnin' around 'em . . . pourin' rain. Purty tough summer, eh? Joe took it purty hard. You know how he is about the livestock. Has a real affection for 'em, hates to see 'em hurt. . . .

"Oh, yeah! Talk about a scandal . . . Zack's wife, Mabel, ran off. Zack had a detective agency lookin' for her, wantin' to serve divorce papers on her. . . . They found her in Tulsa, we heard, with some fella."

Thoughts of Hebbie were floating through John's mind as Gus recounted the details. Finally he had to ask.

"How's Hebbie doin', Gus? I haven't heard from her in some time."

Gus was silent for a little while, and finally spoke in a solemn voice.

"I'm sorry, John. I supposed you knew. She ain't at the 101."

"She's *not?* What . . . Where is she?"

"Well, she got sick. Phthisis, or consumption, or whatever they call it. She was coughin' a lot. The doctor sent her to one of them sani—Whatever they call 'em, the hospital where folks go with that coughin'."

"A sanatorium?"

"Yep, that's it! A 'TB san,' they called it."

"*When,* Gus?"

"Well, must have been in July, as I recall . . . Place out of state somewhere. She didn't write you about it?"

"I've been travelin', Gus."

"What . . . Oh, sure. The Olympics . . ."

"Yes, and then we traveled to some exhibition meets. Lord, I didn't know. . . . I'd have come back, Gus, if I'd had any idea."

"I know you would, John. I'm sorry."

THIRTY-NINE

The letters, two of them, were waiting in the mail room at the ranch, forwarded from Carlisle. By the dates on the cancellations, both had been sent on *before* he had returned from Europe. He sought a place to be alone. . . . Behind the horse barns, where they had often met. He tore open the envelopes.

My dear John,

By the time you read this, it will be after the Olympics. How I hope for the Americans to do well. They will, with you helping them, and we'll read about it here. News travels so fast now.

Things have been good here, though I miss you. Strawberry had her baby, a fine stud colt. He's sort of mouse colored, what the Mexicans call *grulla,* but I think he'll shed off as a blue roan.

I've had a cough for some time, and will go see a doctor in Ponca tomorrow. I'll mail this then. I miss you a lot, John, and I'll be glad when we can be together again.

All my love always,
Hebbie

He tore open the other envelope, which was dated in late July.

My dear John,

Forgive me for not writing sooner. I was waiting

for the doctor's decisions. He was concerned about my cough, and gave me some medicine, which smelled pretty bad and tasted worse. It didn't do much good. He said I have what we used to call consumption, and they call it tuber-something now. "T.B. . . ."

Some folks go to Arizona or someplace for this, but the doctor says they have special hospitals for it now. Some even get well. But, I wouldn't want you to catch this from me, so good-bye.

I will love you forever, John. Don't try to come to me. If I get well I'll look you up. Good-bye, John.

All my love,
Hebbie

He sat numbly, sitting on the ground with his back against the barn wall. A dung beetle a few feet away was rolling the ball containing her eggs toward wherever she'd bury it. The burden was three times her size, maybe as big as the laggin' taw marbles he'd seen kids play with. He'd never understood how such a creature could handle such a weight. But it was nothing compared to the weight that now fell on *his* heart.

In the ranch office in the White House, Joe Miller was sympathetic.

"Yes, I heard about that, John. Too bad, to come home to such a thing from such a triumph as yours. She's a good woman, too."

"I've got to find her, Mr. Miller."

"Of course. Let's see . . . Surely we've got some connections with information like this. Let me send a couple of wires . . . You'll want to take a train, I suppose. A horse would be pretty slow."

"I hadn't thought—"

"You need an advance on your pay?"

"No, sir. I still have a little from my Carlisle job."

Miller nodded. "Good. But maybe we should advance a little, just in case. Now . . . Come back tomorrow afternoon, and we'll see what's turned up. Be ready to travel."

Joe Miller was true to his word. John had always been amazed at the "connections" the Millers enjoyed. They challenged the world with a confidence that they could do anything, and usually did.

But not this time. Miller rose from his chair behind the desk as John entered the office. There was a frustrated look on his face as he motioned to John to shut the door. Then he pointed to a chair and seated himself again.

"John," he began, "we're hitting a dead end, here."

John's heart sank, as he found his seat, and Miller continued.

"Hebbie . . . I understand that's short for Hepzibah?"

"That's what I was told, sir."

"Gawd! Who'd name a defenseless baby somethin' like that?"

"She said it's a Bible name."

"That's no excuse. But let's go on. There are several states beginning to open these sanatoriums to treat this T.B. I understand it's quite a problem. I'd heard there was one in Kansas, but I find it's not even open yet. Several others . . . But, I can't find a trace of anyone with the name of Hebbie Schmidt. Hepzibah, either."

"She may be using another name," John said numbly.

"You know of one she'd use?"

"No, sir. But she'd change both names if she wanted to disappear. There are a lot of Schmidts, but as you said, Hepzibah or Hebbie would be one folks would remember."

"Yes . . ." Miller hesitated a moment. "We have to consider the possibility that she may be dead, John."

"Yes, I know," John said quietly, his voice husky.

"But," Joe Miller went on, "none of the sanatoriums we contacted had any such record. She's just disappeared."

John nodded sadly. "She just doesn't want to be found, sir. If she's in one of those places, it's under another name. She may have changed her name anyway. One thing's sure: She's gonna do it her way. She's tryin' to save me the pain of takin' care of her."

"I'm sorry, John. If you can think of anything we can do . . ."

John took a deep breath.

"No, sir. I reckon not. If she don't want to be found, we're not goin' to find her. She's smart, and she'll cover her tracks."

To himself, he held one more thought. Her letter—the second one—stated plainly that if she did survive, *"I'll look you up. . . ."* *She* wanted to call the shots, and she would.

But . . . If she wanted to find him, he'd need to be available. Where would she look first? Here, on the Hundred and One.

As if in answer to this unspoken thought, Joe Miller spoke again.

"You'll stay with us?"

"Yes, sir . . . I appreciate your help."

"Sorry we can't do more, John. We'll keep some feelers out."

"Thanks, Mr. Miller."

"Glad you're staying. We've got a bunch of two-year-old colts that will need some attention. Keep your mind off things, maybe."

"Maybe so."

But he knew it wouldn't help much. However, it would give him a lot of time to think, and remember some of the best years of his life so far, which had been here on the 101.

With Hebbie . . .

FORTY

Preparations for the 1913 show season were in progress during the winter. The success of the past two seasons had been inspiring to the already-enthusiastic Millers and Edward Arlington, their less-conspicuous partner.

John was astonished at the change in equipment, facilities, and in organization in the short time he had been gone. The show train now consisted of twenty-eight railway cars, brightly painted and exciting to view. There were eight stock cars for the horses, cattle, and a few buffalo, and fourteen flat cars to carry the extensive equipment, canvas, electric generators for lighting; all the accouterments of the circuslike show. The remaining six cars were for the personnel: Pullman sleepers, which would be their homes for the next six months, beginning in early April.

It was good to remain busy, but it did not help entirely. John would waken in the night and find it impossible to return to sleep, thinking of Hebbie, not knowing whether she was alive or dead. Sometimes he thought of going to look for her, visiting some of the sanatoriums to try to find her, but he always realized the futility. Besides, he was certain that if and when she recovered, Hebbie would come to *him*. She had promised. The first place she would look, of course, would be the 101. Even if he was on the road with the show, this would be her contact. He could see no other way.

He threw himself into the work of taming and training the range-bred colts, readying them for use. An operation the size of the Hundred and One, including all of its far-flung enterprises on the West Coast, required hundreds of horses, not to mention the turnover in cattle . . . Roping calves, steers for wrestling, longhorns for the simulated cattle drives, beef to feed the small army of cowboys, Indians, and headliners.

Near the corrals where John was working, Bill Pickett, who never seemed to change in a changing world, worked with horses and steers as he had for years.

Bill said little, but his word carried a lot of meaning.

"Good to have you back home, John."

"Thanks, Bill."

"They's a lot of new folks," Pickett went on.

John had noticed that. With the nationwide publicity, the moves and the extensive train travel of the 101 Wild West Show, it seemed that everybody in the country wanted to be a cowboy . . . Or cowgirl. There must be kids everywhere who were pretending to be Tom Mix, Buck Jones, or Princess Wenona. As they became old enough, a lot of them were making their way to the 101 Ranch to seek employment. This year there were far more than usual.

There were, of course, many who were legitimate cowboys. Some were good, hardworking young men, down on their luck, looking for a steady job. A few were of questionable morality, possibly even on the run from a misunderstanding with the law. The Millers asked few questions. A man who did his work well and was loyal to the Hundred and One was accepted.

A young man was assigned to help John with the two-year-olds. John was not very enthusiastic about it. His work, like that of Pickett and some of the other specialists, was best done alone. But, after the first few hours of gentling, it would take a lot of hours of easy riding to complete the animal's education. As Pickett put it, "a poultice of wet saddle blankets applied daily." Wet, of course, translated to sweaty. A light workout, every day, a few miles under saddle, to finish the animal's training after the preliminary gentling and breaking.

The young man, who called himself "Ed," was from back east somewhere, Illinois or Indiana. He appeared to have little experience with horses, but seemed ambitious.

" 'At's okay," chuckled Pickett. "You kin start 'em out together, train both hoss an' rider."

"That ain't funny, Bill," John observed.

Still, the results seemed acceptable. A day or two of John's "medicine," then a few hours of riding, before he turned the animals over to young Ed. The process was producing some pretty good mounts.

However, there came a day when the deep-seated warnings in the farthest corners of John's subconscious mind began to ring true. The young man had ridden off on one of the green-broke horses and had not yet returned at noon for dinner. This fact almost escaped John's notice. The mess hall was big and always crowded, a lot of people coming and going. Maybe he'd missed Ed in the crowd. But he ought to be sure. . . .

At the corral, he couldn't find the saddle that the young man used. He asked a couple of cowboys working nearby, with no results.

"I seen him ride off," Bill Pickett verified. "Headin' north, like most every day. He was ridin' that dun gelding, about fifteen hands tall, dark mane an' tail, star an' snip on his face, white front foot. . . . Good horse . . ."

Trust a horseman to remember the details of the markings of any horse he saw.

"That's the one," agreed John.

"He ain't back yet? Missed dinner?"

"Guess so."

"Mebbe he's in trouble," Pickett suggested.

"He better be, Bill, 'cause if he ain't, he's gonna be."

"You think he be stealin' that hoss, John?"

Pickett was concerned, but mildly amused by the situation.

"I dunno. But, I figger I better let George know, either way."

"Mr. Miller, that fella we had helpin' with the green-broke colts turned up missin'."

"When was this, John?"

George Miller rocked back in the chair behind the big desk, a look of concern on his face, along with a bit of a question.

"This morning, sir. He didn't show up for dinner. He may be in trouble."

"Did anybody go look for him?"

"I rode out a couple of miles, where he usually goes. No sign of him."

"Any tracks?"

"Sure. Lots of 'em, this close to the ranch. I couldn't tell."

"Of course."

"The saddle's missing, that we use on the green-broke colts. But he could have had an accident, Mr. Miller."

Miller nodded. "Be best if he did. Okay, you go look for him. Take somebody if you want to. But come back tonight. I don't want you out with no supplies. Let me know when you get home."

It was dark when John returned and put Strawberry in the stall, with a reward of oats in the feed bunk before her. He made his way to the White House.

"He's gone, Mr. Miller. I found his tracks, followed him maybe four, five miles. Horse was workin' well, headin' straight north."

"Why, that son of a bitch! Took him in an' tried to help

him. Well, okay . . . I'll send somebody into town tomorrow, have the sheriff wire ahead. We'll offer a reward for this horse-stealin' bastard. Good horse, you say?"

"Purty good, sir. One of the best of that bunch."

"Damn! Prob'ly worth a hundred, or more?"

"Yes, sir. More'n that. And the saddle, too. It wasn't much, but worth mebbe thirty or forty dollars. Bridle, too . . ."

"Yep . . . Well, we'll put a hundred dollars on his head, and describe the horse. He'll try to sell it, I expect."

"Yes, sir."

"You want to chase him, John?" Miller asked with a grin.

"Not in the winter, sir. Mebbe if it was summertime."

"Okay . . . Well, go on with the horse breakin', then. If you learn anything, let me know."

"Yes, sir."

The mild buzz of the curious excitement over the disappearance of the young man from Illinois quickly subsided. There were other things to think about, such as the opening show on the road on April 5, 1913, in Hot Springs, Arkansas.

Meanwhile, however, George Miller, with his thorough efficiency as a manager, published and distributed a "Wanted" flier. It advertised a hundred-dollar reward for the arrest and conviction of the horse thief. The Millers asked few questions about the past of a prospective employee, but one certain requirement was loyalty.

In late January, John was working with a young horse when a cowboy paused at the rail.

"John, when you have a minute, George wants to see you in the office."

John nodded and continued his work, but his mind was racing.

Something about Hebbie?

He decided not. The clue was in the way his presence had been requested: *When you have a minute.*

He tried to continue with the horse, but found it impossible to concentrate. How could he possibly find his way into the head of the already-suspicious animal when his own head was spinning? Finally he gave it up. Leaving the colt to relax in the little enclosure, he called to Pickett.

"I'm goin' up to the White House, Bill. The colt's okay. . . . Back purty soon."

Pickett waved and nodded.

What could George Miller possibly want? It is a worrisome thing to be called before the throne of authority, even when innocent. Was there somehow an oversight, an unseen or forgotten infraction? Well, he would know soon.

He knocked on the door frame from outside the open office door as he peered into the room. John's first glimpse of George Miller as the manager looked up from his cluttered desk was reassuring.

"Ah! Come in, John."

Miller's grin was like that of the cat who has just made a meal of the family canary.

"Sit down, son! Just thought you'd like to see a couple of things, here."

He shoved a letter across the desk, and John picked it up cautiously. He was curious. The letter was friendly, innocent, and appeared quite insignificant. It was merely an inquiry about a relative who, it seemed, was employed at the 101. . . . The younger brother of the writer, it seemed. There was a polite request:

> . . . give him a chance at riding . . . For I truly would
> like to see him gain a high reputation. Surely he ought

to be able to better himself immensely. Hoping you will try to help me make my wish come true.

John was puzzled. Why should this be of any concern to him? Who was the young man referred to in the letter? He looked at the envelope again. Moline, Illinois . . .

A light dawned, and the tight smile on the face of George Miller gave evidence that his thoughts were on the right track.

"Is this the fella?"

Miller didn't answer, but shoved another letter across the desk, his answer to the request:

Dear Madam,

Your letter of January 27th is just received, and I regret very much to have to write this letter.

I enclose herewith a reward card, offering $100.00 reward for the arrest and conviction of a horse thief.

I beg to further advise you that your brother . . . is the man mentioned in this card, and he was captured at Arkansas City, Kansas, on the morning of January 30th, where he was attempting to sell the horse and saddle for $30.00, and he is now in jail at Newkirk, Oklahoma, and will, no doubt, plead guilty to horse stealing.

When caught with the goods, he was probably very fortunate in falling into the hands of the sheriff instead of falling into other hands.

Very truly yours,
George L. Miller

FORTY-ONE

In early spring, when Zack Miller stopped by as John was working with a young gelding. Miller leaned on the fence, said nothing, but merely watched and waited.

When the time came to pause, John left the animal for a few moments and walked over to the rail.

"Mornin', Mr. Miller. You want to see me?"

"If you've a minute, John. Nice gelding, there."

"Yes, sir. He's comin' along purty good."

Miller reached into his pocket and drew out a coin, which he handed to John. It was shiny and new, and on one side bore the profile of an Indian's face; on the other, a buffalo.

"Know what that is?"

"A medal of some kind?"

"That's a nickel, John. New design, just out. But do you know the fella on it, there?"

John paused. Was Zack Miller teasing him? It was well known that to many whites all Indians look the same. It was a quiet inside joke that to Indians, all whites look alike. But joking about this was not like Zack Miller.

"I don't think so," John said carefully. "Should I?"

"I dunno," Miller answered. "Thought you might. You're Sioux, ain't you?"

"Yes, sir. Lakota."

This had never come up since he joined the 101. What was going on?

"Well, this fella on the nickel, here, one of them that posed for the picture, is an Oglala Sioux named Iron Tail."

"But what—"

Miller waved the question aside and continued.

"Iron Tail has been with Buffalo Bill's Wild West show, but has contacted us. I guess things ain't goin' so well with the Two Bills. You knew they'd joined up? Buffalo Bill and Pawnee Bill?"

"I'd heard that."

"Well, some of their people, particularly the Oglalas, are gettin' restless. Iron Tail's contacted us and will be with us this season. . . . Great opportunity for advertising, with the nickel and all."

John nodded. Trust Zack Miller to think of every angle for publicity.

"I've heard my father speak of Iron Tail," he said.

"Good! Well, just lettin' you know. He'll prob'ly bring some others with him. We're bookin' a big season. . . . You know, my brother Joe's over in Europe now. He's workin' on a deal with a German circus for some of our Oglalas to spend a season with them."

"In Germany?"

"Yep. They'll announce it purty soon."

"You'll go there?"

"No . . . Wayne Beasley will run that. I'm goin' south to pick up some cattle we're buyin'. Ten thousand head— about 350 carloads, we figger. Bring 'em up here for the grazin' season. I'll take some cowboys down."

"You want me to go?"

"No, no, John. Joe will need you for the show. Well, see you later!"

Zack Miller turned and strolled away, leaving John with several questions. Was Zack talking about the show season starting soon in Hot Springs, or the show season with the Oglalas in Germany? Or both?

Well, he'd learn eventually.

———

Zack Miller's crew of cowboys were still shipping cattle when the show opened in Hot Springs, Arkansas, on April 5, 1913, with a great parade. Joe Miller led the procession on Ben-Hur, his Arabian stallion. He was riding in a new saddle, designed and built by S. D. Myres, the famous saddle maker of Sweetwater, Texas. The saddle itself was used in the 101 advertising and publicity. "The finest fancy saddle ever made . . . Valued at more than ten thousand dollars . . ." It was of hand-carved leather, decorated with fifteen pounds of silver and gold, and studded with diamonds, sapphires, and rubies.

All three Miller brothers were present; Zack had returned for the occasion. Joe, too, had completed his negotiations in Europe with the Sarrasani Circus, based in Dresden. The entire Miller family, including Mother Molly Miller, and Joe's wife, Lizzie, were on hand for the beginning of a whirlwind season, and rode in motorcars in the parade. Also featured in the parade were a new steam calliope, Professor Donato La Banca's cowboy marching band, scores of floats, and hundreds of riders, including more than one hundred Indians.

The Sarrasani Circus, billed as Europe's "grandest," featured wild-animal acts, acrobats, clowns, and a Wild West Show, patterned somewhat after Buffalo Bill Cody's show, which had toured Europe and Britain. Joe Miller had contracted to furnish fifty Oglala Sioux, to work under Beasley's direction.

Joe Miller approached John while the show was in New England.

"Buffalo, how'd you like to go back to Europe?"

"To do what?"

He was hesitant to leave the country, in case Hebbie tried to contact him. But . . .

"Well, let me tell you about it, John. The ol' Hunnerd and One is goin' international. We've got a deal to supply horses for that war in the Balkans. You know about that?"

"Not much."

"Well, they're usually fightin' one another. The Greek Army is buyin' horses . . . Cavalry and artillery. We're supplyin' three thousand."

"Does the 101 *have* that many?"

"No . . . We're buyin' in Mexico an' Texas, to resell. We'll ship out of Galveston. I'll need a few cowboys to take 'em over."

John's mind was racing. If Hebbie needed him, she would know that he'd probably be on the road with the show. If she happened to be where the troupe was performing, she'd ask the crew, and they'd tell her of his whereabouts. Similarly, if she went to the ranch. If she wrote instead, the message would be waiting on his return. . . .

"I don't see why not," he told Miller.

"Okay. Good! Now, one other thing. You'll be over there—Europe, I mean. You've a little experience. Schprechen a little Deutsch?"

"*German?* Very little, Mr. Miller."

"But you've been among Europeans, got along with 'em."

"Tried to, anyway. But what—?"

"Well, Beasley's havin' some problems with the Oglalas at that circus in Dresden."

"Problems?"

"Yep. Some of 'em don't think they're bein' treated right. Couple of 'em even jumped ship and started home on their own."

"Oh! Well, most of 'em speak some English, and a lot

of the Europeans do. They could work their way home on a ship, I guess."

"Hope they make it okay," said Miller. "Anyhow, here's what I was thinkin'. If you could spend a few days talkin' to them . . . The ones still with the circus . . . I've got some watch fobs, made out of them nickels with Iron Tail's picture on 'em. They look like medals. . . . Like you said. You can take a bunch of 'em over and hand 'em out as gifts. Just try to keep most of 'em there till the contract's finished at the end of the season."

"Well," said John, "why not?"

"Good! You'll need to leave here tomorrow. Head to Galveston by train."

As it turned out, seventeen of the Oglalas had rebelled at the treatment they were receiving, and had "jumped ship."

Anxious to avoid problems with the government, or any damage to the reputation of the Hundred and One, Joe Miller wrote to the Agency at Pine Ridge, South Dakota. Most of the Oglalas in the European contingent were from that reservation. In a letter addressed to Superintendent John Brennan, Miller acknowledged:

> Several of our Indians have got tired of show business and have gone home. . . . Should any of the Indians who come in complain of mistreatment or things not going right with the show, I would be very glad to have you write to Iron Tail or any of the Indians on the show (on the U.S. Tour), and they will tell you that there is no show on the road that takes as good care of the Indians and treat them as well as we do.

John Buffalo arrived in Europe via the ship carrying horses to the Greek Army, and made his way on to Dresden by train. He had no trouble asking his way to the Sarrasani

Circus. In fact, because of his manner of dress—boots, Stetson hat, and Levi's, the natives assumed that he was an American, associated with the circus. He was met with smiles everywhere.

He stepped off the train at the circus grounds, to find the afternoon performance under way. The German employees of Sarrasani nodded to him and motioned him on inside. Still holding his suitcase, he walked up the entrance ramp, listening to the roar and applause of the crowd. There was laughter; there must be a clown act in progress. But there was a thunder of hoofbeats, too. . . . More like the Indian attack and cavalry pursuit in the 101 show. But why the laughter?

He could see the ring now, and the galloping horses as they circled. He heard the war whoops of the Oglalas. Yet what—?

A painted warrior swayed and toppled from his horse, landing and rolling as other horses dodged around his limp form, or jumped easily over it. The crowd roared with laughter, thinking it part of the show. But . . . Something must be wrong. Other riders were swaying drunkenly in the saddle, sliding, toppling. . . . This was not part of any show he'd ever seen.

The fallen warrior scrambled to his feet and staggered toward the ramp where John stood. He tried to evade the circling horsemen, dodging and falling, to scramble up again. John dropped his luggage and sprinted into the arena to help him. The brawny shoulder of a galloping horse struck John a glancing blow. He whirled and dodged another, grabbing the unhorsed Sioux by the elbow.

"Come, Uncle," he yelled at the man in his own language, using the traditional term of respect for an older male. "I will help you."

There was a startled look of surprise on the face of the bewildered Sioux. John slid an arm around the man's waist and half-carried him out of the galloping traffic. There was a whiff of alcohol on the man's breath as their faces came near.

Drinking? How could that be? The Millers were quite strict. John was certain that the Oglalas' contract had a "morality clause" prohibiting their use of alcohol.

He dragged the stumbling warrior onto the ramp and to one side. Someone ran to help him, and he recognized Wayne Beasley.

"Buffalo!" exclaimed the startled Beasley. "What are you doin' here?"

"Joe sent me. What the hell is goin' on?"

"Tell you later—let's get Bear's Hand out of here."

"What about the others?"

"Dunno . . . We'll see. . . . But I sure want you to talk to 'em. Some of 'em quit and went home."

"Yes, I heard. Okay, let's go!"

Away from the arena, with the inebriated Bear's Hand snoring comfortably on a pile of folded tarps, the two men had a chance to talk.

"It's gotten worse since you heard, I guess," Beasley explained.

A young Indian girl, daughter of Dick White Calf, had walked too close to the animal cages of the Sarrasani Circus, and was mauled by a tiger.

"Just flesh wounds," Beasley explained. "I wrote Joe Miller about it. I sent the girl to the hospital. Damn! We didn't need this. The Indians are sort of sulkin' anyway. Glad you're here, Buffalo. Mebbe you can make 'em understand."

It was an uncomfortable position for John. Taking sides in the growing discontent would be disastrous. He spent the rest of the day talking to the Oglalas, and he and Beasley sat down late that night to discuss the situation.

"It's not that they don't understand, Wayne," he noted. "They'd just like to either be treated better, or go home."

"But I treat 'em good."

"I know you do. They know that, too. But the German border guards, when you've made some of the short trips— they sort of look down on our Indians."

"Hell, I know that!" Beasley sputtered. "That riles me, too. But I can't do anything about an uppity border guard or two!"

"I know. But you're white. The border guards are white. The Oglalas need *somebody* to be mad at."

"What do they *want?*"

"Just respect, I guess. Some left, I heard. . . . Went home."

"Yeah . . . Broke their contracts. So, no pay comin'."

John shook his head.

"Did they understand that?"

"Don't know."

"Okay. Let me talk to them some more."

It was much as he had thought, but there was still a lot of unrest. The daughter of White Calf was doing well, but that seemed to be only a small part of the problem. A faction among the Oglalas seemed determined to cause trouble. In talking to Dick White Calf, John learned that some of the troublemakers understood their contracts all too well.

"There's a morals clause," Dick told him. "No drinkin' allowed. So, some figure, if they get drunk, Beasley will have to send 'em home."

It was apparent that a few of the disgruntled Oglalas

were using this strategy. To make matters worse, the German circus fans, fascinated by the Indian troupe, were eager to supply them with all the alcohol they could consume.

"Oglalas and schnapps is a bad combination," observed Beasley.

John agreed. "But," he reminded, "you can't fire them, because that tells all the rest that it's the quickest way home. You don't want that."

"We sure don't."

"Well, most of 'em are pretty sensible, Wayne. I'll hand out these medals made out of Iron Tail's nickels, tell 'em he sends his greetings."

"He's on the U.S. tour?"

"Yes. Doing fine, I guess. I'll tell 'em about that. They'll trust Iron Tail."

By the time Zack Miller arrived in Dresden in September to see how the Oglalas were faring, the situation had improved considerably. All three Miller brothers had attended the August bankruptcy sale of the Buffalo Bill show in Denver. They bought most of the arena stock, wardrobe, electrical lighting plant, and "considerable other stuff," Zack related.

"I tell you, boys, it was a sad day," he told John and Beasley. "A sorry thing to watch such a finish for a grand old outfit like Buffalo Bill's."

"Sure musta been," Beasley agreed. "You still shippin' cattle?"

"Yeah. Ten thousand from Florida just before I came over. So . . . Buffalo, you think our Oglalas here can finish the season?"

"I think maybe so, sir. Things are some better now."

"Looks like it to me," added Beasley. "John's been a help."

"Good work, boys!" Miller nodded. "We're thinkin' about a South American tour this winter. You interested?"

"Depends," said Beasley. "Who's goin?"

"Hell, I don't know." Miller chuckled. "Just thought I'd mention it. We can talk about it when we get home. A lot of our equipment needs repair, including some of the Buffalo Bill stuff, but we'll have enough to put a show on the road. Some pretty good new performers, too, from the Buffalo Bill outfit."

Much of the equipment and canvas was shipped to New Jersey for repair and storage. Meanwhile, Edward Arlington was busy booking the South American tour: Buenos Aires, Montevideo, Rio de Janeiro . . .

FORTY-TWO

On November 1st, John found himself aboard the S.S. *Varsara*, bound for Argentina. Around the Millers, things seemed to happen very quickly.

He was uneasy. It should have been a good feeling, heading toward a winter season in a warm climate. The arena director would be Vern Tantlinger, the respected 101 showman. Headliners were the cream of the crop, restless after the season's close, and glad to stay busy. Pickett, Lulu Parr, Milt Hinkle and his cowgirl wife, Iona, Mabel Kline, Ed Bowman, Chet Byers, Hank Durnell, rodeo clown Billy Lorette with his trained mules. Some of the top performers from the "Two Bills" show, now dispersed, had also signed on for the winter season, along with a number of the Indians. That was one of the reasons for John Buffalo's presence with the troupe.

"You can do double duty," Joe Miller joked. "Help with the horses and look after our Indians."

It was said in an offhand, joking manner, but John knew that it was sincere. That was indicated by the size of his pay envelope. There had been a substantial raise after his help with Beasley's Oglalas in the Dresden circus.

But, from the time he first laid eyes on the *Varsara,* standing at the pier in Brooklyn, he had felt that something was wrong.

"Its spirit is not right," said one of the Indian women, as the water lapped gently on the hull.

"You are not accustomed to water travel, Mother," he told her jokingly, in her own tongue. "Our people did well in Germany last summer, no?"

She gave him a sharp look.

"Some of them, yes. But I am not talking of that. This boat smells of trouble. . . . Bad spirits. I have spoken."

She turned her back to him and walked away.

John had dealt with this lack of communication between the two cultures since his first day in old White Horse's classroom at the reservation school. The white man had tried to ridicule the Lakota belief that the world is peopled with spirits, good and bad, which can help or hurt one's life. Somehow, it seemed to offend the white man's ideas of God. John had never really understood how or why, but he had learned quickly not to talk about it. When he did, he'd usually had his knuckles rapped with White Horse's ruler. It was easier for an Indian student to pretend that he did not hear, see, and feel the presence of the spirits in his life. It kept the whites with whom he worked or studied more comfortable, and avoided a lot of controversy. Many of the Indians that he knew admitted that they no longer followed the old ways. However, he had never heard one say that he did not *believe* in the old ways.

John himself felt caught in the middle of this dilemma. Among whites, it was easier to follow their ways of thinking. At least, to pretend to. It avoided argument, and allowed things to run more smoothly. He could trade the resulting success for the slight, uneasy feeling of guilt that he sometimes felt for having partially abandoned the old ways.

Just now, standing at the rail of the *Varsara*, watching the white curl of foam that blossomed on each side of her bow, he was worried. He had tried to brush aside the reaction of the old woman, but he could not. He felt very strongly that she was right. He had tried to stifle such feelings, but even before she had spoken, he knew. The spirit was bad. There was a feel—almost a *smell*—of tragedy. Now there was the guilt of participating in this venture, which he now felt as a threat to his people and his friends.

Someone moved along the rail and stopped near him in the twilight. He recognized Bill Pickett. The two exchanged nods and were silent for a few moments.

Pickett spoke first, quietly.

"You feel it too, John?"

"What?"

"You feel it. . . . The bad-luck ship."

This time it was a statement, not a question.

"Well, I . . . Some of the Oglalas have a bad feeling."

"Yep. They got a feel for it."

John was silent for a moment. He knew that Pickett, like everyone else, had his own private beliefs. "Superstitions," many whites would call them. No matter that in the background of a great many people, possibly *all* people, are the customs of previous lifetimes. In Pickett's case, several different cultures. For several generations, there had been intermixing of white, Cherokee, and Negro blood in Cherokee country. Pickett had the heritage of all three. Would this dilute his feel for the spirit, John wondered, or enhance and strengthen it? He'd never heard Pickett discuss it. The bulldogger *had* mentioned a feeling of doom before his nearly fatal experience in the Mexico City bullring, but John felt that this was something else.

"I'm glad I sent Spradley back to Oklahoma," Pickett remarked absently.

"You sent your horse home?" John asked.

"Yep . . . Didn't want him on this ship. It smells of death."

Then Pickett turned and strolled away.

Perhaps the first sign of catastrophe was the weather. The sea became rough, the ship tossing on the crest of the waves and then dropping into the wallowing trough of the next. Everyone became seasick. Certain that he was to die, Bill Pickett said later that the only thing that saved him was to think constantly about his family back in Oklahoma, where his wife, Maggie, waited for his return.

John himself was queasy and vomited over the rail a time or two, but escaped the worse of the symptoms by staying on deck when he could, to breathe the fresh air.

Even so, there was one incident which was unnerving yet, in an odd way, reassuring. He was in his bunk, sleeping restlessly, when he awoke in the night. Someone was standing beside him, dimly outlined by feeble light from the ship's electric lanterns. It was a female figure, so hazy and indistinct that he did not recognize her until she spoke.

"It's okay, John. Everything will be okay. . . ."

"*Hebbie!* What are you doin' here?"

He sat bolt upright, his heart pounding, as the figure faded and disappeared.

"Shut up, John," said one of the other supine figures in the bunk room. "You're dreamin'."

He lay back down, but could not sleep. He had to admit it was possible that it *had* been a dream. This in turn confused him further, because in the tradition of his people, a vision may occur asleep or awake. Is there really any difference?

He rose and went on deck, where he stood for a long time, watching the writhing horizon line, where the dark sky met the dark sea. Despite the shock, the heartrending disappointment, he felt a calm, an assurance. *It will be okay. . . .*

But *what* will? What was the nature of this vision? He tried to be objective, to understand what had just happened to him. Suddenly it came to him what he was doing. He was behaving like a white man, trying to dissect and examine and interpret, instead of merely accepting the event as it happened. Hebbie had come to reassure him. . . . From where, how, or why was unimportant. It had happened. He had regained some of his confidence, though his stomach still protested at the abuse. But he knew that in the end, it would indeed "be okay."

It was not many days before the next wave of misfortune struck. Someone on the deck told him that the Indians needed him. Some of them were sick.

"Yes, I know," he said. "I talked to them. They're not used to ocean travel."

"No, not that, John. Somethin' else. They want to talk to you."

Probably need a little reassurance, he thought. The weather had actually moderated a little, and John had no inkling of the seriousness of the situation as he went below. At the doorway of the Oglalas' quarters, he paused. There was an appearance of tragedy on the faces that met him and, in some cases, accusation, as if he had somehow betrayed them. His most shocking impression, however, was the odor of the place. It was not merely the smell of unwashed bodies in close quarters. That was to be expected in such a situation. This was a malevolent stench of sickness and disease. He had smelled that same stench before, but it took him a moment to remember where. He had been quite small, but that is the way with smell. A whiff of a long-forgotten scent, good or bad, stirs primitive memory like none other of the senses. Through smell, even an old person can be transported instantly to memories of childhood, good or bad.

In this case, it was bad. He had been no more than five summers when the people in the lodge next to Yellow Bull's had fallen ill. John had not thought of it for years. Some of that family. had died, and Little Bull had been taken to the white man's doctor at the Agency. All who lived near those with the *poch*—the spotted sickness—had been protected against it with the white doctor's medicine. Little Bull—now John Buffalo—still had a scar on his left shoulder to show for it.

Now, after all these years, these memories came flooding back. He felt the revulsion, the dread that he had seen in the faces of his parents then. It was now his own, and enough to inspire terror in the present situation. Here they were, in mid-ocean, with no way to escape the lurking killer. . . . *Smallpox.*

The Oglalas had concealed their problem. Many of those on board had, like John himself, been vaccinated. But, there were a few others who had not. Six or eight were sick, some dangerously so. In addition, when John approached the ship's doctor, he learned that one of the whites, Hank Durnell, the trick roper, was also sick.

"There is no treatment except time," the doctor explained. "We are not even equipped to vaccinate to protect the healthy. A ship like this is limited in what we can carry. We can expect some deaths."

Four of the Indian performers did die and were buried at sea, to the great concern of their friends and relatives. The songs of mourning echoed from the afterdeck for three days, and then the Oglalas settled back into private mourning.

Hank Durnell was carried on deck for fresh air by his friends. He begged and pleaded that they throw him overboard to end his suffering. Of course they refused, and Hank recovered, scarred but alive.

The S.S. *Varsara* docked at Buenos Aires nearly a month after her nightmarish journey began in New York. Edward Arlington, accustomed to dealing with foreign officials, had scheduled the entire tour. He now took over the questionable and risky part of the disembarking. Incoming ships were subject to health inspection for the very reasons that the *Varsara*'s passengers were now in trouble. But usually, it was merely a formality. Arlington greased a couple of official palms with cash and smuggled his now-recovering smallpox survivors ashore. They had managed to avoid a quarantine for smallpox, which would have destroyed their tour schedule.

But there was one more surprise. An officious-looking man in a government uniform arrived and introduced himself as a livestock inspector. He must examine the horses of the troupe for disease. None would be allowed ashore until he and his two assistants had completed their work.

Arlington offered a bribe, which was received congenially.

"But you realize, *señor,* that I must still perform the inspection, no?"

Grudgingly, Arlington agreed.

"It will not take long," the inspector promised.

It did not. In a very short time, the official and his two assistants reappeared, their faces long and sober.

"Señor," he told Arlington, "I am sorrowed to tell you this, but your horses are infected."

"Infected? What is this? They want more money?" sputtered Vern Tantlinger, the ringmaster.

"No, *señor,*" said the inspector. "I wish it were so. But some of your animals are diseased. 'Glanders,' it is called in your country. They must be destroyed, and the carcasses burned."

Arlington heaved a deep sigh. "Very well . . ."

"How many?" demanded Tantlinger.

The inspector looked at him sympathetically. "You do not understand, *señor*. This is a highly infectious disease. It is necessary to eliminate all possibility of contagion. *All* of your horses and mules must be confiscated and burned."

Members of the troupe were gathering, sensing that something big was happening.

"My trained mule?" sputtered Billy Lorette, the rodeo clown.

"The tour's over," someone muttered.

"Shore glad I sent Spradley home," muttered Bill Pickett as he turned away.

The Hundred and One troupe stood helplessly as their show animals were led away by military personnel. Down the gangplank, along the wharf and away from the shore, to an isolated area out of sight. They winced at each volley of shots.

A few of the performers felt called upon to follow the dozens of doomed animals to the scene of destruction. They must make sure that there was no skulduggery in process, no confiscation for personal profit.

Apparently, there was not. It was a legitimate quarantine and preventive measure. As they turned back toward the ship, greasy black smoke rose in a funeral pall over the death scene.

The death ship had done its evil work.

FORTY-THREE

This ain't over," insisted Vern Tantlinger.

"What can we do?" asked someone helplessly.

"Look," said Vern, "what would you do if your horse broke a leg?"

"Get another'n."

"Sure. How's this any different?"

"He's right," said Edward Arlington. "I'll authorize purchase of replacement animals. I suppose there are horses available?"

"Oh, *sí, señor!*" assured one of the inspector's assistants. "We can help you."

Always a promoter and skilled as advance man for the show, Arlington decided to capitalize on their misfortunes. His press releases engendered sympathy, and the public turned out in record numbers. Extra shows were added to an already full schedule.

Horse traders understood their urgent need for replacement stock and scoured the continent to be of help. Of course, with Yankee dollars in view, even Billy Lorette found a small mule for his clown act. The 101 Wild West Show was back in business for the South American schedule. The whirlwhind tour became one of their best, several times performing three shows a day.

January 1914 . . .

Zack Miller sat on a hilltop outside Presidio, Texas, watching activity across the Rio Grande. He had been on a buying trip, and was waiting to take delivery on a herd of mules. He had negotiated the purchase, amounting to several thousand dollars, and was to accept delivery from Ojinaga, Mexico, to Presidio, where the mules would be shipped by rail to the 101 in Oklahoma.

But, as often where the Millers were concerned, outside events had intervened. There was a revolution in progress in Mexico. Above all else, Zack Miller was flexible. He had long ago learned that in such a conflict, there was money to be made. One of his first such coups had been more than a decade earlier, in California. Starting with a small stake, he had bought, sold, and traded mules. Britain was engaged in the prolonged and costly Boer War, and her demand for mules provided a market for Zack Miller's acquisitions.

This had convinced the horse trader in him. Where there was a war—anywhere—there would be a demand for horses and mules. The other Miller brothers, while horse traders in their own right, were more content with ranching, raising livestock and crops, and with showmanship. They, too, enjoyed the stimulation of a good horse trade, but Zack was the undisputed negotiator of the big trading deals. He had set up the purchase and supply lines for supplying the thousands of horses which they had shipped to the Greek Army in 1913 for their war in the Balkans.

In all of this, he had learned patience. This war in Mexico was interfering with the delivery of his mules. But where there was a war, there might be a profit to be made.

So he sat on the hill outside Presidio, watching the battle across the river near Ojinaga.

The rebel forces were led by Doroteo Arango, who would go down in history as "Pancho Villa." He, too, had a flair for showmanship and had set up this campaign for maximum publicity. He had actually negotiated a contract for movie rights to this battle with Mutual Films, agreeing to fight only during daylight hours for film purposes. All battle plans were to be available to the film company. This could not have happened, of course, except that the rebel forces were in virtually complete control of the situation.

Crowds of newspaper reporters had descended on Presidio, observing and reporting the battle's progress from the safety of the bluffs on the United States side of the Rio Grande. The Villistas were pushing the government troops hard, shelling the retreating columns. Many of the Mexican troops had with them an assortment of camp followers, personal belongings, families, and even pets. Even Zack Miller, with his broad exposure to the seamy side of the world, was appalled at the suffering.

"The screams of the wounded and dying," he later described to a biographer, "were sharp and shrill against the rattle and thunder of the Villista gun-fire."

Refugees began to stream across the river, attempting to surrender to American authorities to save them from the rebels. Within ten days, the Mexican town of Ojinaga had fallen to Pancho Villa's troops.

U.S. Army Colonel John J. Pershing, assigned to defend American interests, asked and received permission to confer with rebel leaders in the captured territory. Since the United States was not involved in the war, the situation was delicate. Pershing could not actually accept the surrender of Mexican troops, but announced his intention to shelter refugees on the American side of the river. This met with the approval of Villa, and the conference was cordial.

Refugee camps were set up along the road north out of Presidio. Several thousand defeated soldiers and their equipment, including weapons, horses, and mules, were scattered along the route. Their status was questionable. Their equipment could not be classified as "spoils of war" because it was in neutral territory. Already, in the freezing weather with no fuel available, the refugees were beginning to burn their military saddles to survive.

Zack Miller had little use for Mexican military saddles or abandoned arms, but realized something else. Each of those saddles had been worn by a horse that had crossed the river. A quick estimate suggested that there must be at least 3,000 horses in limbo, not counting wagon mules, which might number hundreds more. He quickly dispatched a telegram to the Mexican consulate in San Antonio, offering to buy all the livestock and equipment, and bidding $45,000 to complete the deal. He then sent a second telegram, this time to his brother Joe back in Bliss, Oklahoma.

"Yes, sir. You sent for me?" asked John Buffalo as he entered Joe Miller's office.

"Yes, John. I want you to go with me to Texas. Any objections?"

Miller seemed to be organizing quickly, preparing to leave.

"Right now?"

"Yes. As soon as we can get to town."

He was tossing some papers into a briefcase.

"Here . . . read this," he said, handing a John a telegram.

COME AT ONCE HAVE BANK GIVE ME FORTY FIVE THOUSAND DOLLARS CREDIT OR BRING THAT MUCH IN GOLD GOT A HELL OF A BIG DEAL ON

ZACK

"I need somebody I can trust." Joe Miller stated, as he stuffed a few more papers into the case and buckled it shut. "I don't know what this deal of Zack's may be, but we'll see. Go get your stuff together. We have to get to the bank at Ponca. There should be a train outa there."

Why me? John wondered as he hurried to the bunkhouse to toss a few things together.

His question was partly answered on the way to Ponca City in the buggy. The fast team covered the distance in a hurry, as Joe rambled, half to himself.

"Zack's probably got some deal goin' that involves livestock," he pondered. "But it must be sorta tricky. He's dealin' with people, money, and livestock. . . . He wants me to *bring* it, not send it. . . . He's in Presidio, right on the border, so that maybe involves Mexican traders. I know he was buyin' some mules to bring across the border, but this must be a bigger deal. I don't know what he'll need, but you can handle livestock, you can talk to folks, and you come across as pretty honest to people you meet."

He was quiet for a moment, and then ended the conversation with a short statement.

"Vern and Ed Arlington said you did a good job in Germany."

John was honored at this display of trust.

"I'll try, sir."

At the bank in Ponca City, Joe negotiated the necessary bank draft, and they hurried to the depot to catch the next train south.

Meanwhile, Zack continued to walk the thin ice of international intrigue. He had no use for the thousands of weapons and uniforms that were now stacked in piles along the highway to Marfa, Texas, north of Presidio. Joe would be of help with dealing with the myriad of inspectors, customs agents, and minor officials, as well as the Mexican consulate.

One threat was a duty charge of $3.50 per head on livestock crossing the border. This would amount to a considerable cost for the thousands of Mexican cavalry horses which had already crossed the border before the negotiations transferred ownership.

"Maybe Will Bryan can help us," Joe suggested.

They wired their friend, William Jennings Bryan, in Washington, now President Wilson's Secretary of State. Bryan telegraphed the U.S. Customs office in Presidio and ordered waiver of the usual fees in the interests of relations with Mexico.

There was a final coup in Zack Miller's complicated venture into international affairs, and his major purchase of a defeated Army's property. He sold the equipment, uniforms, and weaponry piled along the retreat route out of Mexico back to the Mexican government, even as they loaded horses into boxcars for shipment to the Hundred and One.

But every rose has its thorns. Only a short time later, in the bitter January of 1914, White Eagle, chief of the Poncas and friend of the Millers, died of pneumonia after prolonged exposure as he walked home from the Agency. Joe Miller, especially, was stricken with grief. He recalled a childhood among the Poncas, neighbors to the Millers, and had always had good relations with the Indians. He was sometimes jokingly referred to as the "white chief of the Poncas."

There was a marked disagreement about the burial of the venerable chieftain. Christian missionaries on the reservation demanded a "Christian" burial. The Poncas, equally determined, wished for their fallen leader a traditional "crossing-over."

A compromise of sorts was agreed upon: A wooden coffin, containing the body of White Eagle, dressed in his finery of soft buckskin and intricate regalia, his proud face painted for the crossing. The Poncas bored a hole in the lid of the coffin, through which his spirit could cross over. Burial was on a ridge overlooking the bluestem prairie, the traditional burial ground of White Eagle's people. His grave was covered with offerings of food for his journey, and his favorite horse was strangled nearby to provide transportation to the Other Side. Horse Chief Eagle, son of White Eagle and successor to the old leader, led the days of prayer, dancing, and feasting in his father's honor. Many of their friends from the 101 Ranch were in attendance.

It was a hard time for the Millers, who had lost a friend. Some years later, they erected a limestone monument on the ridge to honor their old comrade, White Eagle.

This year of 1914 was already off to a bizarre start that would be eclipsed by coming events.

In the midst of all this, John learned that some time earlier, Jim Thorpe's accomplishments at Stockholm had been declared ineligible. It was demanded that his medals, on display at Carlisle, be returned to the Olympic Committee. Thorpe had been disqualified, classed as a professional athlete because of having his expenses paid while playing summer baseball in South Carolina.

FORTY-FOUR

The 1914 season began with a three-week stint at Madison Square Garden, with daily shows. The great Barnum and Bailey Circus had closed there only days before, after a successful run.

The Hundred and One boasted an influx of new performers, including some of Buffalo Bill's headliners. There was also a rugged young soldier, just mustered out of the Army, who had wandered into the show at Texas City in October and applied for a job. His name was Charles Gebhart, and he had proved his skill with a rope, on a horse, and as a sharpshooter. He would later become famous as cowboy actor Buck Jones.

The public had more interest in the 101 cowgirls. They became known as the "Oklahoma Cowgirls," astounding audiences with their riding, roping, and shooting. The Millers were determined that their female performers would appear "wholesome," and there were strict rules as to dress and costuming. They were not allowed to wear rouge or lipstick in public.

Inspired by the successes of 1913, in the face of adversity, the Millers elected to take a bold step: They would *split* the Wild West Show, sending the second unit to England and Europe for the season.

Many of the crowd-pleasing headliners were booked for England. Zack Miller himself would lead this second unit, including Bill Pickett, Milt Hinkle, Hank Durell, now fully recovered from smallpox, George Hooker, and top cowgirls Ruth Roach, Mabel Cline, Lucille Mann, and Dot

Vernon. Zack borrowed Joe's fancy parade saddle for the tour.

Although not as large as the main show, the European contingent included a cowboy band, a mule caravan, bucking broncs, longhorn cattle, and buffalo. To emphasize the international flavor, there were not only Mexican vaqueros, but Cossacks, under Prince Lucca of Russia. There were sixty-five Indians, mostly Oglala Sioux. In addition to the Wild West acts, there was a demonstration blending the modern age into the Old West, with souped-up automobiles playing "motor-polo." A matinee and an evening performance were to be held daily through the summer months at the venerable Shepherd's Bush Stadium at London, newly renovated for the occasion.

"John, I'd like to have you in the second unit, the one goin' to England," Zack Miller told him. "You were a big help with Wayne Beasley, settlin' the Oglalas down in Germany last year. Most of them are goin' with us, so I guess they felt treated purty good. You got no problems with a summer over there?"

John had anticipated that this might be the case, and had given it a considerable amount of thought. Hebbie remained a major concern in the back of his mind, but he had heard nothing. Even with the far-flung influence of the Millers, there had been no word, no clue where she might be. It was as if she had dropped off the face of the earth, or as if she had never been. He thought of the dream or vision on board the ill-fated S.S. *Varsara*. Maybe Hebbie herself had been only a beautiful dream all along. . . . No, that could not be. . . . There was too much about her that was warm and human: her laugh, the little crinkles around her eyes when she smiled. . . .

He shook his head to clear it. It would do no good to try to build his life around the slim possibility that she might try to locate him. She was undoubtedly using a different name, which was preventing success in his inquiries. If and when she wished to find him, she would. Their base in common was the 101 Ranch, and she would start there. But there was no point in staying at the home ranch, or even in the States. He *could* be located.

"Yes, sir, I'd be glad to go," he told Zack Miller.

"Good! I figured so. Now, we may subcontract the Oglalas to the German outfit again for a while. You were a big help over there. Well, we cross that bridge when we get to it."

Despite misgivings on the part of some of those who had been on the *Varsara*, the crossing was accomplished with no trouble. The troupe was welcomed to London with such enthusiasm as they'd never experienced. From the first, they were accepted and cheered by the public, and Shepherd's Bush was packed twice daily.

John happened by the chutes one morning to encounter Pickett, leaning on the fence, quietly watching a couple of strange animals. They were light brown, about the size of cattle, with slender horns, and covered with long, shaggy hair. New and exotic animals were nothing unusual around the 101. Zack must have made another deal of some sort.

"What the hell are *them?*" John asked.

"Them," replied Pickett, "are Scotch cattle."

"Cattle?"

"So they say. 'Highlanders,' somebody called 'em."

"What are we doin' with 'em?"

Even as he voiced it, John realized that it was a foolish question. Zack Miller didn't need a purpose for anything new and unusual. If he didn't have one, he'd find one. But these . . .

"Reckon ah'm gonna bulldog 'em," said Pickett.

And he did, further delighting the crowds. Bill Pickett

became a favorite with the British, and his steer-wrestling act became the high point of every performance.

Pleased with their acceptance, Zack leased a mansion on Holland Road, complete with servants and housekeeping staff. He had brought his daughter, Virginia, who was enthralled with the entire British scene. Not only Zack and his daughter, but many of the performers, were wined and dined by British nobility, with chauffeured automobiles and receptions in their honor. Sir Thomas Lipton, the tea magnate, merchant, and philanthropist, entertained on board his private yacht. The Earl of Lonsdale hosted receptions. Lord Robert Baden-Powell, founder of the Boy Scout movement, attended the shows. The Wild West shows were attended by not only nobility, but by the royal family. King George V and Queen Mary were enthralled, and it was said that the King became so excited that he began to cheer like a commoner, and was reprimanded by the Queen. Virginia, Zack's daughter, presented the royal couple with flowers and curtsied before the royal boxes, pleasing not only the "Royals" but the crowd.

It was customary for the royal couple to leave any event early to avoid the crowds, but King George remained until the last dust had settled. He then stationed himself at the main gate, where he officially received the performers, repeating "Most wonderful exhibition! Most wonderful exhibition!" again and again.

It was whispered that His Majesty had never before stayed until the end of any event.

There were, of course, a few problems. A few times in the States the show had been ostracized by humane societies for mistreatment of animals. This was a growing problem for people handling livestock. At what point does restraint become inhumane?

In this case, Bill Pickett's use of his teeth was protested.

There was a list of lesser offenses involving the handling of horses by the hostlers. Ultimately, the London Humane Society persuaded the authorities to arrest Pickett. A hue and cry arose from Pickett's fans, and Zack Miller decided to take advantage of the backlash. He paid Pickett's fine of a few shillings and negotiated a bargain with the authorities. They would charge Pickett each week, and Miller would pay his fine while Pickett continued his act. Between the indignant radical press with their slanderous accusations and the indignant fans of the Dusky Demon, enough publicity was generated to make Pickett a celebrity in his own right. The Earl of Lonsdale threw a huge dinner party in Pickett's honor at his ancestral castle.

The royal family continued to patronize the show. Queen Mother Alexandra and her sister, Dowager Empress Marie of Russia, attended a performance with their entourage of European royalty, cheering their Cossacks as well as the cowboys. Queen Alexandra, an amateur photographer, took innumerable photos. This royal party had been transported in four motorcars to Shepherd's Bush.

Ironically, only two days later, an incident occurred in another part of Europe that would plunge the world into flame. It would affect the lives of everyone, including the performers of the 101 Wild West Show. On June 28, Austrian Archduke Franz Ferdinand and his wife, Duchess Sophie of Hohenberg, were assassinated. As their motor car drove through the town of Sarajevo in Bosnia, Garrilo Princip, a Serbian nationalist, gunned them down. This ignited a tense situation that had been building for years, and would become the "Great War."

Suspicious that this was part of a plot by Serbia to attack her, Austria-Hungary declared war. Russia began to mobilize, and Germany, already eyeing territory which it could claim, invaded Russia, France, Belgium, Luxembourg, and Switzerland. In little more than a month after the assassination, Britain had declared her intention to protect the coast, including France and Belgium, and declared war on Germany. The United States announced her neutrality a day later, but took measures to protect her citizens in Europe with a $6 million fund to help Americans stranded or caught up in the war.

Zack Miller was roused on the morning of August 7 by his butler.

"Sir, there are policemen here to see you. There are soldiers with them."

Zack rolled over sleepily.

"Damn! Did we forget to pay Pickett's fine this week?" he mumbled half to himself. "Tell 'em to go away. We'll pay the fine, but they'll have to make a proper appointment. I ain't even dressed."

The nervous butler relayed the message, and was all but bowled over by the Army's rush up the stairs. The officer in charge handed his official paper to Zack Miller, still in bed. It was a royal warrant:

National Emergency   Impressment Orders
                                   under Section 115
                                   of the Army Act

To Zack Miller, 68 Holland Rd. W.

His Majesty, having declared that a national emergency has arisen, the horses and vehicles of the 101 Ranch Show are to to be impressed for public service if found fit (in accordance with Section 115 of the Army Act), and to be paid for on the spot at the market value to be settled by the purchasing officer. Should you not accept the paid price as fair value, you have the right to appeal. . . . You must not hinder the delivery . . . purchasing officer may claim to purchase such harness and stable gear as he might require with the horse or vehicle.

Charles Carpenter, Sergt.
Place: Shepherd's Bush Exhibition
Date: 7 August, 1914

"What the hell is this?" Miller sputtered. "You're confiscatin' my *show?*"

"I'm afraid so, sir," the officer said stiffly. "You'll be paid, of course."

Zack dressed hurriedly and headed for the arena. There, soldiers were busily occupied in rebranding the 101 horses with the royal cipher. There was nothing he could do but watch as the show animals were led away, along with the rolling stock. . . . Even the stagecoach used in the holdup scene, and the motorcars with hot engines used in the motor-polo act. Efforts at bribes—usually effective—were turned away with cold disdain.

Miller summoned the 101 "gang" and explained the situation.

"The season's over," he said. "Nothin' we can do. We'll work on a way to get home, if we have to charter a boat."

Prince Lucca and his Cossacks were stricken with grief. They must return to Russia to fight for their homeland. It was a sad day as they said their good-byes to board a packet steamer to France for the long trip home. "We shall never see the 101 again," lamented Lucca, his eyes filled with tears.

This proved true.

"Mr. Miller," someone asked, "what about our Indians? They're in Germany."

"My gawd!" Zack exclaimed. "That's right. . . . They're in enemy territory!"

FORTY-FIVE

Zack Miller cabled his brother Joe back in the States, who then contacted some of their German associates to learn the status of the Oglalas.

Even with the transatlantic cable system, communication was slow and unreliable. International law was vague, and the balance of power was shifting. In spite of the Millers' experience in bribing officials, it was risky. Today's government might be ousted tomorrow, and it would never be good to have been supporting the wrong side in such an inflammatory setting.

Germany, above all, trusted no one. Their undersea U-boats with their deadly torpedoes had begun to control shipping, concentrating especially on any vessels flying the British flag, military or not. For the Hundred and One, even contact with their German colleagues was dangerous to both parties. Reluctantly, it was decided to discontinue communication. In one of the last cable interchanges, Zack Miller stated his position to Joe:

GET THEM TO HERE
I'LL GET THEM HOME

ZACK

"What means this?" asked Hans Stosch-Sarrasani, pondering a cable of explanation forwarded from Joe, which only seemed to complicate the situation in Dresden.

It was very touchy, and imperative that they should disclose as little of their potential plan as they could manage.

The cables had mentioned few specific locations, lest the European authorities might be waiting to make arrests.

"Zack's in London," explained Beasley, "but he doesn't want to announce that we're tryin' to take our Indians there."

Stosch-Sarrasani nodded.

"Good," agreed the German. "You know the trouble the odder show had."

Beasley and John Buffalo nodded soberly. Both the Sarrasani Circus and another, Colonel Cummin's Wild West Show, had had European tours featuring American Indians in progress in the crucial summer of 1914. At the war's start, German authorities, suspicious that Cummin's dark-skinned performers might be Serbian spies, had arrested and jailed the entire troupe. Eventually, they were freed only through the efforts of the American consul general in Hamburg. The United States had proclaimed neutrality thus far.

"It is best if ve continue as ve can," suggested Stosch-Sarrasani. "It shows that ve are honest."

The other men nodded.

"Now, ve have some small performances out of Dresden. Let us try to do these, to let the travel of the troupe be seen."

"Will they let us do this?" Beasley asked.

"Ve will see," said the showman cautiously. "Ve must not appear to try to hide."

He turned to John.

"Herr Buffalo, you must make sure that your Oglalas do not try to sep—how you say, 'split up.' A dark-skinned man, traveling alone, might be shot as a spy."

John nodded. A few Indians had taken off on their own the previous season, and had reached home safely, but 1914 was a different story.

The circus man unrolled a map on his desk and began to point to specific locations.

"Now, here, the border is easy, going *out* of Germany. Very dangerous, the odder way. Denmark, Norway, still safe. Ve could maybe schedule a few shows in places near the borders, to Nederlands, maybe. There is still some crossing to Britain."

A complicated schedule was tentatively agreed upon, involving exhibitions already booked and some added because of strategic locations. There were stops by suspicious border guards, verifications by wire of the papers the travelers carried. There was a complicating factor, not mentioned by John to the others: The citizenship of Oglala Sioux was not recognized as that of "Americans." They were not citizens of the United States, and not protected under America's neutrality. Fortunately, authorities in Europe were not so concerned with the niceties of such matters, as with whether there were spies among them. The reputations of both the Millers and the Sarrasani Circus were good, and it helped that the circus had been quite popular on the Continent, even with the onset of the war.

A wandering and devious route through Scandinavia and Holland, crossing only at "neutral" borders was eventually successful. Every member of the stranded troupe arrived safely in England, happy to be alive.

"I'm tryin' to book space," Zack explained. "Some problems . . . Even if the Kaiser's U-boats weren't attackin' everything British, they're not happy—the Brits, that is. . . . With sellin' us tickets. They're puttin' everything into their own war effort. Lots o' folks tryin' to get out of England too, y'know. . . . Get to neutral territory."

Perhaps the most amazing discovery to the European contingent was that the London Wild West Show was still in operation at all. Virtually all their livestock had been confiscated, but the show must go on. With a few animals not suited to military use, and a few more acquired, the troupe reorganized quickly. Emphasis now was on the Cowboy Band, magic acts, jugglers and acrobats, and on the roping and shooting skills of the cowboys and cowgirls of the Hundred and One. The Oglala dancers, fresh from the Continent, again swelled the crowds in the Shepherd's Bush Stadium.

This was simply a diversion, while Zack Miller continued to try to arrange passage home. He seemed to be facing increasingly greater obstacles.

"I'm in touch with the War Department," he told a group of key personnel. *"Ours,* that is. The Navy's comin' to help evacuate refugees, but it'll be more than a month before they can get here. I'm tryin' to get some tickets on some American freighters that are headin' home."

It was early September, and a few 101 personnel were sent on home with a pitiful assortment of salvaged equipment and rejected livestock. Passenger berths were even more scarce. A few days later, Zack Miller called a meeting of all hands.

"Folks," he began, "it ain't good, but it's better. There's a U.S. Mail packet steamer here—the *St. Paul*—bound for a New York run. Now, it's not a passenger ship. She's equipped to carry no more than a couple hundred passengers, but these are hard times. There'll be about 700 passengers *besides* us. The Hundred and One will buy the tickets, and the Germans aren't shootin' at neutral flags so far."

There was a subdued cheer.

"We ought to be in New York in late September," Miller went on. "Now, the main show is still on the road for a couple months. Those who want to join that troupe can do so. They'll close in late November, but open in February at San Francisco. So you got some time to decide."

"What about horses?" someone asked.

Miller turned around with a grin.

"Ever know the Hundred and One to be short on horses? We even supply the British Army." He paused to chuckle. "Wonder how they're doin' ridin' our buckin' stock?"

The total expense of the repatriation had cost the 101 in excess of $25,000, but everyone was headed home.

Hoping against hope that there would be word of Hebbie, John took the train back to Oklahoma with Zack Miller and assorted other employees.

He sat staring out the window at the dark Indiana landscape, listening to the rhythmic *click-clack* that had so impressed him on his first train ride. The sounds of gentle snores from the other passengers drifted through the coach. An occasional point of light identified an isolated farm. The car was becoming chilly in the November night. Maybe somebody would waken and stoke the wood stove. He could, but didn't want to. John shifted his position and tucked a buggy robe around him.

It seemed a long time since he'd had a bit of time alone to think about anything. Working for the Millers was exciting, to say the least. It was always a dizzy whirlwind, almost anywhere. Their interests and holdings and properties worldwide were astonishing. The Miller brothers also seemed to have more respect than most whites for those of Indian heritage. They had given him, John Buffalo, jobs of gradually greater importance, and he had been able to handle them. It felt good. . . . There was only a slight gnawing doubt sometimes that he'd been called upon only when his specific skills were in demand.

But is that not the way of the world for the white man? A need occurs, and someone is found to fill it. Each time he'd been called upon, he felt that he had done well. Better than most could have—especially with the disgruntled Oglalas. Most of them were now quite content. Many from the German circus had actually joined the stateside show units on the road. His own pay would have been good, but he felt that he needed a rest. So he was headed back to the ranch, the place that held more happy memories than any other he could recall. . . . A safe haven against the demands and pressures of the world. It would be good to be in familiar surroundings and with no imminent emergency in sight. Maybe there might even be some word of Hebbie.

There was no word. Nothing. Not that he had expected anything, but he needed something. A letter, a note, even a secondhand rumor. He'd heard the saying that no news is good news. He now began to doubt it. Would it not be better to know?

In the past few years, there had been some women in his life, but no closeness. It was a matter of convenience, a fulfillment of biological needs. Nothing more. For a few years, John had felt that no woman could take the place of the Senator's daughter in his heart. He had now grown beyond that, and had realized that for her it had probably been little more than a temporary fling, now outgrown. In some of his worst moments, he had imagined his lost love telling her society friends about an injudicious kiss with an athlete at Carlisle, for which both had been punished. Maybe, even, an amusing story to them.

Hebbie had been a very different matter. There had never been a time, even now, that he had doubted her integrity. Hebbie was what she was: nothing more, nothing less. Even now, he understood her position. She did not want to encumber his life with her problems.

No matter that in her desire to spare him in this way, she caused even more pain. Of course she could not know that. Could not know that to be able to hold and comfort her would have meant the whole world to him.

FORTY-SIX

Despite the problems of the disastrous 1914 season, the Millers charged ahead with plans for 1915. They would expand the tour, rather than curtail it because of the war. This was accomplished by splitting the show, to run two units simultaneously.

The first, with the cadre of headliners now associated with the Hundred and One, would open in February at the Panama-Pacific International Exposition in San Francisco. Only nine years before, the city had been virtually destroyed by a giant earthquake and the fires that followed. This exposition would celebrate the opening of the Panama Canal, and the vast importance to worldwide shipping that it offered. Secondarily, it would demonstrate the success of the city's resurrection from the ashes. The resilient citizens, already preferring to call the event "The Fire" rather than use the term "earthquake," had done a remarkable job of reconstruction.

There were new acts, too, in the arena performances of the 101 Miller Brothers Wild West Show. The West Coast was becoming a center for the movie industry, and there was never a shortage of extra cowboys, ropers, trick riders, and sharpshooters. There was Cuba Crutchfield, trick roper, who challenged all comers to a roping contest, offering a $1,000 cash jackpot. Joe Miller advertised the dare in *Billboard* magazine, but no challenger ever appeared.

Pedro Leon, another roper, specialized in working with both hands, as Will Rogers often did. Leon's ultimate trick was to rope four galloping horses and riders with a maguey lariat in his left hand, turning to rope four more horses and riders coming from the other direction with another rope, in his right hand.

The arena director for the San Francisco unit was Booger Red Privett, who had had a small Wild West Show of his own until this season. He was an old friend of Bill Pickett and a skilled bronc rider.

"How'd he get his name, Bill?" John asked.

The bulldogger smiled. "When Red was a kid, him an' another boy decided to celebrate Christmas or somethin', with a bang. They stuffed a holler tree with gunpowder and set 'er off. T'other kid was killed, an' Red was nearly blinded. . . . Boogered up some for sure. Ever since, he been 'Booger Red.' "

Booger Red also had a daughter, Ella, a strikingly pretty teenager who was a skilled horsewomen. Ella Privett quickly became one of the crowd's favorites, as well. A number of the cowboys were enamored with Ella, but a bit overawed by her highly protective father, Booger Red.

While at San Francisco, the 101 Show sponsored a ten-mile relay race, involving four riders, each using five horses. They would change horses after each half-mile sprint. Ella Privett, now dubbed Miss Ella, and the only woman rider, placed second behind the great Tom Miller-ick. She also beat Hank Linton, whom she was to marry later in the season. In a horseback ceremony outside a Baptist church in Port Arthur, Texas, while still on the tour, the young riders tied a knot that would last for more than half a century. Booger Red need not have worried.

Not all romances that season on the 101 tour were as favorable. In an ominous prelude to trouble, Joe Miller fell hard for one of his headliners, Bessie Herberg, whose act consisted of a trained horse, Happy. Joe's wife Lizzie sometimes joined the show on the road, but did not really enjoy the nomadic life. Occasionally over the years she had heard rumors of Joe's philandering, but this episode was apparently pretty flagrant. Lizzie packed up her three children and headed for San Francisco. Arriving there, she learned that the 101 Wild West Show had closed and was en route to join the second unit, already on the road.

There were quiet and discreet jokes that Joe Miller had moved the entire operation solely at the approach of his long-suffering wife, but everyone knew better. It had been planned to merge the units when attendance began to fall off at the San Francisco exposition after its early spring opening. They closed in June.

Other events which would profoundly affect the life of John Buffalo had been in progress. In April 1915, Jess Willard, a Kansas cowboy, won the world's heavyweight boxing championship in Havana, Cuba. The fight had lasted twenty-six blistering rounds under a blazing tropical sun, and ended in a knockout by Willard. The newspapers spent considerable space discussing the fight and its implications.

Jack Johnson, the first Negro to achieve the championship, had been resented bitterly by the white sports world. Jess Willard had been heralded as the "Great White Hope," who would demonstrate the white man's superiority once and for all. When Willard's victory took place, it was undoubtedly the biggest sports event of the year. Willard became a national hero.

It was never said that the Miller brothers would overlook a chance at publicity. They hastily added the Great White Hope as a headliner in the Wild West Show. It required some doing: a private railroad car for Willard, his family, manager, trainers, and assorted friends. Included in the deal were an automobile and chauffeur, a chef and a porter, for the exclusive use of the Willards.

"John, you done any boxing?" asked Joe Miller.

"A little, back at Carlisle," John admitted.

He hadn't enjoyed it much, and there was not much emphasis on boxing at the Indian schools. Striking with fists was virtually unknown among the Indian cultures. One would strike an enemy with a weapon or a coup stick, or would wrestle. Competition was keen in running, swimming, and contest sports. This translated well to track and field or competitive games, but not to boxing. It was an unfamiliar concept.

John had heard about the signing of Jess Willard by the Millers, and was not completely pleased by the news that the Great White Hope would be a part of the show. He was prepared to resent this development. But what did Miller have in mind?

"It's like this," Miller went on. "We're settin' up to have an extra private show after each main event. Willard will ride with the cowboys in the arena, but for those who want to stick around and pay an extra quarter, they can watch him in the ring with a sparrin' partner. Now, he's got his own trainin' partner, Walt Monohan. But if we're doin' this a couple times a day, we figger it might be good to have somebody else to fall back on."

"But, I—"

"You don't have to take any real punches, John. Just dance around a bit. They'll be watchin' him, not you."

"I don't know, sir. . . ."

"Talk to him before you decide," suggested Joe Miller. "He's a nice fella, John."

"Okay, I'll talk to him."

———

John was not eager for this interview. He was deeply suspicious about the thing of the Great White Hope and already resented deeply the racial overtones in this situation. It was a pleasant surprise, then, when he first met Jess Willard. The man who extended a hand to him seemed exactly as he had been billed: a big, friendly Kansas cowboy.

"John Buffalo? Howdy. I'm Jess Willard. Mr. Miller tells me you were at Stockholm. You really know Jim Thorpe?"

"Yes, sir." John was completely taken by surprise.

"Must have been quite an experience!"

"It sure was."

"I'll want to talk to you about it later. Now about this sparrin' thing. You're an athlete and at least have an understanding of boxing. Want to try it? Just a show, a little sparrin' for the crowd."

"Maybe so," said John. "Why not?"

Against his initial feelings, he found that he liked this man.

There was a session or two in which he was coached by Walt Monohan.

"Dance around to your right, John, away from *his* right. That's it . . . Parry his left, but don't—Ouch! Remember his one-two. . . . Block, but watch his other hand!"

Willard slipped a left past John's block and landed a fairly solid punch to his jaw. John's head whirled. Almost instantly, he found himself in a clinch, struggling with his arms around the champion's shoulders and chest. He didn't remember having grabbed the man.

"Sorry, son," Willard said in his ear. "Now, when you're in a bit o' trouble, jest grab your opponent like this. . . . Hang on a minute. . . . Wrassle around till your head clears. . . . Referee's gonna break it up, but it gives you a bit o' time. . . ."

The sparring routine was so popular with the crowd that more exhibition sessions were scheduled between shows. It was purely a sparring encounter, and John was grateful that he was not asked to "take a fall," as he had feared. To the spectators, simply watching the champion work out was reward enough.

There were more major developments that summer on the international fronts. The Great War was building rapidly, and the Millers were hard put to furnish horses to the Allies. Shipping became more of a problem almost daily.

Brothers Zack and George were concentrating more on the lucrative business in supplying the war effort, and were, more and more, allowing Joe to manage the show. However, the shipping problem proved a means to serve both efforts. In typical Miller fashion, it was decided to buy their own steamship. A German maritime firm agreed to sell them a vessel at New York for a sum of nearly $500,000, an unheard-of figure in 1915. However, the Millers calculated that four trips delivering horses to Allied nations, would pay for the ship. Then, after the war, the ship could be refitted to carry the entire Wild West Show on a five-year round-the-world tour.

But the best-laid plans go awry. German attacks on shipping were increasing, and in May an American freighter was torpedoed without warning. Only a few days later, the Cunard Line's S.S. *Lusitania,* a passenger steamer out of New York, was destroyed by German torpedoes, with a loss of more than 1,000 passengers, including Americans. For all practical purposes, the United States was at war.

Despite this, President Wilson believed that the country should remain neutral. It would be nearly two years before the mood of the citizens would force the entry of the United States into the Great War.

FORTY-SEVEN

Even after a highly successful 1915 season, the Miller brothers could not agree on whether, with war appearing imminent, they should place a show on the road. Jess Willard had failed to renew his contract, and instead signed on with the Sells-Floto Circus. There was an urgent need for a new special act. Joe Miller was now the "Miller" part of the show offered that year by the Miller and Arlington Wild West Show Company.

There was a great national push for preparedness in case war did come. Once again, Joe Miller keenly guessed the mood of the public. There must be a way to harness the swelling patriotism and national pride.

Buffalo Bill Cody, still struggling to break out of his tragic bankruptcy and other legal entanglements, was able to sign with the 101, the only major Wild West Show still on the road. Unable to buy into the show, Cody was placed on a salary and percentage contract and worked vigorously to prove his worth.

Meanwhile, in keeping with the Preparedness theme, Joe Miller contacted the War Department to see if he could "borrow" some troops for demonstration purposes. His timing could not have been better. A display of "an Army of Uncle Sam's gallant defenders of Old Glory" must have been a recruiter's dream.

General Hugh Scott, Army chief of staff, ordered several regiments to furnish troops for the road show. With Miller's uncanny sense of timing again apparent, the town of Columbus, New Mexico, was raided by Mexican revolutionary Pancho Villa, killing seventeen Americans. The Army dispatched 5,000 troops to Mexico, followed quickly by General Pershing's punitive expedition to pursue Villa.

The Wild West Show was now the "Buffalo Bill (Himself) and 101 Ranch Wild West Combined, with the Military Pageant of Preparedness." The show included a reenactment of the Columbus raid, complete with maneuvers by artillery, cavalry, and parade units, with flags flying and patriotism at its highest.

Buffalo Bill seemed to be a good drawing card, and was pleased to be working again with Iron Tail, his old Lakota friend.

John Buffalo was uneasy. There was always a ripple of excitement in preparation for the opening show of each season, a thrill of expectation. It had been there, but it was accompanied by an odd feeling that something was not quite right.

One thing that bothered him was the attitude of the Poncas. Many of them had objected to the drilling for oil on Ponca land a few years earlier. They remembered that before his death, Chief White Eagle, who had given his approval, had stated sadly that it had been a mistake. "It will mean great trouble for me, for my people, and for you," he told E. W. Marland, the oil wildcatter. By this time, it was being whispered that White Eagle's prediction was a curse. There were stories of ghosts, whose eerie cries and wails could be heard on the wind, mingling with the cries of night birds and coyotes. . . . Ghosts of both Indians and cowboys, the Poncas said. There were stories of 101 riders who had disappeared mysteriously. Usually, they were young loners who had run afoul of the Millers.

John put little credence in these stories. The Millers had treated him well. It seemed to him that cowboys who did not get along with the boss usually moved on. Still, he could not account for the Poncas' uneasiness. They felt something ominous. A pall hung over the ranch, and the ghost stories continued. Maybe it would be better when the troupe hit the road for the season. . . .

But the season was marked by sickness. It was a year of disease. Nationwide, there was an epidemic of infantile paralysis, later called "polio." Influenza was beginning to become serious again. Buffalo Bill Cody's health was deteriorating, though he never missed a performance.

In Philadelphia, Iron Tail fell ill with pneumonia, and was hospitalized. Uncomfortable with the unfamiliar surroundings, the old chief slipped away, bought a one-way ticket to his South Dakota homeland, and boarded the train. He died on the train in Fort Wayne, Indiana, en route home.

The show must go on, and did so in a highly successful twelve days' stand in Brooklyn at the New York Stampede. Among the dignitaries in attendance were former president Theodore Roosevelt and Will Rogers, their old friend from home. Roosevelt pronounced the performance a bully show, and Rogers invited the 101 troupe as his guests to watch his performance as headliner at the Ziegfeld Follies.

John was still uneasy, off balance. He could not define it: a vague feeling that something was wrong. Maybe he had listened to the Poncas' ghost stories too seriously. Or, maybe he had tried so hard to adopt the white man's ways that he was no longer capable of evaluating such a situation.

Among his own people, following their ways, could he have understood? He had been deeply touched, too, by the death of Iron Tail. The old man must have felt something like this uneasiness. Iron Tail's answer was to go home—at least, to make the attempt.

But Iron Tail had had family back in the Black Hills. John Buffalo had none, and nowhere to go. His heart was very heavy.

The show was in Chicago when it happened. The title of the performance had been changed for the Chicago run at the request of local politicians. There was a large German-American population, and it was feared that the militaristic Preparedness pageant might offend some. The military emphasis was downgraded for the series of appearances, and the Indian part emphasized. The entire performance was dubbed a *Shan-kive,* which was interpreted as an Indian expression meaning a "good time."

The mayor, "Big Bill" Thompson, was given a title, Honorary Director General of the *Shan-kive,* and Buffalo Bill was proclaimed Judge Supreme of all rodeo events. Honorary judges included Joe Miller and local dignitaries such as William Pinkerton of the famed detective agency. Once more, John marveled at Joe Miller's ability to evaluate and capitalize on a situation.

In the midst of all the excitement of the Chicago run, John was approached by a 101 employee who had been back to the base in Oklahoma.

"Buffalo! I have a letter for you. Mr. George sent it."

"Thanks, Slim . . ."

He looked for a private spot to open the letter. It was tattered and water stained, but he was almost certain that he recognized the handwriting. The carefully drawn but clumsy-appearing words were certainly Hebbie's. She had tried to raise the level of her literacy to match his own education.

But now, hope sprang alive in his heart. He could find her now and resume his life. In one of the storage tents, he sat on a rolled canvas and opened the envelope with shaking fingers.

My dearest John . . .

 If you are reading this, then it can mean only one thing. I have left it in another envelope, to be opened in the event of my death.

John Buffalo's moan of anguish could not be heard over the cheers and laughter of the crowd in the arena seats, but it echoed into the darkest recesses of his own soul. He had known for years—how many, now?—that this was the likeliest outcome, but could never have been ready.

He sat silently for a little while, tears streaming down his cheeks. Then he made an effort to read further. He found quickly that it was a useless effort. The envelope— even the letter itself—had been damaged so badly that most of it was illegible. It was torn and water stained, and looked as if someone had tried to paste it back together. If it had not been for a fairly clean area on the outside of the envelope where "101" could be seen, it probably would not have been delivered at all. He could see, toward the bottom of the stained page, a few words, including those most important: ". . . love you always, Hebbie."

His eyes brimmed full again, and he turned to the envelope. When and where had this been mailed?

The postmark was smudged, completely undecipherable. He could not read either the date or the location. He looked for a return address, but found none.

There was another roar of approval from the arena as the show continued, but it meant nothing to John. His world was empty. He folded the letter carefully and returned it to the envelope, slipping it into his shirt pocket, and wandered out into the area between the big top and the auxiliary units.

He had to get away . . . But, to where? He had no place to go. For the past few years, his closest thing to a home had been the headquarters of the Hundred and One. Now he could not go there. There were too many memories.

He thought again of Iron Tail, boarding the train for his beloved Black Hills as his life faded away. John could understand that, but he had no comparable place. Still, the vast open spaces of the West, the lands of big sky and far horizons, seemed desirable to him. He thought of the sunsets he and Hebbie had shared. There were few sunsets worth watching in Chicago or Philadelphia.

I have to get away, he thought. *Back to where I can stretch my eyes to as far as I can see. I need to be alone, to think, to remember the good times.*

He made his way to the dormitory-style sleeping tent and tossed his few belongings into a duffel bag. He was just emerging when the main show concluded and the crowd came pouring out. Joe Miller, on his white stallion, came across the grounds toward the stable at a fast walk.

"Mr. Miller!" John called.

The showman reined aside.

"Yes, John?"

"I'm leaving, sir. A personal matter."

"I see," nodded Miller. "Slim said he brought you a letter. Anything we can do?"

"No, sir."

"Well, stop by the office for your pay. Will you be coming back?"

"I . . . I'm afraid I don't know, Mr. Miller."

"Well, there's a place for you at the Hundred and One."

"Thank you, sir. That means a lot."

He collected his pay and headed for the train depot, with very little idea as to where he'd be going. But he carried his saddle. Wherever he might be, he'd want that option.

FORTY-EIGHT

There was much about the next few months that John could never remember later. Sometimes a fragment of memory would startle him unexpectedly. He would struggle with it. Had it happened at all, or was it merely a disconnected thought that had floated to the surface through the dreamlike haze that hung over him?

He was running. . . . From the world, from the tragedy and the heartbreak of reality, from a life that no longer seemed worthwhile. Running as in a dream, and with the same futility. He was pursued, and each painfully slow and laborious step brought him no nearer to escape from the nameless, faceless thing that hounded him. Even knowing that one is dreaming, sometimes it is impossible to escape or to waken. The dream goes on and on, the terror drawing nearer yet postponing the attack that will mercifully end the chase.

John's flight from reality was much like that. He was attempting escape from something that, in the end, was within his own heart and could not be evaded. It would be many years before he was able to even begin to understand. Just now, heartbroken, he sat numbly in the railroad coach and listened to the *click-clack* of the wheels. . . . It seemed to be the sound and rhythm that marked every change in his life, good or bad. Mostly bad. He could remember few train trips that led to anything but disappointment. The travels on the show train did not count. They were accompanied by work and play and the company of friends. This—the solitary travel in a futile attempt to escape—was completely different. He wanted to scream, to shout a protest at the unfairness of life. He did not do so. His dignity would not allow it. The stoic, emotionless defense adopted by the red man in the presence of others would have to suffice. He looked at the other passengers, many of them sleeping in the dim light as the train rushed westward. Could any of them possibly understand the extent of his grief?

He thought of Iron Tail, the proud Sioux chief. The old warrior had known he was dying, and had tried to go home to the beloved land of his childhood. Iron Tail had not succeeded in reaching home before he crossed over to the Other Side, but he had made the attempt.

Maybe, thought John, *he, too, was making such an attempt.* He had given little thought to where he should go in his retreat. He had no home, no family. He had merely headed west because it was from there that he had come.

The thought that he, like Iron Tail, was headed home to die weighed heavily on him. His own death would be not from pneumonia, but from a broken heart. He sighed deeply and stared out the window at the vast blackness of the night.

Afterward, he could not remember just when and how he had started to drink. It must have been on the train, somewhere crossing Iowa or Nebraska. Probably somebody had offered him a bottle and he had eagerly shelled out the cash that was asked.

It might be thought that whiskey would be hard to obtain. There was a hard-fought campaign in progress to outlaw all alcoholic beverages. The major political parties had refused to meet the question head-on in their official platforms. But there was considerable strength in the Prohibition Party and, even without the right to vote, a great many women carried a great deal of power. The Women's Christian Temperance Union and the Anti-Saloon League were bringing pressure to bear. Public drunkenness—and, in many cases, drinking at all—was considered a disgrace. There was legislation making its way through Congress to completely forbid all production, transportation, and sale of beverage alcohol of any type—beer, wine, whiskey, anything.

Under these circumstances, it would seem that it might have been difficult for John Buffalo to have acquired a drinking problem. But it was not so. When he had money, there always seemed to be someone who had, or could obtain, a bottle. Especially in the West.

In the blur of his memory somewhat later, he could dimly remember a series of dusty western towns. Nebraska, Dakota, Wyoming . . . Cattle country . . . People he understood, horses, cowboys . . .

When he ran out of money, he would acquire enough for a fresh start in one way or another. He no longer had his saddle, and was not certain how he had become separated from it. Maybe he had even left it on the train. If he had that saddle, he might have worked as a cowboy. He might have, anyway, except that he didn't feel like it. It would have taken more energy and ambition than he had.

It was easier to make a little money by gambling. Gambling games had always been a favorite pastime among his people. This translated well into the card games of the white man. Poker was a favorite, and lent itself well to the flat, emotionless facial expression often relied upon by the Indian.

John Buffalo was an expert at poker. As a student, he

had had great success in low-stakes games, naturally frowned upon by the school authorities. At the 101, especially in the winter months, poker was a frequent pastime.

Even in his whiskey-troubled mind, John recognized this as a source of money to continue his habit. He was able to stay sober enough when he needed to, to play a skilled hand, collect a few jackpots, and continue his downhill slide.

There were several small towns, indistinguishable one from another in his memory, where this had happened. That he survived was probably due only to the fact that it was summer, and that the drunken portion of the sequence could take place outdoors. He would waken in a street he did not recognize, and begin the destructive cycle again.

In this way, he found himself in a saloon called Happy Jack's, in a town in Wyoming. He was looking for an opportunity for a poker game, casually pretending to drink, while he watched the other patrons. They were cowboys, men he understood. They were having a good time, joking and visiting. Not really a bunch who afforded a good possibility for a poker game, but men he envied, in a way. They were among friends and were having fun.

The conversation was about the European War. Increasingly, there was a feeling that the United States would be drawn into the war.

"I'm neutral, meself," a big Irishman was saying. "I don't care *who* kills the Kaiser, as long as he gets the job done."

"Now, Tom," retorted another cowboy, "I heard the Irish have a secret weapon. . . . A new type of square-barreled cannon that shoots bricks."

"It's true," said Irish Tom seriously, "but the real show-down is comin'. Wait till we get the Irish Navy after them German U-boats."

"Irish Navy? Who ever heard of them?" a cowboy

scoffed. "Ain't they the sailors who go home for lunch?"

"Yeah," said another. "Where is this Irish Navy, anyway?"

Irish Tom lowered his tone and looked suspiciously from side to side.

"An' do ye think," he half-whispered, "that I'd be tellin' *you,* ye damned German spy?"

There was a roar of laughter, and again, John felt a pang of envy. These were friends, having fun. He was an outsider. It was easy to feel that it was because of the color of his skin. He realized, however, that one of the cowboys in the jovial group was probably an Indian, also. The man was quiet and unassuming . . . a tall, handsome man. There was nothing to indicate his tribe or nation.

As the group broke up and passed his table, the tall Indian gave him a slight nod of recognition, and John responded with a nod of his own.

Autumn came, and cooler weather. John was still in the same general area, drawn by the easygoing atmosphere. He was still a loner, rejecting the temptation to make acquaintances. It might interfere with his gambler's vocation.

He considered applying for work at one of the ranches in the area, but kept postponing the decision. He had done well enough at poker that he still had a small stake. Maybe later.

In early January 1917, he was reading a *Denver Post* newspaper that someone had left in a hotel lobby, and an article caught his eye. It was about the war and quoted Theodore Roosevelt at length. Roosevelt advocated immediate entry into the war, with at least a division of volunteers. Among these would be a brigade of hard-riding, fast-moving cavalry, a new unit of Rough Riders who could breach the vaunted German lines. Once in Germany, they would live off the land, move fast and strike hard, and challenge the Kaiser on his own turf. It should not be hard, Roosevelt speculated, to recruit a few hundred hard-riding cowboys who could handle such an assignment.

John thought for a moment of the gang he knew in the 101 Wild West Show. . . . Yes, for many of those, this would be an attractive adventure. He laid the paper aside. He had a more pressing problem. He was running short on cash, and needed a poker game.

In the same general area, a young cowboy named Tim McCoy, who had a homestead on Owl Creek, had read the same article in the *Denver Post*. He was enthusiastically interested in a project like Roosevelt's. *Somebody needs to do something,* he thought. With the brashness of youth and convinced of his own immortality, he took pen and paper and composed a letter to the former president. He offered to recruit four hundred skilled cowboy riders for the cavalry unit proposed by Roosevelt.

Not having any idea where Roosevelt might live, he assumed that someone in the postal system might know. He addressed the letter to:

The Hon. Theo. Roosevelt
New York City, New York

A couple of weeks later, a rider from the town of Thermopolis, Wyoming, rode into the McCoy homestead. He carried a telegram.

"It looked mighty important," the rider explained.

There were six words in the telegram:

BULLY FOR YOU! DO PROCEED! ROOSEVELT.

All of this was unknown to John Buffalo, who had found his poker game and was winning. As the game narrowed far into the night, two players kept jockeying for the big win: John and a nondescript drifter with a week's beard and the shoes of a miner. He carried a small pouch of gold dust, and used it sometimes to cover the cash and chips on the table when the betting became heavy.

John did not trust him, but the gold dust appeared real, and John was on a winning streak. The other man won just often enough to stay in.

The hour was late, the game five-card stud. There were five men still at the table, but three were there more from interest than for serious play. They'd bet just enough to keep the game going, and would fold at the first opportunity. The serious players continued to be John and the miner.

The dealer, one of the other three for this hand, dealt a card facedown to each player, and on top of that, another card, faceup. John took a quick look around the table. Nothing much showing: a jack, a couple of low numbers . . . His own was an eight, the miner's a two, both clubs.

Each player took a careful look at his hole card. Then the bidding began. The player with the jack opened, the miner raised the bet, and one of the others dropped out. John's hole card was a three of hearts. Not much to be proud of.

The dealer tossed cards, faceup, to those still in the game. John drew a three of diamonds. Not bad . . . With his hole card, a pair of threes.

The miner now had a pair of twos showing, with a new two of diamonds.

The dealer dropped, but would continue to deal to the others. The miner, with the highest hand showing—a pair of twos—opened the betting.

"Ten dollars!"

A high bet for only a pair of twos. *He's pretty proud of that hole card,* thought John. A high face card? Not another two, or the miner would have bet higher before this.

"Call," said John, tossing a gold piece into the pot.

On the next round, the miner drew an ace, and John another three, this time in spades. He now had three of a kind—a good hand at five-card stud, but it didn't look like much. . . . A low pair and an eight were all that were showing.

His opponent, with a pair and an ace, seemed overly elated.

John, using his stone-faced stoicism, bet ten. The miner raised twenty, and the third player dropped out.

There was more going on than could be seen as the last card dropped before each of the two remaining players. Two very small cards: a two of hearts to the miner, and another three for John.

Four of a kind. Almost a once-in-a-lifetime hand.

Very quickly, he saw that the miner had overlooked that possibility. He was far too excited about his three deuces and an ace.

John looked over the possibilities. Normally, three of a kind was a good hand, but this miner was far too excited. The man could see that John's threes would top those three twos. This bet, then, would be based on the miner's hole card. What would it be? If it happened to be a fourth two, it would account for the man's excitement. Of course, John's four *threes* would top it.

What could it be? Suddenly it struck him: The hole card must be *another ace: a full house.* Almost nothing beats a full house. A royal flush or a straight flush, both impossible here. Only one other hand could win: four of kind, the hand that was filled by John's fourth three, lying there facedown.

He doesn't realize, thought John. *He's too pleased with his full house!*

John appeared to ponder, and finally faked dejection.

"I'll check," he said in resignation.

"Raise fifty!" said the miner.

"See it and raise a hundred," said John quickly.

The miner took the bait.

"Look," he said, "I got no more cash than this, but here's somethin'. He pulled out a folded paper and spread it on the table. "This here's a deed to a gold claim I own. It's prob'ly worth a few hunnerd dollars. It'll cover whatever you got. How about it?"

There was a little further negotiating, with the dealer and the bartender as witnesses. The miner turned over his hole card triumphantly. The ace of spades—a full house.

Now John flipped over his own card and watched the expression on the miner's face change to one of disbelief.

"Four of a kind!" he breathed. *"My God!"*

FORTY-NINE

The "Boar's Nest," a gold mine . . . It had been exciting, at first. John had rented a horse at the livery stable and followed the directions written out for him by the poker-playing miner.

"It ain't been worked for a while," the man had warned. "It ain't much. . . . There's a tunnel in pretty good shape. About gold, I can't say. I've never really worked it. You know minin'?"

"No."

"Well, you can learn, I guess. All of us did, sometime. You need to go out and take a look, talk to somebody at an assay office. They'll help you. They'll weigh out your dust, too. You got that little bag of dust I was bettin' with last night?"

"Yes . . . That's from the mine?"

"No, not the Boar's Nest. Another place. But there's gold in them hills."

John had taken most of the day to ride out to the mine. Even there, he had trouble finding it. There were bushes and shrubs, even a small tree growing in front of the tunnel opening. Not very impressive.

The day was late, and he made camp in order to get settled in before dark. He could explore later.

He began to investigate as soon as it was light enough. He had brought a coal-oil lantern, and now lit it to explore the mine tunnel.

John quickly realized that it, too, had been greatly exaggerated. It was low, requiring a squatting position. For a man as tall as himself, it would probably be better to work on one's knees or even sitting. Judging from the cobwebs, it appeared that no one had worked this claim for some time. There must be a reason, and he suspected that maybe he—not the miner—had been the victim in that last poker hand.

He scratched around enough to assure himself that he had little interest in mining. He had always had a fear of closed-in places, probably because of his early childhood in a Lakota lodge; warm in winter, cool in summer, but open and free to sky and prairie. This reinforced his feeling that there are things more important than gold.

The next thing, then, was to find a way to get rid of his liability. He spent the day cleaning up around the mine's opening, brushing down cobwebs, and picking up debris from the tunnel's floor. If he were to sell it, it must at least look workable.

Back in town, he went to the assay office, which appeared not to have been very busy for some time. He introduced himself, and asked whether there was much interest in buying and selling claims.

The man behind the counter looked him over curiously: a cowboy, not a miner.

"Not much," he said cautiously. "Pickin' up a little with the war effort. You lookin' to buy a claim?"

"No," said John. "I'm no miner, but . . . Well, I sort of bought one. I either need to learn to work it, or to sell it."

"Where is it?"

"Up north, a half a day. It's called the Boar's Nest."

From the look on the man's face, John realized that he had guessed right. Apparently it had a reputation.

"The *Boar's Nest?*"

"That's what it says on the paper. You know of it?"

"Well, yes . . ."

There was a lopsided grin on the man's face that told a bigger story.

"Maybe I should learn a little about mining," John pondered. "Either that, or sell it, if I can."

"Well, I ain't in business to teach greenhorns to mine," said the assayer. "But there were a couple of fellas askin' about buyin' a claim, a while ago. Are you workin' the shaft?"

"Not yet."

"Well, tell you what. Get you a gold pan over at the mercantile. They can tell you how to get started. When you get a little dust, bring it in. That'll stir some interest in buyin', maybe."

As he left, John realized that he might well have the proverbial bear by the tail. How could he escape? The poorly concealed smirk on the face of the assayer as he turned away was the final insult.

At the store, he bought odds and ends of supplies that seemed appropriate for his purpose. He also asked about a cheap shotgun.

"There's a few grouse up there," he told the clerk. "Maybe I can get some fresh meat."

The old single-shot had seen better days, but the clerk offered to throw in a loading tool for the brass shells.

"You can reload with your own powder and shot," he explained. "Use a cloth wadding. Here, you'll need a box of primer caps. See, you punch out the fired cap and push in the new one with this tool."

John was quite aware of the process of reloading. He'd seen the old men do it many times. This was what he needed.

A gold pan, a short lesson in how to use it . . .

"You'll see this black sand in the pan," the merchant told him. "Now, that ain't gold, but you're gettin' close. That's when you keep tryin'. Now we got a stretch of purty good weather right now, but . . . Say, you got shelter if we get snow?"

John thought of the mine tunnel.

"Oh, yes. I'll be fine."

He actually did spend half a day panning. A few grains of black sand, one sparkling glitter that reflected sunlight for a moment . . . It could have been a fleck of gold dust, he always thought later, but it was gone the next instant, and he never found it again. Like a lot of things in life, he pondered morosely.

Well, time to return to his original plan. He fired a couple of shells from the old shotgun and got a grouse, which he broiled over his fire. While his supper cooked, he took out his reloading tools. . . . Punch out the old primers, replace with new caps, measure the black powder . . . A somewhat lighter load than recommended . . . Tightly packed wadding . . . Almost filling the shell.

With his wad cutter, he had punched several cardboard top-wads out of a lightweight box in which the clerk had packed some of his supplies. One of these on top of the rags . . .

Now he turned to the buckskin pouch of gold dust which had been part of his winnings at poker. Very carefully, he sifted fine dust into the nose of each brass shell casing. He was throwing money away, but he had to think of it as an investment. . . . A thin cardboard top wad, and a light crimp with the tool, to turn the shell's rim over the wad.

His palms were sweating as he took the shotgun and his two high-priced shells to the very back of the tunnel and set the lantern on the floor. He selected a corner with a sort of crevice, and scratched around a bit with his short-handled miner's pick to expose a fresh surface. Then, a few steps back . . .

He fired the first shell, and started forward to examine the results with the lantern. He was stopped by the dense white powder smoke that filled the tunnel. He'd have to wait.

The results were quite pleasing, he thought when he was able to reenter. A bright sprinkle of sparkling gold in a space of a handspan. He backed off another step or two before firing the second shell into the same general area. He rolled in his blankets that night with a solid feeling of satisfaction. Now he was ready to go back to the assay office.

"Is this the real stuff, or am I minin' fool's gold?"

John cautiously tossed a small corked bottle on the counter. Definitely not the pouch he'd obtained in the poker game. The pouch was well worn and greasy, and spoke of long use. That would suggest that he knew more than he was trying to imply. Besides, the stained old pouch held a lot more dust. He had no exact idea of its value, but here was an opportunity to learn. He knew exactly the measure of the gold dust in the bottle. He'd measured it in his gunpowder scoop. This would give him a close estimate of the total worth of his winnings. Then it remained only to rid himself of his useless mine.

The assayer lifted the bottle, glanced at the sparkling powder carelessly, and then took a more serious second look. He pulled the cork, carefully sifted a bit of the powder into a glazed ceramic tray, and poked around with a small glass rod.

"This come from that Boar's Nest claim of yours?" he asked suspiciously.

"I've been workin' it a little," John said casually. And, of course, quite truthfully, without really answering the assay man's question.

He waited while the man ran some tests, dropping fluids from an eyedropper on a few grains of dust, carefully weighing a sample on a delicate-looking scale in a glass case.

Finally the assayer straightened, poured the dust back into the bottle, and set it on the counter.

"That's a good-quality lode," he said, some doubt still in his voice. "Boar's Nest, you say?"

"That's what the papers call it," said John.

"Hmm . . . You mentioned wantin' to sell it?"

"Maybe. I'm not sure, now."

"Well, I can understand that. But in case you're interested, I know a fella or two. . . . Let me talk to 'em."

Suddenly John realized that he had created a dangerous situation. If there were prospective buyers, they'd want to accompany him to the mine. Miles from town, he'd be alone and vulnerable.

But . . . The assay office had to be a reliable establishment. If the assayer referred them, surely prospective buyers would be honest. He needed some sort of assurance.

"How do I know if these buyers are legitimate?"

"Ah, I see," answered the assayer. "You're careful. Miles from town, with strangers . . . Of course! Clever of you to see that. Well, look . . . Your protection is probably the deed. Where is it now?"

"It's safe," John said cautiously.

"Good. But before leaving town with strangers, I'd . . . Let's see . . . You could leave it with the bank, or the sheriff, or leave it in our safe. We're federally bonded, of course."

Of course. John considered consulting someone else in a position of authority; but, being a stranger in town, could not know who might be reliable. The fewer people who knew about the transaction, the better. And it would lend to his own credibility.

"I'll leave it here," he concluded. "I'll have to come back to transfer the deed if you send me a buyer."

"That's right. You want me to send this fella out?"

John's suspicion rose again.

"When do you think you might—?" he started to ask.

"Oh! There he goes now," interrupted the assayer. "Just a minute!"

He stepped to the door and called to a couple of men across the street. They crossed over and the introductions took place.

Then the assayer explained the situation. ". . . so Mr. Buffalo, here, not being experienced in mining, was of the opinion that he might do best to sell."

The two men nodded understandingly.

"You've checked his dust?" asked one. "Good enough for me. Of course, I'd want to see the vein. He drew a gold watch from a vest pocket. It's late. How about we go out tomorrow?"

"Fine with me," John agreed. "Shall we meet here?"

"Good! After breakfast, then?"

They shook hands all around, and John went to check into the hotel. He might as well be comfortable on what he hoped would be his last night in the area.

FIFTY

The three men rode into the camp at Boar's Nest about noon. It seemed a shorter journey now that he had traveled the distance a few times.

"There it is." John pointed to the tunnel.

"Let's take a look," said the man who called himself Johnson, swinging down and heading for the opening.

"There's a lantern inside," John called. "Go ahead. I'll be right there."

He unsaddled his horse and tied it to a pine tree, laid his saddle aside, and walked over to the tunnel. The others had simply looped their reins around the saddle horn. *They must be in a hurry,* he smiled to himself.

The watery yellow light of the lantern showed as a glow from the inner end of the shaft. Johnson was holding the lantern, and Green, his companion, was inspecting the area where sparks of gold dust reflected its rays.

"Look at that!"

"And *that* . . ."

John was pleased. He said nothing, figuring he didn't have to. They were already doing a selling job on themselves.

The two came out toward the entrance, talking softly between them.

"You find where I'd been workin'?" John asked.

"Yes, we sure did," said Johnson. "Way that looks, why you wantin' to sell?"

John shrugged. "I'm not a miner. Don't really know much about it. Just as soon not be tied down."

"How'd you happen to have it?" Johnson asked. "I assume you have a deed?"

"Of course. It's in the vault at the assay office. To tell the truth, I won it in a poker game, sight unseen."

"What do you think it's worth, if we want to buy it?" Green asked, cautiously.

"I don't know, fellas, I told you I'm not a miner," John said. "I'm not lookin' to get rich, here. I figure, the way the bettin' was goin' in that poker game, I've got about five hundred in it. That sound fair?"

The two men looked questioningly at each other.

"Let's take another look at the vein, there," Johnson said.

He picked up the lantern and headed on in. The two men followed.

"Now, where'd you first see the color along here?" Green asked.

"Right there where you see it." John pointed. "Sort of spreads out along the wall toward the corner, there."

"What's your bottom dollar to sell—right now, today?" Johnson asked.

John hesitated. He'd hoped they'd make him an offer. In his ignorance, he might have priced too low and created suspicion.

"Look," he said, "I've told you I don't know mining. I might be too high or too low, and wouldn't know either way. You see what I've got, and you know more than I what it's worth. I said I've got maybe five hundred in it. But I want out, and if you'll agree to four hundred, I'll go back to town and sign the deed."

Then a very strange thing happened. The two men glanced at each other in the dim lantern light, and both nodded agreement. As if in one motion, both drew their guns.

John wanted to make a break for it, but in the narrow confines of the mine tunnel, he knew he'd never reach the open air. This was what he'd feared, but . . .

"Wait!" he called out, hands half-lifted. "Don't shoot! That deed's back in town. This is no good to you. . . ."

His voice trailed off as he saw both men chuckling. Was this some kind of a terrible joke?

"Son," said Johnson, "we don't want to hurt you. We're federal marshals, and you're under arrest."

"For *what?* Tryin' to sell my claim?"

"Well, maybe that, too. . . . One you know is worthless. . . . But, for sure, saltin' a mine with dust from someplace else is a crime. Might say, though, that for somebody that ain't a miner, it's a pretty slick job. How'd you do it? Shotgun shells?"

"Where are you takin' me?"

"Back to town. There'll be a circuit judge around in a week or so. We'll let you gather up your stuff. Green, get the shotgun, there."

He turned back to John.

"I hope you won't try nothin' stupid. You got another gun?"

"No. You can check."

"We will. But it'll go a lot better if nobody gets hurt, an' that's up to you. You're not in a lot of trouble, yet, so just don't *cause* none."

It was nearly dark when they reached town, and the sheriff opened one of the cells for the marshals.

"That's your home for now, Buffalo," said Johnson. "The judge comes a week from Wednesday, the sheriff says. We'll be here."

"What about my horse? He belongs to the livery."

"We'll take him back. The sheriff will look after your gear."

———

The trapped, enclosed feeling in the jail was among the hardest times of his life. He already had a dread of enclosed places, which had shown itself at the mine shaft. This was even worse. There was one small window, high in the wall. He could have seen out by standing on the cot, except that the window was covered by a wooden shutter against the winter winds.

The iron bars let him look down a short hallway and into the sheriff's office. At present, there was no one in the other two small cells.

On the third day in confinement, the sheriff brought a young man down the short hallway.

"You got a visitor, Buffalo," he said simply.

John said nothing. He didn't understand. He knew nobody in the area, except the assayer and the federal marshals.

The man looked familiar, somehow. He was dressed as a cowboy, and looked the part, but . . . Wait! A few weeks ago, in another part of the state . . . In a saloon . . . This was the quiet young Indian who was with the fun-loving Irishmen, joking about the war and the Kaiser.

"John Buffalo?" the young man asked aloud.

At the same time, he was using hand signs. The palm forward sign of friendly greeting, followed quickly by *I am here to help you.*

Still puzzled, John nodded and signed *It is good.*

The visitor smiled, and spoke now in English.

"Good. You know hand signs."

"Out of practice, maybe. Who are you?"

"My name is George Shakespear. I saw you in Thermopolis at the Happy Jack. I was made to think that you were troubled."

"More trouble now." John gestured at the walls and bars.

"That is true."

"Are you a medicine man?"

"No, no. I do a little medicine, is all. I work as a cowboy."

"You are Lakota?"

"No . . .'Rapaho. You are Lakota?"

"Yes. I was, anyway. I went to Indian schools."

"Me, too. That's how I got to be George Shakespear. My brother is William."

"Of course." John smiled for the first time in months. "But, what are you doing here?"

"I heard they were holding an Indian who had salted a mine. I thought it might be the same . . . Same as the troubled one in Thermopolis. So I came over to see."

John stared. "You *do* have a powerful guide."

George Shakespear merely shrugged, and went on.

"I have a friend who can help you. A white man . . . McCoy."

"The big man telling jokes?"

"No, that's Irish Tom. Tim McCoy is small but tough. He was there, but let me go on. He is recruiting . . . Building a war party of cavalry, a Rough Riders outfit to go to Germany. Theodore Roosevelt is sponsoring it."

"I read about that in the *Denver Post,* didn't I?"

"Maybe so. Anyway, he needs cowboys. I am made to think that you know horses, no?"

John nodded. "Some."

"Okay . . . Would you talk to McCoy? With his influence . . . He has a telegram from Roosevelt. . . . They might let you off on this if you'd sign on for the Rough Riders. No promises . . ."

"Why not? It beats sittin' here."

"Okay. I think I can get McCoy to come over."

"Is he a cowboy, too?"

"Yes. He has a homestead, a few cattle. Hires out to other ranches, too, sometimes."

"Why would he help me?"

"He might not, but I'd guess he will. His Arapaho name is 'The Friend.' "

"He's a half-breed?"

"No, he's just a white man who understands. He's all Irish, I guess, but he's all 'Rapaho, too. The old men talk to him."

That, perhaps, was the most significant fact of all. A white man with whom the tribal elders consult must be very special.

"He speaks Arapaho?" asked John.

George Shakespear laughed.

"No," he answered. "He does it all in hand signs."

Tim McCoy, "The Friend," showed up at the jail two days later. He explained the recruitment effort, which was going well. Already, he had enlisted more than 300 potential cavalrymen, with his goal 400.

"I think that your signing as volunteer would impress the marshals," McCoy told him. "No promises, of course. What's your riding experience?"

"Been at the Hundred and One Ranch a few years," said John. "Traveled with the show. We were in Germany when the war broke out."

"*You* were?"

"Yes . . . We had about sixty Oglalas with a circus over there."

"Heard about that! That was *you?* Buffalo, we *need* you."

John signed the enlistment roster, and sat back to wait.

It didn't take long. Apparently, McCoy was skilled in the use of documents. A personal telegram from Theodore Roosevelt, authorizing the recruitment effort, seemed to carry a lot of weight with federal marshals. The jail door swung open.

In a matter of days, John Buffalo was working as a cowboy on a ranch in Wyoming, preparing to be mustered in with 400 other Rough Riders. When the call came to meet the Kaiser on his own ground, the Rough Riders would be ready.

FIFTY-ONE

There is a curious idiosyncrasy in human history: As a nation prepares for war, it thinks in terms of previous wars and prepares for the most recent experience; not for the *next* war, but for the one just fought. This, in terms of weapons, tactics, and preparations. . . .

Teddy Roosevelt's hard-riding American cowboys, the Rough Riders of the war with Spain, were extremely effective in Cuba. Their prowess had stirred the pride of America, and had, in fact, catapulted Roosevelt into national prominence. He served as governor of New York, and was selected in 1900, as vice presidential candidate for William McKinley's second term.

He had been vice president for only a few months when McKinley was gunned down by an assassin. The president was expected to recover, but took a turn for the worse and died a few days later. Roosevelt became the youngest president in American history when he took the oath of office in 1901. The American public, fascinated by his background as a cowboy and soldier, and by the expanding

American West, loved his flamboyant style and no-nonsense approach: *Speak softly and carry a big stick.*

Roosevelt had been instrumental in the creation of the Panama Canal and was elected in 1904, declaring that he would not run again for another term.

But in 1912, concerned over a reactionary drift among the Republicans, he helped to organize the Progressive Party and ran for president. His candidacy split the Republican vote and elected Woodrow Wilson, a Democrat. Wilson's reluctance to enter the "European War" must have frustrated the old Rough Rider to extremes.

Now, there was even more frustration. The latter-day Rough Riders, four hundred strong, were enlisted and signed, ready to serve as Teddy's big stick in Germany. They would "punch a small hole" in the vaunted German defenses and wreak havoc in the Kaiser's backyard, behind his own lines. The Rough Riders waited, poised for action, expecting marching orders.

That, however, was another matter. The special cavalry unit, men and horses, would have to debark from an American port, and the United States was still officially neutral. It would require the permission of President Wilson, Roosevelt's old political enemy, who was still determined to stay out of the war.

There are no official records of the conversation between the two leaders, only that there was such a meeting at the White House in early 1917.

Roosevelt, recounting the meeting to his old friend, General Leonard Wood, later reported:

"If I were president and I told somebody what Wilson told me, I would have meant 'yes.' But since I'm not president and I'm not Woodrow Wilson, I really don't know what the hell he meant."

What Wilson undeniably meant was a definite no. He was determined not to allow any privately organized military units to endanger American neutrality.

In addition, there was another factor. Roosevelt's popularity was again rising with American sympathy for the Allies in the European war. There was a groundswell of pressure for Roosevelt to lead the 1920 presidential campaign as a Republican candidate who could unseat the frustrating Wilson.

For whatever reasons, the Rough Riders' dreams of glory were dashed. In late March, Tim McCoy received a telegram from Roosevelt in which the message was clear: There were to be no marching orders. The plan had been rejected. The Rough Riders would remain cowboys, and nobody was going anywhere.

This, McCoy related in later years, ended the opportunity to have followed "Teddy" in a wild, old-time cavalry charge up the hill. He also conceded that sabers and horses from the last war would have been no match for German machine guns and automatic weapons in this one.

"It's likely that Wilson saved our hides by stopping it," he admitted.

But for now, it was a crushing defeat. Ironically, it was only a few days until the United States entered the war, enraged over the sinking of the *Lusitania*.

The Rough Riders were, as McCoy put it in his biography, ". . . like the man in midair who suddenly discovers that he has no trapeze."

John Buffalo certainly felt this letdown. He had counted on the Rough Riders to give him some sort of a sense of direction. Many of the cowboys he had met recently felt the same. Some were enlisting in the Army. The United

States had initiated a draft, and the cowboys felt that they had a better chance for the choice of cavalry if they volunteered, instead of waiting to be drafted.

As well as every other Indian, John was in a unique position. They were not yet recognized as American citizens, and were consequently exempt from the draft. They could *volunteer* for military service, in the same status as other volunteers, though still not citizens.

Eager to fill the ranks, recruiters sent negotiating teams to the reservations to try to promote enlistments. John Buffalo decided to go along to the powwow on the Wind River Reservation to hear what the recruiters had to offer. He arrived with George Shakespear and Tim McCoy early in the afternoon at the dance arbor, a temporary shelter built to furnish shade for participants and spectators. There were dozens of bluecoat soldiers, many wearing uniforms heavy with gold braid. The high-ranking military men and dignitaries were seated at a table in the center of the arbor, and the Arapahoes, about one hundred in number, sat cross-legged on the ground.

The speeches were flowery and full of platitudes that sounded like some of the old peace commission diplomacy. . . .

"The Great White Father needs the help of his Indian children," one orator gushed.

"We must join together, red and white, to fight our common enemy. . . ."

"The red man and the white man are brothers!"

One after another the speakers rose, voiced their platitudes, and sat back down. Finally, a tall, dignified old Arapaho rose, dropped his blanket, and began to speak.

"That's Lone Bear," George Shakespear whispered to John. "One of our most respected chiefs."

Lone Bear did a very uncharacteristic thing for one of the elders. He spoke in English, and in hand signs as well for those of his people who had no English.

"A long time ago, we 'Rapahoes fought you white men. We were brave but there were more of you. Your medicine was good, and though we fought hard, many of our friends were killed. A lot of bluecoats also died. . . . Then we were beaten and you told us follow the white man's road. You told us putem up our tomahawks forever and pickem up plows. Yeah, 'pickem up plow, live in peace.' That is what you said then.

"But now you come here and tell us, 'Injun, putem down plow, pickem up tomahawk!' Lone Bear is an old man, and maybeso Lone Bear is stupid, but Lone Bear no savvy!"

The old chief resumed his seat.

"I think maybeso Lone Bear 'savvies' pretty good," McCoy said quietly. "That or *I* don't savvy, either."

The recruitment effort met with little success among Arapaho that day.

Not long afterward, Tim McCoy, feeling a strong patriotic pull, left his ranch under the care of George Shakespear and joined a new officer candidate program in the Army.

Other cowboys enlisted, and John Buffalo was restless to be doing something . . . anything.

He could go anywhere he wished. His charges in the matter of the gold mine had been dropped so that he could enlist in the Rough Riders. That had fallen through, but he had been assured that, with the forfeiture of the gold claim his record was clean. There was a nagging doubt that maybe the claim was worth something to somebody, but he didn't care. He was too grateful to be out.

He thought of returning to the 101, but the Wild West Show had been closed until further notice. At least, until after the war. He considered, very briefly, the option of working at the ranch, but that was the locale of almost his entire life with Hebbie. He did not think he could bear to see the familiar surroundings, the places they had loved and enjoyed together. . . . No, it would never do.

Maybe he should enlist. There were white men who had been good to him. The Millers, Naismith, Pop Warner . . . And, what would happen if the United States and the Allies *lost* the war? The Millers had supported the Allies worldwide.

Yes, the 101 was probably not his best option. He could volunteer for the cavalry. He would have no major decisions to make, and could contribute his skills to the war effort. . . . Maybe even learn something.

He wondered where to go to enlist. Thermopolis, maybe. But the recruiter he'd seen there appeared to lean toward infantry, which John hoped to avoid. Somehow, he remembered that the Army's Cavalry School was at Fort Riley, Kansas. Yes . . . He could go there, walk in and offer to enlist.

At the next payday, he collected his pay from the Double Diamond, where he'd been working, and quit.

"Somethin' wrong, John?"

"No, sir. Just need to do something. Thought I'd join the Army, maybe."

The boss nodded. "Lots of cowboys are. I might even consider it myself, if I were younger. Best of luck, John!"

John bought a train ticket and headed south. He'd change trains somewhere, probably Cheyenne. He couldn't recall. He'd check it later.

At least, now, he had some sense of purpose.

FIFTY-TWO

In due time John arrived at Fort Riley and approached the guardhouse at the gate.

"I want to join the Army," he told the guard who greeted him.

He was directed to the proper building, and found himself facing a burly sergeant with a heavy handlebar mustache. The trim on his uniform was yellow. John had already realized that yellow designated cavalry, red, artillery, and light blue, infantry.

The sergeant looked him up and down.

"Cowboy? Where you from?"

"Been workin' in Wyoming," John said vaguely. "Before that, Oklahoma. Hunnerd and One."

The sergeant seemed impressed.

"How you happen to come here?"

John shrugged. "Cavalry."

The sergeant's face beamed with approval.

"Good. You got some experience with horses?"

It was not really a question.

The sergeant opened a drawer and took out a sheet of paper, which appeared to be a form. He dipped a pen into the ink bottle on the desk and poised it over the paper.

"Name?"

"Buffalo. John Buffalo."

The sergeant paused.

"You're Indian, John?"

"Yes, sir. That a problem?"

"No. Can you read and write?"

"Yes. I've been to school."

"Good. Here . . . You want to fill out this form? We get a lot that can't read, you know."

"I'd expect so."

"Here . . . Pull up a chair."

He finished the paper and handed it back. The sergeant blotted the drying ink, turned the paper, and skimmed it quickly.

"Good!" he said. "Now there's a new platoon just forming. I'll get somebody to take you over to Quartermaster where they'll issue you a uniform. Then, down to the barracks. They'll show you."

He called into an adjoining room, and a corporal stepped through the doorway.

"Corporal," said the sergeant, "this is John Buffalo, a new man. Take him over to Quartermaster and then over to C company."

"New platoon, Sergeant?"

"Yes. Are they full yet?"

"Still short a couple, I think."

"Okay, get him settled."

The next few days were a whirlwind of activity. The closest thing that John had ever come to this regimented scheduling was long ago during his first days at Carlisle. Even with the demanding travel schedules of the 101 Wild West Show on the road, there was nothing like this.

To make matters worse, for the past few months he had been in cattle country, an area with strong Arapaho influence. Many of the ranches grazed on leased Arapaho land. It had been easy to fall into the habit of "Indian time": It will happen when the time comes.

Cowboying is often like that, anyway. When something is needed, he does it, sometimes with urgency. Then, a wait, often utilized in planning, but always vigilant and expectant toward the next emergency.

Somehow, John had expected the Army to be like that. He was wrong.

Every waking hour was planned for the recruits. Even the waking was planned, with a bugle call at dawn.... Reveille ... This was accompanied by a yelling drill sergeant, stalking the barracks and shaking the bunks of those who moved too slowly.

"Up! Up! You gonna sleep all day? Outta that sack, soldier!"

Calisthenics, marching, weapons instruction, the issue of horses, saddles and equipment, saber drill "at the heads." An entire afternoon was devoted to instruction in care and grooming of the horses. Some of the recruits had virtually no experience with animals at all. Another lengthy session was devoted entirely to cleaning, care, and polishing of the leather tack used on the horse. Halter, bridle, McClellan saddle, carbine scabbard ... Saddle soap, neatsfoot oil, the old familiar smells. Never, though, had he seen common care of equipment given so important a schedule.

It soon became apparent to the training cadre that John was a recruit with some experience. He could be of use to them. John was given responsibility, a little at a time, and managed to handle it well, assisting green recruits with their handling of horses.

"Try it this way.... Pick up the foot and sort of lean against his shoulder.... So ... That throws his weight on the other foot. Let him keep his balance."

Soon they let him have more responsibility. At the end of the few weeks of basic training, John was rewarded by the addition of two stripes to his sleeve: *Corporal* John Buffalo.

It happened at the parade review. The reviewing stand was packed with dignitaries, gathered to observe and evaluate the graduating classes of trainees. Some of the new cavalrymen were draftees, but most were cavalry by choice, having enlisted as John had done, to gain this advantage.

The military band, seated on a platform near the review stand, was pumping out the stirring strains of martial music to inspire pride and dignity in the troopers. It was a glorious day, one to make any soldier proud. Especially, a cavalryman.

In his position as corporal, John rode at the end of one of the front ranks. As the platoon neared the review stand, the command, "Eyes . . . *left!*" rang out. As one, the heads of all the riders snapped to the left, to look into the faces of the visiting dignitaries. John found himself staring directly into a familiar face, yet one he could not quite identify.

"Eyes . . . *front!*" came the next command, and the moment was gone.

John was bewildered. He was certain that he knew—or had known—that tall captain, apparently an aide to one of the senior officers. But where? How?

The mystery was solved quickly after the ceremonies ended.

"John! John Buffalo!"

The captain was hurrying toward him as John turned and tossed a snappy salute. It was returned almost casually.

"John! What the hell are you doing here?"

Now, with the ready, friendly smile and the familiar voice, his memory came rushing back. How many years? It had been at The Oaks, Senator Langtry's plantation . . . A wonderful, impossible weekend, with Jane . . . Her family . . . Now a world away . . . This, her brother . . .

"Alan Langtry? Excuse me, sir. . . . *Captain* Langtry!"

The captain laughed.

"Yes, finally graduated. But promotion's slow except in wartime. Still just a captain. But where have you been, John? We need to talk. When are you off duty?"

"After retreat, sir. But . . . Isn't it forbidden to fraternize . . . an officer and an enlisted man?"

The captain laughed again.

"It must be permissible for a couple of old friends to talk. What ever happened to you? I expected to follow your athletic career. What happened?"

He doesn't know, John thought. *No one ever told him about it.*

"I was transferred to another school. Haskell."

"You mean out *here?* At Lawrence?"

"Yes, sir."

"But why? That must have been an error of some sort, John."

He has no idea, John realized.

Alan Langtry would have been away at West Point, seldom home for the two or three years following that memorable weekend at The Oaks. There would have been no reason for the Senator to have explained the complicated events by which the life of John Buffalo had been changed. Or, the reason.

"I have to get back to the stable, sir," John said formally.

"Of course. But, do meet me later, John. We can take a walk and visit a little. How about after your mess call— say, about seven? Meet at the parade ground?"

"That's fine, sir."

John saluted, and the greeting was returned casually.

As he reined away, John was amused. Alan Langtry still retained much of his boyish charm and enthusiasm, but now it was heavily overlaid with military discipline. As it should be, he realized. His preoccupation with time called it to John's attention. . . . "About seven . . ."

For the past year, John had been headed in the other direction. Cowboys, especially in the area where he'd been, were largely oblivious to time. Most did not even own a watch. They might as well be Indians, it was sometimes joked. But in the military, time was of the essence. Plans must coincide to bring success.

As he trotted toward the stables to rejoin his platoon, John had an amusing thought. Now that he was in the Army, his life was being regulated again by the clock, as it had on the show circuit. A performance would be scheduled, a time and place. It was necessary to have hundreds of people, animals, and rolling stock coordinated to arrive at approximately the same time, maybe hundreds of miles away. It had become a way of life for him with the Miller Brothers 101.

It had never before occurred to him, though, how much like the Wild West Show the military might be. People, horses, supplies, rolling stock. Even the parade just past . . . A big show, to quicken the pulse and inspire excitement.

About the only difference, actually, was that when each big performance would begin, the results would be not a show, but deadly serious. Both sides would be using live ammunition.

John rather dreaded meeting with Captain Langtry. It would bring back a lot of memories that he wasn't sure he wanted to exhume.

As it turned out, their conversation was much more pleasant than he expected. Alan Langtry seemed genuinely glad to see him. Somewhat to John's surprise, he found that he really liked the young man, as he had originally. His years of bitter resentment toward the family had warped John's memory of a truly wonderful weekend of companionship at The Oaks.

He had determined not to hint at his suspicion—no, his *conviction* as to the reasons behind the transfer of a Carlisle student to Haskell, coinciding with the transfer of Alan's sister Jane to school in Europe.

"Are your parents well?" John asked soon after they met at the parade ground. He should have asked that earlier, he thought. But he had been caught off guard.

"My father is," Alan said. "My mother died a few years ago. Pneumonia."

"I'm sorry."

He truly was. Mrs. Langtry had been good to him. He wondered how much she had been involved in his and Jane's banishment. Or, if she had even known about that.

"Thank you," Alan went on. "It happens, John. We're never ready. However, my father goes on and on. He's out of the Senate; lost out when Teddy's Bull Moose Party split the election and gave it to Wilson. Of course, he wasn't pleased with Wilson's 'neutrality.' Well, we're in it now. My father may take another run at the Senate, I think. But what about you, John? How did you get here? I rather expected you to go to the Olympics someday."

John chuckled.

"I *did*, but as an assistant coach. I was in Stockholm."

"With Thorpe? My God, John. What an experience! You've been coaching, then?"

"Not much. I've been with the Miller 101 Wild West Show most of the time."

Alan roared with laughter.

"As a cowboy, an Indian, or a soldier?"

"Well, all three, at one time or other."

"Really? Incidentally, that's a great show. But how?"

"It's a long story, Alan. Excuse me—I should say 'sir.' "

"Not among friends, Corporal."

John quickly sketched in the events since he left Carlisle, including the abortive attempt at reactivation of the Rough Riders. He omitted his arrest for attempting to sell a salted mine, as well as any references to romance.

"My God, John! What an exciting life! Olympics, Wild West, Rough Riders. And wasn't Jess Willard with the 101?"

"Yes. I was his sparring partner."

Langtry threw up his hands helplessly.

"But tell me more about the Rough Riders. You *met* Teddy Roosevelt?"

"No, no. It never got that far. I guess Wilson stopped it."

"He was right, of course. The day of the old cavalry charge is over, John. And good riddance. But lord, what a thrill! A charge up the hill with Teddy! Just to imagine it . . . Who was your commander?"

"We really weren't that organized yet. A rancher-cowboy in Wyoming put it together. He had the connection to Roosevelt. Tim McCoy."

"*McCoy?* He's here, John. One of those hurry-up tin-plated officers through the special units. They need officers badly, and are rushing 'em through so we can get some units in the field. Incidentally, I'm the general's aide, and up for major. But back to McCoy . . . He's one of the good ones. Promoted to captain right out of school. As you might imagine, that's not popular with some of the West Point crowd, but we *do* need commanders."

They talked of other things. Alan had married his childhood sweetheart, from a good family. They had two children, a boy and a girl. John thought that he could detect little enthusiasm for the marriage. Likely, a "proper" union, with little romance.

As they visited, strolling around the post, Alan finally brought up the subject that John had been avoiding all evening.

"John . . . I've been waiting for you to ask about my sister Jane. I somehow had the idea that you two were quite interested in each other. But I . . ."

It was a clumsy moment for John. How far should he go? Quickly, he decided that the less said, the better.

"I *was*," John admitted. "We corresponded a bit, but it was hard to keep up. Mail service was pretty unpredictable. By the time a letter arrived, the address would be changed. I had a few returned. . . . Wondered if others ever got there."

"Yes, that would be a problem. But you'd think they'd forward mail. Or you could have sent letters to The Oaks. . . ."

Suddenly Langtry seemed to realize . . . He seemed almost too embarrassed to speak. He mumbled and fumbled and at last found his voice.

"My God, John. I never realized. *That* was why Jane was suddenly sent off to school?"

He paused.

"She . . . She wasn't . . . uh . . . in a family way, John?"

"No, no. It never got that far. She did try to write me for a while."

Alan nodded thoughtfully.

"This makes more sense to me now. My father . . . John, he's a good man, but obviously somewhat bigoted. I've thought sometimes that his interest in athletes is like his interest in horses. Fun to watch, but . . . Well, he wouldn't want one to marry his daughter."

The word, even the implication of "Indian" had not even been mentioned, but it hung heavily between them.

"John, I'm sorry."

"It's okay, Alan. Water long gone down the river."

"That doesn't make it right. And you deserve to know . . . Jane married a French artist of some kind. Father was furious and disowned her. That partly accounted for my mother's death, I think."

"Then . . . Where is Jane now? I'd hope she's happy?"

"We don't know, John. She just stopped writing home, a few years ago."

"You don't *know* where she is?"

"I'm afraid not, John. That's what made it so hard on our mother."

"So, she might even be dead?"

"That's about it. . . ."

FIFTY-THREE

John had thought that he was long over the hurt of his first love. How long ago . . . He had been an inexperienced youth, completely overwhelmed by the stimulation of romance. *In love with love,* he had told himself many times. . . . An impossible, impractical love that never could have been.

Over the years, he had managed to convince himself. The natural reluctance to relive the hurt and the shame that had been heaped upon him had assisted in his self-recrimination, and he had managed to see his lost love in a negative light. Well, almost . . .

Now, fanned by the breeze of happy memories of youth and joy and excitement, the smoldering embers began to glow again. He began to remember pleasant memories that had lain fallow for half his lifetime. The sparkle in sky blue eyes, the electric glow of sunlight on the gold of young Jane Langtry's hair . . .

For years, he had managed to make himself more comfortable by convincing himself that he had merely been the object of a girlish fling. He could hate her for her abandonment more easily if he could believe that. For years, this pretense had worked moderately well. He could call up enough resentment to offset the pain of having been mistreated and rejected.

After talking again with Jane's brother, who still seemed sincere and friendly, all his pain had come rushing back. With it was guilt. . . . How could he have misjudged and blamed her for her inability to contact him? Or was this only wishful thinking? Had it been impossible for her to contact him? He changed his theory a dozen times and, as many times, felt even more confused than before.

He encountered Captain Langtry infrequently, and they exchanged the customary salutes of mutual respect. It was not really acceptable to establish any closer contact.

Several days later, he happened to encounter Captain McCoy, on the company street near the Post Exchange.

John saluted, the captain returned the gesture, and paused. There was a puzzled look on his face.

"I know you. . . . Buffalo?"

"Yes, sir. John Buffalo."

"Of course. Wyoming. The gold mine."

There was a half-amused smile on the captain's face.

"The Rough Riders!" McCoy went on. "Too bad that didn't work out. What are you doing here?"

"Had a need to do something," said John. "I signed up."

The captain nodded. "Of course! Cavalry, I suppose. George said you're a good cowboy. Oh, yes, I remember, now. You worked for the Hundred and One."

"Yes, sir. I *did*. I guess they've closed the show on account of the war."

"I'd heard that. Well, for now, we'll go fight the Kaiser, right? Good to see you again, Buffalo. Couple of stripes already, I see. Keep it up!"

"Yes, sir."

John came to attention and saluted smartly. Again, McCoy returned the salute, but then relaxed and extended a hand.

"How about a cowboy handshake on it?" he grinned.

John felt that here was a man he'd like to follow. But likely, he'd never see him again.

He was tired. Completely exhausted . . . There was a lot of illness on the post, thought to be connected to the harsh winter climate. It seemed to be widespread, though. Influenza . . . The newspapers, somewhat inclined to sensationalism anyway, appeared to be going wild on this. They wrote of the frequent cases that were cropping up in various parts of the country, and of the degree of contagion. They began to use words like "epidemic."

Now, with the death toll rising, there was increasing alarm. It seemed that this was a more virulent "flu" than any that had been seen for a generation or more, with a much higher death rate.

To add to the problems with this "new flu," the Great War was in progress. More people were traveling, worldwide, than ever before. Consequently, the disease was spread by people who were contagious for a few days before they realized their coming illness. No one knew where it had started, but military bases were hit especially hard because of troop movements. There was a constant flow of personnel in all directions, to and from all parts of the world. The newspapers were now referring to the "worldwide pandemic." Word leaking out of Germany hinted that it was a crisis there, too.

But John was merely tired. With many of the troops reporting on sick call, the platoon was shorthanded. Some had even been hospitalized at the infirmary on the post. This had resulted in extra work for those still healthy, and more responsibilities for the noncommissioned officers.

The increased work load was frustrating, and in turn, exhausting.

The day was over, and John looked forward to an opportunity to rest. Maybe he'd lie down a little while before mess call. . . . He wasn't very hungry anyway. . . . Maybe even skip supper . . .

He was passing headquarters area, looking forward to reaching his bunk in the barracks. Just then, the bugler sounded retreat, the end of the working day. Everyone on the post was expected to pause to observe the lowering of the flag by the color guard.

John turned automatically to face the ceremony, and came stiffly to attention as the plaintive strains of the bugle call floated across the parade ground. Old Glory fluttered slowly, oh, so slowly, down the pole toward the waiting hands of the color guard. *The flag must be lowered slowly,* he recited to himself, *as if in regret. It is raised quickly in the morning, in jubilation.* Flag etiquette, taught to all new recruits. But surely, they could do it a *little* faster. His knees were feeling wobbly. He'd be okay if he could get to the barracks, where he could lie down. . . .

He tried to focus his eyes on the flagpole and the brightly fluttering Stars and Stripes. It was a blur, a confusing shimmer that assaulted his vision and made his head throb. The top of the pole appeared to be swaying as he tried to clear his thoughts. The gilded knob on the tip was tipping slowly toward him now. . . . Too far away to hit him, though . . . No danger . . . There was a buzzing in his ears. . . . The pole was still tipping, falling slowly . . . *NO! He* was falling, still stiffly at attention. The buzzing in his head became louder, and he no longer had any control of his body. The ground rushed up against him, just before he struck, a brilliant white light flew toward him out of the distance somewhere and exploded in his face.

———

John awakened slowly, his head still buzzing. He was no longer on the parade in front of headquarters, but in a building somewhere. It seemed much like a barracks. But where it should have had rows of beds covered with olive-drab blankets, everything was white. Beds, blankets, walls, ceiling. An irrational thought flitted through his mind: Was he dead, and this the white man's Other Side, the Great Mystery of life and death, which the missionaries called "Heaven"? Since it had a military appearance, maybe this was the heaven of the bluecoats, the white man's warrior society. Some tribes, he had heard, had a special Other Side home for warriors. Maybe . . .

"Oh, you're awake," said the voice of a white-clad angel at the foot of his bed.

Her face and hair were like those of the angels in the biblical picture books that occasionally had turned up at the reservation school. Bright golden hair, with the setting sun from the window across the room streaming through it. The angle of the sunbeam had a tendency to darken the features of the face itself. But he could easily see that she had the most beautiful of smiles. It was gentle, friendly, happy yet concerned. Another irrational thought: *I am dead; so is Jane. Here she is and we meet again.* It was comforting, but such hopes were dashed quickly.

"Glad you're awake!" the angel said. "We need to start your treatment."

"Treatment?" he muttered weakly. "What is this place?"

"The post hospital, of course," chuckled the angel. "You're really confused, trooper."

Then I'm not dead? He started to ask, but realized that it would sound pretty stupid.

"Who are you?" he asked instead.

"My name is Jackson. I'm a nurse."

Gradually, it began to make sense. But he could not lie here, helpless. The platoon was short-staffed, already.

"I have to get back to duty," he told the nurse. "They're short—"

As he spoke, he tried to sit up and swing his legs out of the cot. He found that he could lift his head only about six inches. Nothing else seemed to work at all. He felt a moment of panic. . . . His head fell back.

"Okay, trooper. Now you just discovered what I was about to say. You aren't goin' anywhere. You have the flu . . . influenza."

His head was clearing now. She had mentioned treatment.

"How long, and what treatment?" he asked weakly.

"That's more like it." She smiled. "A long time . . . Maybe three or four weeks, if you're doing well."

"Weeks?"

"Oh, yes. You try to cut it short, you'll be back and a lot sicker!"

"You mentioned treatment?"

"Yes, we'll get you started. Enemas, today, to cleanse the bowel."

She paused at the look of alarm on his face, and smiled.

"One of the medics will do that," she assured him. "Then, hot mustard footbaths . . . Hot packs to the torso to sweat out the poisons. You'll have to drink a lot of fluids. And, just rest while you have a chance. It's back to duty when you're well."

John didn't comment, but the idea of drinking a lot of fluids was not very appealing. His stomach was queasy, and putting anything in it would be a challenge. As for an "enema," he wasn't sure what it was, but he was already reluctant. It sounded far too much like "enemy" to make him comfortable.

He tried to remember what he'd heard about the epidemic. None of it was very good news. As an old gambler, he wondered about his odds, but somehow felt that it would be inappropriate to ask. Probably Nurse Jackson wouldn't tell him, anyway.

He sank back resignedly to wait and see.

FIFTY-FOUR

As the nurse had informed him, he soon received a cleansing enema at the hands of a burly medic, who described it as a "triple-H": High, Hot, and Helluva lot. It was a new experience for John Buffalo, and one not appreciated. He was too weak to resist, and even weaker when it was over.

Schwarz, the patient in the next bed, in somewhat better condition, seemed to take an unholy glee in the discomfort of others. He had apparently been there for some time, and was recovering.

"That's sure somethin', ain't it?" he chortled as John lay exhausted after the enema. "Hell of it is, prob'ly no good. Might as well shove it up yer ass."

He chuckled with his crude attempt at humor. John resented it, but was too tired to even answer.

In the next few hours, he learned a lot. He was in a barrackslike twenty-bed ward. Every bed was occupied. He was too weak to care very much.

He had no interest in the watery gruel that they brought him the next morning. In fact, it reminded him of the soapy fluid that had been used for his introductory enema. He nearly gagged over it.

"Better drink it," advised his obnoxious neighbor.

"They'll get it into ya one way or another, you know. This way's better'n the other end."

He managed a few spoonfuls with shaking hands, and sank back on the pillow. After a while, Nurse Jackson returned, and noticed his plight.

"Here, I'll help a little," she offered.

With her assistance, he managed to swallow a little more, but even that effort exhausted him. He fell asleep.

He woke a little later, to see two men who appeared to be doctors, accompanied by a clerk with a clipboard who seemed to make notes at each bed where they stopped. The nurse, too, followed the trio, and occasionally furnished information in a low voice. At one bed, on the opposite side of the aisle, they conversed a little longer. John could see the charts on the foot of each of the beds in that row. One of the doctors picked up that chart and ruffled through the pages, shaking his head. Quietly, he spoke to the clerk and handed him the chart.

When the clerk returned the chart to the bed, clipped to it was a bright orange card about the size of a man's hand.

"Uh-oh!" said Schwarz under his breath.

John said nothing. In fact, he tried to fake sleep, so that his neighbor would not talk to him. But the party worked its way down the row of beds, and back up the other side. Soon they stopped near John's position, and the leading doctor lifted a chart from the foot of his bed.

"New one, eh? Bad shape?"

"Pretty weak, sir," answered the nurse. "Cooperative."

The doctor nodded. "Well, we'll see. Had his cleanser?"

"Yes, sir."

"Well, get him to sweat, and push the fluids."

"Yes, sir."

The clerk replaced the chart.

"Hi, Doc," chortled the abrasive Schwarz from the next bed. "How many you killed today?"

From the irritated looks on the faces of the party on rounds, the man was well known to them.

"Can it, Schwarz," advised the clerk.

"When can we get him out of here?" asked the doctor.

"As soon as possible, sir," said the nurse.

"Hey, I can't even stand up yet," Schwarz protested. "I'm a sick man."

The party moved on without comment.

There was one other bed, beyond that of Schwarz, where the doctors paused a long time. There, again, John saw the orange card clipped to the chart. It must be a bad sign.

He found that he was tired merely from watching the party on rounds, but Schwarz kept trying to talk to him.

"Tryin' to get me out of here," the man snorted indignantly. "I'm a sick man. I couldn't go back to duty. Besides, the food's better here than in the mess hall."

John pretended to sleep again so he wouldn't have to listen. He finally did fall asleep, and was wakened when somebody else entered the ward.

It was a priest in a dark robe, an official-looking cap on his head, and carrying a container with smoking incense. He made his way down the aisle, glancing at each chart, nodding or speaking to some of the patients, and nearly ignoring others. There must be some indication on the charts, John decided, as to each man's religion.

When he came to the chart across the aisle with the orange card, he stopped and stepped between the beds, toward the head of the patient.

The priest hung his incense on a hook near the bed and took out a small container of liquid of some sort, which he sprinkled on the head of the semiconscious patient. All the while, he was mumbling incoherently.

John had never seen this ceremony, but assumed that it was Roman Catholic. His own contact with missionaries had been with Protestants, who had made it quite plain that "Papists" were to be avoided. They had some radical disagreement in their history, he had always assumed. This he did not understand at all, because among his own people, religion was not something to disagree about. Every tribe and nation of which he had ever heard had some kind of an all-powerful Creator of all things. This God is known by different names among different peoples, because He speaks to each in his own tongue. But to argue and insist that God spoke truth to only one group and falsely to all others would be incomprehensible. "You have your religion, I have mine; it is nothing we argue about."

Yet here two groups of whites, both professing to be "Christians," had never really agreed about what God said. To John's people, this was a source of wonder and not a small amount of amusement.

At the present time, John was in no mood for any distraction. He was tired and sick, his head throbbing and his fever burning. The sickly sweet smell of the incense nauseated him, and he greatly resented the presence of the priest. He did not realize that his distaste for the man was largely due to his sickness. He wanted only to rest, and he could not do so with the gibberish in a language unknown to him rattling on and on.

The priest finished his ceremony and moved on, to another bed at the far end of the room to repeat his ritual. Then to the bed beyond Schwarz, to repeat yet again.

Why these three? He wondered. Was this ceremony only for them? That was fine with him, though he found the repetitious gibberish annoying.

"What's he doing?" he demanded of the nurse.

"Just a ritual," she assured him. "Nothing to worry you."

"It hurts my head," he snapped.

"I know . . . He'll be finished soon," she assured him. "Try to rest."

He did manage to doze off for a while.

When he woke, it was because of activity across the aisle. The face of the patient was covered with a sheet, and a pair of medics were lifting him onto a wheeled cart. The body appeared stiff and lifeless.

In a dreamlike fog of confusion, John watched them wheel away the dead man. What was the connection that seemed to elude him? The last rites? That had come before. . . . Quickly, he looked at the bed beyond Schwarz, who was napping peacefully at the moment. The other bed was empty.

With something like panic, John twisted around to look toward the far end of the ward, where he had also seen the priest pause for the ritual. He propped himself up on an elbow to see better. The bed was still occupied, but the patient seemed to be breathing hard, struggling to get enough air. An orderly or medic stood over him, watching and waiting. John sank back on the bed, completely exhausted from the effort, and still trying to interpret what he had seen. At least two deaths today . . . Probably three, the way the patient down the aisle looked and sounded. But there was still something he did not quite comprehend. All three had received last rites from the priest, but who decided when such a ceremony was appropriate? How was it decided? It was hard to think. His fevered brain pounded in delirium, trying to solve the mystery, or even to decide whether one existed. Maybe it had something to do with the doctors on their rounds. Yes, that must be it. They had marked three patients by clipping an orange card to the charts. Those three were now dead or dying. It did not seem very important now.

He fell asleep still thinking about it. He was also having more trouble breathing. At times he felt that the thick, gluelike secretions in his throat were blocking off his lungs completely.

His confusion deepened. He slept and woke and slept again. There was no longer any night and day. He had no idea how long he had been there. He drifted through a mindless fog of discomfort and a need for air. He longed to be in the lodge of his parents on the open prairie, to relive the memories of early childhood. Then there had been no worries, no cares, few responsibilities. It had been a long time ago.

He dreamed. . . . Or maybe it was all one endless dream, a part of the living and dying and crossing over. . . . What his Arapaho friend George Shakespear called the Great Mystery.

People from his past drifted through the dream sequence. Especially women. His mother, sad and tired beyond her years, as she prepared to send her son away to white man's school. Old White Horse, the teacher. There were many things she had not understood, but she had tried, as she saw fit. . . . Some of the girls at Carlisle: friends, but not really close.

Startlingly plain was his vision of the golden-haired Jane Langtry. She leaned over his bed, smiling, gently encouraging him to try to eat a little more of the broth that she tried to feed him with a spoon. He roused a little. . . . No, his vision focused and the angelic form and figure was not his first love. It was Nurse Jackson. The two had become one in his muddled brain. The hair was the same, the blue eyes. . . . He drifted off again.

There were times when he could not distinguish whether he was asleep and dreaming or awake and hallucinating. Or was there really any difference? Once he saw Hebbie, standing beside the bed as she had once before. . . . The dreadful experience on what he had come to think of as the Death Ship. It was different this time. He knew that she had crossed over, and he wanted to join her. He reached out toward her, and she smiled gently, just out of reach.

No, my dear, not yet.

He was never sure afterward whether Hebbie had voiced

the actual words, or just the thought. He woke, in the darkness of the hospital ward, lighted only by a dim bulb at each end of the room. It was filled with the smells of sickness and death, and sounds of racking coughs and labored breathing. He wondered how many days he had been here, and how many more he had to suffer.

He slept again.

When he next awoke, it was daylight, and the little party of doctors was in the process of daily rounds. They stood at the foot of his bed, talking quietly. One of them stepped to him and placed a listening device on John's chest for a few moments. Back at the foot of the bed, a whispered consultation . . . The clerk took something from his clipboard and reached toward John's chart. There was little effort to conceal what it was: an orange card, the size of a man's hand.

FIFTY-FIVE

It didn't seem to matter much. The party moved on. The orange card had simply become a part of the Great Mystery that had gone on since Creation.

The nurse lagged behind for a moment, smiled at him, and tucked the blanket around his shoulders.

"Try to move around a bit, John," she urged. "Breathe deep. We have to get you moving."

She cares, he thought, and his heart was good for a moment, as he slipped back to sleep. He was too tired to follow her suggestions.

The next morning, he woke with the sickly sweet smell of incense again in his nostrils. The priest was across the aisle, mumbling over another patient in another bed. John could see the chart at the foot of that bed, and its orange card. He dozed off again, only to be wakened by the nurse.

"John . . . Wake up. This is the Army chaplain, Father O'Reilly. He's come to see you. . . ."

John was wide awake now, the figure of the robed priest looming above him like the specter in his worst nightmares. The little incense pot on its silver chain swung back and forth in front of his eyes.

"Bless you, my son," Father O'Reilly said.

John was wide awake, now, and his anger was rising.

"I'm not your son!" he screamed. "I am Little Bull, son of Yellow Bull. I'm not even Catholic." Desperately, he turned to the nurse. "Get this son of a bitch away from me!" he pleaded.

"Now, calm down, John," said the nurse. "He's only here to help you."

"Like hell, he is! He wants to put me under, like he did the others. Get him out of here!"

The chaplain shrugged and turned away, followed by the nurse. They withdrew a few steps and engaged in conversation, then moved on down the aisle.

John sank back on his pillow, soaked with sweat and breathing hard. The effort had completely exhausted him.

After a little while, Nurse Jackson returned, and brought a cup of soup. She sat in a chair next to the bed.

"Now, let's try some of this, John."

"I'm too tired. Maybe later . . ."

"All right. But a little bit for now. Try it for me."

He was weak and still shaking from the rage he had just experienced, but she steadied his head and handled the spoon skillfully. The broth slid down smoothly, and the warmth was good in spite of the soreness in his throat. With much help and encouragement, he managed to take most of the cup of broth.

"Good!" praised the nurse. "Now, get some rest. I'll be back later."

He was already nearly asleep.

By the next morning, the empty beds vacated by the fatalities of the day were occupied by two new victims of the flu. John paid little attention. He had slept soundly after the exertion of the incident with the priest. That puzzled him a little. He had been dimly aware that in the Army there were chaplains: preachers, so to speak, for soldiers of various faiths. There must have been a misunderstanding of some sort. If John had a deep-seated faith of *any* kind, it certainly was not Roman Catholic. If he had been asked about his religion, he didn't know what he would have said. He still had great respect for the old ways of his people. But, in recent years, he had had little contact with any form of religion. The fast-moving life on the Wild West Show circuit, the travel, the long trips . . . His life with the Hundred and One had not lent itself well to either the ways of his people, *or* to the Protestant ethic of the mission schools. He could not even remember some of the more recent years.

He watched suspiciously as the priest entered on his grim daily rounds. . . . Up the aisle, speaking here and there to a patient, a casual nod or gesture. John was watching more closely now. He had become personally involved.

The priest stopped at a bed with an orange tag at the far end of the room and performed his ritual. *Too bad,* thought John, as the sprinkling and mumbling proceeded. He felt his anger rising.

One other stop for last rites on the way back down this side of the aisle, and the priest moved on toward where

John lay, tense and angry. Without hesitation, he stepped between John's bed and that of the obnoxious Schwarz.

"Bless you, my son—" he began.

John flew into a rage.

"Get away from me, you bastard!" he screamed. "You're not sendin' *me* across!"

He rose on one elbow.

"Now, now," soothed the chaplain. "I'm here to help. . . ."

John turned to the nurse, who stood pale and wide-eyed at the foot of the bed.

"Get him away!" he yelled.

The priest turned to the nurse.

"I'll come back later."

"Like hell!" John screamed.

He grabbed a nearly empty soup cup from the bedside stand and threw it. The priest tried to dodge, but the heavy ceramic mug struck him on the shoulder, splattering liquid across his face and robe. Calmly, he wiped his cheek with a sleeve and turned away.

Nurse Jackson paused at John's side.

"*I'll* be back later," she whispered softly.

"Okay . . ."

He was dog-tired from the exertion, and sank back to sleep.

When he woke, it was in the quiet of the afternoon. Most of the major activity of the wards seemed to be centered around mornings, he now realized. The doctors' rounds, the medications, enemas and footbaths and sweats, administered by orderlies and medics. There were apparently two nurses, one who seemed to be assigned to another ward across the central corridor, on the other side of the building. The nurses occasionally helped each other if a male orderly was not at hand to do some of the heavier tasks.

He was still confused, but began to notice things that had escaped his attention before. He was still quite weak, and his thinking still muddled. He was quite frustrated that he could do little more than lift his head or raise to an elbow for a few moments. Such weakness was not a manly thing, and was little short of ridiculous.

Later that afternoon, Schwarz was transferred to an ambulatory ward somewhere, to continue his recovery. He complained loudly all the way.

"I ain't well, Jackson," he howled. "Don't let 'em kick me out. I'm a sick man."

"Come on, Schwarz!" The nurse laughed. "You know you're ready to go. Enough of your goldbricking. You need some fresh air and exercise."

"I'll probably have a relapse," whined the malingerer. "You'll be sorry when I'm dead."

"You're a long way from dead, Schwarz!" scolded the nurse. "Go on, now. Good luck to you."

He went out the door, still mumbling. A few of the stronger patients applauded, and the ward settled down again. By evening, Schwarz's bed was occupied again by a very sick patient.

The next morning John awoke feeling a little more alert. *Maybe I'm better,* he decided. He attempted to sit up and decided that it was a false impression. He was still far too weak, and it was not worth the effort, even to breathe more deeply. It was painful to do so, and his head whirled. He felt as he had when he'd fainted out by the flagpole. . . . The buzzing in his ears, his vision swimming and blurring. *I'll never be well,* he thought dejectedly as he sank back, his breathing shallow to protect against the pain in his chest. Sleep came again. Time seemed meaningless, and he didn't care if it was night or day.

Once more, he was wakened and roused slightly when the doctors came on rounds, and dozed off when they left. He paid little attention to their conversation. He didn't much care.

The next time he wakened, it was again in what had become a familiar ritual. He was approached by the priest with his dark, threatening robe and smoking incense, who loomed above him in a dreamlike episode.

"Don't come near me!" John yelled. "Jackson! Help me. Get this dog shit away from me!"

"Be calm, son," crooned the priest. "I'm here to help."

"Bullshit!" screamed John. "You killed that fella yesterday! Leave me alone, you fat bastard!"

The priest shook his head, puzzled, and moved on.

There was yet one more incident when the priest attempted to carry out his ritual, with the same result. John did not become physically violent, but it was largely because of caution on the part of the chaplain. John merely cursed him at a distance.

The next day after that, the priest maintained a careful space between them. He merely nodded from the aisle as he passed. John Buffalo, already up on his elbows and ready to hurl obscenities, settled back with a barely audible curse under his breath.

The one bright spot in his gloomy world was the golden-haired nurse. She was helpful and kind to everyone. The medics and orderlies seemed to have the highest respect for her. She had a rare quality occasionally found in special people: She made everyone feel better. Nurse Jackson could enter the ward, her presence and her smile lighting the day, and every man there felt that she had come especially to see *him*. It was not a matter of competition for her attention. There was enough of the gift to go around. As the people of John's early childhood years might have said, "She has a powerful medicine." She could even carry it off without creating jealousy among those in her care— possibly the most difficult task of all.

He was gaining a little strength, but progress was slow. Each morning patients at one stage of recovery were subjected to a treatment called "cupping," intended to remove secretions from the lungs which might have accumulated through the night. The doctors referred in this connection to "postural drainage." In simplest terms, it involved the patient's lying prone across the narrow cot, with shoulders and arms lower than the bed's surface. Cupping his palms, an orderly would beat a tattoo on the back of the patient's chest to start the thick secretions flowing. The patient would begin to cough, expectorating large quantities of foul yellow sputum.

"It helps prevent pneumonia," Nurse Jackson explained.

Some of John's wardmates had earthier explanations.

"If you don't cough up enough, they'll pound the hell out of you," stated one experienced individual.

"Naw, it ain't that," argued another soldier. "Them orderlies just like to beat the snot out of a helpless patient."

The orderly grinned. "That's right, Kesterson," he jibed. "More fun to pound on some guys than others. But you're gettin' well, ain't you?"

FIFTY-SIX

Very special to John were the rare times when Nurse Jackson would assist him in eating. He was not strong enough yet to sit up and handle regular food for an entire meal. From the beginning, she had been instrumental in inducing him to eat. She had become so special to him that he would have done almost anything to please her. How could he have refused the request of an angel to drink the broth or finish the gruel in his breakfast bowl?

And he was better now. He could tell, it was actually *happening*. His appetite improved. Not only was he able to chew better food, but his sense of taste was returning. Some things actually tasted good.

"John, tell me about you," she said one day as she assisted him with his food. It was the first meal he had been offered that would have to be cut with a knife and fork, so it was a special occasion. He was tired before he finished cutting, so Nurse Jackson had stopped to help him.

"Not much to tell, ma'am," he said, embarrassed.

"You've been a cowboy?"

"Yes, ma'am."

He was possibly more embarrassed than even his basic shyness would have demanded. He could not forget that he had actually cursed a holy man in the presence of this angel. She had never mentioned it, but it hung there between them every day.

It was especially bad when the chaplain made his rounds. Sometimes the priest would make eye contact, and John could feel the disapproval like a living thing between them. Usually Nurse Jackson would accompany the priest, and John scrupulously avoided *her* gaze. He fully expected that some day, he must face a scolding from her about his behavior. Until then, maybe his punishment would merely be the guilt that he felt when he saw the dark, disapproving glance of the priest.

"You enlisted here," the nurse was saying. "Are you from this area, John?"

"No, ma'am. Dakota, originally."

"But you're educated."

"Yes, ma'am. Indian schools. Carlisle, Haskell."

"I see. But you cowboyed here?"

"Well, no. In Wyoming. I knew Captain McCoy, worked for him a little while. But I didn't know he was here."

"Wait a minute, John. You're confusing me. You started to cowboy in Wyoming?"

"Oh, no. At the 101 Ranch."

"The Wild West Show?"

"Yes, ma'am . . . Most of the time. I left them for a couple of years to work with the Olympics."

Now he was becoming quite uncomfortable. He was afraid that it would sound as if he were bragging.

"Never mind," he said. "It wasn't much."

The look in the eyes of the nurse was one of puzzled astonishment. She started to ask something else, but apparently changed her mind.

John did not see real doubt, only curiosity, but he was glad when she changed the subject.

"John, about tomorrow, I think you're ready to sit up in a chair. That sound pretty good?"

"Yes, ma'am!"

He smiled at her.

"Good!" she said. "I like to see that smile, John."

She rose and moved on, to help someone else, but the heart of John Buffalo was good.

His first few shaky steps the next day were accomplished with the help of the nurse on one side and one of the orderlies on the other. John felt that they half-carried him to the chair. He was exhausted when it was accomplished.

It could not have been done without the help of the beautiful nurse. The sensation of her arm around his body, her shoulder against his chest, and the softness of her breast as it touched him . . . *Aiee!* All the weakness and discomfort of his aching body, the protest of muscles unused for a long time vanished in the ecstasy of the moment. Just then, he could have accomplished anything.

It took some time simply to recover and restore his labored breathing to normal again. Back in bed, he felt as tired as if he had just done a day's work. It *was* a day's work, he realized. About all he could handle with the help of two healthy people. He slept well that night, with the sleep of exhaustion and work well done.

The move to the chair the next day was accomplished with more of his own effort and less assistance. He faced a real dilemma now. He wanted to do well to please the nurse with whom he was rapidly falling in love. But if he did well and became more self-sufficient, he would no longer need her physical help, the steadying of her strong arm and shoulder around his body. Yet he would have done anything to avoid faking a weakness he did not feel.

However, John *did* feel that they were growing closer. Somehow, the smile that she gave him was different, from her routine cheer for others, or from her professional smile for the doctors and orderlies. At first he could not make himself believe such good fortune, but it was undeniably true.

She made occasions to talk to him and seemed genuinely interested in his many varied experiences. She laughed with delight at some of the events on the road with the Hundred and One. There was no question that he grew and expanded as a storyteller with such a delightful audience of one.

One morning she had wheeled him outside in a high-backed wheelchair for a breath of fresh air.

"Nurse Jackson," he said, "I am tired of calling you that. Do you have a name?"

She actually blushed, which John found quite charming in such a capable woman.

"Seriously," he went on. "I am made to think that we are more to each other than nurse and patient."

This frankness was very difficult for him.

The nurse shrugged. "We are friends, yes?"

"More than that, I think," he said seriously. "I think I am falling in love."

Her face was scarlet now.

"John," she said gently, "every soldier who has been sick or wounded falls in love with his nurse."

"I have heard this," he admitted, "but I think we have more than that, you and I."

She was silent for a long time.

"Maybe so," she said softly. "But, back to your question. Do I have a name? Yes . . . Ruth. But it is not considered good manners for a patient to call his nurse by name . . . Publicly, that is."

"And privately?"

He had to know.

"I . . . I don't know how it could be prevented," she murmured.

Now his heart soared.

"John, have you a wife? You've never said."

"No . . ."

"Ever *been* married?"

He was unsure how to answer that. His relationship with

Hebbie, over a period of years, had been more durable and loyal than many marriages.

"Well . . . Not a church marriage. No ceremony. We were together."

"Were?"

"She is dead," said John. "I guess we were more married than most."

"A common-law marriage, then? She was a lucky girl to have you, John," Ruth Jackson said softly.

"I dunno about that," he muttered self-consciously.

He sensed that she wanted to tell him something, but did not know how. How could he . . . *Ah!*

"Have you ever been married?" he asked.

The clear blue eyes looked deep into his.

"John, I *am* married. *Mrs.* Ruth Jackson. You must not fall in love with me. We can be friends—nothing more."

"But . . . Where is your husband? How could he *leave* you?"

"He didn't leave me, John. He had to go. He's in France, fighting the Kaiser. Lieutenant Emil Jackson."

"I . . . I'm sorry, Mrs. Jackson. I had no idea. I apologize if I've offended you. . . ."

She laughed, now, her soft throaty chuckle like music to his ears. Or maybe, spring water over polished pebbles.

"You had no way of knowing, John. I should have told you, but I didn't realize . . . At least, not . . ."

"It's okay," he murmured.

But it wasn't. His heart was very heavy.

"Friends?" she asked.

She stuck out a hand toward him, and he took it in a friendly shake—a strong, capable grip, one he could appreciate.

"Friends!" he repeated huskily.

They were quiet for a little while.

"We'd better get back to the ward," she said. "It's getting late."

She turned his chair and they started back toward the building.

"Shall I call you Mrs. Jackson?" he asked, half-teasing.

"If you like," she answered in the same tone. Then, somewhat wistfully, she went on. "Or 'Ruth.' I have no one to call me that just now. But not publicly. There would be some, maybe, who'd try to read more into it than friendship."

"Okay, Ruth. Friends . . . Friends *only.*"

Their friendship was comfortable. Bringing it into the light of day had illuminated the thoughts and feelings of both. They could now relax and enjoy each other's company without pressure, but with understanding. Friends. Nothing more.

"When can I go back to duty?" John asked one afternoon when she had taken him outside in the wheelchair.

"Are you in a hurry?" she teased.

Then she relented.

"Forgive me, John. It was an honest question. You're feeling a lot better. But the flu is treacherous. Try too much, too quick, and it's almost like starting over. You don't want *that,* do you?"

"I'd get to be here longer."

"Stop that!" she scolded, but with a smile.

"Okay, I understand. But what happens next?"

"You go to an ambulatory ward. What the medics call the 'walking wounded.' You can do a lot of things for yourself now. There are calisthenics to get your strength back. You'll do a lot of things for yourself."

"Do they dress?"

She laughed.

"You're pretty tired of underwear and a robe, aren't you?"

"Right!"

"Well, you'll probably wear fatigues."

"Good."

There came a day before that transfer, however, when Ruth approached his bed with a gleam of mischief in her eye. It was mid-afternoon. Many of the patients, exhausted from morning activities, were napping.

John had been dozing comfortably and was dimly aware that someone had come down the ward's central aisle.

"John, you have a visitor," Ruth told him.

Instantly, he was wide awake, and a little embarrassed to be caught off guard. But who . . . How could he have a visitor? The ward was virtually off limits to visitors, to avoid contagion.

The nurse stepped aside, and a burly man in an officer's dress uniform moved forward. John started to rise in a gesture of respect, but the officer motioned him back. John found himself in an awkward, half-sitting position.

Quickly, he tried to understand the situation, gathering what he could from the uniform. A captain's bars at the shoulders . . . The man looked familiar, but . . .

"Do I know you, sir?" John asked.

The captain smiled. A face somehow out of context . . .

"You should," chuckled the officer.

Just then, in the quick search for identity, John's eyes fastened on the captain's collar insignia, which designated the officer's specialty. The small silver emblem on the khaki lapel was not the crossed sabers of Cavalry, but—

An irrational fear and dread gripped John's heart. The insignia was a small cross. Not crossed weapons, or the winged medical caduceus, but the simple Christian cross of the clergy. A *chaplain*. Now he recognized the man. John had seen him before only in the robes the priest used for ritual.

"Father O'Reilly," prompted the chaplain.

John was caught completely off guard.

"I—I—" he stammered.

He must be guilty of insubordination. He could hardly believe, now, that a few weeks ago, he had actually cursed a superior officer. There must be a court martial awaiting him. And why was the captain taking such *delight* in the shame of an enlisted man? John's anger began to rise over such impropriety.

He might have caused even more trouble, except that at that moment he caught a glimpse of the nurse's face over the captain's shoulder. She was *smiling*.

"Am I . . . in bad trouble?" John asked seriously.

The captain chuckled.

"No, no, Corporal," he assured. "But you *do* deserve an explanation. I'm leaving . . . Transfer to Europe. But Nurse Jackson suggested that I stop to explain. . . . You were pretty sick. They couldn't seem to get you to *care*. You wouldn't move, wouldn't try. The doctors had given you up. The orange card . . . Extreme Unction . . . 'Last Rites.' That was a misunderstanding, apparently."

"I'm not Catholic," John said apologetically.

"So we learned," said the priest with a wry grin. "But it did stir you up. You breathed deep, opened your lungs, worked up a sweat. . . . Nurse Jackson, here, suggested that we repeat the . . . Uh . . . 'treatment.' "

Ruth was chuckling now.

"I . . . I owe you an apology, sir," John said hesitantly.

"Not at all, son," said the priest. "I've taken worse. Just pleased that it worked. Of course, I may have to go to confession myself over it. Not exactly the proper use of ritual. But thank your nurse, here, for seeing the possibilities!"

The captain rose.

"Well, I have a train to catch. Good luck to you . . . *son*."

"Thank you, sir."

They shook hands, exchanged a salute, and the priest was gone. John turned to the nurse.

"I had no idea. . . . Once more, I owe you, Ruth."

His voice was choked, and there was a tear in his eye.

"Thank you . . ."

FIFTY-SEVEN

A few days later, John was transferred to a recovery ward in another building. It now became a problem: how, where, and even whether his friendship could continue with the young woman who had very likely saved his life.

"Don't try to contact me," she had cautioned. "You'll be kept out of the acute wards because of the flu. 'Isolation,' they call it. Keeps from spreading the epidemic. They don't really know how it spreads, I guess. It's not spread by mosquitoes, like malaria, or in food and water, like typhoid. Well, you're not interested in that."

"Not really. How do I manage to see *you?*"

"I'll know where *you* are, John. I know the nurses on those wards, and I can stop by to visit *them*. As you improve, you'll also have the possibility of a pass into town before long. And I can learn when that's a possibility by stopping by your building. We can meet in town."

"Is that permitted?"

"Not really." There was mischief in her eyes. "Look . . . You'll have to be in uniform, but I won't. I can wear civilian clothes. Who's to know who I am?"

She tilted her head, with the perky little smile that she seemed to use more often now. He loved to see her with more pleasure and animation in her face. Her work must be quite depressing at times, he realized. Some joy in success, but so many tragedies. For one in a healing profession, the failures must be a heavy burden to bear.

They managed to meet only twice during the two weeks while John was assigned to the recovery ward. The meetings were similar: an afternoon pass, a meeting at a predetermined location in the town of Ogden. Ruth brought a picnic basket each time, and they walked. . . . Out into the open country, where they ate and relaxed and talked and talked.

"What do you hope to do after the war, John?"

"I don't know. I had hoped to coach . . . Teach sports, maybe. Couldn't find a job. That's how I started cowboyin'."

"But . . . You've told me of your education, John. With so much interest in football, there must be . . . Didn't you say you'd been to the Olympics . . . Where was it? Stockholm?"

"Well, yes. That was a temporary job, as a pretty low-ranked assistant coach."

She sat straight up from her semireclining position on the picnic blanket.

"*Coach?* I thought you went as a spectator. John, these are wonderful credentials! *Why* can't you find a job?"

Her voice was almost accusing, as if he hadn't really tried. Long dormant, his disappointment now came rising in his throat.

"Because they'd rather have white coaches," he said flatly.

It was the first time that he had ever actually said it aloud, that he'd been able to voice his frustration. Now he was embarrassed.

"I'm sorry," he apologized. "I had no right to say that."

She was staring at him in shocked silence. Finally she spoke.

"Oh, John," she whispered. "I had no idea. It's something I wouldn't even have thought of."

She reached over and took his hand. "Is it that way everywhere?"

"Depends. Worse in some places than others. But . . . I don't want to talk about it. What about you?"

"That's not very exciting, compared to you," she assured him. "Grew up near here, married my high-school sweetheart after nurses' training. Emil wants to farm near here, supply the fort. A lot of local farmers and ranchers do that. We were pretty well started. . . . A little place, a few acres. Cattle, hogs, chickens . . . He'd like to raise horses for the Army, too. But when the war came, he felt he had to enlist. So I went back to nursing. It lets me feel like if I'm helping some other soldier, maybe somebody's helping mine."

"No children?"

"None. We want some."

"You mentioned your farm?"

"A neighbor is running it. I still stay at the house sometimes, to get away from my work at the fort. It's lonesome without him, but I want to keep it ready for when he comes home."

"Emil is a very lucky man," mused John.

"Not really." She smiled wistfully. "But I hope *he* thinks so."

If he doesn't, there's something wrong with him, thought John.

Things were changing rapidly in the conduct of the war. It was finally realized that men with sabers on horses would never be a match for cannon and machine guns. The action necessary for cracking the Kaiser's defenses would be artillery. There had begun a rush to train and put into combat a large number of batteries of cannon. Not yet mechanized, these would be drawn by horses. French "75s," firing an explosive projectile a foot long and as round as a man's wrist, were shipped in quantity to the United States for training purposes.

Much to the chagrin of old-line professional cavalry officers, they were converted almost overnight to the command of artillery units. At some military posts, mock funeral processions with black-draped coffins mourned the demise of the proud horse cavalry.

In the midst of this change, Corporal John Buffalo was dismissed from the recovery ward to return to his unit. He found the barracks in a state of turmoil.

"We're movin' out," explained the sergeant major. "They're makin' redlegs of us."

The sergeant was not happy with the change. From the yellow braid and striping of the cavalry to the red of artillery was a major catastrophe to the old soldier.

"We're shippin' to Oklahoma to learn to shoot them French cannons," he said sadly. "Usin' horses to *pull* the damn things, like wagons."

"When does this happen, Sergeant?" asked John.

"Couple o' days, I guess. By train, prob'ly Monday. Good to have you back, Buffalo."

"Thanks, Sergeant. Any chance for a pass Saturday? I've been shut up in the hospital."

The sergeant thought for only a moment.

"Why not? Pretty tough over there? We heard a lot of men are dyin'."

"Pretty bad . . . A lot I don't remember."

"Bad times," the sergeant major said sympathetically. "Sure . . . Make out your pass. I'll sign it."

He planned almost frantically. A quick visit back to the recovery ward to talk to Ruth Jackson's nurse friend.

"Back already, John? Just can't stay away from us, eh?" joked Alice.

"I'm bein' shipped out," he explained quickly. "I'd like to say good-bye to Nurse Jackson. She was good to me while I was so sick. How can I contact her?"

The nurse's face fell. "Oh, John, I don't know. She's not working. You knew about her husband?"

"No . . . What? He's back?"

"No, no. He was killed in France."

"Aw, no!"

"Yes. She just learned yesterday, I guess. They gave her a leave."

"But . . . Where *is* she?"

"She went home, I guess."

"Home?"

"Yes. Her place. Hers and Emil's. John, have you two got something goin'?"

His anger rose at such a suspicion.

"No! Of course not. She's not like that. She's a friend, that's all!"

He surprised himself, that he was so defensive. Equally surprised, Alice backed off.

"Say, John, I didn't mean—Look, no offense intended."

He took a deep breath.

"None taken . . . Sorry. But do you know where their place is?"

"Not exactly. She's wanted to keep it theirs, and separate from their military jobs. North of here, somewhere."

That didn't narrow it much, but he tried to recall. Probably the meadow where they'd had their picnics would be in an area familiar to her. He recalled now that when she spoke of their farm, she had used a hand gesture, as if *over there*. . . . It was worth a try. He hiked out toward the grassy hillside.

As luck would have it, he had not quite reached the point where they would leave the road, when he heard the *clip-clop* of an approaching horse, and the slight rattle and squeak of buggy wheels. He stepped off the road and looked ahead to the point where the approaching buggy would top the hill.

A mail carrier . . . Maybe . . . He waved to the driver to pause, and the man pulled the horse to a stop.

John stepped forward. "Excuse me. Am I on the right road to the Jackson place?"

"Sure are. Over the hill and just around the bend, there. Not home very often, though."

"That's okay. Thanks!"

His pace quickened as he rounded the bend to see a small frame house tucked in against the hillside. Like many with the men away at war, the yard was a bit weedy and untended, but the place looked prosperous. There were good corrals, a hay barn, and a young apple orchard. It could be a good place. Except . . . There was no man here, to live and love his home. Now there would not be.

His heart was heavy as he walked up to the porch and knocked at the door. He could hear music inside, a phonograph playing a sweet romantic waltz. He recognized the melody as one he had studied in a music class at school, but at the moment could not put a name to it.

He knocked again, and heard footsteps approaching the door as the record came to its end and continued to turn with a scritch-scritch sound. The door opened and Ruth Jackson stood there, surprised.

"John! Come in!"

She turned and lifted the needle from the phonograph record, stopping the annoying scritch-scritch.

He had no idea what to expect when he knocked on the door, but certainly not this. There might have been friends or neighbors, but there were none. She might have been drawn and haggard, but it appeared that she was dressed for an occasion. Her hair was arranged carefully, she had used just the right amount of powder and rouge, and wore an attractive party dress. If it had not been for the tragedy in her eyes . . .

"Ruth . . . I heard," he mumbled. "I'm sorry."

"Thank you, John. Thank you for coming."

"You . . . You're alone?" he asked, puzzled.

"Yes. I really have no people here, anymore. I wanted to spend a little time here, alone with some of the happy memories."

"I'll go," he offered, with a glance at the crank-winding Edison phonograph and the stack of wax record disks beside it.

"No, no," she protested. "It was good of you to come."

"Well, I . . . I'm shipping out. Monday, I guess."

There was a look of alarm on her face.

"France?"

"No. Oklahoma. They're converting cavalry units to artillery."

"I heard about that. Fort Sill?"

"I guess so."

"Well . . . John, would you stay with me a little while?"

"Of course."

She stood at the window, gazing at the radiant sunset.

"I was just remembering some of the good times," she said wistfully.

She turned and pointed to the stack of records on the chair by the phonograph.

"Nearly every one of those has a special memory," she murmured. "Here, I'll show you."

She wound the spring tightly, put a new record under the needle, and released the latch to allow it to turn. The strains of a Strauss waltz floated through the room.

"That was the first one we danced to," she said happily. She was swaying to the music. "It's a good memory. Will you dance with me, John?"

She came into his arms, naturally and comfortably, and they danced. He had always felt clumsy and uncomfortable on a dance floor, but this was different. Somehow, this was not for his pleasure, but to fulfill *her* inner needs. It was almost as if some outside influence was making him a better dancer, for *her*.

Her face brightened, her smile became happier, and her eyes shone with pleasure. The record finished and she chose another, and they danced.

Later, thinking back, he could not believe the perfection that he achieved that night with her. . . . *For* her. People mourn in different ways. For Ruth Jackson, reliving the good times was the way to honor her husband's memory. John did not delude himself. She was reliving the good times with her sweetheart, lover, and husband, not with John Buffalo. He was merely a proxy. John knew and understood this, as he knew that she did. It was not necessary to discuss it.

Darkness fell, and Ruth lighted a coal-oil lamp. They danced some more. Finally, as the phonograph wound down on a slow, romantic number, she snuggled close to him. He could feel the wetness of the tears on her cheeks as she whispered in his ear.

"John, would you stay with me tonight?"

FIFTY-EIGHT

John woke in the morning with a burning sense of guilt. There was a smell of coffee and of bacon frying. He did not know whether he could face her. In her moment of bereavement and weakness, he had betrayed his friend, had taken advantage of the situation. How could he look at her this morning?

He turned to the pillow beside him, still bearing the indentation of her head. The memory of her body next to his, the warm softness as she cuddled against him . . . At times she had cried softly. . . . He had held her close and tried to comfort her in her grief. He had given her only what she seemed to want and need.

But these thoughts did not in any way justify what had happened. He looked around the bedroom, attractive, with just the right degree of feminine ruffles and frills. On a dresser, the instruments of a lady's preparation for the day: comb, hairbrush, powder puff . . . The faint scent of sweet perfume wafted from that direction . . . Her party dress lay across a chair. He had been here, in a place he had no right to be. Another man's home, his bed, with his *wife*. A dead man. He had done some things in his life of which he was not particularly proud, but never like this. The guilt descended on him like a cold, wet blanket. He did not know how he could face Ruth. The whole thing was wrong, like the taste of ashes in his mouth. He considered for a moment whether he could dress and slip quietly out the front door, but rejected the idea. He must be a man, acknowledge his mistake, and ask for her forgiveness.

He saw a hint of motion from the corner of his eye, and turned to look to the doorway of the bedroom.

"Oh, you're awake!" she said brightly. "Good. I'll bring you some coffee."

She turned away toward the kitchen. There was no time to answer, but he did not fail to notice that she made only momentary eye contact.

"I'll come out there," he called.

He could not wait to escape the bedroom and its associated guilt. He dressed quickly and stepped down the narrow hallway to the kitchen, where she was busy at the stove, sending wonderful breakfast smells through the warm room.

"On the table." She pointed with a big spoon, but did not look up from the eggs she was scrambling.

John sat at the table and cupped the hot coffee mug in his hands.

"Thanks," he muttered briefly.

There was much more that he had to say, but he knew that to broach any subject while a woman is cooking would be a mistake. That was one of the things he had learned as a small child at his mother's lodge fire.

Silence was wise. Ruth was doing everything at once, dishing up fried potatoes, eggs and bacon, and peeking into the oven to check the progress of what must be biscuits. It all came together with the miraculous timing that allows a really good cook to have everything ready at the same moment. She set two plates on the table and a plate of biscuits between. She added a covered cut-glass dish with a lid, though which he could see a comb of honey.

"Sorry I've no butter," she apologized. "I'm not here very often."

Their eyes had still not met for more than an instant.

"Ruth, I—," he began clumsily.

"Let's eat while it's hot," she suggested. "We'll talk later."

John didn't think he could find the appetite, but once he was started, the primitive instinct to eat when there is food took command. Ruth Jackson was a very capable woman in many ways. With a great deal of regret, he felt that his behavior had now destroyed any chance of a lasting relationship. He cursed himself for being an idiot.

They ate in silence, and she rose once to refill their coffee cups.

"Good coffee," he said clumsily. "Good breakfast."

"Thank you."

Finally he could stand it no longer.

"Ruth," he began.

"John, I—," she stammered at the same instant.

Both laughed nervously.

"Let me," he said. "Ruth, I owe you an apology. I have violated our friendship. I'm sorry. . . ."

Her eyes were wide with surprise.

"No, no!" she insisted. "I owe *you* the apology."

He was astonished.

"How could you think that?" he blurted. "I—"

She placed a finger gently on his lips.

"Hush," she said softly. "*I* asked *you* to stay. I was lonely. . . . Maybe, the loneliest night of my life. You were here for me when I needed someone. I took advantage of you. I *used* you."

"No, no, Ruth. It was not like that. . . . I wanted to do *anything* to help you. I know how it feels. I have *been* there. Besides, I probably owe you my life."

She blushed self-consciously.

"That was my job."

"Not hardly. Not many would have gone that far."

"But that . . . John, I don't want you to misunderstand. I'm not ready . . ."

"I know," he said gently. "Ruth, I wasn't trying to . . . I mean . . . I—I violated your trust."

She laughed a bit nervously.

"We could argue all day," she observed. "I was able to help you in your need. A different need, of course. You were here for me. Some things are meant to be. It does not require anything else."

"Still friends?"

"Of course. Better than ever, John. Maybe even more, later. But not now. I hope you understand. But no hurt involved?"

"Of course not."

They got up from the table and embraced warmly. A kiss . . . Not like the deeply, urgent amorous kisses of the previous evening. Merely a warm, affectionate exchange of genuine esteem.

And it was good.

"You have to get out of here," Ruth observed. "Aren't you due back to duty?"

"Oh, my God!" he blurted. "Of course. I'll be listed AWOL on the morning report!"

"Buffalo! Where the hell have you been?" yelled the sergeant. "I've got you listed . . . Never mind! Get your duffel. The train leaves at noon."

John dashed for the barracks, yanked open his footlocker, and started stuffing the contents into his duffel bag. Fortunately, there wasn't much to pack. The troop had not yet been issued winter clothing, which would have been much bulkier.

He had just finished and buckled the canvas web straps when the sergeant entered the barracks.

"Okay, fall out! Assemble in the street, carrying your gear. Let's go!"

As John passed him, the sergeant spoke quietly.

"John, we're tryin' to get the morning report changed. You were listed as AWOL, but the company clerk will try to fix it. If anybody asks, you know nothin'. Somebody made a mistake, but you're here. Mebbe they had you confused with somebody else, I expect."

"Sergeant, I—"

The sergeant held up a hand to stop him.

"The less I know, the better. I don't even want to hear about it. Whatever it is, I reckon you had a reason. Now, get down there and fall in. We got a train to catch."

The train huffed and puffed its way south across rolling hills covered with lush prairie grasses, now starting to push up tall seed-heads. It would be October before they were fully ripe. They crossed into a region where more farms and crop land formed a green, brown, and black checkerboard across the landscape. The train stopped frequently to take on water for the boilers, but even so, they were making good time.

South of Wichita, the country changed again. The familiar red soil began to make John feel at home. This was much like the country around the 101. He wasn't certain exactly when they crossed into Oklahoma, but he began to see familiar landmarks. How many times he had traveled these same tracks on the Hundred and One Wild West Show trains.

The train stopped briefly at Ponca City, and no one was allowed to get off. John craned his neck to see if he could spot anyone he knew, but it was growing dark, and saw no one.

On southward to Lawton, and nearby Fort Sill, the command school for the Army's Field Artillery training. It was completely dark now, and had been for some time. They detrained and marched in formation, carrying their duffel bags to a distant area of the post. There, they waited in a company street for something to happen. John had often wondered at such situations. What was happening inside the office of the administration building? What could there possibly be to talk about? The commanders had known for days, probably, that new troops would be arriving. They would be assigned to a barracks. An empty barracks. What could there possibly be to discuss, while the troops waited in the street in loose formation in the middle of the night? This was one of the things about the military that he would never understand.

In due time, the noncommissioned officers came out and called the formation to attention. They shouldered duffel bags and marched, this time at rout-step, to an area a half mile away, where they moved into an empty barracks building like all the others.

John fell into his bunk, exhausted from long hours of travel, thinking bittersweet thoughts of where he had been only twenty-four hours ago. He wondered whether Ruth might be awake. . . . Sleeping, probably . . . His heart went out to her in her bereavement. He knew how she must feel. He had overcome most of the guilt feelings, and hoped that he had, indeed, helped her in her loss and her loneliness. Ruth had certainly seemed to think so.

It seemed that he had barely closed his eyes when the strains of reveille floated across the bright Oklahoma morning. Tired troopers were jumping into clothes and hurrying outside. It had been a short night.

This was John's first look at Fort Sill by daylight. It was much like other posts he had seen, but with one notable exception. The signs, designating building numbers and letters, were red, sometimes with white lettering. The little picket fence along the corner of the lawn where the barracks stood was bright red. He had never seen a *red* picket fence before. It took a moment to realize. . . . Red . . . The color designation for artillery, along with the symbol of crossed cannons. He wondered whether an Infantry school would have sky blue fences.

They could see a mountain in the distance. It was symmetrical in shape, an almost perfect cone. Not a mountain that would be impressive in the Rockies, but still certainly worthy of note.

He learned this was Mount Scott, tallest of the range that could be seen in the distance, the Wichitas.

There seemed to be a winding trail, spiraling around and around the cone of Mount Scott.

"Looka there!" One of the newcomers pointed as they

dispersed after roll call. "There's *people* on that hill over there!"

"Sure," said a sergeant who was passing the newly set-tled troop. "Them are the mule packers."

"Mule packers?"

"Yep . . . Mountain howitzers. Seventy-fives."

"They've got *cannon* up there?"

There were human figures walking and leading mules along the mountain trail.

"Yep. Special troops. The gun comes apart, packs on six mules. You'll see 'em, later. I expect that's C-battery up there. Say, you're the new fellas. . . . Maybe you'll be *assigned* to mule-pack."

He moved on, chuckling to himself. John and his fellow cavalrymen did not understand the humor in the situation. Not yet.

FIFTY-NINE

Before the day was over, they learned a great deal more. Every newcomer received a brief physical examination, part of which included detailed measurements of length and girth of their legs.

"What's goin' on here?" someone asked.

"We're forming a new battery," an artillery sergeant told them. "Special troops."

Still, no one answered any questions.

At one point, John was called aside to be interviewed by a young captain.

"Corporal," said the officer, "you *are* John Buffalo?"

"Yes, sir. Corporal John Buffalo, reporting as ordered."

"Hmm . . . Your unit's morning report yesterday lists you as absent without leave."

"Yes, sir. Our platoon sergeant mentioned something about that. I don't understand. I'm certainly here. . . ."

The captain looked up sharply, as if questioning whether this was an insolent remark.

"How's that, Corporal?"

"Sorry, sir. I meant no offense. Only to call attention to my presence."

"Well . . . Don't get smart!"

"Oh, no, sir. Nothing of the sort intended. Anything I can do to help straighten it out."

The officer still appeared to have some doubts.

"Hmm . . . No one seems to know *anything* about it."

"So I was told, sir. Someone said, probably a clerical error at Fort Riley before we entrained."

"That would be a convenient explanation, Corporal," said the captain, perhaps a bit sarcastically. "But . . . Your record's good. Maybe it *is* just an error in recording the report."

John decided that it was a good time to refrain from comment.

"Now, while you're here," the officer went on, "there's this other matter. As you know, your troop is being reassigned to artillery. That's why you're here."

"Yes, sir."

"Your troop will be assigned to the 75s. Several batteries using French guns are in training. Some are already in process of moving to France. But we have another type of gun here. Several, actually, but I mean another 75-millimeter. The mountain pack howitzer. You've heard of it?"

"Something of it, sir."

"Yes . . . Well, we can take it where we couldn't take

wheeled cannon, drawn by horse teams. In essence, the pack howitzers can go anywhere a man can walk. We don't need roads. You can see an advantage in combat."

"Yes, sir."

But what does this have to do with me? John wondered.

"You noticed that the examiners spent extra time measuring legs?"

"Yes, sir. We wondered. . . ."

"Of course. Here's the situation: The mules are handled by a two-man team. Packer and driver, jobs interchangeable, trade off, front or back of the mule."

John was puzzled. He could not imagine where this conversation was going.

"Now, you're cavalry . . . horses. Know anything about mules?"

"Not much, sir. Driven a few wagon mules."

"Yes. Pack mules are shorter and stocky in build. But they walk fast. Basically, faster than a man. Infantry, as you may know, marches at about three and a half miles an hour."

But where does all of this lead? John wondered again. He was very uneasy at the mention of "infantry."

"Now, a mule travels at nearly *four* and a quarter."

John still did not see the point, but kept silent. Surely the captain was going somewhere with this.

"If we hold the mule down to our pace, he has to take short little steps," he went on. "This makes his ankles sore, he goes lame, and we'll have to carry his load. So, the driver and packer have to step on out, match the mule's speed. And that takes long legs. Hence, the extra measurements."

John began to understand. It was a matter of capabilities. A draft horse has a different job than a racehorse. Among human athletes, a tennis player has different capabilities than a bone-crushing football tackle or fullback. A distance runner is entirely different from an expert with the 16-pound shot.

"So," the captain continued, "some of your troopers are being assigned to the pack howitzers. Those with long legs. Shorter men will be placed on the French 75s. We hate to break up a unit, but it's not as if you're a unit of local militia. You volunteered as individuals, right?"

"Yes, sir. Pretty much so."

The officer nodded.

"Thought so. Well, they'll be reassigning, probably this afternoon, some will move to other barracks. Best of luck to you here, Corporal."

The change was a real shock to cowboys, who had seldom traveled anywhere on foot. Now, not only must they walk, but in addition, either lead or follow a mule. There was a lot of indignant complaint.

"Damn' jackasses! I didn't sign on for this!" someone grumbled.

"Not much better for those on the French guns," came an answer.

"At least, *they* get to ride," the other retorted.

"Sure . . . Bouncin' on a caisson with no springs!"

John, who had the traditional height of his people, had realized from the first that he must be in the segment chosen for the pack howitzers.

The new artillerymen were already well versed in care and handling of animals in the military. It now became a matter of learning to use the equipment. There were four guns to the battery, short ugly cannon capable of direct or high-angle fire. Each of these howitzers was served by six mules with their drivers and packers. Set up for firing, these twelve men would become the gun crew for each of the guns.

A mule is a hybrid. His mother is a female horse, a mare. His sire is a donkey. This ignoble breeding, dating back thousands of years, produces a useful, though sterile, animal. He has been the steed of kings, and valued above all else for some purposes. He has the build of his mother, and the long ears, stamina, and voice of his sire. Instead of the usual eleven months' gestation for a colt, a mare bred to a jack donkey will take twelve to produce a mule.

"Takes that extra month to grow the ears an' the beller," explained one of their instructors.

There was a lot of training to be done. Practice drill, taking down and setting up the gun, packing the component parts on the mules. The howitzer could be quickly disassembled into nine component parts, which clamped and buckled onto specially fitted Phillips packsaddles. Everything was designed to fit something else, and each mule and its crew had its specialty. A squat, powerful jack mule carried the barrel, or "tube," the business end of the cannon. It was the heaviest and most cumbersome of the loads. Another mule carried the wheels and the breech mechanism, another the recoil cylinders, and so on. All of these parts must be available in sequence, first things first.

To accomplish this, the mules must stand in formation, facing outward around the gun's location. Fanwise, three facing north, three south. It was quickly apparent that these mules were old soldiers. At the appropriate command, they would run to position. If a new recruit happened to be in the wrong place, he'd probably be stepped on. Some of the more experienced gun crews at Fort Sill could convert from a pack train to a firing artillery position in less than two minutes.

More difficult than this learning process, however, was the conversion to marching at mule speed. Four and one-quarter miles an hour. The morning after the first five-mile hike leading mules—or, more properly, trying to keep up with mules—the trainees awoke with *pain*. From the groin, a band of cramplike fire stretched spirally inside the thigh and to the back of the knee. Troopers dragged painfully out of the bunks, to hit the floor spraddle-legged, limping painfully. The thought of another five-mile march after packing heavy gun loads on the mules was met with authentic groans. It was nearly a week before the new packers could walk normally again.

By this time, they had developed a certain amount of pride in accomplishment. Like other special troops whose work is physically more demanding, they were issued extra rations. The mess hall of the pack units was reputed to be the best on the post.

There was a change in attitude toward mules in the next few weeks. Most cowboys had little use for such a creature, and scorned their appearance and demeanor. It was a double insult, then, to be forced to become "mule men."

"Don't underrate 'em, boys," insisted a grizzled old sergeant. "They're smarter'n a horse. You've heard a mule is stubborn? Nope, just smart. If he wants to balk, he's got a reason. Mebbe his load's slippin'. Mebbe his hide's gettin' sore where his saddle rubs. Mebbe a loose shoe. But whatever it is, *he* knows, an' you'd better find out. If'n you don't, he may go lame, an' then *you'll* be carryin' his load. An' some of them gun loads is purty heavy.

"Now, a mule will never founder, like a horse. A horse that gets into a grain bin will eat until he can't stand, and may never be the same again. A mule jest eats what he *needs.* Tell you what . . . You can leave a penned mule with enough feed for a week. If you'd come back on the sixth day, ol' mule will have one day's feed left. A horse, now, would have et all he could, an' be hungry by day three."

Few of the men actually believed Sarge's testimonials. They laughed about it behind his back.

But one day, most became believers. One of the gun crews was making their way around a narrow mountain trail, with a sheer wall above and a drop-off, a steep slope down to the creek below. The tube mule, carrying the gun's heavy barrel high on his back, misstepped and fell, bouncing and sliding, through the heavy fringe of willows on the creek bank. They heard the massive splash as the struggling animal struck the water and the willows closed behind him. The driver and packer had avoided the fall. No one could see the unfortunate mule, and the sounds of struggle soon ceased.

"This is bad, boys," said the old cadre instructor. "More'n likely his legs is broke from the fall. Even so, he's drownded now, sounds like. But we got to get down there an' salvage the gun. Won't fire without that tube."

It took about twenty minutes to find a way down the bluff, a riffle in which to cross the creek, and back to the scene of the accident.

To the amazement of the rescue party, there lay old Rabbit, the tube mule, on his back in the icy stream, with all four legs in the air. He had stretched his neck to reach the stream's edge, and was calmly cropping grass from the bank, while waiting for rescue. He had hardly a scratch.

"My gawd," said one of the new mule men, "a hoss would have kicked hisself to pieces!"

From that day on, there were fewer complaints about mules.

In addition to the four gun crews in the battery, there was a fifth crew with a remuda of ten mules, forming the "cargador" section, assigned the responsibility of supply in the field. This included transport of not only ammunition, but the field kitchen and blankets, tents, and other necessities.

John related well to all of this. The logistics of moving and setting up a mountain battery of artillery were not markedly different from those of the Wild West Show and its assorted personnel. The necessities were the same: food, shelter, preparation. Only the performance itself took on a somber, deadly tone. When the show was over, many would not be going home.

A couple of the junior officers quickly noticed the apparent experience of Corporal John Buffalo.

"You've done this before, Buffalo?" asked a first lieutenant.

"Not exactly, sir . . ."

John was somewhat unsure of what his previous experience would mean to these professionals.

"I've only been in the Army a few months," he said vaguely. "Part of that was hospital."

"But you seem to know tents. . . . Packing. What was your civilian job?"

"I . . . I worked for the Hundred and One, sir."

"The ranch, or the show?"

"Both, sir. Several years."

The lieutenant burst out laughing.

"Little wonder, then! We've often discussed how in the hell they can move a couple of hundred people and animals around the country like that. Well, we'll talk later. We can use your experience."

When all was said and done, John Buffalo was assigned to cargador, rather than a gun crew, and wore a third stripe on his sleeve. As a noncommissioned officer, he was also assigned a horse, and found himself back in the saddle.

That, too, was good, despite the military saddle. It could never approach the comfort of his old deep-seat stock saddle back at the 101.

SIXTY

Very quickly, the newly formed battery of mountain artillery became a unit with skills and pride in the accomplishment. As a group, having been chosen for length of leg, they were taller than other platoons. On occasions when they marched as a unit, without the gun mules, their demeanor showed their pride. Swinging at a fast march through the streets of Fort Sill, they had a tendency to strut just a trifle. They developed an esprit de corps and communication with expressions based on their work with the mules, the guns, and the packing.

In an emergency, every packer was expected to be able to do the job of any other. This, whether that happened to be on one of the gun mules or a cargo mule carrying regular pack loads. There was a language of communication all its own when packs were being loaded. Even without the experience, it is easy to see that a pack mule's cargo must be balanced, to keep the packsaddle from slipping to one side. It must be loaded by the packers at approximately the same instant, to avoid slipping. Visualize, for a moment, canvas-wrapped bales of hay, for instance, weighing eighty pounds, one on each side of the pack animal, to be lifted into place simultaneously. Some communication was necessary. *One, two, three, hup!* As the two packers lifted the loads to sling them with a tight rope across the pack-saddle. Then followed the intricate application of the famous "diamond hitch," handed down through antiquity to form the final tightening of the pack load. In this situation, the diamond hitch became a two-man job. One packer was responsible for drawing all of the slack out of the hitch and holding it for the few seconds required to yank the last turn tight and fasten it. This required communication. Since the packers, on opposite sides of a tall mule, could not see each other, there must be vocal commands, in sequence, alternating from one packer to the other. *Ready . . . Take slack . . . Hit it.* These, in a rhythmic cadence, would be meaningless to the men of other units. It became the exclusive code of the packers.

On pass in the nearby town of Lawton, Oklahoma, there was sometimes some friction between various units from Fort Sill. Usually these encounters were good-natured. But, with a great deal of pride involved, there was a tendency of the pack units to consider themselves the elite. Add to this, perhaps, a bit of jealousy or indignation over the packers' superior attitude. A few drinks in one or more of Lawton's hangouts, and friendly jibes might become more serious. Sometimes even physical.

Trained or training to fight, but not yet tested, young men have a natural tendency to search for opportunity without realizing it. It is difficult to be the first to back down from a confrontation. There is also the factor of loyalty and comradeship. A man in trouble has the right to accept support and help from his peers.

It was in this way that a custom arose in the darker regions of Lawton on a Saturday night. A mule packer in trouble might call for help from any other mule packer by initiating the packing sequence of communication. A long, loud call for help, *"Take slack!"* would be answered by any packer within earshot as they responded physically, rather than verbally. *Hit it!* Analogous to the circus roustabout's request for assistance, *"Hey, rube,"* this sequence of events sometimes resulted in bloodied noses, blackened eyes, and broken teeth. The Military Police were usually active enough to forestall much serious injury, and the net result was largely an increase in pride and belonging.

John Buffalo usually avoided the areas where drinking was in progress. He had had enough experience with "John Barleycorn" to realize a potential weakness in himself. There was a serious theory that those of Indian blood react differently to alcohol than those of other races. John had seen this in evidence on the reservation at his last visit there. Some of the old men, dejected and dispirited over the changes happening to their people, were drinking heavily and rapidly sliding into oblivion. He saw the possibility that it *could* happen to him, and took pains to avoid it.

Even so, in early autumn he found himself one Saturday night with a couple of other noncoms from the pack howitzer units, walking the streets of Lawton for a change from the rigors of training. The battery had been in the field on a "firing problem," involving a simulation of combat. The officers had been impressed at the speed with which the pack howitzers were able to set up in minutes and deliver a barrage of aimed fire. The targets were three miles away and out of sight behind a range of low hills. It was a good feeling, one of accomplishment, and morale was high. This, perhaps, contributed to a general cockiness on the part of the mule packers.

Add to such a mix a few beers, a few local girls of easy companionship, and a few gunners from the horse-drawn batteries. It was an explosive situation.

The three strolled along in the warm summer evening, listening to the laughter and piano music and loud voices from some of the smoky hangouts along the street. John was wondering. . . . In case the others wanted to stop in one of the bars, should he have a beer or two, or be content with sarsaparillas? He was still pondering that weighty problem when Corporal Vandever stopped short.

"What is it?" asked Staff Sergeant Bonner.

"Listen . . . I thought—"

Then the same sound, a long, wailing cry, *"Ta-ake slack!"*

Vandever was already running toward an open doorway where there were yells and the sounds of a scuffle. A woman screamed. The others followed him.

Inside, the problem was apparent. Two soldiers stood against the bar, surrounded by a half dozen others who were crowding toward them, but cautiously. One of the besieged men held a stout stick that appeared to be part of a broken chair. The bartender held a heavy policeman's nightstick and seemed reluctant to use it. Possibly, undecided on whom to use it.

"Six of 'em," observed Sergeant Bonner. "Well, let's go!"

He stepped forward, speaking as he did so. "Okay, break it up!"

"Like hell!" said one of the more inebriated of the crowd.

He launched a long swing at the sergeant, and Bonner took a glancing blow to the ear. His reaction was quick, a one-two to belly and nose. There was a yell of triumph from the beleaguered pair at the bar, and pandemonium broke out. A crash of broken glass; fists flying; a scream, curses, and a rain of fisticuffs.

John was caught almost off guard as a burly man rushed at him, starting a looping haymaker swing as he did so. He ducked, grabbed the swinging arm, and used the man's own momentum to propel the soldier into the wall, where he dropped limply. John turned to meet another incoming swing, tried to dodge, and succeeded only partially. A fist caught him above the ear, and the room whirled. He clinched with the attacker, remembering Jess Willard's advice: *Wrassle around till your head clears.*

There were whistles blowing now, and the sound of running feet on the wooden floor. A trio of Military Police burst into the room, and the crowds began to scatter. Out the door, the windows, through a narrow back exit beside the bar . . . The fracas was over almost before it began.

"Who started it?" one of the MPs asked the bartender.

"I dunno," said the barman cautiously. "These three tried to break it up."

He indicated the three noncoms.

A tough-looking girl was helping a dazed soldier to his feet beside the bar. A lanky packer from their own battery, one whose back had been crowded against the bar, now grinned sheepishly, if somewhat drunkenly.

"Thanks, Sarge! We knew you'd come."

"Okay," said Bonner. "Let's go home. You're s'posed to be fightin' the Kaiser, not each other!"

Training and practice continued. There began to be rumors about shipping out, mingled with rumors that the war was coming to an end. Corporal Vandever gleefully told John of a prank that a couple of privates in his platoon had carried out. They had deliberately started a completely ridiculous rumor that the battery was to be sent to defend Alaska, and told it in strictest confidence.

Within a matter of hours, the rumor was back, with more details. The battery was to go by train to San Diego, where they would board ship to Alaska.

"I know damn' well it's true," insisted one packer. "I got it from a fella in A-battery who has a cousin in Quartermaster. They're fixin' to issue cold-weather gear. But, he was told to say nothin', and to deny it if he's asked."

"Hell," said Vandever with a chuckle, "by that time, I was ready to believe it myself!"

It was only a few days later that John met a familiar-looking figure on the street at the fort. An officer, with insignia of a major . . . No, a lieutenant colonel, he saw as they came closer. Something familiar in the way the man walked. Straight as a ramrod; not tall, but lean and wiry.

John saluted as they met, and saw the recognition in the man's eyes. At about the same time, he realized—

"Buffalo? John Buffalo?"

"Captain . . . Excuse me, sir. *Colonel* McCoy?"

"Yes . . . What are you doing here, John?"

"Transferred here, sir. From the cavalry. Fort Riley."

"Yes," McCoy chuckled. "I got into the same change-over."

"You're in artillery, too?"

"Yes. French 75s. But, I didn't know you were in the Army, John."

"Yes, sir. When the Rough Riders fell through, I had to do something."

"And you're a sergeant! Good. But it looks like the war's about over now. What will you do then?

"Hadn't thought about it, sir. Will you stay in?"

"Probably not. I'm married, now. We'll probably go back to the ranch. Fella running it . . . Well, of course! You know George Shakespear."

"Yes, sir."

"Well, good to see you, Buffalo. If you're up Wyoming way, stop by!"

"Thank you, sir."

"Mebbe by that time, we can forget the 'sir.' " McCoy grinned.

Only a few weeks later, the war was over. It would take a while to decommission the combat units, but it was time to consider moving on. John thought long and hard about a military career. He could do it, but would probably have to take a reduction in grade. He had always felt unsuited to the strict, time-oriented pace of the Army, anyway. It would be best to return to the more loosely organized schedule of a civilian. But what to do, there? He wasn't sure. Well, he could decide, later. When it's time . . .

At last, the Great War, the war to end wars, was over. Worldwide, there had been millions of fatalities. Ten million, he had heard.

Yet that paled to insignifance compared to the death rate from the terrible influenza epidemic. Worldwide, more than twenty million deaths . . . He realized now that he was fortunate to have fallen ill among such caring people as Father O'Reilly and Nurse Ruth Jackson.

He wondered how Ruth might be doing. Maybe he'd go and see. But first he'd have to muster out, and that process was moving slowly.

SIXTY-ONE

John Buffalo was mustered out at Fort Sill in the spring of 1919, after helping with the decommission of the wartime training units. Hundreds of mules were sold at auction, with large quantities of equipment, no longer needed.

The pack howitzers were covered with canvas tarpaulins, and stored at the fort, in the huge stable facilities. There they would wait for the next war, their iron-rimmed wooden wheels an anachronism in a conflict fought on rubber tires, and by sea and in the air. It is worth note in passing that the concept of the mountain-pack artillery was a good one. Modified with rubber-tired truck wheels, the same howitzers were used to good advantage by paratroops in the *Second* World War.

John had no definite plans. He had a vague idea that he would go back to Fort Riley and visit Ruth Jackson. He still had mixed feelings: shame and guilt, mixed with the bitter-sweet memory of that night. Yet she *had* seemed grateful for his presence in her time of need. Maybe if he could get past the initial embarrassment and talk to her. . . . Become reacquainted . . . Yes, she had left an open door, recognizing that either or both might have quite different feelings after a period of time. Whether they would—or *could*—relate as friends, as lovers, or both, would not be certain until they met again. Maybe the intensity of their relationship would have burned away the chances of returning down that road. Regardless, he must go and see.

Now he recalled that on the trip to Fort Sill, the troop train had passed through Ponca City. Why not plan to pause there before going on to see Ruth? He could see what was happening at the Hundred and One, talk to some old friends, maybe. He wondered whether, in the aftermath of the war, the Wild West Show might take to the road again. Yes, a stop there would give him a much better idea of his options, no matter what the result of his reunion with Ruth Jackson might be.

He said good-bye to a few friends and boarded the train north, with his discharge papers and his mustering-out pay.

It was a relatively short trip to Bliss, Oklahoma, and he caught a ride out to the ranch on a supply wagon. He did not know the young driver, but gained some information en route.

The Wild West Show was not on the road this season. There had not been much talk of it, but the war was barely over. Speculation about next season was beginning to surface.

One trend was toward more drilling for oil on the Ponca lands. There were many more motorcars in use, and gasoline and oil would be needed in large quantities. Henry Ford was expected to develop new models of his auto. Others were rushing to respond to the demand for cars and trucks. Oldsmobile, Moon, Starr, Dodge, Chevrolet, Willys, Cadillac, Maxwell, Buick, Hudson . . . Even Studebaker, the veteran manufacturer of freight wagons for a century, was manufacturing an entry into the booming world of motorcars.

After the fact, it was realized that motorcars had changed the course of the war. German forces had threatened Paris, and the military governor, General Joseph Gallieni, commandeered the taxicabs of Paris to transport troops to the battlefront. The German advance had been stopped at the Battle of the Marne. Military transportation would never be the same again. The demand for oil was increasing by leaps and bounds.

John stepped down from the wagon and thanked the driver. He headed toward the ranch office at the White House, duffel bag on his shoulder.

"John! Good to see you." Joe Miller greeted him. "Wondered what had happened to you."

"Been in the Army, sir," said John, a trifle embarrassed.

He was always nervous around people in positions of authority. Possibly Old White Horse may have been the origin of this trait, but he wasn't thinking of that now.

"You're out, now?" asked Miller.

"Yes, sir, just discharged. Passin' through to go see a friend."

"I see. Thought you might be lookin' for a job. Show isn't on the road this year."

"I heard that, on the way out," John told him.

"Want a job here? We've got some good things goin', John . . . Crossin' buffalo with cattle and with zebu, them humpbacked cows from India. New crops, too. And there's the oil. . . . Big business there."

"Thank you, sir, but I think I'll move on for now. I've got some friends to see. I'll stop back by if I get a chance."

He rose and began to head for the door. Joe Miller extended a handshake, and John turned back to respond.

"Say," said Miller suddenly, "there's a letter here for you. I'd forgotten. Let's see . . ."

He began to rummage in an array of pigeonholes above a desk behind him.

"Didn't know where to forward it. . . . Been some time, now—"

His search was interrupted by a knock at the open door of the office. John turned to see an Indian couple standing in the hallway. Poncas, by their dress and demeanor.

"Oh, yeah! Thanks for comin' in, Elk! Got somethin' for you to sign. . . . You get some oil money. John, you remember Spotted Elk, here, an' his missus."

John nodded noncommittally, and gave a hand sign in greeting.

Miller spread a paper on the desk and set an inkwell and a pen near it.

"Now, sign right there." He pointed a finger. "That says you give permission to drill for oil on the land titled in your name. Now, I'm gonna give you the money."

He counted out some bills and shoved the little stack of paper toward Spotted Elk.

"Could be some more, if we hit it big," Miller suggested.

Odd, John thought. *A strange way to sign an oil lease.*

John was trying hard to look anywhere but at the paper that Spotted Elk had signed, but his eyes were drawn to it. He did not have much experience with legal papers, but something seemed wrong. The paper did not have the appearance of an oil-lease agreement. Actually, it looked more like a deed. Could it be that Joe Miller . . . ? *No!* It was a ridiculous idea to think that there might be any deception on the part of Joe Miller, "white chief of the Poncas."

But, there was also the payment by Miller to the Spotted Elks—in cash, with no apparent record of a transaction. John was very uncomfortable with this situation, but he was certainly in no position to ask questions.

Miller and the Poncas shook hands while John waited, still uneasy. The Indian couple nodded to John and departed, pleased with the transaction and with the handful of greenbacks.

"Good man, that Spotted Elk," said Miller to John. "Now, where were we? Oh, yes, I was looking for your letter. Hmm . . . Should be . . . Yes! Right here!"

He handed the letter to John.

"Come back and see us, John. And there'll be a job when you want it."

"Thank you, sir. I appreciate it."

He was completely puzzled with the business-sized envelope. It bore a New Mexico postmark, and the return address was printed, in the upper left corner: Door of Hope, Loving, N.M. It was addressed to him, John Buffalo, 101 Ranch, Bliss, Oklahoma, in a neat, tight script. Someone accustomed to writing.

Completely confused as to what the communication might be, John sought privacy and slit the envelope with his pocketknife.

The letter was written in the same hand as the address on the envelope. The date was more than a year old. It took him only a moment to glance at the printed letterhead, "Door of Hope Orphanage," in formal, churchly lettering like that on the title page of an old Bible. Now thoroughly confused, he began to read the letter. . . .

My dear Mr. Buffalo,

It is my painful task to inform you of the death of your son, John, from the ravages of influenza.

His heart was racing and his palms were damp from sweat. Did someone have him confused with someone else? He shook his head to clear it and read on.

We had rather hoped to hear from you before such an occurrence made it necessary to contact you. It was our understanding that the people with the TB research group had forwarded to you a letter from your wife. It was to have explained the situation and the whereabouts of your son in case of her death.

John's eyes filled with tears. A son—his and Hebbie's . . . She had tried to tell him in the letter which was too damaged to be read. . . . Slowly and painfully, he began to piece the information together. Hebbie must have wanted to conceal . . . But why, oh *why?*

He wiped away tears and attempted to read the rest of the letter. Now it seemed to him that it was somewhat accusing in tone.

She had indicated that she believed that in the case of her death the boy's father would come to assume the responsibility of his care. This has not happened. There is, however, in the case file, a note that it may be possible to reach you through the 101 Ranch in Oklahoma. Hence, this letter. Your son was buried beside his mother in the cemetery near Carlsbad, in case you wanted to know.

Our sympathy for your loss.

> Sincerely,
> Margaret Jones, Dir.
> Door of Hope Orphanage

It was all that John could do to keep from crying aloud in his grief. There was much to be said, he realized, for the celebration of the Great Mystery by means of the songs of mourning of his people.

He began to realize now how carefully Hebbie had planned. She had not wanted to complicate his life more than necessary. If only she had known how much he had longed to be a part of hers. In her thoughtfulness, her determination not to be a problem to him, she had inadvertently deprived him and herself of so much. A son ... He could see now that the ruined letter would have explained the whole thing. Hebbie had known that when he received that letter, he would come immediately to take care of their son, the product of their love. If only he had *known*. ... But the letter was destroyed.

I'm so sorry, Hebbie, he whispered to the evening sunset.

If only he had known where *she* was, he could have gone there. ... And *then* what? His thoughts kept circling, like a "bull-roarer," the child's toy of his people, whirled around one's head on a string.

Hebbie had carefully set up the letter which would have explained all of this and directed him how to find their son. ... And the letter was lost.

He saw only one thing that he could do now. He must go to New Mexico, must find the orphanage which had housed his son, must inquire as to the circumstances of Hebbie's death, and where it had occurred.

It was growing dark as he shouldered the duffel bag and

started to walk toward Ponca City. He could not have slept, anyway, and he'd be there to board the first train that would take him to Loving, New Mexico.

Loving . . . A cruel twist of fate . . .

SIXTY-TWO

The "Door of Hope Orphanage" read the sign across the front of the house. He walked up the steps and across the front porch to the heavy door, where he gave the cast-iron toggle a twist. He could feel the mechanism whirl and clang against the bell and hear the sound that was generated inside the house.

He heard footsteps, and a well-groomed middle-aged woman, her hair drawn up in a bun, opened the door.

"Yes?"

"I'm looking for Margaret Jones," he began.

She eyed him a bit suspiciously.

"And who might you be?" she demanded. "What is the nature of your business?"

"Forgive me, ma'am," John said. "I neglect my manners. I am John Buffalo, and I seek information about my . . . My son."

It was the first time he had voiced the words aloud.

"John Buffalo?"

The expression on her face scrolled through a range of emotion: disbelief, anger, sadness. . . . Her eyes swept him up and down. He was tired, dusty, disheveled, and, just now, growing impatient.

Her face softened.

"Come in, Mr. Buffalo," she said politely. "I am Margaret Jones."

Seated in her office, John began to feel the discord between this setting, neat as a pin, and his own condition.

"I—I just got off the train," he began apologetically.

"I understand. But how is it that you come here now?" Her attitude was still one of disapproval.

"I will explain, Mrs.—Mrs. or Miss Jones?"

"Mrs. I am a widow. But please go on."

"Yes . . . This is very difficult for me. Until two days ago, I had no idea that I had a son. I came as soon as I received word."

"But I wrote—That was a year ago! And I expected you long before that. You never even responded to the death of your wife, I'm told. What kind of a man *are* you?"

She was angry, now, her voice shrill with disapproval. Visions of Old White Horse flitted through his head. Her behavior over infractions by her young charges had been much like this. Except, compared to the thin and bony frame of the teacher, this woman was quite attractive, even in her anger. She was tall but shapely, and the years had been kind to her. She was dignified and proud in her carriage, reminding him of his own mother in her prime, before she lost everything.

But now, his anger rose over the lack of understanding that this woman showed.

"Mrs. Jones," he began as calmly as possible, "you have no idea of this situation and no right to condemn me for something over which I had no control—no knowledge, even."

He paused, unsure where to begin.

"Go on," she snapped. "I'm listening."

Best he should start at the first, he reasoned. Quickly, he related his experience at the 101 Ranch, and how he and Hebbie met and became common-law partners. How he felt that both were ready for a formalization of their relationship in marriage when he returned from Europe.

But Hebbie had disappeared.

"I am made to think," John said thoughtfully, "that she wanted to spare me the pain of seeing her fail slowly."

The woman's face had softened somewhat, and so had her voice when she spoke.

"You looked for her?"

"Of course. I contacted every sanatorium I could learn of. There was no trace. I was forced to conclude that she had used another name."

Now Margaret Jones was nodding sympathetically.

"This explains much. Please go on."

"Well . . . That was seven years ago. I kept trying for a couple of years, but there was no trace. Then finally, a letter. I could read only a small part of it because it had been torn, damaged, and wet, and part of it was missing. I knew that I was to receive it only in the event of Hebbie's death. I could read that much."

He paused, choking back a tear.

Now the expression on the face of Margaret Jones was one of pure sympathy. "How difficult for you! And you had no idea where the letter had come from?"

"None . . . Yes, it was a hard time. It still is."

"Of course. There's not much I can tell you, but a little. Mary—that's the name she was using—Mary gave birth to your son in Carlsbad. There was a TB treatment center over there, with some huts in the cave. You know about the big cavern?"

"Not much."

"Well, it's huge. Miles and miles of caverns. The theory was that a constant temperature—no change in the air, winter and summer—would help heal the tuberculosis. I don't know that it was very successful, but that's where she was. To protect her baby, she placed him here."

"She never saw him?"

"Only at first. She didn't want to expose him to the infection."

"You *knew* her?"

"Not really. I met her only once. I didn't know about the letter to be sent to you in the event of her death. She said only that if she recovered from the tuberculosis, she would pick up the baby. If something happened to *her,* his father would."

"But how—"

"That letter—the one that was destroyed—must have told the whole story," she pondered. "I was notified of her death, and was puzzled that no one inquired about the child. Finally I wrote you. The 101 Ranch had been mentioned, and I thought it worth a try to write you there. But that was a year ago."

"I was in the Army. Just mustered out, a few days ago."

Now, the woman's face was filled with sympathy.

"How hard it must have been . . . Not to know . . . You did not even know of your son?"

"No, I had no idea."

"Ah . . . Mary . . . Hebbie, you say?"

"Yes. Short for Hepzibah. Bible name, I guess."

"Well, she named the baby for his father . . . John Buffalo. He was a wonderful child, Mr. Buffalo. It was so hard. . . . We lost three of the children to the influenza."

"Yes, it was bad. I was in an Army hospital with it."

He refrained from further details.

"You said in your letter that they are buried at Carlsbad?"

"Yes. The mother was buried there, and we thought it appropriate that her son rest with her."

"I'll want to visit the graves," John said.

"Of course. Where are you staying?"

"Nowhere, yet. I came here directly from the train."

Her eyes swept over his dusty clothes.

"Would you care to stay here? Our census is low, and we have a spare room. You could change and refresh yourself. I have to make a trip to Carlsbad tomorrow, and I can show you the way to the cemetery."

"Well, if it's no trouble . . ."

"Good! It's settled, then."

The "spare room" was comfortable and quiet, and apparently little used. A plump Mexican woman brought him a kettle of hot water. She took the pitcher from the dresser and returned quickly, having filled it with cold water. She placed it next to the basin, laid out towels and a washcloth, and turned to go.

"Gracias, señorita," said John.

The woman blushed and giggled. *"Señora,"* she corrected him with an embarrassed smile.

"Oh! Sorry."

She giggled again and departed, closing the door behind her.

John bathed and shaved, dressed again in the only other clothes he possessed, and tried to brush some of the dust and wrinkles from the coat he had worn en route.

He made his way downstairs and was greeted by Margaret Jones, who now seemed genuinely friendly. John decided that she must have formed a very poor opinion of the sort of person he must be. It could have been no other way. It had appeared to her that he must be a shiftless wanderer who had abandoned a sick and pregnant wife and, in turn, a motherless son. Now she was probably trying to make amends.

"Supper is at six," she told him.

He had no watch, but was accustomed to estimating the time. He had been involved with boarding enough trains and participating in enough shows and military schedules to be pretty adept at it. Now he judged that it would be two or three hours until supper.

"Let me show you around the facility," Mrs. Jones suggested.

"You have no other responsibilities?" he asked. "I don't want to bother—"

"No, no, nothing important," she interrupted, "and I enjoy a change in the routine."

It was a rambling old house, with four-foot-thick walls of adobe. He knew that it would be warm in winter and cool in summer's heat. Comfortable, solid, protective . . . Ideal for an orphanage. The house had been built by a wealthy entrepreneur as his own family residence. He had been orphaned himself, and understood the plight of a child without family. He had married, but had no children of his own, and in his will had specified this use for the estate after his own passing.

"It's really a home," Margaret Jones told him. "At least, we try to make it so."

"Church supported?" he asked.

"No. Most orphanages are, you know. But we are well funded through the estate. Quite a unique situation. The founder was a self-made man. Oh, it's for boys only. He specified that. Frankly, that avoids a lot of problems."

"But . . . You're the director—a woman."

She laughed. It was a hearty masculine laugh, one he could appreciate.

"Yes," she said. "Sort of a contradiction, isn't it? But Mr. Hope—a name he selected for himself, incidentally—felt that he wanted a woman's influence in the operation. Preferably, a married couple. My husband and I . . ."

She hesitated, and John attempted to fill the gap.

"You had children of your own?"

"No ... Yes, one, but he died in infancy. We were unable to conceive again. But I have many sons here." She smiled.

"How long ago ... ?" he began.

"... Did I lose my husband? About six years now, I guess. But back to the operation. We teach the three Rs, have an extensive garden. A full-time couple ... You met Rosa. She and her husband are a great help. Juan can fix anything. A good carpenter."

She paused and chuckled, half to herself.

"Your original question, as I recall, was about church. Mr. Hope insisted that we be nonsectarian. So, we have a priest who comes in for Mass. I'm Methodist, myself, and we have Protestant services, Sunday evenings. Rosa and Juan are Catholic. Our boys are permitted to attend either or both."

The afternoon flew, and it seemed only a little while until a chime sounded, like a smaller version of a church bell.

Margaret Jones led the way to the dining room, where clean-scrubbed boys of various ages were assembling.

There were eleven in all. Three appeared to be under the age of five; two were showing a fuzz of whiskers along the upper lip and jaw, suggesting approaching manhood. Between were six others of varying ages. All seemed to relate well to each other, the older helping the younger. There was considerable good-natured teasing. The whole thing was impressive.

"This is Mr. Buffalo, our guest this evening," introduced the director. "We can sing for him after supper. For now, let us say grace. Aaron, will you do the honor?"

All heads bowed, and one of the older of the boys asked a blessing on the group and the meal.

John found it good that the son that he had lost, without

having ever known of his existence, had lived here.

"Amen," sounded the chorus of young voices at the close of the grace.

John wiped away a tear, hoping to be unobserved.

SIXTY-THREE

The next morning, he helped Juan harness the horse and hitch up the buggy for the trip to the town of Carlsbad. Staying at the orphanage had been a good experience. There were some things that could not escape his notice. Similarities to his own childhood. The whole operation reminded him of a boarding school. More specifically, of his own experience in the first of the government schools he had been forced to attend.

However, the differences were greater than the similarities. The entire atmosphere was pleasant, cooperative. There was genuine love in the approach of Mrs. Jones, and of Juan and Rosa. In the short time that he had been at the Door of Hope, John had felt a sense of belonging on the part of the orphan boys who lived there. They were fortunate to have arrived in such a place. At the age he had been when he arrived at the government school, this would have given him an entirely different outlook. Maybe . . . But no, there was no point in pondering, "What if . . ." There was some satisfaction in thinking that the short life of the son that he had never seen, his and Hebbie's, had had some happy and loving times there.

Margaret Jones took him to the cemetery, a peaceful place with a magnificent vista of landscape. In a area where the markers were close together, simple, or nonexistent, she pointed out two wooden slabs with carving that told the bare facts.

HEPZIBAH BUFFALO	JOHN BUFFALO
1885–1915	1912–1918

Somehow, he felt great satisfaction in the fact that Hebbie had taken his name. John had always felt that when he returned from Stockholm they would have married, except for the disease that had taken her from him.

He was startled from his thoughts as Mrs. Jones spoke gently.

"I knew her as Mary Ellis," Mrs. Jones was saying.

John nodded. "That's why I could never find her. I had suspected . . . She didn't want to burden me with her problems. I would have—"

He stopped, unable to talk.

The woman went on, "I think that she always hoped she would recover. She wanted her son nearby, so that the two of them could return to you."

"He—He was a good boy?" John asked.

"The best . . ."

Now Margaret Jones was having trouble choking back tears. Finally she was able to speak.

"Would you like to stay here a little while? I'll run my errands and come back for you."

"That would be good," he said in a husky voice. "Thank you."

When the buggy was out of sight, he sang the songs of mourning for both of them. It was good to be alone with his thoughts for a little while, with no one to interfere, no pressing responsibilities. There were memories to cherish. . . . He felt close to Hebbie again. He thought of the times when she had appeared to him in a dream or vision, and felt a confidence that brought him peace.

Thank you, Hebbie, he voiced, wordlessly. *I wish that we could have shared our son. . . .*

That had not been fated, but this quiet hour was very meaningful to him, something that he had long needed.

The buggy returned, and Mrs. Jones asked if he was ready to go. He could see that she understood.

They rode in silence for a little way, and she spoke, gently and with understanding.

"Is there anything you'd want to do for them? A head-stone, maybe?"

John thought of the burial practices of his people, the scaffold burial, and smiled to himself.

"No. I know where they are."

"Will you want to visit the cavern? It's a day's travel west, but I could help arrange it."

John thought a little while. He had always had the fear of closed places that is born into the marrow of the no-madic prairie dweller. The thought of a dark underground place was enough to make him shudder. He did not think that he wanted to visualize Hebbie in such a setting.

"The lodges . . . Houses? What is the 'treatment' you spoke of?"

"Mostly, the constant temperature deep in the cavern, I suppose."

"They never came out?"

"I don't know, John. I think that it was not very effec-tive. It is my understanding that there are huts, below the level influenced by the weather outside."

"I don't want to go there," he decided.

"Then will you go back to Loving with me?"

For a moment, John was thoroughly confused. He had been somewhat startled when she boldly called him by his first name. Now her last question caught him completely off guard. *Loving* . . . In the space of a few heartbeats, his mind reevaluated the question. *Loving, New Mexico* . . . The town. He was embarrassed that he could have thought otherwise. He risked a glance at her face and, to his surprise, saw the hint of a blush along her neck. She, too, had caught the nuance. He devoutly hoped that she would not realize *his* thoughts. Margaret Jones *was* a very attractive woman. He *had* left his duffel bag at the Door of Hope, and would need to retrieve it.

"Of course," he said formally.

"Good! You will spend the night before moving on? Where will you go? Back to the 101?"

She appeared to be trying hard to move on to another subject. Maybe he could help.

"I don't know," he mused. "I think not the ranch. I traveled with the Wild West Show, and it's not in operation now. But . . . Well, Hebbie and I met at the 101. It might bring back too many memories, to be in places we shared."

She nodded in understanding, and he felt that she really *did* know his feelings. She, too, had suffered such a loss.

"I may go back to Wyoming," he went on. "I worked there a while."

"In what job?" she asked.

"Cowboyin'. I've also friends in Kansas. I was at Fort Riley, there, in the Army."

He didn't want to be too specific. He had already decided that he would not yet intrude on the loss that Ruth Jackson had suffered. Later, possibly . . . Give her a little time to mourn. A year, maybe. Then see what feelings were left, and whether they would support a relationship other than that of friends.

It was nearly dark when the buggy drew up at the stable behind the Door of Hope. Juan met them and helped Mrs. Jones to dismount.

"Rosa saved you some supper, *Señora,*" he told her. "Go on . . . I will take care of the horse."

It took him a long time to fall asleep. There were jumbled and confusing thoughts in his mind. He dozed, and the images of people in his memories wandered through fragmented dreams. Mostly, women. Hebbie, of course, flashing her shy smile. Jane Langtry, her golden hair almost glowing in the moonlight. Then the image of Jane faded and changed and became Ruth Jackson, the angel who had literally saved his life when he had been dying of influenza.

There were a couple of fräuleins in Germany, their memories passing even more swiftly than the actual relationships. . . . An English girl, near Shepherd's Bush, who, at a later time, would have been called a groupie.

And Margaret Jones . . . There had been no romance, even a hint. But she had been kind and understanding. She was an attractive woman, and her maturity and frankness was a definite advantage. She, too, had known sorrow and bereavement.

He thought of her accidental innuendo—*return to Loving with me*—and smiled in the darkness of the bedroom. He wondered about her age. . . . Possibly a bit older than he, but of that rare charm which seems to make some women age gracefully, actually becoming more attractive with maturity.

What strange thoughts . . . It had been a long and stressful day. He drifted between waking and sleep, possibly dreaming. Was he trying to read more into this woman's friendliness and compassion that what was really there? Probably. But he could not deny that in the short while he had known her, there was a closeness and understanding between them, out of all proportion to the situation.

It must have been about that time that he heard—or

rather *sensed*—someone in the hall outside his bedroom door. Not actual footsteps, but a *presence,* which paused and hung there for a long moment. He had the strong impression that someone was about to enter the room, and he was certain as to the identity of that person. He could even visualize the hand on the doorknob. . . .

The moment passed, and the presence, real or imagined, moved on down the hall.

John awoke with the soft rays of the rising sun peeking through the window. He was refreshed, though he felt as if he had hardly slept. Strange dreams . . . Someone in the hall, deciding whether to enter . . . Had that really happened, or was it merely a wishful thought on the part of a lonely man in his grief?

He dressed and prepared to meet the day, still wondering. He could hear no one stirring yet. Maybe he'd take a walk before the day warmed enough to make it impractical, and before the house awoke to the busy schedule of a herd of small boys.

In the front hall he encountered Margaret, also dressed for the day.

"Good morning," she said quietly, "I was just going for a walk."

"I, too," he said with a smile. "Shall we?"

They slipped outside into the quiet of early morning.

"You slept well?" she asked conversationally.

"Yes, ma'am. Some dreaming . . . A lot of memories."

"Of course," she said thoughtfully.

They walked in silence for a little while.

"John," she said finally, "would you consider staying here for a little while, helping with the boys? It wouldn't pay much, but they need a father figure. Juan is a good man, but—" Her voice trailed off, leaving a lot unspoken.

He took a deep breath.

"I don't know that I'd be much of a father figure," he mumbled self-consciously.

"Oh, John, I'm sorry. That's not what—Now I've hurt you. I didn't mean . . ."

She paused and chuckled ruefully. "I guess I'm pretty transparent. I was being selfish. I was prepared to hate you, but . . . Well, it's apparent that we have . . . Oh, John, you know what I'm talking about."

He nodded thoughtfully.

"Of course. But . . . Margaret, this has happened so quickly. A few days ago I didn't even know I had a son. You have been kind, and very gracious to me. I will always treasure your help when I needed it, as well as your care for my son. If I'm in your area again, I *will* come back."

Maybe I'll come anyway, he said to himself.

Then he continued aloud.

"I'm not sure where my life is going now," he finished lamely. "I need to take some time to decide."

"I thought so," she said with resignation. "But, after that . . . Well, you know where we are."

SIXTY-FOUR

John was on the afternoon train, heading north. He did not want to spend another night at the Door of Hope. It could easily come to look far too attractive, and he needed some time alone, without any outside influences. Maybe he'd cowboy a little. The long hours alone on horseback would provide an opportunity to think.

For that matter, the train trip yielded some time for

thought, if he managed to avoid chatty passengers. For the present, he had abandoned the idea of returning to visit Ruth Jackson. There were other things that he needed to consider. Not decisions, necessarily, but events and possibilities that required some thought, before they could be put in their proper places. Besides, his thoughts were too preoccupied with memories of Hebbie to think of anyone else just now.

He reached into his shirt pocket and drew out a small photograph, given him by Margaret Jones. It depicted a small boy with light-colored hair, an infectious grin, and freckles. He had looked at it a dozen times since she had handed it to him on the depot platform as he boarded the train.

"You should have this," she said.

On back of the Kodak likeness was written in a firm feminine hand,

"John Buffalo II, age 6, 1918"

John had the impression that across the eyes, the boy resembled him. However, the hair and the smile were purely Hebbie's. He could plainly see the shy yet mischievous nature of the boy's mother in his grin. The hair, light in color and curly along the forehead and over the ears, was also a true picture of the unruly hair that Hebbie always fought to control. Usually, she had simply tied it back or jammed a cowboy hat over it. On a boy, it could be controlled by cutting, but . . . It didn't matter now, he realized with a heavy heart.

John was still unsure what he wanted to do, and where. Idly, he picked up a newspaper that a fellow passenger had left on the train, and passed a little time in reading. The sports page was always of interest to him, and he found it so today. There were familiar names. Jim Thorpe was discussed as a professional baseball player in one article. The sportswriter was defending Thorpe's skill, which had apparently been criticized by another writer: "Can't hit a curve ball?" the writer questioned indignantly. "Look at Thorpe's batting average!" There were statistics and opinions.

He learned that Naismith was no longer at the University of Kansas. He had turned the reins over to his friend Forrest "Phog" Allen. Allen's basketball team was doing better than Naismith's had done. John smiled to himself, remembering Naismith's scorn of his own creation: *You don't coach basketball, Forrest, it's just a game!*

There were times when he thought of going back to see if there might be a position at Carlisle that he could fill. It had been several years since he had any contact there, but there should be someone who would know him. Even a lesser job as an assistant coach or trainer would be sufficient for his needs. He wasn't sure whether Pop Warner or McGregor, his old coach, were still there, however. The Great War and the influenza had caused a lot of changes. That was a long way to travel, just to inquire, and his modest mustering-out pay would not last long.

Possibly he could find an athletic job in the area around Haskell. He had only a speaking acquaintance with Phog Allen, but there were several colleges in the area, and Allen could probably tell him of any openings. It was only a passing idea, and he did not consider for very long. Such a move would not give him the solitude that he needed right now, or the time to be alone with his thoughts.

No, the more he thought, the more appealing became the picture of riding alone under a big sky. He had once heard a saying that now came back to him. About a horse . . .

There's something about a horse that is good for the inside of a man.

He wasn't sure that was quite it, but it was close enough. A horse can furnish companionship when one needs to think without interruption. Long days and nights on the range would give time for thought and self-evaluation, while the horse handled his end of a rather routine job.

The more he thought along these lines, the better it looked. A cowboy's job in Wyoming had a lot of appeal to a man just recovering from several emotional crises of different kinds. It would give him an opportunity to sort things out in his head, to overcome some of the guilt that kept coming at him from different directions.

The thought that finally decided him was the fact that he had already been offered a job. Colonel McCoy had sounded quite specific.

Now, John began to wonder. Had his own decision already been made at some other level? Here he was, on a train heading in that direction. Had his actions been anticipated? Who was it who once told him, *John, there are no coincidences?* The longer he lived, the more likely this seemed. He wasn't sure, but it was a comfort, somehow, to feel that in the confusion of the vast world, there was some sort of a pattern. Maybe, even, a purpose.

He fell asleep, lulled by the familiar *click-clack* of steel wheels on the rails.

When he reached Wyoming, John learned that McCoy was not at the ranch on Owl Creek.

"No, he's not here," said George Shakespear. "You need to see him?"

"Well, I—" John mumbled, caught off guard. "I talked to him at Fort Sill. He asked about what I'd do after the Army. . . . He sort of . . ."

"Offered you a job?" George chuckled. "Sure, we can use you. But the boss got himself a job in Cheyenne."

"A *town* job?"

"Well, sort of. When he left the Army, he stopped in Cheyenne to see an ol' friend, who happened to be the governor."

"Governor of what?"

"Of Wyoming. You didn't know Bob Carey, I guess. They'd cowboyed together, years back, before the War."

"So what's his job?"

"Adjutant General."

"Of *Wyoming?*"

"Yes. Our colonel's wearin' a star on his shoulder."

"He's a *General?*"

"Yeah. Had to have the rank to take the job."

John was astonished at such news.

"So . . . He's living in Cheyenne?"

"Well, he's out here quite a bit," George admitted. "You knew he's married?"

"Yes, he told me that."

"Yeah . . . Oh, yes, he has a new name."

"You mean 'General'?"

"Well, that, too. But you 'member, the 'Rapaho called him *Ba,* 'The Friend'? Well, the old men decided he needed a real name. They had the ceremony, the feather hat and all. He's a real Arapaho—'Soldier Chief,' to honor his general's star. In 'Rapaho, *'Banee-i-natcha.'* Well, you want to go to work? I can use you."

"Sure."

Time passed quickly. The work was hard, the days sometimes long, but the reward of hard work is good sleep. During waking hours in the saddle, he was able to sort out in his mind many of the events that now seemed only dim memories: some good, some bad, some a bittersweet mixture. Once more, he noticed the selective nature of memory. The unpleasant is more easily forgotten, while the good is stored away carefully, to be drawn out and cherished from time to time. The experience that is good is relived. Sometimes with regret, of course. *If I had only realized then . . .*

The winter descended like an icy blanket thrown over the world, chilling man and beast to the bone. It had been a long time since John had wintered in the northern plains. This was one of the unpleasantries that had been selectively forgotten during the winters farther to the south in Oklahoma. Sometimes, in Mexico or South America, he had dodged winter entirely.

Old injuries, forgotten in the warm days of summer, awoke with each cold front, stirring up the selectively forgotten memories. He began to understand more fully the remarks of the old men: *My bones tell me a storm is coming.* He had only half-believed it until now, but the signs were plain. He would awaken sometimes in the night with aches and pains in a knee or shoulder. The one, perhaps, on which he had landed from the "hurricane deck" of a high-bucking bronc. It was no longer a surprise, now, to have such weather indicators followed in half a day by a dark cloud front moving in from the northwest, with a threat of snow.

He seldom saw McCoy, who was occupied with government matters while George Shakespear continued to manage the ranch. As the weather began to open up in the spring, however, the visits to the ranch became more frequent. It was plain that the love of big sky and wide-open horizons was talking to the general as he carried out the business of government.

"John," Shakespear told him later that summer, "the 'Rapaho are gonna give Soldier Chief a new name. You wanna come to the ceremony?"

"Sure. But, *another* name? Isn't that unusual?"

"Not unheard of, John. The old men decided that *Banee-i-natcha,* Soldier Chief, doesn't tell his whole story. He needs a better one."

John had attended some Arapaho ceremonies as a guest, with George Shakespear. Some were much like those of his own people, or at least similar enough to recognize their significance. John spoke no Arapaho.

"That's okay," George told him. "Soldier Chief doesn't speak Arapaho."

"But he *is* Arapaho, by adoption."

"Sure. He uses hand signs. And the old men talk to him in English."

"Your elders talk English?"

"Most of 'em. If they don't want to, they pretend not to understand."

John smiled. He was familiar with this subterfuge. Sometimes, as a child, he had even used it himself.

On the appointed day, they rode out to the reservation with McCoy. As adjutant general, he had spent a lot of time traveling to visit other tribes. He was well respected by not only whites and Arapaho, but Lakota, Blackfeet and Cheyenne, communicating with hand signs. He had earned a reputation, "the good white man."

Yellow Calf, one of the elders, served as a holy man to the Arapaho, a medicine man in his priestly function. Yellow Calf had also been, in his younger days, a "caller of buffalo," a profession no longer necessary with the disappearance of the great herds.

After dark, the council fire was lighted and the old men gathered around it in a circle. Outside of that circle, friends and observers sat or stood.

Yellow Calf began by explaining why a new name was needed.

"Once, we called our friend Soldier Chief. In those days that was good enough, and when anyone said *Banee-i-natcha,* all of us knew who that was. But now, time has passed, and *Banee-i-natcha* has gone to the tribes of the Four Directions. He has traveled much and learned many things. It is as if he were a bird, an eagle, able to soar into the sky and look at all of the people of all the tribes. He needs a new name now. We have met in council and smoked on it. Now I will give him the name we have agreed on and he will be known from now on as *Nee-hee-cha-ooth* . . . High Eagle."

The medicine man placed the ancient ceremonial bonnet on McCoy's head and began to sweep his hands across the general's shoulders and down his sides, "peeling away" the old name. He rolled it into a ball and symbolically dropped it to the ground.

Then an unheard-of thing occurred. Out of the crowd darted a young man, Charlie White Bull, son of the venerable old leader, White Bull. Charlie knelt to scoop up the discarded name from the dust, cupping it in his hands hugged tight against his chest to keep it warm and alive.

There was a brief conversation with Yellow Calf.

"What's happening?" asked John quietly.

"Charlie is asking to keep the name," George explained. "Since *Nee-hee-cha-ooth* won't be using it, he asked to keep it for himself, to honor *Ba,* our friend."

The medicine man glanced around the circle of elders, and they nodded in assent. The young man ran proudly off into the night with his new name.

Probably no one felt more honored than *Nee-hee-cha-ooth,* High Eagle, the blue-eyed Irish 'Rapaho.

SIXTY-FIVE

Working on the ranch at Owl Creek was good. John could go into Thermopolis with George Shakespear and some of the other cowboys to spend an evening at Happy Jack's. There were always interesting people to listen to, and discussion of the news of the week. Sometimes he did this, mostly listening.

Sometimes he wanted to be alone. The other cowboys respected his feelings. He was invited—but not urged—to join in anything that might be occurring. Probably George understood him better than anyone because George's reaction to their varied amusements was much the same as his own.

Sometimes he played cards. It was a diversion, an interesting way to pass an evening, do a little socializing, and keep up on the news. His skill at cards, considered by his friends to be "luck," stood him in good stead. He was careful not to do *too* much winning, which would have attracted attention, and possibly resentment.

Best of all, however, were the days of solitude, when he had time to think as he rode and worked alone, counting cattle and new calves, fixing fences, checking windmills and watering places. It was for such solitude that he had chosen this job, and it was a comfort.

From time to time, he thought of Ruth Jackson, or Margaret Jones in New Mexico, or of friends at the 101 in Oklahoma. After the surprise and agony of learning about Hebbie and his son, both now lost, he had really intended to retrace some of those trails. He did not do so at first because of the enormity of the burden of his loss.

As time passed, it became easier to postpone such a pilgrimage. He told himself sometimes that he was needed at the ranch. This feeling was gradually replaced by a misplaced sense of guilt that he had not yet attempted to communicate. He could avoid this by throwing himself wholeheartedly into whatever he was doing.

He seldom saw McCoy, who was living in Cheyenne with his wife and children, in the course of his position as Adjutant General of Wyoming. On the occasions when McCoy did visit the ranch, John had the strong impression that the boss would far rather be there than in the office in the State House. At Owl Creek or when visiting his Arapaho friends, the Irishman could change his high-collared Army uniform and knee-length military boots for a Stetson, Levi's, and cowboy boots, and relax in comfort. The general still stood ramrod straight, but he was more relaxed.

It was more than a year—possibly nearer two—when it happened. John and George Shakespear joked frequently about the luxury of working on "Indian time": *When it's time, it will happen.* They wondered how this could possibly work for the Adjutant General who, in many ways, was more Indian than the Arapaho themselves.

Apparently, this was a problem recognized by McCoy himself. He arrived at Owl Creek unexpectedly and revealed that he had resigned his office as Adjutant General. He had been asked to assist Famous Players–Lasky, a motion-picture company, in the filming of an epic. He called George Shakespear in to talk about it.

"You too, Buffalo. I need your skills on this, too. You've handled a bunch of Indians for the 101 Show, right?"

"Not handled, exactly, sir. We had a party in Germany when the war broke out."

"Yes, that's what I meant. Oglalas, right? And you can drop the 'sir.' We're not in the Army now."

"What is it you need to do, Tim?" asked Shakespear.

"Well, this film outfit is makin' a picture based on an Oregon Trail novel, *The Covered Wagon*. They want it to be authentic, so they need 500 Indians with old-style hair and dress, along with teepees and families. Oh, yes, ponies, too."

"Whew!" George whistled. "Tim, there aren't that many 'long-hair' Arapahoes in the whole world."

"I know," said McCoy. "They don't have to be Arapahoes as long as they fit. . . . Long-hairs, in buckskins and blankets. I figure we can use Shoshones from the other side of the Wind River Reservation."

"Now, that's askin' for trouble, maybeso," said George. "You know there's bad feelings between 'em. Goes back a long way. It's been tried before, to get 'em together. Last time, it caused the Battle of Tabasco Sauce."

"What?" asked John Buffalo.

"Oh, yes," explained Shakespear. Then he related the story.

Somebody had decided that since the two were on the same "rez," they ought to get along. They invited two of the most important leaders from each tribe: Washakie and Otai from the Shoshoni, Sharp Nose and Black Coal from the Arapaho. They had a big dinner in the officers' mess at Fort Washakie, with the chiefs seated across from each other.

Things were going pretty well till some young officer figured he'd have some fun. He took a big bottle of Tabasco from the table, put his thumb over the hole, and pretended to take a drink. Then he handed it to Washakie. The old chief figured it was a ceremonial drink, so he took a big swig. His eyes began to water.

"Why does Washakie weep?" asked Sharp Nose, across the table.

"I was thinking of my brother," said Washakie. "He was killed by Blackfeet a long time ago."

He handed the bottle to Sharp Nose, who took a big gulp or two.

Very quickly, he, too, was crying.

"Why does Sharp Nose weep?" asked Washakie.

As soon as he was able, Sharp Nose answered. "I was thinking," he said thoughtfully, "it is too bad that Washakie did not die with his brother at the hands of the Blackfeet."

With the help of Paul Haws, the agent at Wind River and a friend of McCoy, they set up a celebration for the Fourth of July, involving both Shoshone and Arapaho.

McCoy had been supplied with a convertible automobile by the film company, and they crisscrossed the Wind River Reservation, extending the invitation to feasting, dancing, and entertainment. McCoy, though a bona fide Arapaho, still spoke no Arapaho or any other Indian tongue. However, he was skilled in the hand signs, while many modern Indians were not. This impressed the elders greatly and, as they traveled to extend the invitation, High Eagle told of the opportunity for employment, just for being themselves: Indians.

John and George Shakespear were astonished at the pay offered by Famous Players–Lasky: On the basis of a seven-day week, each adult, man or woman, would receive $5 a day. For each child, fifty cents. One dollar a day for each horse, and for a teepee, another dollar. Thus, a couple with one child, a horse, and a teepee would draw $87.50 a week. Most Indian families would not see that much money in a year.

"They'll feed you, too," McCoy assured the potential actors.

"Huh! *What?*"

"Beef, bread, canned fruit, coffee. Just what I'll be eating myself."

"You'll be there, High Eagle?"

"Of course!"

Quickly, nearly every long-hair on the Wind River Reservation, Shoshoni and Arapaho, had agreed. The offer was too good to refuse.

"But, Tim," protested Shakespear, "you're still about three hundred short. There aren't that many long hairs!"

Over in Idaho, the Indian reservation at Fort Hall contained a large number of Bannock Indians, relatives of the Shoshones, Bannocks were big and muscular, and a great many followed the old ways in dress and hair. They would fit in well with the Wind River Arapahoes.

There was one major problem. The Lasky people had already been there, and had signed a number of Fort Hall Indians to play in *The Covered Wagon*. However, the agent at Fort Hall refused to issue passes for them to leave the reservation.

With his basic confidence and ways of getting things done, McCoy felt that there must be a way. He left John and George Shakespear at Wind River, working with Ed Farlow, another friend of McCoy's, organizing the transportation of Arapahoes, Shoshones, teepees, ponies, and families.

He sent a couple of telegrams to some of his military and political connections, asking their support, and boarded the train to Fort Hall. On arriving there, he found that the agent had received telegrams from such influential persons as General Winfield Scott and Senator Warren of Wyoming, father-in-law of General Pershing. The agent was asked to give the project his full cooperation.

"The extent of his cooperation," McCoy said later, "consisted of not getting in my way."

McCoy spoke no Bannock, of course, but was skilled in hand signs, which were universal. The novelty of watching a blue-eyed Arapaho converse with their own elders in a mode many of them did not know fascinated the Bannocks. Gradually, with the help of an English-speaking Bannock named Black Thunder, plans began to come together. Thunder, whose white man's name was Randall, was hired by McCoy as one of the assistants authorized to help with the Indian encampment at Milford, Utah, where the filming of *The Covered Wagon* would take place.

The logistics involved in transporting the Indians to Utah were enormous. The three hundred Bannocks, families, and horses were loaded onto Union Pacific cars at Fort Hall in mid-October. The railroad ran directly through Fort Hall.

Arrangements were not so easy at Wind River. The Arapahoes and Shoshones were transported to Rawlins, Wyoming, by truck. There, they met the young Arapaho who had driven three hundred horses overland to board the train.

Again, McCoy's contacts as Adjutant General helped to clear the tracks for the two special trains: thirty coaches and fifteen stock cars in all. Five hundred Indians, four hundred horses . . . Baggage, teepees, poles . . .

At Salt Lake City, they detrained for the overland trek to Milford. Again, the people were loaded in trucks and the ponies driven overland, the eighty-five miles to the site where Famous Players–Lasky would establish the tent city that would be the base for the filming.

There were some five hundred tents, not even counting the teepees of the Indians. Altogether, more than 3,000 people, besides the Indian "extras."

This would be the greatest production on film yet attempted, and the longest. Ten reels in all, running nearly two hours. The budget—originally $100,000—soon stretched to five times that, but there was no turning back.

The director was James Cruze, hired by Jesse Lasky to organize the actual filming. Cruze, a veteran Shakespearean actor in traveling companies, was not emotionally prepared for dealing with conditions like those at Milford. He was well aware of the financial strain of so many people on location for a period of several weeks. The food bill alone was enormous.

Added to all of this, the fact that Cruze had no idea at all as to how to go about dealing with Indians.

"Did you see him when he discovered that they'd carried off a side of beef from the cook tent?" chuckled Shakespear. "They were cuttin' strips and dryin' it for jerky on racks outside their lodges. Tim convinced Cruze that it would make great film."

SIXTY-SIX

A tougher problem arose when Cruze decided on a scene in the Indian encampment.

"Now, look, Tim. I want to shoot a scene tomorrow morning, and I want those teepees in a circle, with entrances facing each other, just like the old days."

John and Shakespear listened with amusement as Mc-Coy tried to explain.

"But that's not the way it was in the old days. They always had the entrances facing east."

"Why?"

"To greet the rising sun."

"The rising sun? Oh, for Chrissakes!"

"Yes, the rising sun."

"Well, that may be true, but it's also bullshit, because this scene can't be filmed that way. Now, you just go and tell 'em what I want, how they gotta put those goddamned tents of theirs, and we'll have a few minutes of film in the can, ready to send to Lasky."

"No."

"What the hell do you mean, 'no'? I want the tents the way I want them, and that's the way they're going to be!"

"Fine, *you* tell the Indians," McCoy said angrily. "It's taken me a long time to build some friendships with these people, and I'm not goin' to ruin everything overnight by asking them to do something they're not goin' to do anyway."

Cruze was pacing angrily.

"Great, just great!" he yelled. "We hire a technical director, an 'Indian expert,' and he's not gonna tell the goddamned Indians what to do. That's just terrific! Okay, you goddamned red-faced Irish son of a bitch, *I'll* tell 'em."

He did a lot of yelling and motioning, and gathered a circle of Indians. He demanded that Black Thunder translate in hand signs.

"Tomorrow, everything the same, tents in circles, but entrances all facing each other, *not* east!"

Black Thunder converted Cruze's demand into hand signs. There were nods around the circle, and a few mumbled, "Yeah, yeah." The gathering dispersed.

Cruze whirled on McCoy.

"You see? All you gotta do is ask 'em right!"

John Buffalo and George Shakespear watched from a distance, amused at the scene.

John shook his head. "Tim could have explained to him that the teepee has to face east or the smoke won't draw."

"Sure," George agreed, "but don't you think Tim's way of pointin' that out is more fun?"

"Right . . . Let's not miss it in the morning."

They were up at dawn, headed from the tent where they were staying toward the Indian encampment, when they heard a wail of anguish.

"Kee-rist!"

They ran toward the sound, to find Cruze, surrounded by cameras, equipment, actors, and crew, almost ready to weep. All the teepees still faced east.

"Jimmy," McCoy was saying to Cruze, "they're not goin' to change tens of thousands of years of habit for this picture."

"But," Cruze protested, still missing the point, "don't they realize this is an *epic?*"

Despite such misunderstandings, the filming went on. In a few weeks, a sizable body of work had been accomplished. Then came another problem: weather.

A blizzard came howling over the mountains to the northwest. Cameras were rolling in an attempt to finish the scene before snow struck, but in vain. By this time, having realized that one cannot change either the weather or Indian custom, Cruze decided to keep filming as long as they could. The fortunate result—almost an accident—was some excellent footage of pioneers laboriously pushing Conestoga wagons across the mountain trail in a blinding snowstorm.

The snow and ice continued. The three thousand crew,

actors, and extras huddled in their tents, wet, cold, and miserable. Except, of course, for the Indians, who had wintered for generations in their teepees. They were oblivious to the world outside, cooking, eating, visiting each other's lodges for a social smoke, singing, and playing on their drums. The teepee, with its central fire, its insulation via the lodge lining, and its east-facing smoke hole to make the fire draw properly, kept them quite warm and dry. Some invited white friends to join them.

Several days later, as the snow continued, Goes in Lodge, a senior chief of the Arapahoes, suggested to McCoy, who was staying with him, a possible solution. He finished a song, laid his drum aside, and turned to McCoy.

"High Eagle, maybe so you ask Yellow Calf about this weather?"

"Why Yellow Calf?"

"He might be able to do something about it."

Yellow Calf was respected as a powerful medicine man, but . . .

"What can Yellow Calf do about it?" McCoy demanded.

"You ask Yellow Calf about his Turtle Medicine," answered Goes in Lodge.

The conversation was over.

It was a major decision for McCoy. The old men were fond of jokes, and it might be that he was being set up for a wild-goose chase. But, he decided, it would do no harm to try. Only embarrassment . . .

He made his way through the snow to the lodge of Yellow Calf, where he scratched at the doorway.

"Who is it?" came the question from inside.

"High Eagle. May I come in?"

"*Whoahai!* Come in," called Yellow Calf.

They smoked and visited, and after a polite length of time, McCoy broached the subject on his mind.

"I have been with Goes in Lodge, and he says you might be able to do something about the weather."

Yellow Calf shrugged.

"This weather, he's strong," he chuckled. "What could I do about it, High Eagle?"

"Goes in Lodge said something about Turtle Medicine."

"Oh, yeah . . . It's been a long time since I used that power. I don't know if it will work, but maybe so we give it a try."

He picked up his drum and began to sing, apparently lost in the rhythm and cadence, maybe in the unintelligible words of the chant.

After an hour or so, with no apparent results, High Eagle excused himself and returned to the teepee of Goes in Lodge. Later in the afternoon, Yellow Calf came to the lodge, looked in, and spoke.

"You ready?"

Accompanying the medicine man were a small crowd of Indians, including George Shakespear and John Buffalo.

"We gonna try the Turtle Medicine," announced Yellow Calf.

Wrapped in a blanket and carrying an ax and his drum, Yellow Calf led the way through the storm to the center of the teepee circle. With the handle of the ax, he drew out in the snow a ring, about five paces across, then sketched a rough representation of a turtle about four feet long, in the frozen snow.

He sang some songs, glanced around at the cluster of observers, and announced, "Now we try Turtle Medicine!"

Stalking into the circle with great dignity, Yellow Calf raised his ax high and swung a mighty blow into the back of the turtle figure. There was a crunch of ice and frozen snow, and Yellow Calf turned to the spectators.

"Pretty soon now, we'll know if it works. Not too long. Just wait."

One of those present later recounted the next development:

Within five or ten minutes the snow and wind stopped, the sun came out from behind the clouds for the first time in several days. And within a short time, the ice turtle had melted and vanished. We were all believers.

About eight weeks had been spent in filming, and the project at Milford was finished. The process of striking camp and transporting five hundred Indians, their lodges, ponies, and baggage was at hand. Tim McCoy insisted later that it was necessary to book two extra railroad cars to carry all of the canned goods and beef that the Indian extras carried home to the reservations. He figured they had earned it.

Back on the ranch at Owl Creek, McCoy approached John Buffalo.

"John, these movie folks want me to come to Hollywood to be a 'technical director' on this film."

"I thought it was finished."

"Basically, it is, I guess. But they want to shoot a few more scenes to patch in. You know anything about training oxen to the yoke?"

"No . . ." John thought of Bill Pickett, bulldogging with his teeth. "Nothing at all," he said quickly.

"But you're good with animals," said McCoy. "These folks want some footage of that kinda thing. To them, anybody that knows one end of a steer from the other is an 'expert.' You want to come along?"

John thought about it for a moment. Maybe this was what he needed. He was restless. The past months had been busy and occupied, and now he was wondering whether to return to Kansas or to Oklahoma, maybe even New Mexico.

"You don't have to decide now," McCoy was saying. "Think it over. Sleep on it."

"No," said John. "I've thought about it. I'll go."

It was little short of amazing, the diversity of people and of expertise involved in the making of motion pictures. John had had some such contacts before, as the Hundred and One had always been involved in the rising film industry. He had even appeared as an extra in some Bison 101 films. Most of these, however, were filmed at the ranch or, like *The Covered Wagon*, on location.

A motion-picture studio was an entirely different and new experience for John Buffalo. The entire area was filled with specialists. Cameramen, electricians, actors, prop men, those with experience in handling livestock, cowboys who would take a fall that would kill a lesser man . . .

Even the animals were specialists. A scene might call for a horse that was trained to fall on cue, as if he had been shot. Roping, cutting, and bucking horses were, of course, familiar to John, as well as those used in harness or as pack animals. One trait was crucial. A horse must be able to remain calm and pay attention to business in spite of distractions. Most horses would be alarmed at bright lights, gunshots, and snaky-looking electric cables. In that respect, there were similarities to the Wild West Show.

The movie director's job was to bring all of this together and create order out of chaos. It was immediately apparent that the film community known as Hollywood was growing rapidly. Several companies were leading the way, and the specialists easily moved from one to the other to carry out their specialized jobs.

Famous Players–Lasky started with three men: Sam Goldfish, a glove salesman, Jesse Lasky, a playwright and brother-in-law of Goldfish, and Cecil B. DeMille, a director. Sam Goldfish had sold out his share some six years earlier, changed his name to Samuel Goldwyn, and joined a theater operator from Massachusetts, Louis B. Mayer, to become Metro-Goldwyn-Mayer. Famous Players–Lasky would eventually become Paramount.

The already-famous green barn where Cecil B. DeMille had filmed their first motion pictures was no longer a movie stage, but had been demoted to a prop room.

But for now, Famous Players–Lasky was concerned with finishing *The Covered Wagon*. They were still filming gold rush scenes in northern California, and wanted McCoy up there.

"But . . . there aren't any gold-rush scenes in the script," McCoy protested.

"There are now," Lasky corrected him. "Go on up there with Jimmy Cruze. You're the assistant director."

SIXTY–SEVEN

Hey, John! John Buffalo! What are you doin' out here? Want a job?"

John turned, to see a familiar figure from the 101 Ranch days.

"Yak? Yak Canutt? What are you doin' here?"

"Workin'! Easy as fallin' off a horse, an' I'm serious about the job."

"Well, I sort of have a job, but . . . Well, what is it?"

"Like I said . . . Fallin' off a horse! The movie folks need fellas to double for the pretty-boy actors in the stunt scenes. They'll pay fifty dollars and up for a fall. We used to work a week for that kinda pay, din't we?" Yakima chuckled. "A lot of the boys are here. Some are actin', some are cowboyin'. You remember Buck Jones and Tom Mix?"

"Sure."

"Hoot Gibson . . . Young fella named Ken Maynard from 101, too. Jesse Briscoe was doin' stunts, like me. Got himself killed when a horse fell last year. But what are you doin', John?"

John made a mental note about Briscoe, and the "easy" money in Canutt's new art. He'd worked with Jesse Briscoe.

"Well, I hadn't really thought about it, but I guess I'm sort of in the movie business, too. I've been helpin' the Famous Players–Lasky folks film in Utah. We used five hundred Indian extras. A picture called *The Covered Wagon,* from a book by Emerson Hough."

"Yeah, we heard about that. Well, you were wranglin' Oglalas in Germany when the war broke out, weren't you?"

John nodded.

"Who directed in Utah?" Yak asked.

"Jimmy Cruze."

Canutt slapped his knee and roared with laughter.

"Now *that* woulda been worth seein'. How did he get along with five hunnerd Indians?"

"There were some problems," John agreed ruefully. "We had a fella handling the Indian part. Tim McCoy. *General* McCoy . . . Arapaho. I work for him."

"Oh, *that's* the connection."

"Yes . . . He's up at Bishop; they're shooting some gold-rush scenes. I'm helping with some livestock scenes here, finishing up."

"I see. So you haven't been at the Hunnerd an' One for a while?"

"No. I've been in Wyoming, cowboyin'. A hitch in the Army."

"It *has* been a while, hasn't it? Well, a lot of the old bunch are here. We sort of hang out at The Water Hole . . . Hollywood and Cahuenga streets. A little poker and some tequila and whiskey. Stop by!"

"Maybe I will!"

John doubted that he'd do much drinking. That had given him some grief before.

"Do you think the 101 will put the Wild West Show back on the road?" asked Canutt.

"Hadn't thought about it. There were some good times, weren't there?"

"Sure 'nuff. Say, remember Will Rogers, the roper?"

"Sure. We were with him that time in New York. Nice fella."

"Well, he's comin' on big. Radio, newspaper column . . . Made a film or two."

"Times are really changing fast, aren't they?" John observed.

"Yep . . . You hear about 'talkies'?"

"What's that?"

"Puttin' talk in a movie."

"Aw, c'mon, Yak . . . You're funnin' me."

"No, really. You know, some theaters are usin' phonograph records for background music instead of a piano or organ."

"I'd heard something like that."

"Well, what if they could make a record of the talkin', the gunshots, war whoops, hoofbeats, whatever?"

"Yak, I don't think it could ever work. They couldn't get it matched up right."

"Mebbe not. But some of 'em are workin' on it. I figger they'd have to hook it to the film on the reel somehow. But John, it ain't long since movin' pictures were just a curiosity. We're livin' in modern times. Fast trains, airplanes . . . Folks have flown across the ocean, you know."

"Some got killed."

"I know. But it *can* be done."

John remembered having heard a newsboy in Denver hawking papers with a headline about a failed transatlantic flight. Two European military pilots had gone down in the Atlantic.

An old woman, passing by, had paused to read the headline, and sniffed indignantly.

"Serves 'em right, for thinkin' they could fly!" she snorted, as she shuffled on down the sidewalk.

Yes, we live in fast times, John thought. *Maybe, too fast.*

It was an interesting winter, warm in Hollywood, unreal in many ways. On the studio streets, it was not unusual to see couples in evening clothes meeting and nodding to a knight in armor, an Indian in war paint, or a dark-cloaked vampire. There was a calmness about such things that belied the general tension and excitement in the air, which pervaded the entire community. There was a feeling of expectancy, a reluctance to be anywhere else. To be absent from this strange make-believe world might be to miss the next development or happening. The fact that no one knew what that might be only added to the mystery and suspense.

The location unit at the gold-rush site near Bishop finished that sequence, and returned to Hollywood. McCoy seemed satisfied with the work they had done there, but approached John with a proposition.

"John, they want to make a big show out of introducing this *Covered Wagon* thing. It'll be at Grauman's Egyptian Theater, which is about the biggest thing around. There's been only one movie presented there before: *Robin Hood,* with Douglas Fairbanks."

John wondered what this had to do with anything, but McCoy continued.

"Now, Lasky wants a live prologue, onstage, with a few of our long-hairs, and me, using some hand signs. Could you stick around and sort of help me with arrangements for the Indians' encampment? They know you, and you can talk with the movie folks."

"I don't know much hand talk," said John.

"You don't have to. Most of them speak English. You know them, John. Goes in Lodge, Left Hand, Charlie Whiteman, their wives. Broken Horn and his wife, Lizzie. You remember her—a redheaded Arapaho . . . Indian name is 'Kills in Time.' It's a four-month contract, pays pretty well."

"Sure, why not?" agreed John.

The Arapaho camp was established at Cahuenga Pass, a mile from Grauman's Theater. John helped with the arrangements for transportation of the thirty-five Arapahoes and their lodges, and McCoy moved his wife and their three children to Hollywood, at least for the season.

The grand opening on April 10, 1923, was spectacular, with aerial searchlights and costumed Egyptians stalking the parapets. Admission tickets sold for $1.50, a princely sum at that time, when skilled workmen drew only about $10 per week.

The houselights dimmed, the crowd quieted, and an announcer spoke from the orchestra pit:

"Ladies and gentlemen, Famous Players–Lasky presents *The Covered Wagon*. This film, which is dedicated to the memory of Theodore Roosevelt, stars Miss Lois Wilson, Mr. J. Warren Kerrigan, and a cast of thousands, directed by Mr. James Cruze. As a prologue to this epic film, which may very well be the finest ever made, General Tim Mc-Coy will now present for your elucidation, edification, and entertainment, a company of America's native sons, over thirty Arapaho Indians from the Wind River Reservation in Wyoming."

Then the electrician brought up the lights, illuminating the stage. The audience gasped. There, appearing to have generated out of the darkness, stood thirty Indians in various stages of dress or, in some cases, of undress. McCoy had told them only to "show the white-man audience how they looked when they felt beautiful." There were eagle feathers, warbonnets, shell chokers, gold earrings, hairpipe breastplates, Washington peace medallions, fringed buckskin shirts, beaded leggings, and quilled moccasins. According to McCoy's later account, this scene "erupted into a volcano of pure, joyous color."

McCoy, dressed in a white shirt, dark tie, trousers, and boots and wearing a white Stetson, then introduced each of the Arapaho in turn. Each told his or her story briefly in hand signs, which the general translated into English.

Goes in Lodge, who fought against the white man and later became a scout for the Army.

Charlie Whiteman, captured by Utes from a wagon train in the 1860s, later captured from the Utes by Arapaho. His fellow Apaches teased him about being "one-third Ute, one-third Arapaho, and one-third white man." He considered himself an Indian.

Lizzie Broken Horn, wife of Broken Horn. Captured from her family's wagon train in 1865, by Cheyenne and Arapaho "dog soldiers." Her older sister was ransomed, but when Lizzie was finally located in 1902, she could not speak or understand English. She was all Arapaho.

Left Hand, who had fought Custer, but wore a blue Army jacket to show his later service as a scout.

Red Pipe, six and a half feet tall, created a sensation merely by his appearance.

Twice a day, this prologue was presented, at 2:30 and at 8:00, before the showing of *The Covered Wagon*. It was vastly popular and a great attention-getter.

During the next four months, the Arapahoes were wined and dined, invited to lavish dinners, attended movies, and enjoyed side trips by bus to see the ocean.

"Big lake," said Goes in Lodge. "Can't see across."

There was one near-disaster. Attempting to load the bus for a tour, Grauman's stage manager committed a major breach of Arapaho etiquette. He attempted to seat some of the men next to their mothers-in-law. The entire group refused to board until such a flagrant error could be straightened out by Tim McCoy and the Arapahoes could be seated properly.

As the contract for the onstage prologue drew to a close, McCoy was approached by Victor Clark, Lasky's right-hand man. *The Covered Wagon* was to open in London in September, he explained. Would he consent to take the Arapahoes to London?

McCoy was willing, and convinced John Buffalo to go along.

"You know your way around there, John. I don't. You could be a big help."

Convincing the Arapahoes was another matter. Goes in Lodge finally made an impassioned speech, and with ceremonial burning of sweet grass, singing, and dancing, the troupe from Hollywood boarded the train again at Wind River to head to New York. Ed Farlow and John Buffalo would go along to assist as needed.

The teepees were erected on the lawn of the Museum of Natural History, across from Central Park. There were only a few days to process passport applications, including photos.

The day before the ship was to sail, Ed Farlow made a disturbing discovery.

"Some of the 'Raps are missing."

"*Missing?*" McCoy snapped. "Ed, they're supposed to be here, getting photos taken for passports. No photo, no passport; no passport, no trip. Where *are* they?"

"I don't know! Off in Central Park or in some bar, I reckon. But they sure as hell aren't here."

There were supposed to be thirty-five, but only thirty-two could be found. McCoy, Ed Farlow, and John stood helplessly, wondering what could be done.

Just then Goes in Lodge, wearing his eagle-feather bonnet, came out of the photographer's tent.

"Look," said Tim, "borrow Goes in Lodge's bonnet, put it on Yellow Horse, tell 'em it's Shavehead or one of the other absentees."

"Uh . . . ain't that kinda illegal, Tim?" asked Ed.

"Ed," McCoy pointed out, "will this be the worst thing you've ever done?"

Thus began a game of "musical warbonnets," as it was described later. A headdress would be placed on the head of a man who had already been photographed bareheaded. Taking advantage of the white man's belief that "they all look alike" the feather bonnet would be pulled down over the brow and the photography would proceed.

In a short while, there were thirty-five passport photos, and the next morning, thirty-five Arapahoes boarded the S.S. *Cedric,* a modern White Star Line luxury liner. There were no questions about "they all look alike."

SIXTY-EIGHT

The stay in London, which lasted nearly six months, was a great success. Initially, they erected the teepees on the grounds of the Crystal Palace, Piccadilly. It became apparent within a couple of weeks that teepees, while ideally suited for the heat, cold, and storms of the prairie, they were no match for the constant rain and fog of London. Appropriate rental quarters were found, and the troupe settled in for the winter.

The Arapaho were accepted with even more generosity than they had been in Hollywood. They were wined and dined by nobility, and honored constantly. Lord Robert Baden-Powell, the hero of the Boer War in South Africa and founder of the Boy Scout movement, was particularly impressed. The Arapaho of Wind River were invited to his estate, and later to the International Boy Scout Jamboree, held that year at Gilwell, England, outside London. Scouts from all over the world were instructed in Arapaho crafts and archery.

In mid-March 1924, the contract was over and the delegation from Wind River returned home. As they disembarked in New York, they were met by a swarm of reporters. The traveling Arapaho from Wyoming had become celebrities. By this time, such interviews had become familiar to the Arapaho, who rather enjoyed the notoriety, as well as the naïveté of the reporters questions.

"What was it like in London?"

"Did you really fight Custer?"

Goes in Lodge probably summed it up, when he related the London experience to home.

"All same as Wind River."

The old chief was talking in hand signs, though he spoke English well. Hand signs always made more of an impression on whites.

"Like the subway," he signed.

McCoy finally came to the rescue of the confused reporters.

"What has that got to do with an Indian reservation?" one asked.

"All same," Goes in Lodge signed. "Prairie dog go down one hole, come up another."

Back in Wyoming, John Buffalo was faced with a decision. What now? The McCoy ranch on Owl Creek was a safe refuge, operated by George Shakespear while Tim McCoy was off on various jobs for the movie people. Currently, he was off somewhere tracking down potential defense witnesses for a lawsuit against Famous Players–Lasky. A descendant of Jim Bridger, the mountain man, had taken offense at the depiction of Bridger in *The Covered Wagon*. But there were still people alive who had known Bridger, and could testify to the character of the man.

McCoy's long-range plan was to build a house for his family and settle in on the ranch, now being called Eagle's Nest. Meanwhile, the cattle operation was thriving, and cowboys were needed. John was not unhappy working there, but he was restless. He felt that there were things left unfinished.

Finally he talked to Shakespear.

"George, there's something I have to do. Somebody I need to go and see."

"Uh!" George grunted assent. "You comin' back?"

"I dunno. Maybe so."

"You on Indian time?"

It was a gentle jibe. John smiled.

"Guess so. I just don't know how this will turn out."

"I see. Well, you know the way back."

"Thanks, George."

John's excitement grew as he traveled back to Kansas. He bypassed Fort Riley when he detrained, and headed directly to Ogden and on toward Ruth Jackson's farmhouse. His anticipation grew, but his uneasiness and doubt did, also. *I should have written,* he thought.

Ruth might not even live here now. In his mind, he had not considered the fact that it had been several years since that fateful night. *I should have written.* But in a way, Ruth represented for him something solid, dependable, and permanent. In an ever-changing world, she was the stable, predictable factor. She had saved his life.

There was a feeling of guilt as he walked up the road and around the bend from their picnic spot. Why had he not kept in touch? He realized that it was because of the guilt of their night together. He still felt that he had betrayed a friendship.

When the little farmstead came in view in the darkening twilight, he almost turned back. Ruth might be working an evening shift at the hospital. He should have checked there. But now he saw a light in the window. He stopped for a moment. A beautiful, comfortable, homey picture, with smoke curling gently above the slender brick chimney. That would be above the kitchen. . . . The supper fire . . . The name Jackson was still on the mailbox. Good.

His heart warmed as he walked up the path. It was a homey feeling. Had he at last found where he belonged?

Almost eagerly, he knocked at the door.

"John! How wonderful! Come in!"

She gave him a quick hug and a sisterly peck on the cheek.

"Where in the world have you been?" she went on. "I thought something had happened to you."

She was beautiful, almost radiant in her beauty. Her golden hair had not changed, but her face had. Where there had been lines of sadness the last time he had seen her, now there was only happiness and contentment.

"Come on in!"

She took him by the hand and led him inside, talking over her shoulder as she did so.

"I want you to meet my husband."

She raised her voice slightly.

"Ned!" She called into the kitchen, "John's here! John Buffalo!"

His head whirled in confusion. Who was Ned, and was he, John, supposed to know him? And . . . Ruth had said *husband*. Was her husband not named *Emil?* He had never met the man, but—And Emil was dead!

She must have remarried. Ned? He was sure that he knew no one by that name. But it *had* been a few years. . . .

The old guilt came rushing back, the embarrassment and regret over the night that he and Ruth had shared in each other's arms. She had attempted to make him more comfortable with what he had done, by trying to let him think that he was fulfilling *her* need in her bereavement. But now . . . How could she appear glad to see him?

She had used his name, John Buffalo, when calling to her husband, which made him very uneasy. How much had she told "Ned"? *Everything?*

Down the hall from the other part of the house strode a man that John had never seen before. There were two remarkable things about him. One was his size. That was bad. He must be well over six feet tall, big across the shoulders and heavily muscled. Not an ounce of fat on that frame. He was tanned. A farmer's tan, his forehead white above the line that would mark the position of his straw hat.

That almost-frightening impression was offset by another remarkable quality. It was a big, friendly grin; somewhat reassuring.

Ned stuck out a paw the size of a side of bacon, and John met his friendly grip.

"Ruth's told me about you!"

How much? John thought.

But the man was still smiling.

Not everything, John concluded as their eyes met. Not the whole story.

Ned went on, "I want to thank you for your kindness when she lost her husband."

Definitely not the whole story.

"I . . . I did what I could," answered John vaguely.

There was a sound from the hallway from which Ned had appeared before. That, John remembered, led to the kitchen.

He turned, to see a towheaded toddler just entering the room. The handsome young face was ruddy and healthy-looking, and became a trifle shy when confronted by a stranger. But not measurably so. Mostly, the child's face expressed curiosity.

"John, this is our son, Emil . . . Emil John Jackson."

A cold hand grasped John's heart. Emil . . . Ruth's dead husband . . . But *John?* Could it be that the child was named for him because—His head whirled in confusion. No, not possible. This boy could be no more than three years old. The night before he had shipped out on the troop train would have been at least four years ago.

Ned was smiling at the confusion on John's face.

"Yes, he's named for you," Ruth was saying.

"And 'Emil' for her husband. I suggested that. I knew

how much he meant to Ruth, and she had told me of your kindness during her loss."

John did not want to meet her eyes just then. He was glad that because of the time span involved, there was no question of young Emil's parentage. The way the boy sidled up to his father promised a good father-son relationship. He found himself jealous on more than one count.

"I'm honored."

He smiled at the youngster. Again, he was persuaded that the husband knew most, but not quite all of the story. Ruth had an understanding of people that was quite sensitive. As always, she had been able to choose just how much information could or *should* be shared. Ned was a very lucky man. If circumstances had been only a little different, this could all have been his. He knew, Ruth knew. But she was happy.

His eyes met Ruth's, and he saw in her face only happiness and contentment. No alarm, no apprehension. She must have been somewhat vague in her narration of how and what kind of help had been involved.

"She has the highest regard for you, Mr. Buffalo," Ned went on.

This further emphasized a couple of points: that Ruth had not been specific in her description of their relationship, and that she held no grudge that John had dropped from sight without trying to stay in contact.

But Ned talked on. "I want to thank you on behalf of my brother," said Ned.

"Your *brother?*"

John was thoroughly confused.

Now a puzzled look crossed Ned's face.

Ruth laughed, delightedly. "Of course!" She chortled. "John doesn't know. He couldn't. John, Ned is Emil's brother."

That explained a lot, very quickly.

"His *brother?*" John blurted again.

"Yes, I'd always been a little envious," Ned said teasingly, slipping an arm around Ruth's slender waist. "Emil was older than I, and when he married Ruth, I knew I could never find a woman half so desirable. I came when I heard of her loss. I do want to thank you, though, John. You were here when we needed someone."

I'm not sure you'd thank me, John thought.

"The least I could do," he mumbled, embarrassed.

For some reason, this struck Ruth as quite amusing.

"Not *really,*" she said, laughing. "But come on in, John. We're ready to have supper. Tell us all about where you've been. You were headed for Fort Sill, weren't you, the morning after . . . After I heard of Emil's death?"

There was just a hint of a blush as her eyes met John's for an instant.

"Yes. A lot has happened since then," said John. "I was transferred to Artillery. . . . Mule pack, mountain howitzers."

"So you know mules!" Ned exclaimed. "Good! We'll talk of that. I'll want to show you some mules in the morning."

In the morning?

"Of course. You'll stay with us, won't you, John?"

SIXTY-NINE

It was a very uncomfortable situation. John tried to protest the invitation to stay the night, but both of the Jacksons were insistent. Ruth seemed to be quite genuine in her wish to have him stay over. She did not share his discomfort over the memory of their last time together. He was even more embarrassed that she did not seem to read anything negative into that situation, or this.

He felt some new guilt over some of his thoughts and repressed desires. He wondered if Ruth felt the old attraction, as he did. Probably not, but if she did, he felt that she was handling it better than he.

John lay for hours in the feather bed in their spare bedroom, staring into the dark ceiling, lost in his own confusion. He was tired, but unable to sleep yet as he tried to sort out the disorganized bits and pieces of his life. For a brief time, he had thought that there was some sense of direction taking place, but now that, too, was shattered. He forcibly thrust aside his thoughts of Ruth with another man. They had been so close! He had made a bad mistake in leaving her, he now realized. He had had no choice in his departure, but he should have kept in touch. Maybe things would have turned out this way, even if he *had* written, but . . . These thoughts were like oats long since run through the horse, as his cowboy friends would say. The loss of a woman with whom he could have been very happy was a great disappointment. It might not have developed into a life together anyway, but he had missed a golden opportunity, and his heart was heavy, the memory now like the taste of ashes in his mouth.

What should he do now? Never in his life had he been able to actually make any plans, he realized. Most of his happy memories were linked to some other events, and ended with the thoughts of *if it had only been* slightly different, in some way. It was easy to feel that never in his life had he made a *right* decision. He was a failure.

Still, he had to admit that the failure of whatever he tried was usually due to events beyond his control. It was simply a world in which he did not belong.

Where, then, *did* he belong? At times, it had seemed that things were going well. At the Hundred and One, with Hebbie . . . On the road with the Wild West Show . . . He *had* done some pretty good things, some accomplishments of which he could be proud. Helping to rescue the Oglalas from Germany at the start of the Great War . . . Looking back, he could hardly believe some of the achievements of which he had been a part. The time Zack Miller bought virtually the entire Mexican Army and resold what the Hundred and One could not use . . . He smiled in the darkness.

There *had* been some good times. The Olympics, with Jim Thorpe and the other athletes . . . He wondered where Jim was now. . . .

He had enjoyed the isolation of his cowboy jobs in Wyoming. Finally, toward morning, he fell asleep, and dreamed jumbled dreams with fragmented scenes that seemed to go nowhere. Hebbie appeared to him briefly, saying nothing, but with a wistful smile that was somehow a comfort. He slept better after that reassurance.

John rose with the sun, and with at least a semblance of a plan. While he was in the area, he'd stop by Haskell and Kansas University. He doubted that he would still know anyone there, but maybe someone in their athletic departments might even know of a coaching job for which he could apply. It was worth a try. Failing that, he could stop by the 101 Ranch. Out of curiosity, he wondered what was happening there. A few seasons ago, the ranch and the Wild West Show were constantly in the news. Now there was nothing. *Why?*

Well, maybe he'd stop by there. . . .

His departure from the Jacksons' was difficult and embarrassing for him. Ruth gave him a hug and kissed his cheek, whispering quickly into his ear, *"Thank you, John!"*

He wished she hadn't done that.

Ned Jackson shook his hand warmly and urged him to come back anytime. That, too, was hard. He doubted that he'd do it. The memories were too intense.

John patted little Emil on the head and lifted his duffel bag. At the bend of the road, he turned for a last look.

Ruth waved.

At Lawrence, he could find only one person whom he knew: Forrest Allen, now at the University of Kansas. "Phog" was interested in John's activities during the intervening years, but they really had little in common. They discussed the whereabouts of mutual acquaintances.

"You haven't been coaching, then?" Allen seemed surprised.

"Too busy at other things," John admitted. "I had a hitch in the Army, too."

"Yes, that affected a lot of us," Allen agreed. "Well, stop by when you're in the area."

All in all it was a pleasant visit that, in essence, went nowhere.

John was not ready to return to the Hundred and One. Not yet. Thinking to himself of how he had quite possibly ignored the possibility of a wonderful relationship with Ruth Jackson, he began to think again of Loving, New Mexico, and the Door of Hope. There, after all, was a woman who had actually known *and loved* his own son. The only person, as far as he knew.

He thought of writing to Margaret Jones, but immediately realized a problem. He could never know whether she might answer such a letter. He had no place in which to wait and see. No, better to go back to Loving (he was not unaware of the suggestive play on words) and see what evolved. He was certain that Margaret Jones had indicated an interest in him by her actions. She was a handsome woman. Somewhat older than he, but probably not an important difference. It would do no harm to go and see.

En route on the train, he found himself thinking about other options. He had always avoided any thoughts of returning to Carlisle because of the circumstances of his leaving. But maybe . . . He'd think about it after he had checked out the situation in Loving.

He did not realize that in this decision, he had already assumed failure.

In Loving, he found that the Door of Hope seemed to be thriving. He was welcomed warmly and courteously by Margaret Jones.

Things were going well, she said. They had three more boys than when he had been there before. The big house was in good repair. Juan and Maria were still there, serving their purposes well.

It took only a few hours to see that he may have misread the situation. On his first visit, Margaret Jones had been kind, helpful, and accommodating, but it was probably out of sympathy. She had only been trying to show her regret for the accidental lack of communication.

Still, he could not forget the day they had spent together on the trip to Carlsbad. She *had* been warm and friendly. And there *had* been his feeling of someone outside his bedroom door late that night, deciding whether to enter. He had left the Door of Hope with a strong inkling that both of them knew there was a potential relationship here.

But something had changed. She was polite and friendly, but distant. Surely he could not have misread her attitude so badly on his previous visit. And to add to his confusion, Margaret Jones seemed a trifle embarrassed around him.

The mystery was quickly solved when he found himself

alone for a moment with Juan. Juan wanted to show him something he was building with the help of the older boys. But maybe there was another motive. . . .

"The *señora*," Juan began, flashing his beautiful grin and assuming a conspiratorial air, "she have *un hombre* . . . How you say? Man friend?"

"Ah!" said John. "A gentleman comes to see her?"

"*Sí, sí! Esta un bueno hombre,* Senor John. She is happy."

"Then I am happy for her," John told him.

"*Sí.* Me, too. *Señora* needs a man."

And she had found one. He was glad for her, but once more, floundering, himself.

After much thought, he decided to return to the 101 Ranch, primarily to see what was going on. At his last visit, he had been quite uneasy and unable to account for it. Something was in the air, something he needed to know more about. He'd have a look, anyway. Maybe even work there for a while. All the traveling with no real home base was depleting his funds. He'd have to work somewhere.

He was somewhat startled to see that the town of Bliss had been renamed. "Marland" was the new name painted on the sign under the gable of the railroad depot.

The reason was apparent to anyone familiar with the area. Marland was a name well known in the oil fields of Oklahoma. It was E. W. Marland who had begun the exploration on the Poncas' land, leased to the Millers for grazing.

John thought for a moment of the attitude of the Ponca elders and the "Ponca curse." Was this a part of the uneasy feeling he'd been experiencing? He also recalled with uneasiness the episode in Miller's office, and the signing of the lease by the Ponca couple.

At the 101, he was astonished to see some of the changes. An elephant stood patiently in a new, heavily built corral to the south of the other facilities. There was a new large barn, and new equipment, tractors, and machinery in evidence. There was a buzz of activity. The old excitement over preparation for each road season washed across him.

But . . . An *elephant?*

He sought out Bill Pickett, who was breaking horses in one of the corrals.

"Howdy, John! Good to see you. Where you been?"

"Lotsa places, Bill. But what's goin' on here? I saw an elephant!"

Pickett chuckled. "Yep. We goin' on the road agin', I reckon. They done buyin' a circus."

"A *circus?*"

"Reckon so. Figger the crowds is wantin' somethin' beyond Wild West. So, you know how Mistah Zack is. They buyin' the Walter Main Circus, gwine mix it with us. There's lions an' tigers an' all. I dunno what's goin' on the road with us. All of it ain't even here, yet. But I tell you . . . That elephant shore spooked some hosses."

"You gonna bulldog him, Bill?" teased John. "He's shore got the nose for it!"

"No, suh! I ain't got the teeth for that much nose." Pickett laughed. "But serious, now. You comin' back?"

"Hadn't really decided, but why not? Might be interesting to see how this circus turns out."

SEVENTY

As Pickett had said, it was indeed a circus. Even without the purchase of the Walter Main Circus, there had been some major events at the Hundred and One, John learned gradually.

In the summer of 1923, a major flood on the Salt Fork had isolated the ranch and the town of Bliss for some time. Water had even entered the first floor of the White House itself. With classic Miller style, the 101 ranch established a ferry service at their own expense to serve the town and the area.

Oil production was hampered somewhat, and the Poncas whispered again of the ghosts and restless spirits and of old White Eagle's "curse" when the first oil well came in a decade before.

"It will mean great trouble for me, for my people, and for you," he had told Marland.

Eventually, though, the waters had receded. Repair and rebuilding quickly took place, and the Millers were looking ahead. In September 1924, they announced that a bigger and better Wild West Show would open the following season.

Billboard carried the news. Their headline read:
101 Ranch Wild West Will Again Take to the Road.

The show was retitled "The 101 Ranch Real Wild West and Great Far East Show."

This, to accommodate the expanded scope of the three-ring circus and its equipment and personnel. There would be more than five hundred people involved in the traveling show, to open in April 1925. Attractions ranged from Ezra Meeker, a ninety-five-year-old pioneer with an ox team, to Selina Zimmerman, "the elephant girl," with her highly trained troupe of elephants.

There were Indian riders, Cossacks, a Zouave drill team, and reenactments of buffalo hunts and stagecoach robberies. There were also sideshow and carnival features: sword swallowers, midgets, snake handlers, fortune-tellers, magicians, and Oriental dancing girls, the Frog Boy, and "Montana Hank," an eight-foot, 360-pound cowboy.

To transport and supply this huge organization required dozens of railroad cars. Every ten days, fifteen tons of fresh produce from the ranch would be shipped to the show lots on the road in refrigerator cars. Meat, fruits, and vegetables, direct from the ranch. It was said that the cooks could feed hot meals to the five hundred show train personnel on forty minutes' notice.

Of the Walter L. Main Circus animals, only the elephants and camels would take to the road. The assorted trained monkeys, lions, tigers, miniature horses, and bears were either sold or remained at the ranch. A black bear that drank soda pop was a fixture, chained in front of the ranch store, and became a favorite.

The 1925 season started with great fanfare, but developed problems quickly. They presented the "opener" in Oklahoma City in April, and bad luck dogged the tour through twenty-nine states and one Canadian province. Weather, always a major factor in a tent production, ranged from too cold for comfort in the early season to beastly hot in Boston later. The customers "stayed away in droves," someone remarked.

In Indiana, a tornado ripped through the grounds, and in Pennsylvania, the big top was shredded by a freak windstorm.

In St. Louis, after an evening of hard drinking, some of the cowboys were discussing the problems of the season.

"What we need," said one, "is some pulbicity." His speech was slurred.

"Naw . . . You're tryin' to say *putiblicy*," another giggled. Everyone laughed.

"Whatever," said another. "You guys are drunk. But you're right. We need some newspaper coverage."

"The Millers are spendin' a lot on advertisin'," somebody pointed out.

"But that ain't workin' . . . We need some *free* coverage. Somethin' that will have the papers writin' about the Hunnerd an' One!"

"Yeah, like if somebody tried to steal Colonel Joe's fancy saddle, or somethin'. It's worth about twenny thousand dollars, they say."

"Not that much, but it's worth quite a bit," said another. " 'Nuff to get some attention. Mebbe we can find somebody dumb enough to try stealin' it."

"Lissen," said one of the more inebriated, "*we* can help out. Mebbe we jest pertend to try to steal ol' Joe's fancy saddle."

"Yeah!"

"Good idea!"

"No risk, like there'd be with real crooks!"

The plan, if such a scheme could be considered planning, was hatched quickly.

"You in, Buffalo? Help the bosses out?"

John had been listening in amazement. He had imbibed very little, but was along for the companionship. He was astonished at how quickly this harebrained scheme had developed. Now, he was in a spot.

"Fellas, I want no part of this. You'll get in trouble, or get somebody hurt."

"You're skeered!" somebody hooted.

"Damn right! I'm stayin' out of trouble."

"You ain't gonna rat on us, John?" one asked suspiciously.

"You know better'n that, Tex. I'm sayin' nothin', except that it's a crazy idea. An' now I'm leavin', 'cause I don't want to hear any more."

He turned and walked off to seek his bunk in the sleeping tent.

Some time later, he was wakened by some yells and what could have been gunshots. He wanted no part of what might be happening and pulled the blankets over his head in a futile attempt to sleep.

He never did hear all the details, partly because those most closely involved had very foggy memories of the events of the night. Partly, because he already knew more than he wanted of the scheme.

It never made the papers—at least, not in any way favorable to the Hundred and One. There had been shots fired by the police; there had been arrests made; there had been trips made to the jail and bail money paid to extricate the wayward employees. But Joe Miller's jewel-studded saddle was intact.

In Georgia, late in the season, the 101 Show found itself in heavy competition with the Ringling Brothers–Barnum and Bailey combined circus, which was also touring the South. Their bad luck continued. A couple of sleeping cars on the show train near Gainesville caught fire and burned.

To bring an end to a losing season, the last two weeks

of the show tour were canceled after they arrived at Birmingham, Alabama.

And 1926 was no better. Their bad luck continued. Weather was again a major factor, cutting attendance to unprecedented levels. Equipment was continually damaged by wind, which shattered tent poles and shredded canvas. One customer in Erie, Pennsylvania, was killed by a falling pole. Many of the season's performances were late, shortened, or canceled entirely.

The season was to close in a tour of neighboring states close to home, but an epidemic of hoof-and-mouth disease closed it even earlier. The show returned home in an unprecedented series of rain and thunderstorms. Salt Fork flooded again, drowning hundreds of cattle. Another season of financial disaster . . .

If there was any bright spot in the year for the Millers, it was Joe Miller's remarriage, having divorced Lizzie, to a bride half his age, Miss Mary Verlin of Grand Rapids. They had met in Ponca City, while Mary was visiting relatives there. The wedding was in Chicago, while the show was there on tour.

John Buffalo was becoming more and more depressed over the bad seasons on the show circuit. Not that it was a personal loss, but that he was a part of what appeared to be a worsening situation. He was also concerned with the fact that the Poncas were still talking about the "curse." He wasn't certain that it was at all wise to remain in a situation that carried such a bad possibility.

But around the Millers, it was easy to succumb to the idea that bad luck is only temporary. Next season will be better. . . . He decided to stay on for one more season.

But 1927 was no better. The same specters haunted the 101 Show: Competition, weather, rising costs, and another bugaboo, legal problems. There had been enough accidents and injuries, both to the 101 show people and support staff, but also to spectators, to make legal expenses a major factor. The season again closed on a losing note, and returned to the ranch in October.

John was still trying to find a way to tell the Millers gracefully of his decision to leave when tragedy struck.

On October 21, Joe Miller had driven to the home he had built for his bride and their new son, a few miles north of the White House. He had told Zack that he intended to work on his car, which had been "acting up." Miss Mary and their five-month-old son had been in Grand Rapids, visiting her mother, and had not yet returned.

At about three o'clock, Will Brooks, a cousin of the Millers who worked with them, stopped by the house. He heard a car engine running and found Joe lying in the garage beside the car. The hood was up, and he had apparently been tinkering with the engine. He was dead, the doctors said, from carbon-monoxide poisoning. The garage doors had been only partly open.

The Poncas took an active part in the funeral ceremonies, dropping eagle feathers into the casket, beating drums, and chanting the death song. Horse Chief Eagle spoke for the Poncas.

"Our brother Joe, he is one of us. . . . He is gone. When he went away, it meant more than anything to the Indian. The Indian weeps. . . ."

Joe was buried in the family plot near Ponca City, next

to Mother Molly Miller. Things would never be the same at the Hundred and One.

Still, the old Poncas shook their heads and mumbled about the "curse."

"The show will go out as usual," George Miller told the assembled gamely. "That is what Joe wanted."

There was some question about that. It was well known that there had been a certain amount of disagreement among the brothers as to how to overcome the past three money-losing seasons. But this was not the time or place for argument. Everyone was in agreement at this point. It was announced that plans were under way for the 1928 season.

This time there was no question in the mind of John Buffalo. He felt that he *must* separate himself from this ill-fated extravaganza, which seemed to be headed for disaster at ever-increasing speed. Even without the shadow of the words of old White Eagle, it was easy to see the direction in which things were headed.

John's plan was to head for Wyoming, but he realized that winter would soon be coming on. Maybe it would be better, he thought, to stop a little while in Hollywood, see some old friends, maybe work a little while as a horse trainer. Yakima Canutt and some of the others of the old 101 gang would help him find something.

Thanksgiving, 1927, found him on a train, headed for California.

SEVENTY-ONE

Hollywood was as exciting as ever. The sense of unreality was even stronger, the buildings bigger, the charade more outlandish.

John sought out Yakima Canutt.

"John! You come back for that job?" Yak greeted warmly.

"Not the fallin'-off-a-horse job," John responded with a grin. "Some kinda job, maybe. Handlin' livestock?"

"Still wantin' to cowboy, huh? Well, you can prob'ly find somethin'. Stick around till we finish this scene."

The scene involved a fall—not by Canutt, but a younger stuntman. John watched with interest as they set it up. A hobble was buckled around the horse's front foot and attached to a slender cable, coiled on the ground and fastened to a stake.

Canutt explained, "When he hits the end of that wire at a gallop, the horse trips and falls, an' the rider goes flyin' over his head. Now, here they go."

The cowboy spurred the horse into a gallop, as the coiled cable unwrapped behind them in a blur like that of a striking snake.

"But won't that—," John began.

He was interrupted by the managed "fall." The cable snapped tight, the horse tripped and fell, and the stuntman sailed forward over the animal's head. He rolled and came to his feet, apparently unhurt. Others rushed forward to where the horse struggled on the ground. Everyone had heard the crack of breaking bone, like a pistol shot, when the horse went down.

"Damn!" said Canutt. "I hate when that happens!" He turned to another man. "Jim, you got a pistol?"

"Right here," answered the grim-faced cowboy, as he started toward the crippled horse. The animal had struggled to its feet, but a foreleg flopped uselessly, at a joint where there should have been none. A pistol shot ended its suffering, and the horse collapsed in its tracks.

"Get it outta here," yelled the director. "We have a film to finish!"

John was appalled.

"Yak, that's *gonna* happen. Don't you kill a lot of horses this way?"

"Not as many as you'd think, John. Usually, no broken bones. Sometimes it goes bad, like this. Sometimes the rider breaks a bone, maybe. But they've got the picture in the can."

"But—My God, Yak! To deliberately set that up . . . Don't that bother you?"

Canutt was irritated.

"Of course it does, damn it! You know, there's accidents on a ranch, too. Folks that work with horses do it because we love 'em, and we always hate an accident. Besides, it's expensive."

"But in this business, they don't *care?*" John realized slowly.

"It's not exactly that, John. They spend money to make money. You know a better way?"

"Maybe I do. You can train a horse to do a lot of things. You've seen some of the trick horses in the 101 show. They'll lay down, play dead, like a pet dog. These Hollywood horses are specially trained anyway, to ignore spotlights and loud noises and all."

"But they generally don't use those trained horses for the falls, John. They're too valuable. Any horse—"

"That's the point, Yak. A horse could be trained to take a fall, without gettin' hurt with that damn wire."

"Who's got the time to do that?"

"Well, I have, for one. If I can find somethin' to keep me goin', I'll train a horse or two on the side. Can you find me the horses?"

"Sure! Look, there's a lot of rigging in this stunt game. You can help me with that, and we'll get you a horse to work with. What you want? A colt?"

"Prob'ly a two-year-old gelding. Solid color . . . Sorrel or bay."

"Don't be too picky," Yak teased. "But you're right. You wouldn't want a horse with flashy coloring. That'd limit his use."

The training was time consuming and slow. John worked with the young horse away from the movie lots, first gaining its confidence and getting in tune with its spirit. Pal was a middle-of-the-road animal in build, sorrel in color, with a white star on his forehead. Not a horse you'd pick out of a crowd. He'd learned that in the Army. The military had always frowned on animals with distinctive coloring. They could be described and identified too easily. The same principle applied here. It was not prudent to have a horse so distinctive that he would steal the scene from the rider.

There were exceptions. Tom Mix, from the old Hundred and One, already had a cult following for his horse, Tony. Later, Roy Rogers would do the same with Trigger. Mix's career had lasted long enough to stretch beyond one horse's lifetime, so now he rode "Tony Jr."

Fred Thompson's horse, Silver King, was actually fitted with his own toupee, an artificial mane to ensure his recognition.

———

In a few weeks, John summoned Yakima Canutt to watch his accomplishments with the young gelding. It was a Sunday, and Canutt was enjoying a rare day off. There was often filming on weekends.

John put the horse through the walk, trot, canter, to warm him up, and then demonstrated a few tricks. There was a thin wire attached to a front leg and running to the saddle horn. It was more of a signal than a trip wire. At an easy canter, he gave the wire a tug, and the horse rolled, without injury, as a gymnast would. At a walk, the same wire could signal for a limp.

John put the horse through several such tricks, then dismounted and stepped around in front. He pointed a forefinger at the animal's head like a pistol, and spoke softly.

"Bang!"

The horse dropped in its tracks, like a marionette with the strings cut.

Canutt laughed.

"How'd you do that?"

"Just like teachin' a dog to play dead," said John.

"Well," the stuntman admitted, "it's got possibilities. You'd train a horse for a particular scene?"

"Sure. Just like the two-legged actors."

"Yeah. You know, John, time's comin' when the humane society could give us a lot of trouble."

"I figured that," said John.

He was remembering that there had been protesters in London who objected even to steer wrestling, a virtually harmless event.

"But, the main thing is, you'd have a trained horse that could learn new tricks if the script calls for it. And it'd save the cost of shootin' a horse when there's an accident."

"Maybe you'd still have accidents."

"Sure, but not as many."

"Okay. Now they've got a scene comin' up with knights in armor on horseback, jabbin' one another with them long spears. Lances! That's it. Mebbe they'd like one horse to go down."

"Sure, I can train him to do that."

This opened the door for a new career for John Buffalo, that of animal trainer. Within a few weeks, he was besieged with requests for a parrot that could sing "Yankee Doodle Dandy," a chicken that laid eggs on cue, and a variety of other unattainable animal actors. John was bewildered by the bizarre assortment of desires.

"They just don't understand, Yak!"

"Of course not. This is Hollywood!" chuckled the stuntman. "None of it makes any sense. 'Mr. Buffalo, can you teach this dog to fart "The Star-Spangled Banner"?' "

"Aw, lay off, Yak!" John complained.

"Don't worry about it," Canutt said more seriously. "Do what you can, and tell 'em no on the rest."

"Guess I'd better stick to horses and mules," John decided. "Maybe steers, but nobody wants much from them."

"An ox team, sometimes," Yak pointed out. "But I think this'll work for you. There are already people trainin' dogs and monkeys. Everybody's a specialist now."

Canutt was getting a great deal of enjoyment out of John's efforts and the situation in general. And he was quite helpful in introducing John to people who might use his help.

The Watering Hole, now known as Gower Gulch, was especially attractive to the cowboys, both real and movie types. It was about as rough as any of the frontier towns depicted on celluloid, and there were several shootings and other assaults at or near the Gulch. Still, nearly everyone went there sometimes. It was the cowboys' hangout. There one might run into an acquaintance from almost anywhere else.

"John Buffalo!" called a familiar voice, on one of John's infrequent visits there with a couple of the stunt men.

John turned.

"General McCoy! I thought you were in Wyoming."

"I was," McCoy chuckled. "And I thought you were in Oklahoma or somewhere. Why is it everywhere I go, you turn up?"

"I don't know. Are you filming the Arapaho again?"

"No, not this time. We did shoot another picture up at Wind River. . . . Did a prologue for *The Iron Horse*, John Ford picture. Prologue like the one we took to London."

"That's what you're doing now?"

"No, no."

McCoy seemed somewhat embarrassed.

"I'm here doing some screen tests," he said cautiously. "Seriously, John, I wouldn't cross the street to see *this* face on the screen, but that's what they're doing. What are you up to?"

"Training horses."

He explained what he was doing, and why.

"It's a good thing, John. That's bothered me considerably, to see a good horse crippled or shot . . . or both. Full speed ahead!"

They visited, and when they parted, shook hands warmly.

"I'm over at M-G-M," McCoy told him. "May our trails cross again soon!"

SEVENTY-TWO

1929...

Word came by way of a couple of disillusioned cowboys that spring. They had left the 101 after yet another show season with heavy losses. Knowing that many of the old gang were in Hollywood, they had come, looking for jobs.

The crowning bit of bad luck back at the ranch: George Miller, manager and bookkeeper, the stabilizing influence of the operation itself, was dead. One of his favorite extravagances, a powerful Lincoln roadster, had been his downfall. He had been drinking and playing cards with friends at the Arcade Hotel in Ponca City until past midnight. Driving too fast on icy highways, en route from Ponca City to the 101, he had gone off the road. He was found the next morning by a couple of local men. Miller had apparently been thrown clear, but his head was crushed beneath a front wheel. He was only forty-seven.

Matters worsened considerably in October of the same year, with the crash of the stock market and the onset of the Great Depression.

The 101 Ranch Wild West Show had again experienced a losing season on the road. Creditors were pushing to be paid, prices on farm products were dropping, but expenses rising. The ranch was mortgaged to the extent of $500,000 just to stay afloat.

Again, there were whispers about the Ponca "curse."
1930...

"Naw, you gotta swagger a little. . . . Swing yer arms and sort of walk with a swing in yer stride . . . Like this. . . ."

Yakima Canutt strolled a few paces, turned, and stalked back, a swing in his step. He paused to speak to the approaching John Buffalo.

"Howdy, John. Just coachin' a friend, here. Marion, this is John Buffalo, the horse trainer."

The lanky young man stuck out his hand in greeting.

"Haven't I seen you around?" John asked.

"Yeah, probably. I've spent some summers here," said the other. "Marion Morrison."

"He's from Iowa," Canutt said. "College football player. Been spendin' the summers here, playin' an extra, some odd jobs. Couple o' stunts, but he's like you—not really into the stunt thing. He'd really like to act. Play a cowboy."

John reflected that there were a great many young people with such an ambition.

"He's got a shot at it," Canutt went on. "John Ford's recommended him to Raoul Walsh, who's directin' a picture called *The Big Trail*."

"You a friend of Ford's?" John asked.

"Sort of," Morrison said. "Met him here a couple of years ago. He likes to talk football."

"Trouble is," said Canutt, "he's playin' a cowboy, but he don't walk like one. Walks like . . . well, like he's from Iowa!"

"I *am* from Iowa."

"Yeah . . . Well, anyhow, I'm showin' him some pointers about ridin' a horse an' how to walk so's to look like a cowboy. Oh, yeah! He don't think Marion Morrison sounds like a cowboy's name, either."

He turned to Morrison.

"You and Ford decide on that name yet?"

"Pretty near," said the young man. "I'm about settled

on 'John Wayne.' Now, lemme try this walk some more, Yak. Like this?"

He swaggered a few steps, turned, and swung back toward them.

"Yeah!" said Canutt. "Now, that's comin' along. You'll be lookin' like a cowboy, yet!"

Someone once observed that the days pass slowly, but the years, quickly. It was true in John Buffalo's life. He was busy. It was also true that the deceptive climate made it difficult to distinguish the season. There was a certain sameness the year round. John never quite became accustomed to the fact that in April, when the prairie grasses were greening and preparing to grow to six feet and taller, the California hills were becoming dry and yellow. They would remain so until October, when greening again began in the hills behind Hollywood.

1931 . . .

The worst year yet for the 101. John read about it in the papers. The 101 Ranch Wild West Show had closed forever, on the road, in Washington, D.C. August third was their last parade. Rising bills and falling attendance made further struggles useless.

In September, the ranch was placed in receivership. The land would be divided and leased to individuals to farm. Personal property would be auctioned off.

1932 . . .

The auction occurred in March. Zack Miller, sick and suffering from a "nervous breakdown," referred to the auction as "legal robbery." He was arrested and confined for a short while after firing a shotgun over the heads of approaching lawyers.

Less than a month later, Bill Pickett was dead. He lingered two weeks in a Ponca City hospital after being kicked in the head by a 101 horse which he was breaking.

Pickett was buried on the ridge near the resting place of White Eagle, the Ponca chief—he who had voiced the pronouncement that became known as the "curse."

One of the old cowboys gave a left-handed compliment to his long-time friend.

"If ever there was a good nigger, it was Bill Pickett."

John Buffalo would have made the trip to Oklahoma, to attend the funeral of the man who had been a good friend, but learned of Pickett's death too late, after the funeral was over.

Also in 1932, Zack Miller negotiated with the Capone family of Chicago to buy the ranch. Al (Scarface) Capone was still in federal prison for tax evasion, but the family was negotiating seriously. News reports and rumors were rampant.

The ranch, it was said, was to be divided into forty- and eighty-acre plots. It would be used for truck farming in a cooperative farm, run by Italian immigrant families in hundreds of co-op units.

The deal finally fell through, after months of haggling, and Zack Miller again faced disaster. In addition, Zack's recently divorced second wife, Marguerite, filed suit for overdue child support, lawyer fees, and alimony. Zack was jailed briefly at Newkirk, Oklahoma, for contempt of court.

1933 . . .

Miller managed to put together a troupe of cowboys and cowgirls who performed under the banner of the 101 Ranch at the Century of Progress exhibition in Chicago. Frantically, he tried various schemes to keep the 101 alive.

He tried to interest Babe Ruth, the New York Yankee slugger, to invest in the operation as a partner. Zack envisioned the show back on the road, with the great baseball icon putting on an act and autographing baseballs after each performance. The "Bambino" was not particularly interested.

1934 . . .

The country was still in the depths of the Depression, but Hollywood was in another world.

For a nickel or a dime, the American public could escape their troubles for a couple of hours in the movie theater. There, anonymous in the darkness, they could escape their own tawdry existence for a little while to live the adventures depicted on the silver screen.

Talking pictures had been a reality for several years now. After starring in a number of films as the strong and upright cowboy hero, Tim McCoy had finished a cowboy serial. It would be in twelve episodes, each to consist of two reels, which ran twenty minutes. One episode would be shown each week, with a cliff-hanger finish, a la *The Perils of Pauline*. The title of this first talkie serial was *The Indians Are Coming*.

John Buffalo was doing well. His work was held in high regard. While the rest of the country suffered from the Depression, Hollywood seemed exempt. There was usually money from somewhere if someone needed it to make a picture.

But John was restless. He was past forty, and still felt that his life had no sense of direction. He could see the years passing at an ever-increasing speed. He had no family. He was neither a hermit nor a ladies' man, though he had had some relationships of convenience from time to time. Though he realized that the industry in which he found himself was suspected of debauchery, most of the people with whom he worked were good, upright citizens, with homes and families.

Yet he had none, and there was an empty spot in his life.

He was walking down Sunset Boulevard when a voice called his name.

"Buffalo!"

He turned. There were a lot of people whom he knew, but it took him a few moments to place this man. It had been many years.

"Mac? Coach McGregor?"

The two clasped hands warmly. Mac had aged some. He was balding, and the fringe of hair over his ears had changed from brown to gray.

"You're in the movie business?" he asked. "I thought you'd be coaching."

"Didn't work out," said John. "But you?"

"Still coaching. On a vacation just now. I'm taking a year off. Lost my wife last winter."

John was somewhat embarrassed that if he had ever known anything about Mac's family life, he couldn't remember.

"I'm sorry, Coach."

"It's okay. I'm doing better now. Our kids are grown and gone. It's a good time for me to see the world. You married, John?"

"No, sir. I was . . . Lost my partner, too."

"Sorry . . . Guess that makes us a sorry pair."

A flash of an idea crossed his face.

"Say, John, why don't you go to the Olympics with me? Like old times!"

"You're coaching them again?"

"No, no. I'm just going as a spectator. No responsibilities. Berlin . . . It'll be like old times, but with no cares and troubles. . . . Just to watch . . ."

It did not take long to decide. Maybe this would be just what he needed, to shake the uneasy wanderlust out of his system.

"I'll do it!" John said.

SEVENTY-THREE

They were on a train, headed for New York.

"I'm afraid I haven't followed athletics much for a few years." John apologized. "Hollywood's such a different world, Mac. It's easy to get into that, and forget there's a *real* world out there. What's goin' on?"

McGregor laughed. "Sounds easy, John, the make-believe . . . What's going on? I dunno. Baseball's still the national game. You know about Babe Ruth, I guess. Folks say he can call his shots—not only whether he'll hit a homer as he comes to bat, but *where* it'll go over the wall. I dunno . . . Some good players comin' on. Couple of brothers named Dean—they call 'em Dizzy and Daffy. Dizzy's prob'ly the best pitcher."

"What about football?"

"Yeah, college football is really big. Army, Navy, the Ivy League schools. You knew about Knute Rockne, coach at Notre Dame? Killed in a plane crash a couple of years ago. Pity . . . He was a good man. A lot like Pop Warner, I guess. Some professional football, getting a bit more attention. You knew our friend Jim Thorpe played pro for a few seasons?"

"Yes. I heard that. What about Pop Warner? Retired, I suppose? He'd be past sixty."

"Not on your life!" Mac laughed. "He's still goin' strong. Let's see . . . He's coached at a lot of schools since Carlisle. Georgia, I think . . . Nope, maybe Cornell. I don't remember, John."

"How about track and field? This Olympics?"

"Yeah . . . I think maybe there's some increase in public interest. That Cunningham . . . Glen Cunningham . . . Distance runner . . . Great story, a few years back. He set a couple of records. A 4-minute, 4.4-second mile, indoors. You know, John, I'm thinkin' some day we'll see a mile under four minutes."

"Really?"

"I'd bet on it. But the runner we'll be lookin' at in Berlin is a sprinter. Jesse Owens . . . A colored kid. John, last year he set *three* world records on the same day: 220-yard dash, 220-hurdles, and broad jump! *Same day,* he *tied* the 100-yard dash. He'll be one to watch. I think he's probably the best track man I've seen since our boy Jim."

"Really? I'll look forward to that! Does he play football?"

"Don't think so, John. Athletes are more specialized now. Fewer of 'em in multiple sports like we used to do. But I'm sort of behind on following some of this myself. My wife's illness and all, you know."

"Yes. I understand." *You don't know how much I understand,* he thought. That would supersede everything.

"The football player I like is at Texas Christian, Mac went on. "Quarterback with a great arm for the forward pass. Sammy Baugh. They call him 'Slingin' Sam.' "

"Coach, you mentioned Rockne's death. Do you think air travel will ever be really practical?"

"Oh, sure. But not with airplanes. Too complicated. You heard about Will Rogers and Wiley Post last year?"

"Sure did. I knew Rogers, through the 101. A real tragedy, Mac."

"Yeah . . . Well, that's what's wrong with air travel by airplanes. The airship, lighter than air, is the future. Reminds me . . . I tried to get us tickets on one of the German dirigibles. They've got some transatlantic passenger service now. They're building a really big one, I understand. The *Hindenburg* . . . Over four hundred feet long."

"Hadn't heard about that. But, you remember, we saw airships in Europe when we toured with Jim."

"That's right, we did. Of course . . . You're well acquainted with airships."

"Not really, Mac. I hadn't paid much attention to them. Everywhere I've been there have been a lot of people and livestock to haul."

McGregor laughed. "Guess you wouldn't like to haul horses on one. They do have a flight deck, though."

"A *flight deck?*"

"Sure. They can land and carry up to three scout planes on a sort of hanging platform under the air bags. John, we live in marvelously changing times."

"We sure do."

"I started to tell you, though. I tried to get us on one of the German airships, but they're booked far ahead. I surely would have liked to ride the *Hindenburg,* though."

"We're going by ship, then?"

"Yeah, I guess we're stuck with the old way. But you said you'd been to Germany—since we were there with Jim?"

"Yes! Right after the war broke out. The 101 Wild West Show had about sixty Oglala Indians under a subcontract to a circus in Dresden. We had a time gettin' 'em out."

He related some of the events involved.

"My God, John, you've had some adventures!"

"Guess you'd say so. But tell me . . . You've checked into the situation in Germany. They've got this new Chancellor . . . What's his name?"

"Hitler. Adolf Hitler. A strange one, I guess. A lot of show and pageantry. Talks about racial purity. Aryan bloodlines, better'n anybody. Wonder how he'd have gotten along with Jim Thorpe."

They both laughed.

"Not as well as King Gustav, I'd say," said John.

"Pageantry" was an underestimation. John had never seen such an enormous crowd. The packed stadium was bedecked with scarlet banners and patrolled by uniformed soldiers.

"Never saw so many uniforms," commented Mac.

"Or so many swastikas," John added.

Some of the American Indians he had known used a swastika in their traditions. But this frightening design was everywhere: a stark black cross with broken arms, in a white circle, placed on a scarlet background. They were on the armbands of the military, on the flags that flew over the arena, on the bunting with which the reserved boxes were draped.

There were marching units of the Nazi elite guards, goose-stepping with a stiff-legged gait that appeared to John the most uncomfortable gait in the world. The jarring thud of hundreds of heavy jackbooted heels on the pavement sent a chill up John's spine. He could not quite understand the vague feeling that something here was very wrong.

In a way, however, all the pageantry *did* lend excitement to the Berlin Olympiad. It was interesting and different to attend purely as a spectator. McGregor was acquainted with some of the coaching staff of the American team, so they did have a casual contact with the events, without the responsibility. It was a good feeling.

It was apparent that, although the Americans were expected to do well, their major hopes centered around Jesse Owens, the short-distance runner.

Owens was an immediate favorite with the crowd. His style as a runner, his modesty, and his undeniable ability held the spectators on the edge of their seats.

World's champion at the 100-meter dash . . . The crowd applauded wildly.

"Wonder what happened to the pure-blooded Aryans?" commented Mac. "Damn, that boy is good, John."

The scene was repeated with the 220-meter competition. Again, Owens took the gold medal.

When the broad jump, another of his best events, brought Owens yet a third gold medal as world champion, the crowd went wild. After the customary rise to their feet to honor the winner, they stayed standing, continuing to applaud.

"Look," said Mac. "Hitler's not standing."

John was shocked.

"Did he stand before?" he asked.

"Not for Jesse," said McGregor. "How low can you get, over a prejudice?"

The next few years would produce that horrifying answer.

On the trip home, John festered under the scene in Berlin. With time on his hands to think, he spent many hours at the ship's rail, going back over his life. He stared out over the endless ocean, restless and unhappy. There were some good times and bad, some mistakes and triumphs, joys and sorrows.

There were times when he had felt that life was unfair. Life *is* unfair, he told himself. Nobody said it's all supposed to be good. It is the way of things.

Coming back at him was another facet of his life, however. In retrospect, there had been some pretty good things. Most of them, however, had at some point stopped short, for no cause that he could have avoided. And, too often, it had been because of the color of his skin.

He thought of Adolf Hitler, refusing to stand to honor

the accomplishments of a man of color. This bothered him increasingly as he ruminated and he was making no effort to stifle such feelings.

Sensing that John was working through some major crisis, McGregor thought it best to leave him alone. Only once did he offer his help.

"Anything I can do, John?"

"No. Thanks, Mac."

"Okay . . . If you need me . . ."

In most of his low-tide experiences, there were white men. *Biased* white men . . .

His youthful romance with the Senator's daughter, and the Senator's determination that it should not proceed.

His experiences with job hunting . . . He was certain that, more than once, his skills had been overlooked because there was a white applicant.

His Army experiences . . . The sidelong glance that told far more than words.

There were some good whites, he knew. Mac, for one. He thought that the Miller brothers had treated him fairly. Then he thought again, and remembered that they had been indicted for stealing land from the Poncas. So, even the Millers were not immune to this bias.

If there was anyone in his life whom he had felt that he could trust completely, it would have to be Hebbie. He guessed there were a couple of others. Ruth Jackson, McGregor, Tim McCoy . . . However, McCoy was a special case. John thought of him as an Arapaho, although McCoy had been born white. He held the same status as Charlie Whiteman or Lizzie Broken Horn.

There had been whites in Hollywood who respected him and his work, but others who were blatant in their attempts at demeaning humor. One, in particular, had been a source of irritation, calling him "Chief" since they first met. John had maintained his stoic, unmoved quiet with that one. But he hated to do that. It was causing himself to be a part of the man's bigotry.

SEVENTY-FOUR

By halfway home, he had made his decision.

"Mac," he said at breakfast one morning, "I've figured it out."

"Good," said McGregor. "It's about time. *What* have you figured out?"

"I'm goin' back to the blanket."

"What the hell does that mean?"

"It's an expression the old-timers use," John explained. "They've tried white man's ways, and have figured they don't work very well. So they just go back."

"Back to *what?*"

"To the old ways. It's hard to explain, Mac. It's something that you learn as a child ... A mixture of religion and spirit and life and death and faith and trust ... You don't know what I'm talkin' about, do you?"

"I haven't got the faintest idea," mumbled the startled McGregor.

"Well, I'm afraid it can't be explained," said John. "Some whites find it ... I think you have to find it for yourself. Nobody can really tell you about it. Maybe it's what whites call our 'medicine,' though there's really no English word for it."

He paused and took a deep breath. McGregor was still staring at him in astonishment.

"We're taught in the 'Indian' schools to be ashamed of it," John continued. "I never realized what they took from me, till now."

"So, what are you gonna do?" asked Mac, looking as if he expected to be scalped.

"I'm goin' home."

"To where?"

"To the reservation. Or some other one. I'm qualified to teach. I'll find a job, teaching my own people. Give 'em back some of their pride."

"That's good, John. At least, I guess so. But you always were a good teacher."

"Thanks, Mac. I knew you'd understand."

Mac chuckled.

"At least, I understand the joke."

It was years since he had seen the prairies and far horizons of the northern plains. His heart quickened at the sight of familiar-looking landmarks.

John rented a horse at the livery and rode out across the prairie toward the Agency. He drew in great lungfuls of the clean air, scented slightly with sage and sweetgrass. His chest expanded and his shoulders straightened.

It was good, to be astride a horse in the country where he now realized that he belonged. Here was *home!*

At the Agency, he introduced himself.

"I am Little Bull, son of Yellow Bull. You may have me on your rolls as John Buffalo."

The white secretary rummaged through a dusty file folder from an ancient cabinet, and came up with a sheet of paper.

"Yes, here it is. You went off to school and never came back. Your parents are dead?"

"Yes . . . I'm back now."

"To *stay?*" she asked in astonishment.

"Yes. I'd prefer to resume my own name, but . . . Well, I'm a teacher. I'd like to teach in a reservation school. How do I go about applying?"

"I guess you'd contact the schools. We don't have many teachers who apply here, you know."

She was a little sarcastic.

"You know where the school is?"

"The one where I went? Sure."

"Try there, then. The principal's name is Ranier. Mrs. Ranier."

"Thank you."

The buildings hadn't changed much. Some repairs were needed, but he knew that the Depression was being felt everywhere.

He walked down the hall to the principal's office, feeling the dread he had felt as a child. Any reason for a trip here *must* be bad.

A woman was bending over a file cabinet, searching in a lower drawer. He could see that she held a yellow pencil in her teeth as she used both hands to aid her task.

"Mrs. Ranier, I'd like to apply for a teaching job if you have one. Phys ed or athletics."

"Yes, yes," she said, her voice muffled by talking around the pencil. "Just a moment, here."

This was a far cry from Old White Horse, he thought with amusement. Hers was a trim figure, with well-shaped hips. Well-turned calves and slim ankles were visible beneath a skirt that came a few inches below the knee. She'd have to be his own age or older, he figured, but certainly well shaped. Maybe she'd have a face like a horse. . . . That would be a pity!

The silence was uncomfortable. He felt a need to say something.

"My name is John," he began, then hesitated. If he wanted to be Little Bull, now was the time. "John Little Bull," he said.

The woman straightened and turned, a stack of papers in her arms. She looked toward him and gasped. The yellow pencil dropped unnoticed to the floor.

"John Buffalo!" she said.

John was equally astonished. Could it be?

"Jane? But they said 'Ranier.'"

"Yes . . . My married name. Jane *Langtry,* when you knew me."

She hadn't changed much. The blue eyes, the golden curls . . .

"So you're married?" He tried to remain calm.

"I *was.* A disaster. I was too young. Divorce."

"You kept the name—"

"So my father couldn't find me."

"I saw your brother once."

She laughed. "He didn't know where I was, either. But . . . I *did* look for you, John. That's how I landed here. They didn't know where you were after you left school, but offered me a teaching job. I figured if you ever turned up . . ."

Now she was embarrassed.

John smiled. This was possibly the best day of his life. So far, anyway.

"Jane," he said, "we have a lot of catching up to do."

EPILOGUE

I really hadn't wanted to attend the reception, held at one of the local hotels. Basically, I'm a rather private individual. But it was a civic duty, I figured, to put in an appearance and support the Chamber of Commerce at such a function.

My wife and I entered the hall and began to make small talk with friends and acquaintances. I picked up a couple of cups at the punch bowl and delivered one to my wife, who was busily engaged in conversation.

A woman waved at me from across the room and began to make her way through the crowd toward me. I'd known her for a number of years, though not very well. A friendly, speaking acquaintance. Our paths had crossed occasionally at social gatherings like this one. She was a stylish professional woman, fortyish, and capable in her field.

She walked up, spoke a brief greeting, and then gave three quick motions, which I recognized as Indian hand signs.

"Do you know what this means?" she asked.

"Sure. That says you're Sioux . . . *Lakota*."

"Yes! But I didn't know that!" she went on excitedly.

I was a bit confused, but she laughed and began to explain. She had always known that she had some Indian blood, but her family would never talk about it.

That wasn't surprising. A generation ago, Native American parentage was something to be ashamed of. Children in Indian schools had their knuckles rapped with a ruler for speaking a few words of their *own language*. They were taught to reject their heritage, not to take pride in it.

"How did you find out?" I asked.

The woman then began to unwind a bizarre tale, one in which I was proud to have a small part. She had heard me lecture, several months ago, she said, on the Humanities Council circuit. I had been relating some of the research I had done in the American Indian cultures, and she began to think that she should try to discover her own roots. She had only one fact to go on: the hand sign.

"Wait!" I interrupted. "How did you know that?"

Well, she related, her father was the Indian connection, but he always completely refused to talk about it. However, his mother lived with them for a while. The old woman would take her little granddaughter on her lap every day, hold and rock her, and every day repeat the hand signs over and over.

"When you grow up, and someone asks who you are, you do this!" she told the child.

The woman repeated the signs as she had learned them, with quick slashing strokes. She went on to tell how, only a few weeks before, she had gone over to Haskell Indian Nations University and found someone who could tell her what the signs meant.

"Now," she went on with excitement in her eyes, "I know who I am! I am Sioux! Lakota!"

Although certainly no expert in hand signs, I was picking up something here that told a little more than she realized. It is possible to express one's tribe or nation with two hand signs: First, a circular touch with the forefinger of the right hand on the back of the left indicates "the nation of . . ." The sign for the individual group follows this. It can be done very calmly, a bland statement of fact. That was not the way this lady was performing the signs. Her motions were sharp, quick, and slashing, with a great deal of decisiveness. And she was adding an extra sign at the beginning, the sign for "mother."

My mind reached back to imagine an old woman, her culture falling apart underneath her. No one cares. Her son has rejected his heritage. She has one thing left, a tiny child. Every day, she takes the little girl on her lap, and over and over repeats the hand signs that will become the magic key to that child's heritage. And the *way* in which she teaches it: Not bland and quiet, but with a defiant slash that fairly crackles with pride and rises to a screaming challenge: *"The mother nation is Lakota!"*

I explained this and saw the realization dawn in her eyes. The two of us stood, oblivious to the crowd around us, the tears welling up in mutual understanding. . . .

And from somewhere on the Other Side, Grandmother looked down and smiled.